PRAISE FOR NOVE

Hope Beyond the Waves

"Embrace your emotions because *Hope Beyond the Waves* is going to touch each of them deeply. Heidi Chiavaroli paints a beautiful portrait of loving the unlovable, of forgiving the unforgivable, and of finding hope in the least likely places. This is a story that lingers."

KAREN SARGENT, author of IAN Book of the Year, *Waiting for Butterflies*

"If ever the world needed books offering hope in the midst of tragic and isolating times it is now, and Heidi Chiavaroli delivers just that. I was mesmerized by the history of Penikese Island, Massachusetts, and the heart-rending shame, isolation, and fear of victims of Hanson's Disease—and Atta and Gertie's made me feel like I was living it right along with them. Their journey captivated me from the first pages and kept me enthralled and rooting for them—and the handsome Dr. Harry—until the end. The parallel story of Emily, her Grams, and Sam, offered an equally poignant and compelling story of shame and isolation when people misunderstand and mistreat each other, and how one person's secrets can lead to another's freedom. Combined with Chiavaroli's trademark eloquent prose and her talent for weaving in forgiveness and redemption, *Hope Beyond the Waves* provides readers with a tear-jerking, super satisfying ending. I can confidently say this is my favorite novel of hers yet. A must-read for lovers of time slip, historical fiction, as well as books with a medical thread to them, and a simply outstanding escape of a read!"

AMY SORRELLS, award-winning author of *How Sweet the Sound* and *Before I Saw You*

"Love is love—even if love is loving an outcast—in any time period. Not a believer in miracles? This story may change your mind! And as for forgiveness? We are all capable should we choose—with the help of Heaven. This story and its characters will not soon leave my heart."

DONNA ANUSZCZYK, author of *Pomegranate Lane*

The Orchard House

"Chiavaroli delights with this homage to Louisa May Alcott's *Little Women*, featuring a time-slip narrative of two women connected across centuries."

PUBLISHERS WEEKLY on *The Orchard House*

"*The Orchard House* is a historical novel made for Louisa May Alcott fans, with plentiful references amid a touching story about homecoming and forgiveness."

FOREWORD REVIEWS

"This is a story I had a hard time walking away from, even after reaching the epilogue."

T.I.LOWE, Bestselling Author of The Carolina Coast Series

"As a longtime fan of Louisa May Alcott's *Little Women*, I was eager to read *The Orchard House*.... [It] invited me in, served me tea, and held me enthralled with its compelling tale."

LORI BENTON, Christy Award-winning author of *The King's Mercy*

"*The Orchard House* is a captivating story of sisters, difficult relationships, and the mending of broken hearts....Heidi Chiavaroli has written *The Orchard House* with depth and soul."

ELIZABETH BYLER YOUNTS, Carol Award-Winning Author of *The Solace of Water*

The Tea Chest

"Captivating from the first page....Steeped in timeless truths and served with skill, *The Tea Chest* is sure to be savored by all who read it."

JOCELYN GREEN, Christy Award-winning author of *Between Two Shores*

"*The Tea Chest* is timeless and empowering. Long may Heidi Chiavaroli reign over thoughtful, effortlessly paralleled fiction that digs deep into the heart of America's early liberty and the resonance of faith and conviction she offers as its poignant legacy."

RACHEL MCMILLAN, author of *Murder in the City of Liberty*

"*The Tea Chest* is not only a story of America's birth as a nation, but also one that reflects the clamoring in humanity's heart to soar unfettered by the weight of chains that bind."

JAIME JO WRIGHT, Christy Award-Winning Author of *The House on Foster Hill*

The Hidden Side

"*The Hidden Side* is a beautiful tale that captures the timeless struggles of the human heart."

JULIE CANTRELL, *New York Times* Bestselling author of *Perennials*

"This page-turner will appeal to readers looking for fiction that explores Christian values and belief under tragic circumstances."

BOOKLIST

"Filled with fascinating historical details, Chiavaroli connects two women through an artifact of the past. This heartrending tale will engage aficionados of the American Revolution and historical fiction."

LIBRARY JOURNAL

"Heidi Chiavaroli has written another poignant novel that slips between a heart-wrenching present-day story and a tragic one set during the Revolutionary War. I couldn't put this book down!"

MELANIE DOBSON, Award-Winning Author of *Catching the Wind* and *Memories of Glass*

"Chiavaroli's latest time-slip novel does not disappoint. Both story lines are fully developed with strong character development and they are seamlessly woven together."

ROMANTIC TIMES, Top Pick

Freedom's Ring

"First novelist Chiavaroli's historical tapestry will provide a satisfying summer read for fans of Kristy Cambron and Lisa Wingate."

LIBRARY JOURNAL

"Joy, anguish, fear, and romance are seamlessly incorporated with authentic history, skillfully imagined fiction, and the beautiful reminder that good can—and does—come out of darkness."

ROMANTIC TIMES

Hope Beyond the Waves

HEIDI CHIAVAROLI

HOPE CREEK PUBLISHERS, LLC

 Created with Vellum

Also by Heidi Chiavaroli

The Orchard House

The Tea Chest

The Hidden Side

Freedom's Ring

The Edge of Mercy

The Orchard House Bed and Breakfast Series

Where Grace Appears

Where Hope Begins

Where Love Grows

Where Memories Await

To John and Pam McPherson, my parents in the faith

And to Frank and Marion Parker, who gave all they had to the outcasts of Penikese Island

"But I will restore you to health,
and heal your wounds,"
declares the Lord,
"because you are called an outcast."

Jeremiah 30:17

Chapter One

Osterville, Massachusetts
April, 1993

I stand rigid, arms pinned to my sides as my mother wraps me in a loose hug in Gram's foyer.

"I'm so glad we thought of this arrangement," she says.

Arrangement. As if shipping me off and hiding me away is a plan we'd come up with together.

My father kisses me on the forehead, but it's awkward. Probably a show for my grandmother. He's kissed plenty of babies on the campaign trail, after all—this is likely no different.

"Be good, Sweet Pea." He turns to my grandmother, who barely comes up to his armpits. "Keep in touch, Mom. Don't hesitate to call if..." His gaze flicks to me and he doesn't finish his sentence.

What? Does he think I'll find a cute boy in Gram's retirement village? One who will get me in bigger trouble than Bryan already has?

"Oh, we'll be perfectly fine, won't we, Emily?" Gram smiles up at me, her lips the color of the Radio Flyer wagon I had as a child.

As much as I want my parents to leave—and don't want them to leave all at the same time—I can't bring myself to answer.

My father's smile wavers. "We better hit the road. We'll talk soon."

And then they're gone.

A twisting ache beneath my breastbone catches me off guard and I whirl around and race up the stairs to my new bedroom. I hardly know my grandmother, and I refuse to let her see me emotional.

Once in my room, I watch my parents' Honda Accord grow smaller from behind the gauzy curtains.

The car stops at the end of the road, and a crazy hope they'll change their minds and come back floods me. But no. Dad spins the wheel right and Mom doesn't turn her head to look back at the house even once.

They'll drive back to our perfect suburban home in Maryland in their spotless car and have their friends over as if nothing has happened. If asked about me, a lie will roll off their tongues. (Lying is permissible only in the *direst* of circumstances, which my mother has told me countless times, this absolutely is.)

I can hear her now. *"Emily is spending the summer with her grandmother. She's long overdue for a visit."*

Maybe not a complete lie, but certainly not the whole truth.

I step away from the curtain and flop on the twin bed, covered in a hideous floral bedspread. It's uglier than the pale yellow wallpaper peeling off the walls. The scent of mothballs and Avon perfume coat the entire house. I try to imagine my father growing up in this small coastal home, but I can't.

I glance at the phone on the nightstand beside a stack of books I've brought with me. A new book called *The Giver* by Lois Lowry. *Island of the Blue Dolphin*s by Scott O'Dell. *The Outsiders* by S.E. Hinton—a reading assignment for my new school. And *The Thorn Birds*. Mom didn't let me read the latter when I was a freshman but had recently made a snide remark about me and the heroine having something in common.

I'd tried not to care what that was but couldn't contain my curiosity—I bought the novel from Waldenbooks with the birthday money my great-uncle sent last week. Now, I scan the room for a picture of him, but don't see any family photographs. Not that I would recognize him, anyway. All he does is send money and cards.

I push a lock of my shoulder length, light brown hair from my eyes and reach for the phone before realizing my mistake. I've received enough lectures from Mom to earn a college credit in how-to-act-at-Gram's.

"No calls back home," Mom had said. "Your grandmother doesn't have a long-distance plan."

But Ashley.... Just to hear my best friend's voice would make all of this better. Surely I'm imagining the space between us since I told her my secret. I've always had a good imagination—too good, really. I used to imagine E.T. hid in the depths of my closet when I was in elementary school. I probably imagined Bryan actually meant those three little words he'd told me in the back seat of his Dodge Viper.

Yes, that had to be it—my imagination had gotten the better of me. Ashley's parents must have heard rumors. They'd warned my best friend to stay away, but of course Ashley was totally on my side. Best friends forever, right?

I run a finger along the chain at my neck to the pendant—half a heart with the letters *Be* and *Fri*. Ashley gave it to me the summer before high school, taking the other half of the heart for herself and promising that no matter what high school brought, we'd get through it together.

No matter what.

I scoop up the phone and dial the long-ago memorized number, praying that Ashley—and not her parents—will answer.

She would be home from school by now but her parents should be at work—a perfect time to call.

"Hello?"

Relief washes over me. "Ashley, it's me. Thank God you answered. I'm dying over here." I pause to catch a breath and roll over on my back, settling in for one of our long conversations. She'd want to know what Gram's house is like, if the neighbors have any cute teenage sons, if the beach is as beautiful as I imagined. Of course, we'd also dump on Bryan. Affirm how all boys with flashy sports cars, football letters, Homecoming King titles, and smooth words should be annihilated from the face of the earth forever.

"Emily...hey."

The phone freezes in my hand. She sounds...distant.

I swallow. "Is your Mom right there?" Was that why she was being so careful?

Ashley clears her throat. "Listen, Em. I'm going to be super busy these next few weeks with graduation and prom. And I also have to think about college...maybe we'll have time to catch up when you get back."

When I get back? But by then she'd be at college, living the dorm life, finding a new best friend to give a necklace to. I shake my head. "I—I don't understand—"

"I'm sorry, but we're in different places in life right now, you know? You've got a lot going on, and so do I. Take care of yourself, Emily."

The line goes dead, but I can't bring myself to return the phone to its cradle. My breaths come fast and heavy and Gram's walls threaten to close in around me. Is this what a panic attack feels like?

I wind my hand around the broken heart at my neck. No, it can't be true. *No matter what.* That's what kind of friends we were supposed to be. How could the one person I thought would support me to the end abandon me?

I drape my arm over my forehead and close my eyes, my breaths carrying away with themselves, taking me to a place of despair. A tear slips its way down the side of my face.

"Emily!"

I swipe at the wetness and jolt up in the bed, shoving my emotions aside. I can never let Gram know how upset I am. "Yes, Gram?"

"Come help with dinner, please."

I sniff and hang up the phone. I can't afford to wallow in self-pity. Things would get better. By the end of the summer, all would return to normal.

I sit slumped on the edge of the bed. Though I have a few fond, hazy memories of my grandmother and this house during my growing up years, once we moved to Maryland and Dad won the election shortly thereafter, our time with Gram had waned. She sent birthday and Christmas cards with money, but when Mom gave me the choice to write or call with a "thank you," I always chose a short, impersonal note over an awkward telephone call.

After a few deep breaths, I drag myself to my feet and over the threshold. I pass her room on my way to the stairs and hesitate. While Gram knows my big secret, I know next to nothing about her. She hasn't bothered to visit us much. And now, I'm supposed to be grateful she has taken me in, go along with her rules and help her move her bedroom downstairs so she doesn't have to navigate the stairs any longer. I walk in, noting the floral artwork on the opposite wall.

A pan clatters downstairs as my gaze sweeps over the room. Gram's comforter is only slightly less hideous than mine—that same yellow color as my wallpaper. There is a single bureau across from the bed, a small writing desk between two windows, and a nightstand with a Bible, a rosary, and a journal on top of it. Above the headboard is a picture too small to tastefully be placed there— a black-and-white wedding photo. I lean against the bed for a closer look.

I recognize traces of my grandmother in the youthful face of the bride. Hard to believe someone so old could've ever been that young. She is holding a huge bouquet of calla lilies and wearing a simple bridal cap with a veil that melts into the rest of her dress. My grandfather—a man who died before I was old enough to remember him—stands beside her tall and proud and handsome in a tuxedo and slicked-back hair. They are both wearing small smiles, as if they know a secret the rest of us don't.

My gaze drops to the nightstand and I slide open the drawer. A fifty-dollar bill is tucked in the side, but I pass it by for a worn, black-and-white picture of two women and one man in front of a clapboard cottage.

I pull it out. The woman on the right wears a long dress and blouse. Her face looks a bit disfigured—her nose too big. The woman on the left—about my age, maybe a little older—wears a jacket over her dress.

She looks slightly familiar, but I can't say for certain it's my grandmother. The man in the middle holds what I think is a mandolin with deformed hands. Why would Gram keep a picture of a man other than her husband in her bedside table? I flip the photo over.

Penikese, 1917

I know this name, don't I? Yes, my grandfather opened a school for troubled boys on the island off the coast of Massachusetts. Dad used that bit of positive family history in his campaign. Did my grandmother visit there when she was younger? She'd been a nurse at one time—that fact had made its way into Dad's campaign, too. Maybe the island used to be a hospital of sorts?

"Emily!"

I jump and drop the picture back in its place, closing the drawer as quietly as I can. "Coming!"

I take my time going down the stairs, acting as if I've just dragged myself out of bed. Gram stirs rice on the stove. Her gray hair is short and curly. I wonder if she wears curlers to bed. She moves around the kitchen well for being eighty...eighty-something, I'm not exactly sure how old she is.

She raises an eyebrow at my arrival. The gesture draws neat, crinkly lines on her forehead. "I would appreciate your help with dinner every night."

"Yes, ma'am," I say respectfully.

"And if you'd like a tour of my room, next time I suggest you ask me to be your guide."

I open my mouth to make an excuse...I saw what I thought was an abandoned earring on the floor or I wanted to see what sort of furniture we needed to move downstairs this summer—but the lies stop up behind my lips at the look Gram is giving me. She apparently hasn't lost an ounce of her mental clarity.

"Yes, ma'am." If I'm not careful, she might figure out a whole bunch more about me than I want her to know. "What can I help with?"

"After you wash your hands, you may cut the broccoli."

I slip my hands under the faucet with a pump of soap. How am I going to manage with Gram watching my every move for the next several months?

I take the broccoli and knife and saw off the little green florets.

"Child! You're mutilating it. Here." She takes the knife from me and demonstrates how to cut the broccoli into neat little trees. "Didn't your mother teach you how to cook?"

I snort. "You don't know my mother, do you?"

Gram smiles for the first time since she saw my father earlier this afternoon. "That's right. Anne never did have much talent in the kitchen. How did you survive all your growing up years?"

I shrug. "Our chef."

Gram makes a *tsking* sound as she shakes her head. "My son has done quite well for himself, hasn't he?" A moment's pause. "Although I suppose if he'd concentrated more on his daughter than his career...."

I plop the head of broccoli down on the cutting board. "Look."

She raises an eyebrow, as if in challenge.

I take it. I might as well let her know right off that just because I let my parents talk me into this banishment doesn't mean that I plan to slink around in shame.

"I'm sorry my parents dumped my pregnant self onto you. And I get why I'm here—I'm an embarrassment to them. An embarrassment to my school, my community. Dad's *career*. I'm a freakin' outcast. But what's done is done."

Gram's mouth turns into a hard, grim line. "Dear, I shouldn't have implied...but, I promise I won't belittle you for your mistakes. In return, I expect you to use decent language while in this house. Is that understood?"

I sigh, but say, "Yes." If she's upset over the word "freakin'," this is going to be a long summer.

"And as far as being an outcast...I'm not sure you have the slightest clue what being an outcast involves."

As if she knows. And she'd just promised not to belittle me. I glance down at the unfinished broccoli head and plunk down the knife. "I'm not hungry." I leave and stomp up the stairs to my room.

I half expect her to demand I come back and help. But my mini temper tantrum is met with silence.

Once in my room, I close the door behind me—not quite a slam, but with enough teenage angst to be sure Gram hears.

But as soon as I'm alone in my room, the fight immediately drains out of me. I stare at the phone, willing it to ring. Willing Ashley's voice to be on the other end, to say she made a mistake in severing our friendship. Heck, I'd even take a call from Mom letting me know she misses me, but she wouldn't be home yet.

My hopes are met with nothing but silence.

I am completely and utterly alone. One bad decision—a moment that couldn't have lasted more than ten minutes—has cast me from my home, my school, my friends. It threatens my chance at going to college, my hopes of being an English teacher...everything.

I think of my parents' driving away without looking back. Part of their punishment is making sure I know just how ashamed they are of me.

If only they knew I feel enough shame for all of us.

Chapter Two

To say I am surprised when Gram asks me to take her 1974 Volkswagen Golf into town for a few groceries is an understatement—I hadn't gone downstairs the night before, hadn't apologized for my behavior. I had expected a loss of privileges, not a get-out-of-the-house-free card. Not to mention that I don't have much experience driving, but I don't admit that to my grandmother. She offers me the keys and hands me a grocery list and some cash with directions on how to get to *Fancy's Market*.

After my shopping is done, I tuck the bag of groceries on the passenger seat beside me and turn left out of the store's parking lot toward the neatly-landscaped shops and postcard-perfect people adorning the sidewalk. A sign tells me to take another left to get to the library and I don't hesitate.

When I enter the old building, I breathe in the scents of musty books and secret knowledge. I tug my loose black T-shirt down and casually drape the sides of my open button-down shirt across my stomach. Soon I will be so big there will be no use hiding it.

I readjust my pocketbook over my shoulder, cross my arms, and walk into the depths of the library. The main floor is lit with tall windows and a beautiful children's room. I walk down the split staircase to peruse the fiction titles. I soon have a generous pile of books that will last at least through the following week. *Jazz* by Toni Morrison and the first three books in the *Flowers in the Attic* series by V.C. Andrews. I hesitate when I see a new book in the Nancy Drew Files series—*Dangerous Relations*. Though I haven't read Nancy Drew in years, I add the book to the pile. Unlike my real friends, fictional friends have never let me down. Ashley may have left me alone, but Nancy would always be there for me.

I approach the counter on the main floor. A boy about my age, maybe a little younger, mans the desk. His dark curly hair and thick black glasses make him look intelligent in a non-nerdy way.

"Find what you were looking for?"

I prop my books on the counter, effectively hiding my midsection. "Yes, but I don't have a card, but I'll be here for...awhile. I'm visiting my grandmother." The baby's due at the end of August. So until then, at least.

"I'll just need your address."

I give him Gram's address, and my gaze wanders to the banner above his head. Cartoon drawings of musical instruments advertise an outdoor music festival at a nearby park. My eyes catch on the drawing of a mandolin, and I think of the black-and-white picture in Gram's drawer.

"Do you have any information on Penikese? I think it's an island."

The librarian—is that what the boy is?—flicks his gaze from his computer to me. His eyes are a deep blue, clear and sharp through the lens of his glasses. "It is," he says.

I inch closer to the desk. "You know about it?"

He smirks. "Every boy around here has been threatened at one time or another with being sent to the school there. It's for delinquent boys."

The school my grandfather helped start. But that picture in my grandmother's drawer was too old to be part of the school. I study the boy. "You don't seem the type to give your parents grief."

He smiles, and I notice a faint dimple. "You'd be surprised."

"Oh, really?" But he doesn't volunteer more. "So, any good books on Penikese that I might be able to check out?"

He types something into his computer. "I'll be right back. Here." He slides a library card toward me. "Sign this."

I do. In a couple minutes, he's back, adding a book called *Castaways* to my pile. "That's all we have." He avoids my gaze, seems as if he wishes to say something, but doesn't. Instead, he begins scanning my books.

"You like working here?" With his thick glasses and knowledge of books, this boy seems the very opposite of Bryan. Was it possible to be friends—and only friends—with a boy? I'd never given it much thought. But how was I going to make it all summer without Ashley? Without someone I trusted to reassure me that I was doing the right thing?

"Yeah. I like checking out all the new books first, seeing what everyone else is reading."

"I've never met a boy librarian before."

He shrugs. "What can I say? I like books and it's a decent job." He holds up *Flowers in the Attic* and raises his eyebrow.

I try to keep a blush from climbing my neck. "I figured I'd find out what all the hype is about."

He shakes his head, but a smile tugs at one corner of his mouth. "You want a great read?" He digs beneath the desk and pulls out a white book with a black, skeletal T-Rex on the cover. "*This* is reading."

I scrunch up my nose. "I'm not much for science fiction."

He taps the book. "Movie's coming out next month. It's always best to read the book first."

"Thanks, but I think I'm already overloaded. I won't have time to read all these before they're due."

He adds *Jurassic Park* to the top of my pile. "That's my copy.

Keep it as long as you want. Maybe when you're done, I'll take you to see the movie."

A sharp guard goes up inside me at the thought of anything resembling a date. This kid doesn't know me. And soon, it will be apparent that I'm not the type of girl a nice boy who works at the library will want to be seen walking around town with.

"I have a boyfriend," I blurt out, and immediately hate myself. "I mean...I did have a boyfriend."

He looks as if he might laugh. Instead, he slips a printed paper with the due dates into the copy of *Jurassic Park*. "Okay...you can still borrow the book. If you don't like it, I won't hold you to the movie. Deal?"

"Deal."

He picks up the books to place them closer to me. I notice the slight ripple of muscles beneath his T-shirt.

"Hey, I'm looking for someone to move some furniture for my grandmother. It's a paying job." At least now it is—hopefully Gram will approve. "You interested?"

He shrugs. "Sure. I have a buddy who's always looking for odd jobs. I'm sure we could manage with the two of us."

"Great. I have to pack some stuff first. But I guess I know where to find you."

He smiles, and it's a nice smile. The kind of smile you feel all the way down to your toes. Not in a romantic way, but in a way that makes you feel like everything's going to be okay.

"I guess you do."

I return his smile and gather my books. "Thanks for your help." I turn toward the doors.

"Let me know how you like the book!" he calls a little too loudly for the library.

Once in the car, I roll down the windows and breathe in the fresh spring air. A hint of salty sea swirls around me. I sink into the warmth of it all and grab an apple from the grocery bag beside me. I flip open to the first page of *Jurassic Park*.

I read the title of the Prologue: *The Bite of the Raptor* and flip it shut. I can't. Not even for Cute Library Boy.

I kick myself for not asking his name as I dig out the book on Penikese. It's written by a man named George Cadwalader. I flip through it, perking up at the sight of my grandfather's name in the introduction. He, Mr. Cadwalader, and three other men recruited a group of "well-educated social drop-outs" as teachers to experiment in the rehab of juvenile delinquents at their island school.

I turn the page, my eye catching on a quote.

Society has made them its enemies. Therefore, weak though they be, they will wage such war as they can.

> — DR. FRANK PARKER WRITING IN 1905 OF
> THE LEPERS WHO WERE THEN
> QUARANTINED FOR LIFE ON PENIKESE
> ISLAND.

The word *lepers* draws me in.

Penikese had been a leper colony?

I remember the deformed hands of the man holding the mandolin in Gram's picture. I skim through the next few pages, searching for more information.

Could that have been Gram's connection, then? Had she been a nurse at the leper hospital all those years ago? I do a quick calculation in my head. She wouldn't have been old enough, I don't think....

Her words from the night before come back to me.

As far as being an outcast...dear, I'm not sure you have the slightest clue what being an outcast involves.

I swallow and fumble the keys of the car while jamming them into the ignition. Gram can't possibly understand what it's like to be in my shoes, but what did she mean when she said I didn't know what it was like to be an outcast?

❦

"DID you find everything at the market?" Gram asks when I enter her house with my library books and the grocery bag.

"I think so. I made a stop at the library, too."

I put the books on the table with *Castaways* on top, in hopes she'll notice.

She doesn't disappoint. When she sees it, she picks it up and smiles wistfully. "Now what on earth made you choose this one?"

I decide not to disclose the extent of my snooping last night. "That was the school Grandpa helped start, wasn't it?"

She runs a finger over the scarlet title. "I didn't think your father talked about it."

"He doesn't. But someone mentioned it during one of his campaigns, I think."

She releases a short sigh and nods. "I see. Well, it warms my heart that you're interested in your grandfather's work, dear."

"I—I am." I grab the bag of apples out of the grocery bag and open the refrigerator door, my heart thudding. "Did Grandpa ever hear from any of the boys from the school? You know, after they left?" Had my grandfather helped the juvenile castaways find a better life? If there was hope for them, could that mean there was hope for me as well?

Gram nods. "Some. Though many of the boys didn't want to be helped. That was half the battle." She eyes me, but her gaze doesn't stay long, and I sense she is stopping herself from veering into a lecture.

I slide a bag of carrots into the vegetable drawer. "Did you know the island used to be a leper colony?" I don't look at her as I say this, but I sense her hesitation.

"I do."

I swallow before I speak. "I saw the picture you have in your nightstand last night."

She hands me a bag of oranges and I meet her ocean-blue gaze, shrouded with secrets and maybe something like hurt.

"I'm sorry for snooping," I whisper. "But could you tell me who was in that picture? Was one of the women you?"

She lowers herself to a chair. The sun from the kitchen window splashes bright rays on her plaid, button-down shirt. "Your father would not like it if I tell you."

Now I *really* want to know. "But I'd like you to tell me...."

She covers her mouth with one hand and I'm afraid she's going to cry.

"Gram, it's okay. You don't have to—"

"Her story should be told. I've thought so for a long time."

I pull out a chair and sit. "Her story?"

"Atta. My sister."

I lean forward. Gram had a sister?

"Not just her story. *Our* story. Our family story."

My forehead crinkles. "Then why wouldn't Dad want me to know about it?"

"Your father...feels social stigmas, like horrible sicknesses and"—she raises her eyebrow at my stomach—"other such dilemmas, are best left buried when you lead a public life. I've never put up much of a fight with him, but having you here, dear...well, I'm beginning to question if I should have."

"He doesn't have to know that I know. Please tell me."

Her bottom lip trembles. "If I don't, the story may very well die with me." She reaches out her hand to grasp mine. "I don't want it to die with me, Emily. I want it to live on."

I nod, quiet, unwilling to break the moment.

She continues. "It's a tough story. But I promise you, it is full of one thing very dear to my heart."

"What's that?"

"Hope."

My insides warm. Gram's words remind me of a storybook or a novel that promises a satisfying ending. Why does my father not want me to know about our family's history if it's full of hope? "Tell me, Gram. Please?"

"Perhaps a cup of tea is in order?" She gives me a small smile before she stands and heads over to the stove.

I hold my breath in anticipation.

Gram hands me a mug and an assortment of tea bags. "After our mother died, my sister was all I had. I couldn't imagine life without her. But it seemed fate had other plans."

Chapter Three

Taunton, Massachusetts
1916

Atta Schaeffer's fingers gripped the edges of the metal exam table, her senses magnified a hundredfold by the cuff of a crisp white lab coat brushing her skin, the harsh scent of iodine and carbolic acid stinging her nostrils...the anticipation of the cold steel point of a scalpel.

As Dr. Browne descended upon her with the dreaded instrument in hand, she squeezed her eyes shut and burrowed her head into the wide, pleated collar of her shirtwaist.

"Miss Schaeffer, please relax." Dr. Browne pinched one of the rose-colored spots on her leg between two fingers. "The incision will be quite small. You'll hardly feel it."

Atta opened one eye, just as it began a steady, rhythmic twitch. She watched as the doctor made a small cut with his scalpel, scraped the spot, and rubbed a thin smear on a glass slide. Her breathing turned shallow as her corset pressed against the top of her ribcage.

"There you are. All done." Dr. Browne wrapped a piece of cotton gauze around her leg and secured it with a safety pin.

She pulled her petticoats over her knees, but still, the muscles in her thighs failed to loosen.

"It almost looks like an allergy. Have you eaten anything unusual lately?"

She clutched the excess fabric of her skirt. "N-no."

"Well then, I'll send the smear out for a few tests just to be sure. Other than that, I declare you right as rain." He dropped his scalpel into a clear solution. "I hear congratulations are in order. When's the big day?"

She rose on wobbly legs, her volatile heartbeat already calming at thoughts of her fiancé, Robert. "In August, we're hoping. As soon as the house is built." As soon as Papi agreed to let Gertie live beneath the roof of that house.

Atta made an effort to look into the doctor's coffee eyes. To her surprise, his gaze darted to the glass slide on the table. "Tell Robert if he needs any help with the house, Thomas would jump at the chance, what with school almost out and all."

Atta mumbled a "thank you" and dashed out of the room, down the hall, and outside. She gulped in cleansing breaths of the warm June air. The earthy scent of horses mixed with the smell of exhaust from a black Model T chugging past.

What a horrid place. As feeling returned to her shaky legs, she veered left onto a path in the woods. Towering firs embraced the needled trail, blanketing her in their protection.

Her eye stopped twitching as the pine-scented air quelled the demons nipping at her heels. She breathed easier and reached out to caress the soft needles of a fir.

She'd take a bath when she got home. Gertie would still be in school for another two hours, and if Papi stopped at the tavern—which surely he would—Atta would have plenty of time to heat some water and take a long soak in the tub, to wash away any telltale sign of that doctor's hands upon her. Then she'd make some

Berliners for Papi. He wouldn't raise a hand to Gertie if he were busy raising it to his mouth.

Again, she laced her fingers through the green needles as she passed, gleaning solace from—

Strong hands grabbed her waist. She shrieked. They dragged her beneath the boughs of a tremendous pine, enveloping her in a cave of darkness. The rough bark of the tree scraped against her back as the hands pressed her there.

Familiar, deep laughter sounded in her ear, and she opened her eyes.

"Robert David! You've taken a week off my life, you have." She gulped in a breath and settled her fingers at the top of her collar.

"I couldn't resist, dear Atta. Forgive me?"

Her fiancé's playful sky-blue eyes danced before her and she took in his dimpled chin, his blonde hair streaked with sunshine. Her Robert. Her savior. By the end of summer and before her twentieth birthday, they'd be married and in their own home. Gertie would be safe beneath their roof.

"You know I will. I suppose I don't know any better." She reached for the coverall strap on his shoulder and fiddled with the rough fabric. "Did Peter like the quilt?"

"Did he! He vowed to never let it leave his sight. Some of the older boys at the club teased him, but he'd have none of it." Robert angled his broad shoulders so his face was level with hers. "You, my Atta, have the sweetest heart I know."

Atta smiled at the thought of little Peter in his leaky tenement house, savoring a present. Her handiwork showed a tangible love—one that would be remembered every night and naptime.

"Mrs. Bassett stopped by today. She's looking to start a Girls Club." The corner of Robert's mouth crept upward.

"That's wonderful. I'll pay her a visit tomorrow to see how I can help." The Woman's Christian Temperance Union had rejected Atta because she was Catholic. Well, she'd find other ways to better humanity. Impulsively, she ran her hand over Robert's forehead, sticky from sweat. "We have so much to look forward to. A home of our own, a lifetime of serving others and St. Mary's church. I dare say we'll be content forever."

But as the words left her mouth, one doubt licked them all away. She bit her lip and gazed into her fiancé's grinning features. "Will you speak to him soon, Robert? Please."

His smile fell. "I suppose I've been avoiding it too long. It's just —it's a miracle your father's agreed to our engagement, what with his feelings for my father. He still treats me like I'm some kind of leper. What'll we do if he says no?"

"I refuse to leave Gertie alone in that house. If it means we have to wait longer..."

Robert hung his head. "Your sister's only six. Would you have us wait until she's married off?"

"Of course I wouldn't expect you to—"

He placed a calloused finger over her lips. "I would."

A lock of hair fell over his forehead and she smoothed it back. She truly was blessed. No matter that she was small and plain, the daughter of German immigrants—this man loved her heart.

"I'll talk to him this very day, Atta. I promise."

She placed her hands on his muscled bare forearms and stood on tiptoe to plant a kiss on his cheek. He smelled of sweat and wood and hard work. When his mouth caught her own, she didn't resist, but melted into the warmth of his kiss. Only with their recent engagement had they earned the privilege to be without a chaperone. The newfound freedom was...thrilling. As always, though, responsibility begged for attention.

She pulled back. "I should get home."

He led her from beneath the pine tree and onto the path, but kept her small hand clasped in his larger one. "First, I have something to show you."

"Pray tell, Mr. Lincoln."

"Oh no, it's a surprise."

"But Gertie. And Papi will—"

"—stop at the tavern when he gets out of work, which isn't for"—he dug out his pocket watch from his coveralls—"another three hours. Can't I have you all to myself for a bit?"

Didn't he deserve as much? Didn't she? Besides, Gertie was still in school. "Okay, but we'll have to hurry."

Up the trail he led her until they came to Summer Street. They bore right and turned down a dusty road—their road. Atta's finger curled around Robert's pinky. Their patch of earth, their little slice of heaven, their freedom lay just beyond that big oak.

"Robert." Her fingers fluttered to the buttons at her throat. Walls. And an honest-to-goodness roof. "It's more than grand. How in the world did—"

"I bribed the boys. They helped me the last three days in exchange for a boxing match at the club this Friday. They'll do anything to prove themselves the next Jess Willard." He leaned against a maple tree and shoved his hands in his pockets, a smug grin painted on his face.

"Well show it to me, you goose." She nearly jumped up and down as she dragged one hand out of his pocket.

He laughed—a deep, melodious, wonderful sound—and offered her his arm in a formal fashion. "It will be my pleasure to give you a complete tour, Miss."

She circled his arm with her own and allowed him to escort her up the temporary steps and through the front door. Wooden partitions separated the first floor of the small farmhouse into sections. Open holes in the walls denoted windows, while another larger one in back, a door.

He showed her the now-hollow kitchen and parlor then led her to a smaller section in the middle of the house. "And this will be your very modern water closet and bathroom, soon to be fully installed with indoor plumbing so you can take those long baths you love so much."

"And how, may I ask, did you happen upon such personal information?"

He tapped her nose. "Gertie let it slip one day."

Dear Gertie. Joy bubbled up in her throat as her fiancé led her up the wooden staircase to the second floor. Robert swept his arm toward the room on the right. "Our bedroom."

Atta cleared her throat. "And this one?"

"Gertie's room, of course. She'll have to share once the little ones come along, though."

Heat crept up Atta's neck and settled upon her cheeks.

Robert ran a finger under her chin. "You're adorable when you blush."

"And you enjoy making me do so all too much."

His baritone laugh echoed through the hollow rooms and he led her down the stairs, careful to hold her hand as there were no railings on either side. "That I do—but come outside, I have one more place to show you."

There were no steps out the back door, so he jumped down first before placing his hands on her waist. She sank into the soft ground.

"*The* tree." He gestured up at the tall, stately pine—the very reason Atta had been set on this patch of land. "It'll give plenty of shade in the summer."

Atta clasped her hands against her chest and looked up at the tree, four trunks thick, vibrant and green. "It's all perfect, Robert. I couldn't imagine anything better."

He pulled her hands around his taut back until she laid her head beneath his neck. "I can't wait to share it all with you, Atta."

After a moment he drew back and guided her beneath the tree, where he sat on abundant brown needles. He patted the spot next to him and for a half-second she resented her younger sister—the reason she always needed to hurry home. She resented Mami for leaving them five years ago...God for allowing it to happen. Most of all, she resented Papi for not taking care of them.

But to blame Gertie was ludicrous. Unlike her, Gertie was innocent. She deserved protecting—she *needed* protecting.

"I can't, Robert. Gertie will be home in a couple hours. I planned on making *Berliners* for—"

"Only for a moment, Atta. Then I'll come home with you. I'll continue Gertie's fox-trot lessons while you make your precious *Berliners*, and when your father comes home, he and I will have that talk."

If he's sober enough. Yet maybe, for once, the rum that Papi's blood thirsted for would prove advantageous. Beneath the foggy haze of the alcohol, there stood a chance Papi would agree to their arrangement.

Atta lowered herself on the soft needles and snuggled into the crook of Robert's arm. It was cool and comfortable beneath the tree, the back of their little house sitting directly in front of them. Quiet. Solitude. Here, she could almost forget Papi, forget "the Great War" raging in faraway lands—forget the fear that it could one day grasp Robert and wrench him from her life. At this moment nothing mattered but the dear house and the love that would soon fill it. She'd sew at that darling window...she'd hang their laundry over in the sun. Gertie could help her start a garden in that square of earth over yonder.

For the first time in many days, peace lapped at her soul like waves along a sandy beach. Soothing, smooth. Her eyelids grew heavy.

She and Robert would spend their nights cuddled just like this in that room...the moon would shine in that window....they'd all sleep safe...Robert would protect them....

ATTA WOKE WITH A START. Long shadows advanced across the shell of their house. The last of the sun shone through the trees. Her blood flowed cold, her throat constricted.

She clutched at Robert's pant leg. Scrambling to her feet, she took in her fiancé's panicked reaction as he too, realized they'd fallen asleep.

He cursed, then took her hand and began long, jogging strides past their dark house and down the lane. He stopped at the house at the end of the road, dashed through the yard, and knocked on the door.

Atta gazed longingly at the mare in the barn. *Forgive me Father, for I have sinned.*

How could she have fallen asleep? Robert knocked again, and then explained with frantic gestures to a silver-haired man they barely knew.

In a moment, Robert and Mr. Ferguson—if she remembered correctly—walked to the barn. The older man cinched up the saddle while Robert looped the bridle over the mare's head. With Robert atop the horse, he waved to Mr. Ferguson before stopping to help Atta up onto the warm horseflesh behind the saddle. "Hold on tight."

She clutched her hands together in front of him. Robert pressed his legs into the mare's sides and the horse tore fast down the road.

Atta crushed her face against Robert's shirt. Neither the scent of homemade soap nor the mare's steady lope beneath their bodies brought comfort. How could they have fallen asleep in the afternoon shade? How could she have left Gertie alone...with him?

Forgive me Father, for I have sinned. She imagined herself in the small confines of St. Mary's confessional, rosary beads tight in her hand, Monsignor Coyle's muddled face through the latticed screen between them. Monsignor would probably tell her to pay penance by praying the rosary two times. Even now, she longed for the comfort of the smooth beads and the cool metal of the crucifix, Jesus's bent knees pressed into her palm as she began the first prayer.

I believe in God, the Father Almighty, the Creator of heaven and earth...

She was on her second Hail Mary when Robert tugged the reins. Atta peered from behind his shirt, her legs growing numb at the sight of Papi's Tin Lizzie in the drive. Robert hopped down and pulled her off with one strong arm. They ran to the front door, toward the sound of Papi's loud, slurred curses.

Was Gertie safe in their bedroom? Had she been able to secure Atta's hope chest against the door by herself?

Flour coated the kitchen counter. An overturned bowl. The jar of jam Atta used to make *Berliners* open and tipped, a gelatinous blob smearing the counter. Their shoes crunched on granules of sugar as she and Robert hurried to the stairs.

Papi's voice boomed above. "You worthless, girl. Killed my Katharina...worthless...now you gonna pay."

Gertie must have made it to her room.

"Papi! We're home." Atta attempted comforting tones to calm the beast inebriated by demon rum.

The stench of cigarettes and whisky caused her stomach to curdle. On wobbly legs, she stumbled up the stairs before Robert. Around the corner and—

Papi's heavyset form stood in front of their bedroom, a large rolling pin raised in his right hand. Gertie crumpled on the painted floorboards. A large red welt melded with the tears on her face. Her tiny fingers clutched the handle of Atta's hope chest.

She hadn't made it.

"Worthless piece of—" Papi brought the rolling pin back.

"No!" Atta's guttural scream made Papi pause long enough for her to lunge across the hall and throw herself on top of her sister.

THE BLOW NEVER CAME. Robert had seen to that. They were both gone now, Robert probably finding a way to sober up her father.

For a long time, Atta sat on the floor with her sister,

smoothing her blonde tresses. "I'm so sorry, Gertie. I should have been here. It's all right now. I'm here. And as soon as Robert and I are married, you're going to live with us. How would you like that?"

Gertie's soft whimpers sounded from within the folds of Atta's skirt.

Forgive me, Father.

Atta stood and lifted Gertie in her arms, careful to avoid any tender spots. She carried her downstairs and sat her on a chair. She dipped a washcloth in a basin of water and tended first to her wounds, and then to the flour and jam smeared on her hands and beneath her fingernails.

"You know if I'm not home you shouldn't be down here cooking. You know you should be up in our room. You know it." Atta tried to keep the frustration from her voice, but she found herself digging harder than necessary to loosen the sticky jam beneath Gertie's small thumb.

Her sister winced. Atta placed the cloth down.

"You didn't come." Gertie's innocent blue eyes implored her. "I knew Papi would want his *Berliners*. I thought I could"—she hiccupped back a sob—"make him like me."

All the *Berliners* in Germany couldn't accomplish that feat. Atta sighed and clutched Gertie's hands. A sticky spot on her sister's dress stuck to Atta's pinky. "*You* have nothing to be sorry for. I should have been home. But I give you my word, Gertie. It will never, never happen again." She stood. "Now dry those tears. We have plenty of cleaning to do."

Gertie stood, wiped her nose with the back of her sleeve, and took the kitchen broom from the small closet. "How come you never cry, Atta?"

"I suppose...I suppose all my tears dried up after Mami died." Sometimes, when her burden felt too heavy, she longed to cry—begged her eyes to shed a tiny bit of wetness. But the tears never came.

"Tell me about her again. Please."

"Mami was lovely. Prettier than Mary Pickford, even." Atta rung out a dishcloth in the steel sink and ran it over the counter. "You look just like her. Same blue eyes, the color of the sea. You have her smile too. She loved you so much. She used to sing to you."

"*Schlaf, Kindlein schlaf?*"

Atta smiled. *Sleep, child sleep.* "Yes."

"I didn't mean to make her die, Atta. I didn't."

Atta flung the dishcloth down and took Gertie by the shoulders. The child's eyes widened. "You forget that nonsense, Gertie Schaeffer, you hear? *You* did not make Mami die."

"But Papi says she got real sick after I was born."

"You don't listen to Papi for one second. He's a foolish, selfish...oh, never mind all that. You put such nonsense straight from your head."

Atta stood and wiped the counters. Her bottom lip trembled. How did she live with herself? With her guilt? No, Gertie hadn't killed Mami.

The stain of that sin lay on Atta's soul.

AN HOUR LATER, after some toast and eggs and a chapter of *The Secret Garden*, Gertie was settled in bed beside her ragdoll, Rosie, while Atta finished the *Berliners*. When the door opened, she tucked the rolling pin behind her back.

Robert. He walked stiffly to the table and sat, almost in a daze. "He's passed out in the barn." His gaze met hers. "He agreed. I can't believe it myself. It wasn't easy. He'll always hate me, hate my father, I know that. But he agreed to let Gertie live with us."

"Thank the Father." Atta collapsed against the side of the counter.

"I'm working double-time on our house. The boys from the

club will help me. I'll finish it early, talk to Monsignor Coyle about moving up the wedding." His head drooped and she ran a hand through the blonde locks, damp from sweat and releasing the faint scent of livestock.

He lifted his head and clasped her hand to his chest, where his heart pounded out a steady rhythm. She relaxed beneath its melodious sonnet.

He brought her fingers to his lips and kissed them. "You and Gertie need to get out of this house. I need to get you out of this house."

His dogged determination soothed her, and a sudden tranquility stirred the walls of her heart. Everything would be fine. She would never fail Gertie again. Neither would Robert.

Not until later that night, when Atta slid into bed beside her sister's warm little body, did the checkup with Dr. Browne slither into her mind.

The rose-colored spots on her legs. The glass slide with her skin on it. She hadn't even asked him.

What was he testing it for?

Chapter Four

Boston, Massachusetts
1916

Doctor Harry Mayhew cringed as an orderly pulled a sheet over his patient's pale face, the gesture cementing not only Albin Zielinski's death, but Harry's own bleak future.

Pneumonia. He'd associated Zielinski's cough and fever to tuberculosis, but his patient must have been developing pneumonia before Harry had considered collapsing his lung. Most likely, Zielinski would have died either way.

Most likely.

Harry tapped his foot against the linoleum. Losing patients came with the territory of a medical degree. He'd known it from the beginning. But would Dr. Wright view it this way? Would Harry's father?

"Sad, isn't it?" His nurse, Helen, came up beside him, her Florence Nightingale cape fastened at the front for the trip home. "And with two little ones, no less."

Zielinski had children. Maybe he should have listened to Dr.

Young. Would his patient's chances have been better in a sanatorium?

No, everything he learned at Harvard pointed to the benefit of inducing pneumothorax in a patient like Zielinski. Harry had only done what he thought best.

The mental pardon did little to dispel the imagined faces of Zielinski's wife and children, grieving their husband and father.

"Dr. Wright said he'd like to see you before you leave, Doctor."

The old codger. No doubt Harry was in for a lecture that would put the brightest Harvard professor to shame. Perhaps he deserved it.

He bid Helen goodnight and strode down the halls of Massachusetts General Hospital, his rubber soles squeaking against the linoleum.

Massaging a kink in his right shoulder, he gave two rapid knocks on an imposing walnut door.

"Come in."

Harry entered the spacious office. Behind the desk, Dr. Wright raised his eyebrows when he saw him. "Shut the door, Harry."

He did so and sat in a Hepplewhite armchair, his feet planted on a plush area rug. Two tungsten lamps hung on the wall, above a grand mahogany desk. All of it made him feel small, and he straightened his spine as he faced the older man.

"Nurse said you wished to speak with me, sir."

The older doctor sighed and leaned back in his swivel chair. Swivel. Huh. Apparently, the board spared no expense when it came to Dr. Wright.

"I think you know why you're here, Harry. Dr. Young spoke to me regarding one of your patients"—he flipped through a pile of papers on his desk—"Albin Zielinski. Tuberculosis. Dr. Young suggested Mr. Zielinski be sent to Gallops Island for sanatorium treatment. You took it upon yourself to collapse his lung." He snapped the papers and inspected Harry through thick spectacles, as if he were a bacterium under a microscope. "His death ensued."

"I'm not convinced his death was a direct result of the pneumothorax, sir. At the time it seemed the only logical course of action."

"Logical to go against your attending physician's orders?"

Harry flexed his right foot, the tightness of the scars left by inadequate stitching from years earlier pinching his calf. He'd graduated top of his class at Harvard Medical School. One didn't walk away from such an accomplishment to bow down to the orders of some mediocre physician only two years his elder.

"With all due respect, sir, Mr. Zielinski is—was—*my* patient. I didn't agree—"

"With all due respect, Dr. Mayhew, you passed your licensing exam just last month. You don't have to agree. An order's an order. I pride myself on running this hospital—and running it well. Dr. Young is a fully capable physician. I'd put my life in his hands." The older man raised a single bushy eyebrow. His expression softened. "I'm sorry, Harry. I have no choice."

Unfamiliar panic seized his chest. No choice?

Dr. Wright handed him an ivory envelope, an image of the front of the hospital embossed in the top corner. "I've discussed appropriate discipline with the board and the review committee. There's—"

Harry stood. "Dr. Wright, please. Just a minute, now. Mr. Zielinski's health had improved considerably since I induced pneumothorax. He was young. A unilateral case with cavitation. Surely, you would agree with my treatment."

"Whether I would have agreed or not doesn't matter. You're a bright young man, Harry. But respect for those in authority needs to be maintained. This is not the first time you've disregarded hospital protocol."

Bitter bile gurgled in the back of Harry's throat. Respect for authority. How many times had his father shoved those words at him? But respect was something to be earned, not wielded about like a shiny sheriff's badge.

Dr. Wright removed his spectacles. "Dr. Frank Parker, superintendent of the Penikese Island Hospital, is in need of an assistant. Dr. Walbach—you remember him from Harvard, I'm sure—has been in communication with both Dr. Parker and the Board of Charity. Your discipline will require you to remain on the island for one year to assist Dr. Parker in any way he sees fit."

The old man had gone off his swivel. "Dr. Wright—you can't possibly. If I go to Penikese for a year, it'll be suicide to my medical career. No patient will willingly seek me out after I've worked with —with lepers." He spit out the last word as if it were dirt on his tongue.

"Surely, a doctor specializing in bacteriological training isn't frightened of leprosy, Dr. Mayhew." He replaced his spectacles. "And if you get along on Penikese, you may be assured you will have a position waiting for you here at the hospital. Dr. Parker and I graduated from Tufts together. He is a fine man and a fine doctor. You will learn much from him."

Learn? What did he need to know of leprosy? They didn't treat such cases in Boston's hospitals. Reaching into the recesses of his desperation, he clutched the only weapon available to him.

"My father won't allow this."

How he hated to call on his father's position. Hadn't he always prided himself on getting by on his own accomplishments? But this....

"I've already spoken with your father. He was none too pleased. But even the chairman of the board can't argue with your irresponsible choices."

Harry shoved his chair back and strode out of Dr. Wright's office without another word, the envelope tight in his grip. He wouldn't live among lepers. No, he'd open his own practice. Blast, he'd join his father if he must.

SEVERAL HOURS LATER, Harry dragged himself up the steps of his parents' house and onto the wide veranda, where he placed the box of his office supplies and medical bag on a wicker chair. Tucked deep into the side of the small box was the letter Dr. Wright had given him. That letter would not—could not—dictate his future.

The scent of honeysuckle and lavender reminded him of his soft, coddling mother, the complete antithesis of the man she'd married.

"Dr. Mayhew." The familiar young voice caused Harry to look toward the bottom of the stairs into wide, expectant green eyes. "I've been waiting for you near an hour, Dr. Mayhew. Did you save any lives today? Did you, did you?"

"Timmy." On days like this, Harry wondered why the nine-year-old boy idolized him.

Timmy shoved his hands into the pockets of his knickers and trotted up the stairs. "So did you, Dr. Mayhew?"

Harry started to shake his head and tell the boy that no, he did not save any lives. In fact, he may have taken one. But the boy's hopeful face beneath sun-reddened hair made Harry bite his tongue. "There was this one man..."

Timmy almost jumped out of his polished shoes. "What was wrong with him? Cholera? Tuberculosis? Diphtheria? The typhoid?"

"Polio." Harry turned his mouth into a grim line to match the desperation of the story he was to conjure up for the boy.

"Polio?" Timmy's freckled nose wrinkled. "That's bad...how did you save him?"

"He couldn't breathe when he came in. Couldn't speak. If I didn't act soon, he'd surely die from asphyxiation." Harry's voice grew animated, even as he questioned if lying to the boy was better than telling him a man in his care died today. Certainly better to borrow from this half-true story, for he had saved a man with this problem while in medical school, as Dr. Wright kept a watchful eye over the procedure.

"Yes, yes? And how did you save him?"

"A tracheotomy."

"A trache—what?"

"A tracheotomy. A fairly simple procedure, but a rather nerve-wracking one considering all it involves."

Timmy leaned forward. "What—what did you have to do?"

Harry paused, the effect dramatic. "Cut his throat open with my scalpel."

Timmy's hands flew to his throat. Realizing the gesture, he shoved them back in his pockets and cleared his throat. "And then he could breathe?"

"After I inserted the tube into his trachea, yes. He could breathe easily."

The boy stared into the space beside Harry, his jaw hanging open. "No fooling."

Harry couldn't help the smile pulling at his lips. A small lie was a minor price to pay for saving the boy's dreams. "No fooling." He sifted through the supply box. "Now listen up, Timmy. I won't be around for some time, and I want to give something to the aspiring doctor." He held out the instrument, the black tubing familiar and comfortable around his fingers.

Timmy reached for the device tentatively, his mouth working but no sound coming out.

"Oh, I almost forgot. The case. You don't want it getting knocked around when you're off to see your patients, now do you?"

"But—but don't you need it?" Timmy finally grasped onto the black tubing.

"I have another." Harry's father had given him his old stethoscope when Harry graduated from Harvard. He'd been reluctant to use it, though. Bad memories and all. But in this moment, the joy on Timmy's face seemed worth a few bad memories.

Timmy propped the ear tips in his ears and probed around his chest. Harry stifled a laugh when the boy pressed the chest piece about three fingers too high of a clear hearing.

"Here, Doctor. Let me show you." Harry knelt down and slid the chest piece lower. "Hear that?"

"No foolin'...that's my heart?"

"Sure is. It's working hard to keep that young blood flowing."

Without warning, Timmy threw his arms around Harry, forcing him to fall back on the top step. "Thanks so much, Dr. Mayhew. This is the best present I ever got." He pushed himself off Harry and jumped the last three steps. "I'm gonna go show Mother. She'll think I'm a real doctor, now."

The boy rushed away. It was on Harry's lips to remind Timmy he wouldn't be around to say goodbye, but he didn't call out. Better for the boy to remember him a hero, to remember the belief Harry had in him to accomplish his dreams—a belief he wished his own father had supplied him with at a young age.

Leaving the box on the chair, he entered the house, the smell of steak churning his stomach instead of enticing it. Voices tinkled along with china, and the door to the kitchen swung open, sending a wave of heat from the ovens.

"There you are." A sweep of dark ringlets disappeared behind the door. Carrie. "Mother, he's decided to come home at last. Would you like me to have the maid pour the chardonnay?"

Mother. Was the endearment necessary considering they weren't yet engaged?

"How was your day, dear?" Harry's mother stepped in front of Carrie and kissed him on the cheek, her pale blue gown brushing his shoes.

"Well, Mother."

He glanced at his father already seated at the head of the table, his broad shoulders filling the seat. The older man jerked his head toward Harry's chair, indicating for him to sit. "We'll speak in the smoking lounge after dinner."

"Yes, sir."

The sound of glass beakers shattering on tile would have been preferable to the tight silence shrouding the gleaming silverware and china that night. His mother must have sensed something amiss, for she spoke in one-sentence conversations, with only Carrie giving nods of acknowledgment.

"I called on Mrs. Beal today."

"The filet is cooked to perfection, is it not?"

"Mrs. Strong's niece is to be married this summer. Isn't that lovely?"

And finally, "Carrie, would you play that lively piece Harry loves this evening—oh, what is the name of it again, dear?"

Carrie smiled at Harry, her straight white teeth shining beneath the light of the chandelier. "*Nola*, by Felix Arndt. And it would be my pleasure, Mother."

His career hung on a shaky rock of a craggy precipice and all he could hear was Carrie's all-too-familiar endearment of "Mother." Each time pushing him further toward his unsteady future. His lack of control over his own destiny.

"Father and I have business to attend to in the lounge. Perhaps later."

Carrie's bottom lip started to protrude but she caught herself, ever the genteel woman her parents had groomed her to be. "Later, then."

Once in the lounge, Harry's father took a hand-rolled cigar from his leather case, rolled it between his fingers, and lit it.

He didn't offer Harry one.

Neither did he sit in his usual oak Morris reclining chair, but rather stood looking out the darkened windows, bordered by heavy velvet drapes.

"I learned something interesting today, Harry. Do you wish for me to enlighten you?"

Harry tapped his right foot on the hardwood floor, the sweet scent of tobacco heightening his senses.

"My son, whom I've always demanded obedience from...my son, whom I provided an Ivy League education and who has not wanted for anything...my son, so I find out today, can't take orders. 'Has no respect for authority' were Dr. Wright's words. And now, my only son finds himself in quite a predicament." He softened his words as his dark gaze met Harry's. "And for the first time in my life, I don't know what to do about it."

Harry closed his eyes. He'd expected discipline. Degradation. But vulnerability...his father? Never. His last sentence provoked thoughts of sympathy and repentance. Harry would have none of it.

"Sir, I've already decided I'm not going to Penikese. I will not subject my career to such a setback."

His father raised an eyebrow, a few faint gray hairs glinting off the dim light of the oil lamp. "And what do you propose to do?"

Man, he'd have to grovel. He'd rather do anything than beg—anything except live in a leper colony.

"I could work at your practice."

The man who raised him puffed long on his cigar then blew a thin stream of smoke toward the ceiling. "You will only harm the practice I worked hard to build. Your name has been tarnished. Because of irresponsibility, you have a patient's death on your hands. Again."

Harry sucked in a sharp breath, as if he'd been punched. And hadn't he, in a sense? "Father, I was eight. Can't we—"

"I bring it up not to cause you pain, Harry, but to point out that there are some things you haven't learned in fifteen years. Dr. Wright may be correct in thinking you will benefit from time on a remote island, amidst needy people. Some personalized instruction with an experienced physician can't harm your senses, either."

His ears rung. His own father would send him to his doom. He was indeed eight years old again, scooping up a roll of catgut material his father had thrown to him, searching for a needle to sterilize, all so he could stitch up his own leg.

Why would his father help him now?

"I'll open up my own practice, then. We'll be in competition." A lame threat, but no way in Hades would Dr. William Mayhew survive the social stigma of his only son competing with him.

"With what money? You've been out of medical school for all of four months." He swiped an open palm into the air. "But by all means, try it. Don't expect to be living under this roof while failing, though."

Boxed into a corner again. Harry would never win against his father, and they would never be on the same team. He felt the heavy gaze of disapproval on him, sure that whenever his father looked at him, all he saw was total and absolute failure.

"You're quiet tonight." Carrie ran a hand down Harry's arm. Dusk hung over them, and one of those new electric lamps flickered on, casting a shadow over the bumpy cobblestone that led them to her home.

He should tell her now. It wouldn't get easier, and he'd be leaving in two days.

"Your mother invited me to go calling with her tomorrow."

How did the female species survive on such little trivialities and purpose? Embroidery, tea, wedding plans, social clubs, gossip. Did they ever long for more? His mother and Carrie didn't seem to.

"The Travis' are hosting a ball in two weeks' time. Won't that be lovely? We haven't danced in so long."

He smashed his teeth together. She knew he hated dancing, knew he'd choose a plain old vaudeville show over a fancy ball any day of the week. Though every young couple in the city signed up for fox-trot and tango lessons, he'd avoided them like the plague.

"Carrie, can we sit?" He pointed to their usual bench, shadowed from a streetlamp, two houses away from her three-story home.

"Of course." She adjusted her skirts around the wood, and when he sat, she leaned toward him, mouth parted. The scent of jasmine wafted to his nostrils.

Well, isn't that what they usually did on this bench? He gazed down at her soft mouth, his body already responding to her willingness. Softly, he brushed his lips against hers, but then pulled away.

Her lips puckered, as if she tasted an extra bitter lemon. *That's all?*, her expression seemed to ask.

Horsefeathers, there was no easy way to say it. No easy way to admit his failure. "I won't be working at Mass General any longer."

She raised dainty fingers to her lips. "Harry, no. What happened?"

Dr. Wright. Dr. Wright happened. It was *not* Harry's fault Albin Zielinski died! But how much should he tell Carrie? They'd courted for two years, but little, if any of their discussions had ever been of a personal nature.

"I've been blamed for a patient's death and given an ultimatum from both Dr. Wright and my own father. I don't see any way around it."

Carrie stared at the cobblestone beneath her shadowed feet, her chest rising and falling softly. "What's the ultimatum?"

"Complete one year of work on Penikese Island or..." Or what? Could he afford to start his own medical practice by means of a loan? Maybe live in a boardinghouse while making a go of it? But then there was the issue of clearing his name. Blast, he wanted respect. He deserved respect. But the board at the biggest hospital in the city wouldn't allow him that privilege unless he bowed to their whims. "Or forfeit my medical career."

Carrie shot to her feet. "They can't do that. You graduated top of your class at Harvard, for Pete's sake!"

His affection for her grew in that moment. She understood. She still thought him deserving. Carrie was on his side.

"I don't see any other way around it. I'll have to go. It'll only be for a year, and then the hospital will return my job to me."

She gnawed on her bottom lip, seeming to forget etiquette for the moment. "No, Harry. Not Penikese. It's an asylum. A madhouse. Don't you remember the horror stories they told us as children? God Himself has cursed those people. And if you go there, He'll surely curse you too."

The words stung his soul, for they had been lying beneath his thoughts since that afternoon. "Do you think I'd choose this path? I haven't a choice, Carrie. My father won't take me into his practice. In a very real sense, I'm already cursed."

She shivered and tucked her arms around herself. "Anything else would be better. Anything. Perhaps my father could get you a job at the firm." She turned to him, her gaze tentative for the first time that night. "If we married, you could live with my family."

God help him, he considered it. Was he ready to settle down with a woman he wasn't sure he loved? Could he walk away from the medical profession after all the hard work he'd put into it? Could he give up being a doctor?

No. He wouldn't. As much as his father had forced him into his chosen profession, he loved it. The excitement, the risks, the knowledge he possessed, and even the people he helped. Yes, Penikese was his only option.

"I'm sorry. I have to go. Maybe after I'm back home..." Still, he found himself reluctant to make promises of marriage.

She drew herself up and tilted her chin. "Fine, have it your way. But let me give you another ultimatum, Harry Mayhew. Mark my words, if you step one foot onto that cursed piece of land, *I* will not be waiting for you upon your return."

Chapter Five

1993

The solution comes to me at the beginning of Pre-calculus, right after Mrs. Graber, my new math teacher, insists I stand up and introduce myself to the class.

I could get my GED.

I should have insisted my parents let me drop out of school while still in Maryland. Surely, I could attain my GED without too much trouble. It could have been part of our *arrangement*. They could have locked me in my room, fed me meals through a doggy door, not allowed me out in the sun. I would have promised not to show my face to anyone in town for the next four months.

It all would have been preferable to this torture.

The weight of twenty-two pairs of eyes—twenty-three including Mrs. Graber's—feel heavy upon me. I lick my lips. I refuse to stand and expose every square inch of myself—especially when I suspect my stomach has grown twofold overnight. My jean shorts are suddenly too tight, and even my X-large T-shirt and striped button-down won't hide my secret for long.

"Hi. I'm Emily. I just moved here from Maryland." I hope my

clipped words get the point across—*ignore me. Pretend I don't exist.*

Lucky for me, Mrs. Graber doesn't push. She smiles, her face growing abnormally wide with the gesture. "We're so glad to have you here, Emily."

My only hope for this new school is that everyone will be too busy planning proms and senior skip days and graduation parties and college roommates to worry about the new pregnant girl. I refuse to be naïve and think I will make new friends. No one my age will understand me.

When the bell rings, I take my time putting my books and notebook into my bag. Three girls toward the front of the class linger. Finally, I stand. One of the girls nudges the other, but when I dare to meet their gazes, they erupt in giggles and pretend they don't notice me.

I rush from the room into the hall to search out my locker. I can't possibly be imagining the looks I get in the hall. The high school isn't small—so why am I such an anomaly here? Or is my unfortunate state really that noticeable?

After a third attempt at my combination, my locker clicks open. I fumble my math textbook onto the top shelf.

A figure leans against the lockers beside me. "Hey, you're new here, right?"

I look up into green eyes and a tanned face. Gelled hair, casual stance. This guy is good-looking and he knows it.

"I guess."

He holds out his hand. "I'm Greg."

I study his hand for a moment before shaking it. No sense in being snooty. "Emily."

He glances at something behind me, but I don't look. Instead, I search for my English book. "So, Emily...if you're ever missing anything—or anyone—back home, I just want you to know I'd be happy to show you a good time." He erupts into laughter.

My face burns. "Get lost." But I'm too late. He's already gone, poking his elbows into the sides of his friends as they all glance back at me and howl on their way down the hall.

I am an idiot. I'm an idiot for not realizing how obvious my pregnancy is. For not preparing myself for humiliation. It has been two weeks since I last attended my old school—a slew of sick days and April vacation had seen to that. Apparently, two weeks was enough time for the tiny human inside of me to make things obvious.

My bottom lip trembles and I sling my bag over my shoulder and close the locker door, not bothering to cover my stomach with my button-down shirt this time. What does it matter? They all know. And those who don't will know soon enough.

I blink back tears and head for the door. Forget graduating. I *will* get my GED. There has to be another solution than to walk these hallways of hell every day for the next several weeks.

I crash through the door before I remember that I don't have a car. The day is warm and I seek out a secluded spot on the side of an open metal trailer filled with tractors and landscaping equipment. I sink to the cool dirt and rub the heels of my hands over my eyes. I refuse to spend my tears on any more stupid boys. It's quiet here. I could stay out here until the end of the day when the buses come to take students home.

"This isn't going to work."

I blink and squint up at the shadow standing above me. If it's the boy from the hall, I'm going to die. But it's not.

It's Cute Library Boy.

I'm not sure whether to be delighted or horrified. If everyone in the school knows my secret, then he must too.

I bring my knees to my chest as well as I am able and turn away from him. "Go away."

He drops a bag on the ground and sits next to me. "This spot —it's not going to work."

"What—why? I don't care."

"You see, in about two minutes when fourth period starts, Mr.

Panchak has a free period. He loves his cigarettes as much as he loves quadratic equations. Since he can't wait another hour for lunch, he comes to this very spot and lights up. He thinks no one knows."

I peer at Cute Library Boy above my arms. His hair is disheveled today, but it suits him. I lean my head back on the trailer. "Two minutes, huh?"

"One minute, forty-seven seconds, actually."

"I can't go back in there."

He doesn't speak.

"You should go, though. You don't want to get in trouble," I say.

"Who's to say I don't?"

His gray T-shirt has a picture of a pie on it along with the math symbol. Surrounding the pastry is a bunch of numbers, beginning with 3.1415...

This kid is *not* the sort to get into trouble. More likely the sort to suffer an aneurism if he missed a test question, never mind the beginning of class.

I shake my head. "I'm fine. Thanks for checking on me."

"Greg Rydale's his name, biggest d-bag in school. He once spiked my Gatorade with a fast-acting liquid laxative. Not pretty."

What did that have to do with anything?

He taps his watch. "Thirty-eight seconds." He holds his hand out to me, changes his voice to be stiff and robotic. "Come with me if you want to live."

I roll my eyes at the line from *Terminator*. Cute Library Boy is a downright dweeb. And yet I've been a bad judge of character before....

Still, I slip my hand in his at the same time that I whisk my T-shirt away from my body. He pulls me up with ease, and we round the corner, but then he dashes inside the trailer, jerking me with him. "My timing must be off today." He leads me deeper inside. We pass a weed whacker and he assists me over a riding lawnmower, unhooking my backpack strap from the clutch when it gets stuck.

When we're in the depths of the metal trailer, he crouches down and I follow suit. The scent of fertilizer and grass seed and gasoline surround us. He's still holding my hand and I release it to cover my mouth from an impromptu giggle climbing my throat. This is not what I expected to be doing on my first day of school.

Cute Library Boy—I really need to find out his name—elbows me, raises his eyebrows, and holds his finger to his lips.

A tall, balding teacher passes the trailer. A moment later, I hear what I think is a lighter. Another burst of laughter climbs my throat, threatening to come loose. It's the hormones or the gasoline fumes. Maybe both.

Cute Library Boy's mouth twitches, too. When the teacher named Mr. Panchak starts breaking out in Sir Mix-a-Lot's *Baby Got Back*, I smother my mouth against my sleeve, certain I will not last however long it takes to smoke a cigarette and sing Sir Mix's lyrics.

Beside me, Cute Library Boy shakes with silent laughter. The sight of him makes the entire situation even funnier. I steady myself on the handle of a rake, and it moves against the wall of the metal trailer enough to make a small, squeaking noise.

My laughter ceases, as does the singing. I clasp Cute Library Boy's arm, become as stiff as the statue on the water fountain that graces my front lawn back home.

Mr. Panchak sings one more verse, a little more quietly, and must snuff out his cigarette before walking back toward the school.

We wait for what feels like a solid minute before giving our laughter full rein. It echoes against the wall of the container but manages to loosen my shoulders and neck. It feels wonderful.

Cute Library Boy takes my hand again and leads me out of the trailer and back to our original spot, out of view of the school.

"Thank you," I say. The small adventure served to put my day in perspective. Maybe I would be able to face the rest of the day, after all.

"For almost getting you expelled on your first day?"

"No, for making me laugh."

He grows quiet.

We should get back to class. I readjust my backpack.

"How's Isla Nublar?"

"Isla—what?"

He slaps his forehead. "You mean you haven't even read page one?"

Oh, right. *Jurassic Park*. "Sorry. No. I've actually been reading that book on Penikese. My grandmother—" But I didn't know where her story was going. Or maybe I did. My great-aunt Atta...a leper?

While I liked this boy and while he'd shared the laxative story with me, I wasn't quite certain I needed to open myself up to more ridicule. It was hard enough being the new girl. The pregnant girl. Did I also need to divulge incriminating family history?

"Your grandmother...?"

I like the way he looks at my face. As if everything he needs to know about me is right there. Does he know I'm pregnant? It will disappoint him if he doesn't already know.

"My grandmother's telling me about how my grandfather helped start the Penikese Island School."

His gaze flickers. "Cool."

"Yeah, I wish I had known him."

Or did I? Maybe he was just another version of my father. Obsessed with doing things that looked good and worthy—*were* even good and worthy, perhaps—but without enough time to invest in his own family.

"Do you know your grandfather?" I ask in a sudden change of subject. I don't want to go back to class.

"My grandfather raised me. I still live with him."

"Oh, wow." I wonder what happened to his parents, but I don't ask.

"I don't know your name," I say instead.

"Sam."

I smile. "This was fun, Sam. We should do it again sometime."

As soon as the words are out of my mouth, I doubt them. I had assumed this kid was safe, clean. A good choice for a friend. Yet, he seems far too adept at skipping class, far too nonchalant about it. He even knows perfect hiding spots. How many times had he done this before? Maybe Cute Library Boy isn't as straight-laced as I thought. Maybe it is better to stay away, after all.

But he's already nodding his head with enthusiasm. "We should definitely do this again sometime."

WHEN THE BUS drops me off at Gram's house, I walk up the short driveway. Gram is on the porch, husking corn.

"Hey." I let my backpack drop to the planks and stretch. My lower back protests, and I rub out a knot.

"How was school?"

I flop on the rocking chair beside my grandmother and grab a corncob to begin peeling. "About as fun as a root canal."

The corners of her mouth twitch. "Your father is going to call at four. He wants to speak with you."

I groan.

"He received a call about you skipping class today."

I rip off a husk and throw it in the paper bag at Gram's feet. "It wasn't on purpose. I just needed a minute."

Gram continues husking. "You don't need excuses with me, Emily. Do you want to graduate?"

"Of course." Graduating wasn't the problem. Going to school with hundreds of my peers was.

"Then I'm assuming you'll do what you have to do to accomplish that goal."

From inside the house, the phone rings.

I stand. "I'll get it." No sense delaying the inevitable. I go inside and pick up the corded phone sitting on the kitchen counter. "Hello?"

"Emily." I'm beginning to hate my name when he says it. He might as well have answered with, "Shame on you."

I remember how, when I was younger, I asked my parents to call me, "Em." They had refused. I never met people more stubborn about nicknames than Michael and Anne Robertson.

My father clears his throat.

Would he understand if I told him about the laughing girls in math class, the guy in the hall? No. No, he wouldn't.

"Emily Grace, you best start talking."

A slow flame builds in my chest. He's never even tried to see my point-of-view. "Or what? You're going to dump me off somewhere else? Somewhere farther away?"

"Now, that is not fair. None of us like this predicament, but you can only blame yourself, Sweet Pea." Funny how calling me *Sweet Pea* didn't violate their no-nickname rule. "We're doing what we think is best."

"Best for you."

"Best for *everyone*. In a few short months, it will all be over and you can go on with your life. But you need a high school diploma to do that. I care about you, Emily. Your mother and I both do. Can't you see we want the best for you? It's why I'm calling."

I inhale a deep breath. Try with all my might to believe his words. Or at least believe *he* believes his words. Really, all I want is to get off the phone.

"It won't happen again." And it won't. I simply need to finish high school. To finish out this summer and this pregnancy. Hand the child over to the adoption agency. Then all can go back to normal.

"Very good. Now, how was your first day of school?"

He'd never once asked about my school day before. Now that I'm hundreds of miles away from him, he's going to show an interest?

"It was fine." It's what he wants to hear.

"Good. Your mother says hello. Be sure to help your grandmother and stay out of trouble, okay?"

"Yes."

"Love you, Pumpkin."

I return the phone to its cradle, close my eyes, and take a deep breath before heading back to the porch and returning to the rocking chair. Gram is done husking the corn. I had hoped she'd tell me more of her story tonight, but suddenly I'm not sure I can stomach it.

"My father was a hard man to love, too," Gram says.

Gram's father. Dad's grandfather. "Is this part of Aunt Atta's story?"

She nods. "And mine. Are you up for a walk on the beach?"

I appreciate that Gram doesn't judge me, as she promised. She doesn't scold me for cutting class. She even gave me a head's up that my father knew about my misdemeanor.

I remember what she said about her story being one of hope. If I'm in need of anything right now, it's hope.

I nod. "I'd like that."

We leave the corn husks on the porch and head east toward the shimmering ocean.

Chapter Six

"*Ach*, you Americans need to learn how to make decent beer." Niklas Schaeffer sniffed the light-colored brew in front of him, imagining instead the malty, clove-scented Weizenbock of his youth.

"Suppose a Hun like you can teach us?" A man beside Niklas snickered, drawing out more laughs from around the tavern.

"Easy, Bradbury. Niklas is one of my best customers." The bartender stuffed a cloth in a wet beer glass and swished it around the bottom. "He's just trying to lighten things up today, ain't you Niklas?"

"*Ja*, Jimmy. But not with this stuff." He slid the beer toward the back of the bar. "Give me some of that spiced rum, will ya?"

Jimmy poured him a shot before casting a glance of annoyance at the tavern door. "Aw, not again. I tell you those crazy Temperance women are gonna drive me out of business."

Niklas swallowed down a large gulp of the spicy liquor and twisted to view the window. "They singing?"

51

"Yup. Hymns, if you can believe it. And there ain't a thing I can do about it. Between them and the Prohibitionists I might be owning a speakeasy in my basement instead of a tavern on Main Street."

A man with a straggly beard raised his glass. "And I'll be your first customer, Jim!"

"*Ja*, I second that." Niklas allowed another mouthful of the liquid to burn down his throat. Any man that worked as hard as he did deserved a drink or two at the end of the day. And he made enough money to enjoy the luxury. As a skilled silversmith, he could hold his head high on these streets of America. When men mocked him or blamed him for the trouble over in Europe, Niklas could always fall back on the pride he held in his work. At Reed and Barton, he was revered and accepted. At peace.

It was home that haunted him. How many men were burdened by their own home? Yes, he deserved the calm some spiced rum could give before heading home to his two daughters. But not for long. Soon they'd both be out of his life. Gone to live with that *dummer Mensch*'s son. Both of them. His Atta. His Gertie.

Gertie. Even now, those blue eyes taunted him. Reminding him of Katharina. Of her life, of her death. Of the events preceding Gertie's birth. Doubts assailed him and he pushed his empty glass toward Jimmy for a refill. Could it be coincidence that Gertie looked nothing like him and all too much like...

"Drink up, Niklas. It'll help block out that awful singin'."

Blocking out singing was the least of his problems. What were those Bible-thumping women crooning anyway? Their voices rang out as one through the open windows, the words clear, but the message as foreign to Niklas as an immigrant fresh off Ellis Island.

> "Let not your heart be troubled,
> His tender words I hear,
> and resting on His goodness,

I lose my doubts and fears...."

Anger roiled beneath his skin. These old biddies had no right to show up at a man's place, singing songs that strummed at the rusty chords of his heart.

"His eye is on the sparrow,
and I know He watches me."

He watches me. Humph. Well, let the good Lord watch him take another drink. He hadn't watched over Katharina, and Niklas doubted the Almighty watched him drink himself haggard now.

By the time Niklas stumbled out of the tavern, the late-summer sun hovered over the horizon. Only two of the Temperance women remained. They blurred before him, but not enough for him to make out that neither were the "old biddies" he'd assumed.

He must have been staring while in his stupor because their song frittered out and the blonde vision on the right stepped forward. "Looks like this one needs some help sobering up, Ruth. What do you say?"

Niklas sneered. "Out of my way, ya cackling hens. Go find a husband to nag." He pushed through them and fumbled the key of his Model T out of his pocket.

The blond woman slid between him and the car. She smelled like lilacs.

Katharina used to smell like that.

The thought angered him. This woman angered him—the fact that she would interfere in his personal business *and* conjure up memories of his dead wife made his blood steam.

"Sir, my conscience would not bode well for me if I allowed you to drive in such a condition."

Niklas hacked up a wad of phlegm and spit on the ground near her shoe. "Is that a fact? So happens my conscience wouldn't give a second thought to runnin' you and your friend over on my way out of here."

She raised her eyebrows but stepped to the side. Niklas pushed past her.

"Sir?"

He turned. A blast of cold water slammed him in the face, awakening his senses. Sputtering, he wiped his eyes and nose but to no avail, for another cool explosion followed it. Niklas cursed, calling the women all manner of indecent names. Laughter from the door of the tavern further plucked at his pride. The blond woman stepped forward and offered him a handkerchief. He didn't take it, raising his hand instead. Oh, to slap that pretty little smirk off her face. But he hesitated long enough for Jimmy to hurry from the tavern door.

"Whoa there, Niklas." Jimmy laid a steady hand on his arm. "Maybe we're all a little tired. I'm thinking on closin' up early." A round of protests from the tavern caused the two Temperance women to pull themselves up straighter. "Why don't you head home to those beautiful daughters of yours, eh Niklas? I'll see you tomorrow when that old whistle blows."

"*Ja*," Niklas spat. He walked to the front of his Model T and used the hand crank to start the engine. When he drove out of Jimmy's Tavern, he spotted the women climbing into their buggy. He headed straight for them and swerved at the last minute, effectively spooking their horse. That would make them think twice before coming back.

The act proved fleetingly satisfying, however, for an image of Katharina watching from her high seat in heaven appeared in his mind's eye, tarnishing his enjoyment. All because of those women sticking their noses where they didn't belong.

Ten minutes later, he turned into his drive. Both Atta and Gertie would be tucking themselves into bed. He shouldn't have to see either one of them. Safer that way, anyway.

The Model T coughed up the drive. He rounded a bend and a

wave of nausea passed over him at the sight of a black Ford in front of the house. White letters on the side shouted in the inky twilight. BOARD OF HEALTH.

Last time he'd spoken with the Board of Health commissioner it had been regarding Katharina.

Katharina. Atta. Gertie.

Niklas tore out of his automobile and stalked over to the commissioner, who stood at his front door with the man Niklas hated more than any other—the man who happened to be the law of the town.

The sheriff adjusted his hat and both of the men turned to Niklas, face masks over their noses and mouths. *Um Gottes willen...*

"What do you want? I thought I told you I never wanted you on my property again, Lincoln."

"Glad you're here, Mr. Schaeffer." The commissioner nodded to him. "I need to speak with you regarding your daughter."

ATTA HOPED the knock hadn't woken Gertie. She was too tired to read another chapter of *The Secret Garden*. She opened the door and blinked at the health commissioner, the sheriff—Robert's father—and Papi all on the front steps. The sight of the masks whisked her back to the events surrounding Mami's death.

"Sheriff Lincoln? What—what can I help you gentlemen with?"

All three ignored her.

"What about my daughter?" Papi sounded angry, and from what she could gather, fairly sober.

The commissioner glanced at Atta. "I'm afraid we have some bad news, Mr. Schaeffer. We received some laboratory tests from the state this afternoon. The results...they're not good."

The glass slide. The rose-colored spots. The scalpel. Atta's chest tightened, comparable only to an iron band squeezing the life out of her. Was she to follow in her mother's footsteps? Could they diagnose tuberculosis from such a small sample of skin? She felt fine. Maybe—no—perhaps this visit had nothing to do with her. Dr. Brown had visited the school last month. What if something was wrong with Gertie?

She squeezed her eyes shut and grasped the fabric of her double-skirted dress.

Please let it be me.

"Out with it, Rowlings. You didn't show up here with masks over a bit of a cold, *ja*?" Papi seemed calm. Sturdy, like a rock. Atta never recalled garnering protection from her father. Was it only because she felt so horribly weak now that she was grateful he'd come home early? But no, she couldn't lean on him, even now. If only Robert were here.

"No easy way to say this, Mr. Schaeffer. Miss Atta." He nodded in her direction. "The good Lord knows I hate this part of my job, but the results turned up positive. I'm sorry. It seems Atta's been diagnosed with a most unfortunate malady."

Atta combed through the words in her mind, tried to make sense of them.

"What malady?" Had Papi's voice trembled?

"Leprosy, Mr. Schaeffer. Atta has leprosy."

Leprosy. The word didn't register at first, so far removed from anything she'd expected.

Leprosy. The word belonged in biblical times. It had nothing to do with her.

Slowly though, it swelled like an offending ink blot in her mind. *Atta has leprosy.* She recalled the lepers from Christ's time, haunting visions wrapped in white cloths. Warning bells. *Atta has leprosy.* Lepers. Punished. Exiled for the remainder of their miserable lives. Cursed.

No. It wasn't possible. Leprosy...her?

Cursed. In an instant, it all made sense. She dragged in large gulps of air, then stumbled backward and sat with a thump on the kitchen floor. Robert's father made a halfhearted effort to reach for her, with a gloved hand.

Papi shoved the sheriff off the threshold. "Get away from her. She doesn't need your help."

"I know this is upsetting to both of you, but we must act responsibly. We needn't make this any worse on Miss Schaeffer." The commissioner's words spoke of care, but he stayed on the front steps.

Her father ran the faucet and filled a cup. He handed it to her. She refused it, and he stared accusingly at Sheriff Lincoln. "Get off my property."

"Easy now, Niklas." Robert's father stepped forward. "This isn't a picnic for any of us, and you know my boy's gonna be devastated."

"He'll be devastated, all right. But *you* won't, will ya, Charles? After all you've done, now you gonna take my daughter!" Papi lunged at the sheriff who, seeming to expect as much, expertly grasped his wrists and cuffed them.

The sheriff leaned low. "I didn't want to use force, Niklas. But the safety of the community is at stake."

Papi struggled for only a few seconds before hanging his head. When he looked up, his eyes gleamed wet. "Please, Charles. She's a girl. What harm is she to anyone?"

The sheriff sighed and released Papi from the grip of the cuffs. Even in her desperate state, she understood how this deed tormented Robert's father. No matter what Papi insisted, Charles Lincoln was a decent man. Just like his son.

Her heart physically ached at the thought of her fiancé. Were all their plans for naught?

Mr. Rowlings rubbed a mole above his eyebrow. "She's a lot of harm, I'm afraid. We'll have to transport Atta to Penikese Island immediately. You've heard of it, haven't you? It's one of the best treatment facilities in the country for this disease. Harvard University has invested in the hospital. Atta is fortunate to live in Massachusetts. Her chances of recovery are hopeful here, especially with the disease being caught at such an early stage."

Fortunate? Recovery? But she felt fine! She wrung out the hem of her dress until it was soaked with the sweat from her hands. The scent of livestock sweltering under the hot summer sun wafted into the house. Normal, comforting. But it failed to soothe.

Penikese Island. Mr. Rowlings called it a facility—as if the place was some fancy health resort. But she'd seen the newspaper articles about the unfortunates sent there. She knew it for what it was.

A leper colony.

A place where outcasts went to die. A place for the living dead.

"Miss Atta, why don't you go and pack your things? The sheriff and I will wait."

Atta's throat threatened to close. Her breathing came in rapid spurts. Now? They expected her to leave now? Robert...Gertie... what was to become of them? There must be a way out of this mess, an escape. Maybe Dr. Browne had made a mistake. Maybe the laboratory had. She would demand another test be done. She'd—

"Tomorrow." Papi stepped outside and closed the door halfway, shielding Atta from the men on the steps.

"Mr. Schaeffer, that's not possible. While Atta is here, the town is at risk. She must—"

"I said tomorrow." Papi's voice was clear, his English surprisingly strong. "Give us that much, Charlie. She's had the disease for some time, *ja*? What is another day? I'll see to it she doesn't step out of the house. You have my word."

Atta peered around the door. Sheriff Lincoln's gaze flitted to Mr. Rowlings'. They walked to the barn, speaking in hushed tones. When they came back, the commissioner spoke. "Tomorrow morning, Mr. Schaeffer. We'll be back at dawn. Meanwhile"—he reached in the Ford for a block of wood, a hammer, and some nails—"we'll have to quarantine the place."

He handed the wood to Robert's father. Atta read the bold, red letters. QUARANTINE. The sound of hammer on wood threatened to shatter what small shred of sanity she still possessed.

The curse had begun. Maybe she deserved it. But Gertie didn't. Robert didn't. She'd asked Monsignor to forgive her countless times. He'd absolved her of her sins but here, clearer than the latticed confessional at St. Mary's, was God's answer. She was not forgiven. She would finally be punished.

When Robert's father finished, Mr. Rowlings adjusted his drooping mask. "We'll see you tomorrow, then. And while this may be little consolation, I'm confident this is what's best for Atta. She'll be well taken care of. She'll be with others who share her—her situation."

The words still hung painfully in the air when the men bid goodbye and walked to the Ford. Robert's father turned at the last minute. "Atta, if you'd like to write a message to Robert, I'll see that he gets it."

Atta nodded and pushed herself onto wobbly legs. She watched the black night envelop their car.

"I have to go out for a bit. Why don't you get some shuteye?" Papi said.

He was leaving? The one time in her life she longed for her father's arms around her and he would abandon her, most likely for his alcohol.

The tires of the Tin Lizzie crunched down the driveway and with it, Atta's head cleared. There wasn't time to be sorry for herself. She must come up with a plan, a way to protect Gertie.

She dug out a sheet of stationery from the large roll top desk in the sitting room and sat down to write her letter to Robert. Not only would the letter be filled with sorrowful goodbyes, but more importantly, it would contain a desperate plea—one for the well-being of her little sister.

Chapter Seven

Long into the night, Atta shivered on the hard floor of the bedroom she shared with Gertie. Her muscles jumped and twitched, her stomach trembled, and quite suddenly she didn't feel fine in the least. Indeed, she sensed a terrible disease possessing both her mind and her body, spreading its impending doom deep within her soul.

Forgive me Father, for I have sinned.

Afflicted images in white rags appeared before her eyes as she prayed. They called out to her—accused her with their words. "Unclean, unclean!"

How could she, who loved baths so much, who loved to be free of every speck of dirt and drop of sweat, be unclean? Her mother had been pregnant with her when her parents braved the trip across the Atlantic. Might she have somehow caught this illness from the unclean condition of their ship?

As if to correct the idea that she could have caught the sickness from another person or circumstance, the words of a respected man of the church resounded in her ears. He'd been speaking with a group of men at a church barbeque. "Disease is the whip of God for the sin of man."

The sin of man. The sin of Atta Schaeffer.

A sense of imminent disaster, heavy like death, spread through her soul, and her shivering grew more violent.

"Forgive me...Father, for I—I have sinned." But she could not draw peace from the words. A high, long wall existed between her and God. He himself had cursed her.

She sat up and covered her mouth with her pillow before squinting to see Gertie's shadowy outline beneath the covers. She pictured her sister's silky blonde hair, her long eyelashes, her small mouth puckered with sleep. Perhaps Atta should wake her now. They could cherish their few precious hours together. She could remind Gertie to stay out of Papi's way, remind her to place the hope chest against the bedroom door every night. Should she enlist help from one of the church ladies? Plead for help to keep Gertie safe?

No, she'd written her letter to Robert. He would ensure Gertie's safety.

Her chest ached. Would she ever see Robert again? Suddenly, a letter didn't seem adequate to say goodbye, to ensure her sister's future.

Atta crept out of the bedroom and downstairs, past Papi asleep on the divan, probably passed out cold. She stopped short at the package on the counter, a box from Olivia's Bakery—the blueberry scones were her favorite. A part of her was touched that Papi would go out in the early morning hours to secure her favorite baked good on her last morning home, but anger vied for position over the softening in her heart. Her father was the reason she feared for Gertie's safety in the first place. She didn't desire any blueberry scone as much as she desired peace of mind regarding her little sister.

Atta held her breath as she opened and closed the back door. A crescent moon lightened the cloak of night, and she hurried down the drive and onto the deserted road. The pine trees that usually offered comfort now partially concealed the earlier apparitions from her bedroom. Their faces were but a black hole amidst rags and dirtied bandages. They hobbled out from behind the pines, calling out to her, "Cursed! Unclean!"

She walked faster but tumbled to the ground when she twisted her ankle in a hole. If ever there were tears within her, surely, they would make their appearance now. But no. She wasn't hopeless. She must get to Robert. He would take her in his arms and reassure her they'd be together soon. He'd have a plan for Gertie. He'd convince her she wasn't cursed—that she would get well one day soon.

Half limping, half running down the road from the shadows, she finally reached Sheriff Lincoln's farmhouse. She trod with careful steps, cognizant of every twig beneath her feet. Robert's father would take her into custody if he found her, and she'd miss her chance to tell Gertie goodbye. She'd never forgive herself for such a circumstance.

With light steps, she walked to the back of the house and stooped to pick up a pebble. She hurled the stone at Robert's bedroom window. One more and—

"Atta!" Robert poked his head out and spoke in a loud whisper. For a moment, he stared at her. Then finally, "I'll be right down."

A moment later, he opened the back door, his posture stiff at the threshold. Atta stopped herself from running into his arms. He wore a thin white t-shirt and a pair of coveralls. The moonlight glinted off his light hair. Oh, surely everything would be all right for them in the end, wouldn't it?

"Atta...you shouldn't be here."

She took a single step toward him. "I know, but I had to see you. Did—did your father tell you?" Shame shrouded her words, yet perhaps this was the reason for Robert's rigid demeanor. Perhaps he thought she breeched propriety to come to him at night.

"He did." Robert looked behind his shoulder and stepped

outside. "Let's go in the barn. I don't want to wake him." He led the way, quickly.

He didn't reach for her hand.

He always held her hand, no matter how short the walk. Oh, why didn't he hold her?

The barn smelled of fresh straw and livestock, reminiscent of the scent Robert carried. She ached for his arms around her, but the embrace didn't come. He left the door ajar.

"I'm sorry, Robert. I'm so, so sorry. I have no idea how it happened." Yet she did, didn't she? It was because of her transgressions.

His Adam's apple bobbed, his profile beautiful against the moonlight streaming through the barn window. "I don't know what to say, Atta. I can't believe this could happen to you. To us."

"Mr. Rowlings said the hospital on Penikese is very up and coming, with all the latest treatments. He said my chances of recovery are good."

"Recovery? From leprosy?"

She shivered at the word, surprised at how dirty it made her feel. "Must you say it?"

"Does not saying it make it not true?"

His harsh words bit the night air, cutting through her. Would he give up on them so easily? Give up on her? Her strength and hero...he was failing her. Or maybe she had failed him.

"I am sorry. I wish I could make it all right. I keep hoping I'll wake and find it all a dream." Oh, that it was.

He shoved his hands in his pockets and breathed in the air coming through the open window.

The fresh air.

Air not contaminated by her breathing.

And yet they had shared intimate kisses before this night. The same breath. They'd planned to share so much more. Would one ugly word drive them apart?

Robert's horse, Goliath, stomped a single foot as if to assure her that yes, *this* one ugly word was enough to separate them.

"Gertie." Atta dug her fingernails into the waist of her blouse and gulped down a breath. "Will you watch over her, Robert? Please? I'm so scared."

Emotion passed his face. Pity? Compassion?

"You know I will." He walked toward her and lifted a hand to the arm of her blouse, stopping short of touching it. His eyes shone with unshed tears, and she sensed how difficult it was for him to hold back. Surely, he would succumb and touch her after all.

But a moment passed, then another. And he did not give in. He stood firm, too firm to be of any comfort. No tender caress, no light touch of his lips to her temple.

"I still love you, Atta Schaeffer."

His words made her heart flutter, but his actions spoke louder.

And that, more than anything, assured her of the curse upon her.

ATTA scurried home to the chorus of birds coaxing pale pink rays from the eastern sky. She didn't have much time to say goodbye to Gertie, to speak some sense into her father. Perhaps her time would have been better spent doing these things. At least then she wouldn't have felt the barricade Robert had so effectively erected between them.

But he had assured her he'd look after Gertie, and Atta trusted he'd keep his word. Still, short of taking Gertie to the Boys Club with him every afternoon and keeping her at his house at night, how much would he be able to protect her?

The scent of coffee didn't tempt her as she opened the back door. Papi stood at the kitchen counter, pouring two cups.

"Atta." He didn't seem surprised she'd left the house. "Have some coffee. And scones."

"No, thank you. I'm not hungry." The commissioner would be here any minute. The press of time squeezed around her in an invisible wall of steel. She must talk to Gertie. But first...

"Papi."

He grunted.

"Look at me, Papi. Please."

He obliged, his dark eyes almost warm at times like these, when they were not possessed by the poison of whiskey.

"You need to stay sober, Papi. You need to find a way."

"*Ach*, don't go tellin' me what I can and cannot do, girl." He slung back a gulp of coffee.

She raked her mind for something that would hold enough weight to change his heart. If she and Robert hadn't come home when they did a few weeks earlier, he would have...

"You'll kill her, Papi. You'll kill her if you don't stop drinking."

Her cheek stung with the impact of Papi's hand, but she hardly paused to nurse her wound. He could hit her all he wanted. She wouldn't stop.

"You hate Gertie when you're in the bottle. It's—it's abominable. Please let it go. Please promise me you'll at least try to stay sober. I'll never ask for anything else in my life. I'll gladly be cursed forever if...oh, please Papi!"

Slowly, as if in defeat, he lowered his hand. "Promises," he spat the word as if it were detestable. "You know girl, I made a few promises to your Mami before she died. Want to guess how well I've kept those?" His fingers quivered, but he subdued them with another swig of coffee. He waved his hand toward the stairs. "Go."

Atta considered pressing him further, but if Papi himself admitted his pledges to her mother were as pure as fool's gold, what use would one be to her? Heart sodden with grief, she climbed the stairs, attempting a cheery disposition as she pushed open the door of her bedroom.

Gertie slept soundlessly, her blond hair pooled around her head like golden rays of sunshine. Atta sat beside her before realizing her mistake. She jumped up and moved against the wall, as far as she could from her sister.

"Gertie," she whispered, hoping to break her little sister from her sweet dreams gently. She longed to give her tiny shoulder the usual touch that accompanied their morning ritual.

Gertie stirred. Her blue eyes focused, and Atta forced a smile to her lips.

"Good morning, sleepyhead."

"Mornin' Atta. It seems so early. Do you need help with breakfast?"

"No, but I do need to talk to you."

Her sister sat up, brushed a lock of hair from her eyes, and pulled her hands beneath the sleeves of her nightgown. "What about? Do you need me to stay home from school to help you today?"

Raw emotion scraped Atta's throat, but she stood her ground. Away from Gertie.

"What's wrong, Atta? Why are you all the way over there?"

"I can't sit with you, Gertie. That's—that's what I need to talk to you about. Some men came last night. They said I have to leave for a little while. They need some help with...with an experiment." Not a lie. Wasn't the entire realm of treating this disease an experiment?

Gertie's eyes widened with alarm and she shook her head back and forth. "What do you mean? You're leaving me?"

"Only for a little. We'll be together soon, I know it. Please be brave for me, Gertie."

Her blue eyes turned glassy. "No. No! I'm coming with you."

"You can't, darling. I'm so sorry, but you can't go where I'm going."

"No, Atta. Please don't leave!" Tears streamed down Gertie's soft, round cheeks as she jumped out of bed and hurled herself into Atta's arms, wrapping tight legs around her waist and clutching her neck with a viselike grip. Atta couldn't summon the willpower to do more than hold her breath and cling to her sister, relishing her tight little hold.

She hummed the tune to *Schlaf, Kindlein schlaf*, savoring the pleasant weight of Gertie in her arms, the scent of the Canthrox shampoo she'd worked into her hair the night before.

After a moment, though, the crunch of wheels sounded on the gravel drive below. Sniffing, she placed a now limp Gertie back onto her bed. "Listen to me, Gertie. You need to remember what I'm about to tell you. You'll remember, won't you? Please promise me."

Her sister's bottom lip trembled and she wiped her nose with her sleeve. Tears clung to her lashes. "I promise, Atta."

Car doors slammed and the voices of the sheriff and the commissioner rumbled outside the window.

"I've talked to Robert. He'll watch out for you. You go to him if you need anything, Gertie. Anything at all, you hear?"

Her sister nodded, her wet gaze now filled with fear.

"Don't leave for school until Papi's gone for work. And—"

"But Sister will rap me with the ruler, Atta." Gertie rubbed the knuckles of her left hand and Atta stopped herself from running over and kissing her small fingers. Still, a smack on the knuckles was the lesser of two evils that could await her little sister.

"I'll write a letter to Sister for you, explaining the situation. If you run fast, you should make it on time."

"Atta!" Papi's voice bellowed from below.

She couldn't leave yet. Not until they practiced with the hope chest. She strode to the door and opened it a crack. "I'll be right down!" She shut the door and pointed to the heavy chest—a chest of things she would not be using now, maybe ever. "Show me how you can put this in front of the door by yourself, Gertie."

The tears started again. "Please, Atta. Don't go. Don't leave me like Mami did."

Atta ignored the burning beneath her eyelids. She stripped her pillow of its case and started throwing undergarments in it. Her pincushion. Her rosary. Tears would not come in this moment. She wouldn't let them. They'd only serve to frighten Gertie further. "You come straight home from school. Don't worry about taking care of Papi—he can take care of himself. You come up here no later than six o'clock and you put my chest in front of the door. Do you understand?"

Silence.

"Gertie Schaeffer, do you understand me?"

She nodded, but still did not move from the bed.

"Now come, I want to see that chest in front of the door."

For a moment, it seemed Gertie might refuse her—something she'd never done. Instead, she slid off the bed and began to struggle inch by inch with the chest. The ordeal continued after five minutes, and Atta turned away to finish packing to spare herself the heartbreak of watching Gertie work so hard.

Footsteps on the stairs. But no, she needed to see that Gertie could secure the chest against the door. She dove into the hall.

"The commissioner is getting impatient, Atta. Time to go." Papi looked tired, and older than she'd ever remembered. Gray hair seemed to have sprouted at his temples overnight.

"Three more minutes, Papi. Gertie deserves that much."

His jaw set and he nodded. "Three minutes then they come up here themselves." He turned and went downstairs, his footsteps slow and heavy.

Atta hurried back into the room to see Gertie sobbing into her arms, which rested on the chest. "I can't, Atta. It's too heavy."

"You must, Gertie. We won't move it all the way near the bed after. We'll put it much closer. Please, keep trying."

Shove by shove, it must have been much longer than three minutes before Gertie secured the chest in front of the door.

"Well done." Atta resisted kissing the tears from her sister's cheeks. She moved the hope chest back a few feet from the door then lowered herself in front of Gertie. "I love you, Gertie. Do as I told you and you'll be fine. I'll be back soon. I promise."

She'd never broken a promise. Until now. She'd promised Mami she'd take care of Gertie. Forever. How would she live each day knowing her sister was in danger? Knowing she disappointed her mother in heaven...again?

Gertie threw her arms around her and whispered into her neck, "I love you, Atta. Come back soon. Please."

"I'll write as soon as I can, darling. Remember to check the mail every day. And don't go wandering over to the Shepherds' if their dog's loose. Please remember all I've told you. I love you, Gertie."

Gertie stifled a sob, nodding through a fresh wave of tears. Atta grabbed her pillowcase and left the room without glancing back.

Her sister's soft whimpers chased her down the stairs where Papi waited. The commissioner stood outside with Robert's father, both with masks and rubber gloves in place.

Atta took in her last breath of freedom and looked at Papi once more, knowing any words she spoke would be inadequate. She barely knew this man she called her father. Felt nothing toward him but resentment. Maybe even hatred.

"Please, Papi..." She grasped for words. *Make wise choices. Think of Gertie. Stop being so stupid!*

His mouth hardened and he turned away. "I'll have Gertie light a candle for you at Mass. Goodbye, Atta."

She walked into the fresh morning light and stepped into the Board of Health car, a newfound determination overtaking her. She would survive this ugly illness. The real question was, would her family?

Chapter Eight

The girl was almost attractive. Almost.

Absurd, of course. Harry refused to think of the words *attractive* and *leper* in the same sentence.

He leaned over the rail of the *J.T. Sherman* tugboat. The salty sea air whipped through his short curls. The girl on the deck below —the one he'd been told would be a patient on the island— allowed her gaze to flitter up to him. Just as quick, it returned to the blue abyss beneath.

For a moment, he allowed himself to consider the petite, plain-looking girl, whose shoulders slumped within her blouse, whose very demeanor resembled that of a wounded puppy. What, or who, had she left behind? While Harry's stay was not permanent, hers would be complete exile.

He moved to the other side of the boat, contemplating the use of the cotton stowed away in his medical bag. A well-known pathologist from Harvard who had worked with lepers in Hawaii only a few years earlier was known for sticking cotton up his nose when in the vicinity of the unclean. Rubber gloves were also employed. Harry should have put them on before boarding the boat. Or at least asked the captain if the tug was fumigated after each leper transportation.

A speck of land on the horizon loomed closer, and sour bile coated the back of his throat. There it was. The smallest of the Elizabeth Islands. The most insignificant. The single blemish of Cape Cod.

Penikese.

Once he stepped on land, there would be no turning back. Carrie's offer still stood in his mind, tempting at this point. He thought of their last conversation. The girl was spoiled, used to getting her way. Sentencing himself to a lifetime with her, perhaps giving up his medical career, was almost as bad a verdict as a year in a leper colony.

He'd attempted one last ditch effort yesterday and signed up for the Medical Reserve Corps. But they hadn't whisked him away to some army base. Instead, the lieutenant he'd spoken with assured him they'd be in touch. The officer hadn't so much as raised a brow when he gave the name of his new address. While not certain war would be more desirable than living among the cursed, Harry put his hope in Wilson's desire—America's desire—to stay out of the combat raging overseas. Besides, he was quite certain a hospital tent behind front lines was preferable to the piece of land emerging in full view before him.

He gazed into the cloudless blue sky above the island's horizon, wondered if some Almighty laughed at his circumstances. God. *Humph*. What did the Mayhews need of a Creator? Sure, they attended their local church every Sunday, but wasn't that more for the sake of appearances than for spiritual matters? No sir, the Mayhews made their own good fortune out of life, at least until now. Harry thought of Albin Zielinski, whether his patient was in heaven this moment. Did he watch his family grieve his death? Did he blame Harry? Did one concern themselves with such things in the afterlife?

Harry opened his medical bag and pulled on a pair of rubber gloves.

"Doctor?" A young deckhand with sunburned skin approached him at the rail. "You needn't worry about the gloves. We'll be dropping you off at the administration side, where Dr. Parker makes his home. The lepers aren't allowed on that half of the island."

Harry didn't remove his gloves, not willing to look foolish in front of the seaman. He jerked his head toward the other side of the boat. "What about her?"

"We'll bring her around on the patient side after we've dropped you off, sir. The *Sherman* doesn't normally go all the way to Penikese—only to Cuttyhunk. But because of the situation"— he nodded toward the patient below—"we're docking at Penikese."

Harry nodded, and the man left. The tug's motor slowed as they chugged closer to his new home. A small cove lay to his right, a thin strip of land connecting it to the main part of the island. A band of rocky sand separated land from ocean before giving way to tall, wispy grass. Large brush covered the island, not one tree in sight. No place for shelter, no place for hiding. Barren, much like his life was about to become. Strange how the ocean's beauty seemed robbed here. As if some invisible blanket covered it in loneliness.

The tug cut into the smooth water, and its motor died out. A large two-story building to the right reminded Harry of the main house of a southern plantation, its stately presence somewhat assuring. On the wharf, a ruddy-faced gentleman waited. He wore black pants and a white shirt beneath a vest. He searched the boat expectantly, his hands tucked behind his back. Neatly combed white hair stuck out the sides of his bowler cap. It matched his trimmed mustache, the ends of which curled upward.

Harry stepped away from the rail, removed his gloves, and shoved them into his medical bag. When he descended the stairs to the lower deck, the leper was nowhere to be seen. She'd likely stood in this same spot at some point in the voyage. He fought the temptation to hold his breath as the captain and deckhand wished him well. Harry climbed the stone steps to the pier.

The gentleman on the wharf smiled and extended his hand. "Frank Parker. Pleasure to have you with us, Dr. Mayhew."

"Thank you, Dr. Parker."

"Frank, please. We don't stand much on formalities here." Dr. Parker reached for a burlap bag in the captain's hand. "Thank you, Bill. They've been anxious for their letters. I'll drop these off then meet you on the other side." He turned to Harry. "This way, Dr. Mayhew."

Luggage in hand, Harry matched Dr. Parker's long strides as they stepped off the wharf and onto the sand. Seagulls called above —lonely, haunting sounds. The scent of sea air mingled with that of warm grass. The sun beat down upon them and Harry regretted wearing his tie. Who did he have to impress, anyway? This was a one-year punishment. Dr. Wright's letter hadn't said anything about being released early on account of good behavior, much less good impressions.

"I must say, I'm delighted you've decided to come," Dr. Parker said.

"Thank you, sir."

They veered right down a path covered on either side by large brush. Bird droppings littered the ground, and Harry chose his steps with care.

"When I requested the board send me a doctor who had equal or perhaps more bacteriological training than my former assistant, Dr. Honeij, I didn't expect to receive such a blessing. Not many such men choose to study at a leprosy hospital, though I'm glad you're in the minority. Nothing big or showy here, but these patients need doctors. Doctors who care."

Warning flags went off in Harry's head as the brush ahead of them gave way to the white administration building. Dr. Parker had been misinformed about the circumstances of his arrival. Although the facts would cause him further shame, he refused to mislead the man before him. If they were to work together for the next three hundred and sixty-five days, it would be easier if the truth were laid out on the table.

"Dr. Parker, I'm afraid there's a slight misunderstanding."

The older gentleman stopped and tipped his hat. The sound of the wind beating a flag holder against its pole broke the long silence. "Oh?"

"While I do have proper bacteriological training to undertake this endeavor, I must tell you I am not here of my own accord."

Dr. Parker's brow puckered, causing the wrinkles around his eyes to deepen. "And how is that, Dr. Mayhew?"

Somehow the address in front of his surname now seemed like a demerit instead of the distinguished promotion it should be. Why had he spoken? Yet the answer came clearer than the cerulean sea surrounding him. This was his last chance. He need only be honest with Dr. Parker, and that may be enough to send him back on the *Sherman* and on to Boston. No doubt Dr. Wright had left out this important detail in hopes of smoothing things over with the gentleman before him. But if Dr. Parker knew....

"I am being disciplined, Doctor."

"Disciplined. How so?"

"I am to be here for one year as a punishment of sorts. Dr. Wright was none too pleased with some orders I disregarded." Harry stopped short of informing Dr. Parker of Albin Zielinski's death. The man's figure beneath the white sheet was still too fresh in his mind. The imagined faces of his wife and children still too fresh in his dreams.

Dr. Parker slapped a hand against his thigh, and Harry braced himself for the inevitable. A stern reprimand. An expression of disappointment. All followed by an order to wait on the dock for the *J.T. Sherman* to carry him back to the mainland.

But the order never came.

"Huh." Dr. Parker let out a humorless laugh, the corners of his mouth tight. "I ask for an expert and they send me someone else's mistake." He continued toward the house. "Well, it can't be helped. I'm afraid we're stuck with one another, Dr. Mayhew. You have the training. I expect you to use it to the benefit of my patients. And you better not botch it up. Sounds as if you're walking on thin ice with the well-to-dos back in Boston."

His comment hit too close for comfort, one of the said "well-to-dos" being his own father.

"Can I share something with you, Dr. Mayhew?"

Harry nodded.

"Fishing."

"Sir?"

"I love fishing. Do you know the key to a great catch, Dr. Mayhew?"

"No, I'm afraid I don't." William Mayhew had preferred spending father-son time berating his son in regard to the finer points of doctoring. Harry had never fished in his life.

"Good bait. I'm about to offer you some good bait, Dr. Mayhew, so listen up." Dr. Parker's gaze demanded his attention. "This island may not be all that pleasant. You may find the patients frightening at first. But we are all they have. And for a promising young doctor such as yourself, Penikese may be a perfect place to advance your career. Maybe make up for past wrongs, eh?"

Zielinski's face flashed before him. The old scar on his calf tingled as a younger version of his father stood before him, yelling, mocking, belittling.

"What are you alluding to, Dr. Parker?"

"Just that, if anyone, anywhere were to be successful in cultivating—perhaps even annihilating—the leprosy bacillus, it would be a doctor with a fine education such as yourself, who has the opportunity to study the disease firsthand, and who has a first-rate laboratory available to him, not to mention contacts from the most distinguished medical school in the United States. You still have friends at Harvard, do you not, Dr. Mayhew?"

Harry coughed, the wheels of his brain turning. "Yes, of course."

"Then who better than you to apply yourself...to meet this challenge head on in order to lengthen the strides of medicine?"

Hmmm. Dr. Parker did make some valid points.

"I'm going to be quite candid with you, Dr. Mayhew. I've been here for near ten years. I came with high expectations of a cure to be found. I've poured my blood and sweat into this island—into these poor souls, and I am no closer to a cure. But I'd like to think I've made their stay here more bearable, that my wife and I have been a comfort to those the world sees as outcasts. In my mind, that may be just as important as a cure."

Harry stared at the stucco administration building. Two one-story additions on either side huddled up to the main part of the building.

"If a cure were to be found, the medical community would not be quick to forget such an accomplishment. Imagine, a cure to the most feared malady known to man. A cure for the dreaded disease that only Christ could make well. Wouldn't you like to be in such good company, Dr. Mayhew?"

Harry released a strained sigh. The way Dr. Parker spoke, he was being given an amazing opportunity—an opportunity to earn accolades from his peers, from the country, from the world. An opportunity to wipe the past clean, to make his father proud.

Dr. Parker stood on the steps of the administration building, a sparkle in his sea-blue eyes. "Good bait, Dr. Mayhew?"

Humph. Good bait, indeed.

Chapter Nine

"You must be Atta. Pleasure to meet you, dear."

Atta wasn't sure what kind of greeting she'd expected upon her arrival at Penikese, but it was nothing like the one before her. A stout, pleasant-looking woman in her late-fifties extended a hand—a bare hand—to her. Hesitant, Atta took it.

"I'm Marion Parker. My husband is the superintendent and attending physician on the island." The woman squeezed her hand, but only for a moment before Atta snatched it back. Mrs. Parker's brown gaze softened. "I know you've been through a lot in the last day, dear. It isn't right. But you're here now, and I intend to make your transition as smooth as possible."

Why did the older woman not hesitate to touch her? The gesture both calmed and unnerved Atta at the same time. Hadn't she expected never to be touched again? Never hugged, never kissed, never caressed. Even Robert, whom she loved with fierce devotion, had shunned her. She was now an untouchable.

"I'll show you where you'll be staying." Mrs. Parker walked off the dock with all the grace of a finely-bred lady. Atta hung several feet behind and hugged her stuffed pillowcase, reluctant to leave the tugboat, her last connection to the mainland. Gertie would be at school now. Had she been able to braid her hair by herself? Had she remembered her schoolwork from the night before? A quiver climbed Atta's throat.

"Come now, dear. Dr. Parker will see you soon. He has business on the other side of the island to attend first."

Whether it was the mention of seeing a doctor or the gentle hand that again reached for her elbow, Atta snapped from her silent mode. "Mrs. Parker, I insist you cease touching me. You must realize you're putting yourself in danger."

Mrs. Parker studied her beneath a hat adorned with several feathers. "So they say, Miss Atta. So they say. But I have been here for nearly ten years. I've cared for the patients. I've read to them. Shared parties with them. Eaten with them. Of course, the necessary precautions are put into place. But the fact of the matter is, Hansen's disease has been highly stigmatized. In fact, my husband is one of the few who believe that more than ninety percent of the world's population has a natural immunity to the disease."

Atta's heart sank. "I'm afraid you've been misinformed, Mrs. Parker. The disease the health commissioner accuses me of carrying does not go by that name."

"They are one in the same, dear. Only calling it Hansen's disease is a bit more gentle to the ear, wouldn't you agree?"

Atta stroked the fabric of her pillowcase. The material already felt different, saturated with salt from the thick humidity swelling off the sea. "Changing a name doesn't change the circumstances though, does it? Whatever you call it, it's still torn me away from my life, from those who love me, those that *need* me."

To Atta's surprise, Mrs. Parker's eyes became misty. "I am so sorry for all you've lost."

They stared at one another for a moment, Atta feeling understood for the first time since she'd been diagnosed with the awful "it."

"Come now, you've had a long morning." When Mrs. Parker touched her elbow again, Atta didn't jerk from her fingers.

The wind tugged a few strands of hair loose from her chignon. With the exception of a handful of pitiful saplings, there were no trees. No shelter. Only a big hunk of desolate grass that pricked at her ankles. Bad enough to be cast away from Robert and Gertie, but to be cast forever onto this lonely piece of land? Would she never again sit beneath a pine tree and watch the limbs dance in the breeze?

What was left for her? If she couldn't take care of Gertie, couldn't live a normal life with a husband who loved her, couldn't so much as enjoy her favorite parts of God's creation, what was left?

Despair clutched at her stomach, twisting and jerking until it became a physical knot of pain.

No.

She'd promised Gertie she'd be back soon. She would get well. She would find a way back to her sister.

Mrs. Parker led her toward a large, two-story wooden building beside two cottages, all surrounded by a wire fence.

"The cows kept tramping through the patient's gardens. Dr. Parker and Lee—he's a patient here—installed the fence to keep them out." Mrs. Parker picked her way over the rough terrain ahead of Atta.

"Mrs. Parker...the health commissioner back home said I could be cured here. How long might that take?"

The older woman's frame seemed to deflate, her shoulders slouched. "Unfortunately, I am not suited to answer that question. Once you're settled, Dr. Parker will speak with you."

"Will you be present?"

The feathers on Mrs. Parker's hat waved in the breeze. "That's not our standard protocol, but if you'd like to request one of the nurses to be with you, I'm sure my husband will see to it. I'll speak with him before he attends you."

"No, that's fine." Atta caught a slight slithering movement out of the corner of her eye. It pushed down a narrow path of grass before her. "Oh!"

Mrs. Parker took her hand and pulled her in the opposite direction. "Only a garter snake, dear. They won't bother you. The island has many. Best get past your fear now."

An island of snakes. How fitting a cursed lot should dwell with the legless beasts.

"Dr. Parker and I have arranged for you to stay in one of the cottages. For now, you will be alone, although we can't know for how long. Would that suit you?"

Atta nodded and Mrs. Parker walked up the steps of a quaint little cottage with a small porch and pushed open the door. The scent of disinfectant stung Atta's nostrils. Mrs. Parker busied herself with opening the salt-encrusted windows. A small hearth sat in a larger room, along with a crude table, two chairs, and a kerosene lamp. A worn wardrobe with a hat cupboard on one side took up another corner. Atta walked into the room, the sand beneath the soles of her shoes gritty on the wood floor.

Two side rooms held a neatly made bed and the other, a small kitchenette. Atta placed her pillowcase on the bed, struggling to picture herself in this desolate cabin day and night.

"The patients used to cook their own food, but now they all eat together in the dining hall in the hospital building. Betsy is a wonderful cook. She prepares miracles with Lee and Toy's catches, not to mention their gardens. Breakfast's at seven, lunch at noon, and dinner at six. Betsy will ring the bell. Reverend Bailey comes every other Tuesday to hold services."

Reverend? "I'm—I'm Catholic, Mrs. Parker."

"Attendance is not required, of course. But the service is all we have, and the patients have come to enjoy it—even Toy, who is a follower of Zeno, and Solomon, who is Jewish."

"I understand," Atta croaked.

"Dear, I believe there is one God who created the heavens and the earth. Catholics believe the same, do they not?"

I believe in God, the Father almighty, the creator of heaven and earth...

"Yes, yes of course."

"Then maybe we would all benefit to focus on that for now. For surely, God sees our sorrows and will take us under His wings. Surely, He will carry us when we are too weak to walk."

Atta marveled at the beauty of the words. Would God truly carry her? Hadn't He cursed her?

"If you please, Mrs. Parker. Where do I bathe?"

"That would also be done over at the hospital. Come, I'll take you there and introduce you to the nurses."

Atta shut the cottage door and rubbed her arms. The wide expanse of sea stood gleaming before her, a hundred yards away. Papi had taken her and Mami to the beach once when Atta was nine. But it had been sheltered by a horseshoe-shaped cove. Here, it was nothing but vast, endless blue water kissing the horizon.

No chance for escape. A perfect place to dispose of outcasts.

She searched the skyline again. In the distance, a faint gray line smudged the horizon. She hadn't time to search out a map before they'd left. It might soothe her to know her placement in the inky ocean.

Shivering, she turned to the right and hastened to catch up with Mrs. Parker. The woman pointed. "There's a fence of barbed wire at the top of the hill. The administration building is there. The patients are not to go past the wire in order to avoid"—she didn't meet Atta's gaze—"you see, there's a large cistern there and it could be dangerous."

Atta's mouth tightened. Mrs. Parker's unspoken words were clearer than the ocean beyond. The barbed wire was not so much for her protection, but for the protection of those who staffed the island.

The hospital linked two cottages together to make up a large two-story building with plentiful windows. They entered the door and walked down a corridor toward the sound of soft music. "This is the amusement room. Many of the patients find it their favorite."

The long, narrow room overlooked the water by means of half a dozen windows. A billiard table dominated the center of the room. An organ sat to one side, along with three phonographs placed around the wall, one which wound down a tune.

Atta wrapped her arms around her waist and studied a woman on the bench opposite them. Her hair lay graying and unkempt, her skin dark. Though difficult to tell her age, Atta guessed her to be in her late forties. She rocked back and forth, mumbling to herself. With vigorous strokes, she rubbed at a spot on her fingers, drawing Atta's attention to her claw-like hands. The woman then slapped at her hand, as if trying to rid it of the disease.

Pity erupted in her belly. But the woman must have sensed Atta's gaze, for she looked up and threw her a smoldering look.

"Leper!" Her voice came out throaty and heavily accented. While not much above a whisper, the words packed a strong punch as her gaze seared through Atta. "Leper! Stay away from me!"

The pity vanished as Atta fought the urge to run from the hospital building, to plunge herself into the cool salty sea, to swim back home if necessary.

Mrs. Parker placed an arm around her as a nurse knelt beside the ranting woman and spoke in soothing tones. The woman quieted, and Atta dared look at the rest of the room. An orderly stood in the middle, and another nurse walked toward them.

"This is Nurse Edith Nason, Atta. And Mrs. Tufts, her assistant, is over there by Mary. Don't let Mary frighten you, now. She's harmless. Some simply don't adjust well. We try to do what we can for her."

Nurse Edith smiled, but Atta's nerves remained on edge. Ranting women, pretty young nurses in crisp white outfits—it was all too much to comprehend.

Mrs. Parker showed her the dining hall and the bathrooms,

supplied with both fresh and salt water. She explained the strict water restrictions before leading her to a separate room in the hospital.

"Dr. Parker will see you now. You take care, dear, and let me know if I can get you anything. The boat will come in another three days for the mail. I'll be sure to get you some stationery so you can write your loved ones."

"Thank you, Mrs. Parker. I appreciate your kindness."

The woman smiled and turned to go, leaving Atta alone in an examination room that smelled of iodine. She squeezed her eyes shut, attempting to shut out the harshness of her new reality.

Knees weak, she lay back on the high table, but shot up at the realization that the other patients had laid in this same spot. Could being around them progress the course of the disease?

A cough gurgled up her airways and she buried her face in the sleeve of her shirtwaist until it subsided.

"Robert," she whispered into the quiet room. "Please wait for me. Please believe I will get better. Have faith enough for both of us."

Chapter Ten

"You are the first native-born citizen we've had as a patient, Miss Atta. The first American." Dr. Parker removed the gloves he'd used to examine the pale-pink blurs on her leg and studied her, his gaze pensive.

Atta eased her fingers from their tight grip on the edges of the metal exam table.

"I'm sorry you're uncomfortable with the exams, but we only wish to help. And your case has been caught early. The greatest service you can do for yourself is to try not to be too anxious. Keep your hands busy. Do you like to garden? Or maybe knit?"

Atta attempted to push words past her dry tongue. At least Dr. Parker's hands were no longer upon her. At least she had the comfort of her long skirt to hide herself.

She avoided his gaze and looked to one of the four spacious windows along the wall. Nothing about the older man should frighten her. He was none too big, with a kind demeanor and friendly eyes, crinkled at the corners. His white hair and matching handlebar mustache reminded her of a wise old sea captain. Perhaps she'd think of him as such. Yes, a kindly sea captain, head of the island. Not a doctor, but a commander of a ship.

The absurd thought served to loosen her tongue. "I like to quilt."

Dr. Parker gave a nod that hinted of satisfaction. "Good. I'll see Mrs. Parker orders you some material. It may take a week or two to arrive."

"Is that to be part of my treatment, Doctor?" She couldn't help the sarcastic bite that sneaked into her words. But how was making a few quilts going to lighten the curse upon her? He should prescribe her medicine. Something, anything rather than sit and wait for her hands to shrivel, for her limbs to become deformed beneath rotting flesh, for her mind to succumb to insanity.

The doctor smiled. His mustache hid the ends of his mouth—very becoming of a sea captain. "True, the majority of the medical community may not agree with my assessment, but nine years of observations has shown that the more actively the mind and hands are employed, the more beneficial the result in treatment."

"So what you're saying is that if I concentrate hard enough on busying my mind, my body will rid itself of this—this thing?"

"I'm afraid I can't make any such bold claims as that, Miss Atta. But I do believe it will slow the progression of the disease."

"The progression. But what of a cure?" She looked to the labeled bottles on his desk. Strychnine, chlorate of potassium, arsenic acid, chaulmoogra oil. "I was told my chances of recovery would be best here. I've promised my little sister I'd be home soon." Had the health commissioner proclaimed such fabrications to get her on the island without argument? Was there any hope for her at all?

"I will be honest with you as I always am with my patients. There is no known cure for Hansen's disease at this time. A doctor with extensive bacteriological training has studied here for the past few years, but with no real advances. We've been unable to successfully inoculate animals with the bacillus. Do you understand what that means, Miss Atta?"

She closed her eyes. "If you can't test on animals, then that would leave only patients with the disease left for experimentation."

Her mother's face, white as bleached flour, flashed before her as did another doctor's face. A coarse brown beard. Beady eyes.

A chill crawled up her spine. What did any of these doctors know, even those who looked like kind sea captains? The majority of experiments ended in failure, at least from her experience.

"You are correct and very quick to come to that conclusion." Dr. Parker turned to the small table at his side and made a note on a chart. Atta knew all about charts. She remembered her mother having one. Charts meant long-term doctoring. Meticulous recording and monitoring. Her name on a chart was the beginning of a long, hard journey—a journey that may end beneath a white sheet.

"There is one medicine known to slow the effects of the disease. In fact, there have been cases in Hawaii that give credit to chaulmoogra oil for curing Hansen's disease. Yet, I will wait for Dr. Mayhew's opinion on the matter. He's just arrived and will see all the patients tomorrow."

The doctor on the boat. Atta had seen him from a distance. Somehow though, she knew; she would fail to soothe herself into thinking him a sweet, old sea captain.

"DIDDLE, diddle, dumpling, my son John. Went to bed with his stocking on." Gertie stopped singing to Rosie, her ragdoll, to listen for the sound of Papi's Tin Lizzie rolling up the driveway. Nothing. "One shoe off and one shoe on, diddle, diddle, dumpling, my son John."

Rosie's black-stitched eyes looked back at her with an empty expression. Gertie scrunched her eyes shut and wished with all her heart that Rosie were real. When she opened them, the same vacant stare awaited her. She sighed, the breath of air fanning the front of Rosie's dress.

"You're such a goosey Lucy, Rosie." She hugged her doll tight. "At least you'll keep my hiding place secret, right?"

She peered out from the thick forsythia bushes behind her house. She loved when they turned the color of lemon drops in the spring, though the abundant green leaves now made for a better hiding place. Like Mary Lennox in *The Secret Garden*. This was *her* secret garden—well, maybe not a garden, but it was still a secret.

But she shouldn't think of Mary anymore. Mary made her sad. Mary made her think of Atta, and how she'd read to her each night before bed, and how she wouldn't be there to do so anymore. She liked best how Atta read the talking parts of Martha's and Dickon's and Ben Weatherstaff's. It sounded magical. A Yorkshire accent, Atta had told her. As much as she struggled to read with the Yorkshire accent herself, what with its missing letters and apostrophes, Gertie wished she had such a dialect. It sounded grand and dreamy and faraway fairytale-ish to her. She'd have to wrestle those words by herself now.

The clock inside the house rang out through the closed windows. One, two, three, four. Four o'clock. She needed to stay outside for three more hours. The Health Man said she couldn't go in the house until seven o'clock. Said they needed to fume gate the house, or something like that. She remembered *seven* because it rhymed with *heaven*, and that's where Mami was.

Gertie picked at a scab on her knee and remembered Dr. Browne poking at it only hours ago. He'd come to school—said he needed to make a special trip there just for her. And it did make her feel special, especially when he gave her a tiny brown bag of spice drops at the end. She still had three left. All red, because red was her favorite and Atta always said, "Save the best for last," when she tucked her in at night and kissed Rosie first, saving Gertie for last.

The burning came to Gertie's eyes again. She pressed Rosie's black yarn hair against her face to stop the sensation. Atta never cried. Gertie wouldn't either. Besides, Sister said crying made for a disagreeable child, and she didn't want to be disagreeable.

"Gertie...." Barely above a whisper, the voice seemed to surround her all at once, making the tiny hairs on the back of her neck stand stiff.

She clutched Rosie tighter. "Who—who's there?"

"Aye. What art tha' doin?"

A small dark-haired girl stood at the entrance to the hiding place. She wore the loveliest dress. It was pale yellow and looked to be made of cotton soft as the clouds. Gertie had never seen her before.

"I'm hiding," she answered, embarrassed to be caught behind the forsythias.

"I can see that plain enough. But why art tha' hidin'?"

Gertie shrugged but slid over enough for the little girl to join her. "Did you just move here? I've never seen you before."

"I live just down th' way."

Gertie offered the girl one of her cherished gumdrops. "Nay," she said.

"Are you from Yorkshire? I like your accent."

The little girl nodded. "Tha' an' me are a good bit alike, I'll warrant."

"How so?" Gertie asked. "I'm not from England. And I don't know your name."

"My name is Kat."

They were quiet for a few minutes. Gertie rolled the hem of Rosie's dress until it was up to the doll's neck, then she rolled it down again.

"Art tha' goin' to be tellin' me why tha' art hidin'?" Kat asked.

However much she wanted a best friend, and however much she liked Kat's Yorkshire accent, Gertie couldn't bring herself to tell Kat why she was hiding. But before she could think of an excuse, she glimpsed a figure on horseback coming up the long drive.

"Robert!" Nearly pushing Kat aside, she scrambled out of her hiding spot and down the drive, holding Rosie tight in one fist.

Robert slid off Goliath and Gertie launched herself into his arms. He felt solid and big like a warm stuffed bear.

He put her down all too soon.

"Hey there, Little Britches. How was your day at school?"

"Dr. Browne gave me spice drops today."

"Did he now?" Robert's blue eyes darted to the house. He looked sad, but Gertie didn't want to think about being sad right now.

"I made a new friend. Do you want to meet her?"

"Sure thing."

Gertie ran to the forsythia bush and stuck her head in the secret entrance. "Kat?" No pale yellow dress as soft as the clouds. No Yorkshire accent. No best friend. She straightened. "I guess she left. Maybe she's shy."

"Maybe." Robert slipped a brown paper bag from a pocket hanging from his saddle. He handed it to her. "Brought you supper, straight from Joe's Kitchen."

Gertie unrolled the bag. The corners were wet with grease and she inhaled the sweet scent of sausage. "Yum!" She pulled out a big roll with a thick chunk of sausage down the middle of it. Selecting a patch of grass nearby, she sat, folded her hands, and said grace like a good girl. Then she took a big bite of sausage. The juices burst on her tongue. "Joe sure is a good cook," she said, her mouth full.

Robert sat down a few paces from her. "Gertie, did you talk to Atta this morning?"

The sausage turned hard and kinky in her mouth, and she put the sandwich on top of the paper bag, rolling the ends to keep the ants away. She put Rosie on guard beside it.

"I mean—did Atta explain what was happening?"

She forced herself to swallow the bite of sausage. "She said she had to go away for a while, but that she'd be back, and that you were going to take care of me."

Robert's eyes looked shiny then, like big glossy blue jewels one might find as treasure at the bottom of the sea. "That's right." His voice sounded funny.

"Are you sad, Robert?"

He nodded, his mouth in a very grown-up, straight line.

"Me too. I miss Atta so much already, my heart aches something awful."

"Me too, Little Britches. Me too." He scooted closer and put an arm around her. She burrowed her head in his white shirt.

"Robert?" She spoke into his shirt, scared to hear his answer, but daring to ask it anyway. "Am I still going to go live with you and Atta soon in the house you're building? Will you still get married?"

He was quiet for a long time, and she lifted her head, just enough for the scent of nearby hydrangeas to reach her nose.

"I'm sorry, Gertie...but I don't think Atta and I will be getting married."

A great big sadness dug a hole through her stomach. If Atta were gone, if Robert didn't want to be her big brother anymore...then who was left to love her?

Chapter Eleven

1993

I blink, the movement forcing me back to reality. Back to waning daylight and corn cobs nibbled to the bone, drops of melted butter long ago hardened on our plates.

I shake my head. "You were all alone. You must have been so scared."

"Don't pity me, child. It was a long time ago now. I survived."

"Did you ever see Aunt Atta again? But you must have if you know her story."

Gram smiles and stands. "It's late. I need my beauty rest." She winks at me. "And we don't want you missing the bus tomorrow."

I want to hear more. At the same time, my limbs are drained from our long walk on the beach, from the emotions of the day and Gram's story. I don't want to care about my cursed aunt. I don't and I do.

When I get off the bus the next day, I grab Gram's mail and enter the house to see a note on the kitchen table.

Helping set up for the church craft fair. Be home soon.

I take in the shaky handwriting, still neat despite the visible wobbles in it. I place the mail beside the note but my eye catches on the return address of the envelope on top.

Cuttyhunk Historical Society
Museum of the Elizabeth Islands, Massachusetts

I pick up the envelope, studying my grandmother's name. The screen door rattles and I drop the mail.

"How was your day, child?" Gram walks in, her gait a bit more crooked than usual.

"Fine." I attended all of my classes, anyway. No rude boys bothered me in the hall. I sensed a few stares and whispers, but for the most part it seemed Barnstable High had moved on with more fascinating topics than the pregnant new girl. And though I hadn't seen Cute Library Boy—Sam, rather—all day, I'd found a note in my locker. On the top of the torn notebook paper was a horribly drawn picture of a T-Rex.

Movie releases in 13 days. Read the book. You won't be sorry.

I was pretty sure I would be. Besides, was it wise to take Sam up on his offer of a movie? Why did he even want to be seen with me? Was he as lonely as I was? Desperate for a friend? Desperate for female attention?

But then I think of him holding his hand out to me, telling me to come with him if I wanted to live. He didn't *seem* desperate. A little nerdy, but genuine. Maybe the high school girls here didn't appreciate guys like that. Maybe before now, *I* hadn't appreciated guys like that.

Unless, of course, Sam isn't as genuine as I want to believe. I think of him cutting class alongside me, and though part of me wants to throw caution to the wind when it comes to Sam, the last time I'd thrown said caution into the wind, I'd wound up pregnant.

"And did you make any friends?" Gram asks.

Her question makes me feel I'm fresh off the bus from my first day of kindergarten. I shrug. "Not really. But it's okay. Four more weeks and I'll never see these kids again. Oh, I think I found a couple guys to help us move your bedroom furniture."

"So you have made some friends, then."

"Just a kid I met at the library." I wonder if Sam will accept payment in food. "We might have to pay them, though..."

"That's not a problem. I'll start cleaning out my drawers this weekend." She scoops up the mail. I watch as her gaze takes in the return address of the Cuttyhunk envelope. She lays it aside along with some credit card advertisements. "Waste of paper, all this junk mail." She tosses the entire pile in the trash bin below the sink.

"Wait!"

"Whatever is the matter?"

I point to the trash. "There was something that looked like it had to do with Penikese in there."

Her mouth firms into a tight line. "They won't stop sending me things."

"Things? Like things having to do with the school?"

"It's nothing, really. Now, I'm not sure if I'm up for a walk today, but if you don't have plans, how about a rousing game of pinochle?" She reaches in the kitchen drawer for a red pack of Bicycle playing cards.

For a minute, I simply stand there. Who am I to demand anything of her? Yet, something inside of me twists at the thought of that envelope in the trash. Is it really nothing, as Gram claims?

I think of my Aunt Atta cast off on Penikese because no one wants her—because she is feared in every sense of the word. Suddenly, it's very important to me that I know what's inside that envelope.

Gram is already heading for the door. "Child, if you don't like pinochle, I could manage rummy."

I shake my head and follow her out the door. "Pinochle's fine."

WHEN GRAM THROWS a small amount of leftover tomato sauce in the trash after dinner, I inwardly cringe. Paper napkins and a lemon peel follow. When she finally announces she's tired and wishes to retire early, I bid her goodnight even though I want to ask for more of her story. What happened to Gram after my Aunt Atta went to the island? Was my aunt ever cured? What part did the young, cocky doctor play in it all?

When I hear the shower running in the upstairs bathroom, I whip open the cabinet under the sink and pull out the trash. I rummage through sauce-covered lemon peels and dirtied napkins. A thin spaghetti noodle sticks to my forefinger. I shake it off and reach for the envelopes. Luckily, a mailer for a local landscaping company has taken the brunt of the tomato sauce. When I find the Cuttyhunk envelope, I tear it open and lay the single sheet of paper on the counter. I wash my hands and flip on the light above the sink.

An invitation to Gertrude Robertson.

An invitation to Penikese.

From the sound of it, it is not the first one sent to my grandmother.

The second line states:

RE: Commemoration of the Penikese Island Leper Colony and the Work of Dr. and Mrs. Frank Parker.

It is to be held on Saturday, July 31st. Gram is invited to stay the weekend at the Penikese School. They only request that Gram responds no later than June 15th.

Why wouldn't she want to go? The lady walked at least three miles with me back and forth on the beach yesterday. Surely, she's up for a weekend trip for such a ceremony?

I jump when Gram clears her throat on the stairs behind me. "Going through one's mail is a federal offense, young lady."

I scrunch my face in a sheepish manner. "Even if it's mail destined for the dump?"

She comes down the last two steps in a fluffy yellow bathrobe. The woman likes yellow, that much I've learned. "Yes, even if it's mail in the trash. If your name isn't on it, it's not meant for you." She snatches the letter from my hand.

"Gram—I'm sorry. How can you expect me *not* to be curious after everything you've told me?"

"Real apologies don't come wrapped in blaming the party you're apologizing to."

I bite my bottom lip at the same time that a sudden, obvious shift takes place in my abdomen. "Oh!" I place my hand on my growing side, the letter forgotten.

Gram steps toward me. "What is it?"

"It's moving." My tone is filled with wonder. I can't help it. I've tried to ignore the existence of the child within as best I can, but it seems he or she won't have it any longer. I move my hand along the outside of my stomach, but can't quite feel the quickening I know inside myself. It's amazing and weird and frightening all at once.

Gram picks up the kettle and fills it with water from the sink. "As old as I am—as old as your father is, I can still remember that feeling. Your father was a real kicker. He's fought hard for what he's wanted ever since."

She'd known that about him before he was born? To think my baby has a personality already, one that I'll never know...

"Why don't you want to go to the ceremony, Gram?" I need to keep my thoughts off the little one inside me any way that I can.

She sighs, takes two teacups out of the cupboard, then digs in her tea canister for two bags of tea.

"I suppose it makes it all the more real," she finally says.

"What? The leper colony?"

She places her hands on the counter. The faint line of a scar cuts down the flesh between her thumb and forefinger. Her skin is wrinkled and spotted. I think of her smooth hands holding the calla lilies in her wedding photograph, and then of the deformed hands on the mandolin in the Penikese picture.

She looks out the dark window when she speaks. "Your grandfather spent a lot of time on Penikese, right up until the day he died. Many a night, we'd have movie or dinner plans and we'd get a call from the school saying he was needed on the island. One of the boys had turned violent or someone needed to be calmed down. Often one of them would need to be brought back to Penikese after committing a crime on the mainland. One horrible night, a boy hung himself."

"That's awful."

"Your grandfather would never give up on them, though. Seven years after Penikese opened, we followed up with the hundred-and-six boys we tried to help. Would you know that only sixteen had managed to turn their lives around? The rest stayed on the path of crime, drugs, and destruction. More than a handful died from their bad choices."

"I'm so sorry," I whisper.

"I never once complained to your grandfather about his long absences. When he grew discouraged about the small fraction of boys he was able to reach, I told him if he could help one soul, then it was worth it. Atta had taught me that." She glances down at the letter. "Dr. and Mrs. Parker taught me that. They ministered to thirty-six patients. Thirty-six patients and only one fully cured."

One fully cured. Was that *one* my aunt?

"Your grandfather and I felt we had a legacy to continue. And so I did not begrudge his time away." She blinks. "After he died, I found it easier to pretend he was just a boat ride away, on the island... I haven't been back since he passed. I don't want to know the place without him. I suppose, with my sister buried there, the place holds much pain for me as well."

My heart sinks. So my Aunt Atta *had* died on the island. So much for being fully cured.

"But you said the story was one of hope." I cling to the prospect of a happy ending. I refuse to give it up. This was Gram's story, for goodness' sake! It was my story. I needed a happy ending.

"The story *is* one of hope, dear. But hope is often birthed in the midst of pain." She places a cup of tea in front of me and sits with her own. "Are you up to hearing more?"

Something in me is scared, and something in me wants Gram to stay up all night telling the story of my aunt. "If you're not too tired."

"It appears I've found a second wind." She pushes the letter from the historical society aside. "Now, where were we?"

Chapter Twelve

1916

Atta forced her eyes open to escape the depths of her murky nightmares. She blinked at the oil lamp sitting on the small table beside her bed.

So she hadn't left her nightmare after all. Gertie wasn't by her side, Robert wasn't down the street. She even felt Papi's absence, although she couldn't be certain whether she actually missed *him* or the thought of home.

With only the remnant of her nightmares for company and a growling belly, she clutched her rosary to her chest and tried not to imagine the former occupant of her bed beneath these same covers. She'd skipped both dinner and a bath last night, unable to face the other patients—and what may soon be her own fate.

A quiet knock sounded at the door, and she dragged herself from the bed to pull on a fresh shirtwaist and dress. Sweat and salt slicked her skin, and she wished she'd asked for a bathing pitcher last night.

The knock again.

"Yes? Who's there?"

"My name is Lucy," the voice called through the cottage door. "Nurse Edith thought I might accompany you to breakfast."

Another nurse? Or...

Atta grabbed the handle and peered around the creaky cottage door. A fine mist sprayed her face. A thin, tall, not quite middle-aged woman stood at the top of the steps. Her dark hair piled atop her head. She'd be almost pretty if it weren't for the blatantly flat nose that smudged the middle of her face, giving her a lionish appearance. Atta's gaze wandered to the woman's hands. While not claw-like, they appeared swollen.

"Thank you. That's very kind of you. But I can fare by myself."

The woman wavered but bobbed her head. "I will see you there then?" Her scratchy voice barely broke through the sound of the waves crashing on the shore.

"Yes, I will be there."

The woman named Lucy turned in the direction of the hospital and regret pinched Atta's nerves. She shouldn't put off the possibility of a new friend. But should she further expose herself to the disease?

She wriggled her fingers. Would they one day turn into swollen, painful appendages, ridden with sickness?

"Lucy!"

The woman turned, the gesture revealing enlarged ears. Atta forced her eyes away from the abnormality. "My name is Atta. It is nice to meet you."

Lucy smiled, which seemed to take a bit of effort considering the lack of space between her nose and mouth. "I'll see you in a bit."

Atta closed the door on the briny air and picked up her brush. As she smoothed out her long tresses, she imagined Gertie getting herself something for breakfast about now. Papi would be gone for work, her sister would be cracking eggs over the stove—

Atta stopped brushing mid-stroke. Gertie didn't know how to work the stove. What if she burned herself? Or worse, what if she hadn't been in her room when Papi came home last night? What if she were hurt, without anyone to help her?

The room blurred and Atta slumped into a nearby chair, dragging desperate, deep breaths into her lungs.

Robert. He'd promised to watch out for Gertie. Her sister would be safe. Robert was a man of his word, wasn't he?

Yet Robert had promised to love her forever. To cherish her. Would he keep his promise to look after Gertie?

She scrunched her eyes shut and beseeched God to lift this curse from her, repeating the prayer over and over as she finished her toilette and walked through the light drizzle to the hospital building. The humidity clung to the air like a thick, hot blanket. A few stray hens pecked the rocky ground. Little relief awaited inside the hospital. The clinking of dishes mingled with soft voices, and Atta followed them, her pulse knocking against her temples.

White-washed walls encompassed airy windows. A man not covered in bandages or lesions opened one of the hospital doors off to the left. The new doctor. Her knees began to tremble, her breaths came in short puffs.

She wrapped her arms tightly around herself, imagining what misery this doctor had in mind for her. Would it be worse than the swollen, festering limbs consuming her nightmares?

Holding her breath, Atta entered the dining hall. Two long tables took up the middle of the room. The weight of eyes lay heavy upon her.

Fumbling for the seat closest to the entrance, she sat with a small group of disfigured women, her gaze fixed on the wood of the table. The scent of coffee and baking bread did little to calm her stomach.

"Mary, Flavia, this is Atta."

She exhaled her pent-up breath and glanced up to see Lucy sitting beside her.

"Atta, this is Mary." Lucy gestured to the woman across from them—the woman Atta had seen yesterday. Thankfully, she wasn't raining curses down today. Still, her gaze held suspicion and she began to swat at her left hand as if a colony of ants clung to her skin.

"And Flavia."

"Hello," the middle-aged woman said, her accent heavy with the one word. "*Un piacere.*"

A moonscape of pink, bumpy nodules covered the woman's face. Her right eyelid was swollen shut. How would Robert ever see past such repulsiveness if such a fate was to be hers? How would anyone?

"Flavia speaks very little English. She used to live in Italy. She draws us pictures of the beautiful Tuscan villas there." Lucy sighed. "I suppose it's the closest any of us will ever get to them."

Atta dragged out a smile for Flavia before a heavyset woman in a white apron bustled over and placed a plate of scrambled eggs and griddlecakes before each of them.

"My oh my, child, but you're nothing but skin and bones. It'll sure be a pleasure to feed ya. My name's Betsy. I'm the cook here."

"Nice to meet you. Mrs. Parker was complimenting your skill to me yesterday." Strange how she could push out the right words when her mind and heart rode the swells of her turbulent emotions.

Betsy's red cheeks puffed with a smile. "That woman's near the dearest thing the Lord put on this earth. God bless her soul." Humming, she left for another stack of plates.

The steam of the eggs rose to greet Atta's nose. Oh, but it did smell good. The three women around her picked up their forks and began eating off the blue-enameled tin. Atta dipped her head in respect to God, saying a short prayer of grace.

After she finished, she glanced down the table at three Asian men. White wrappings bound one man's arms. A white growth had taken over an eye. Another had elephantine ears. A queer pigmentation covered both their skin, which in many places, looked to be rotting off their bones. The third was the worst. His fork was tied to his hand, for his fingers seemed to be gone, replaced by a swollen stump of a mitten hand covered in bone-white patches. Atta shivered, her stomach churning as she fought to drag in small, stuffy breaths of air.

Forcing down a small portion of her meal, she avoided looking at the other five patients who completed the motley dozen—a dozen that included herself.

After the Asian men left the table—one shuffling along on shoes too big for him—she let her fork clatter to her plate. She mumbled an "Excuse me" and stumbled from the room, down the hall, and out into the fresh air.

With her head down she jogged to the pavilion in front of the hospital and leaned into one of the posts. She scanned the horizon, making out a smudge of gray land in the distance. A boat of some sort bobbed in front of the smudge.

If only that boat would come and take her away. If only Robert were at the helm of the ship, ready to rescue her. She slid along the post until she sat on the ground, damp from the morning mist.

No one would care enough to rescue her. But the chances of her escaping? Perhaps she could get on the ferry the next time it delivered mail. She'd noticed a bin of lifejackets on the boat that had taken her here. Maybe she could stow away while the sailors were occupied, escape back to Gertie.

A seagull flew overhead, dropping a not-so-sought-after gift at her feet. She shifted her body away from the waste.

Even if she did manage to return to Gertie, she wouldn't be able to hide from Robert's father or the health commissioner for long.

But to stand by and do nothing while Gertie was at the mercy of Papi? Disease or no disease, her sister needed her. One chance encounter with a drunken father and Gertie may not make it to see seven years old. And yet...being with Atta wasn't in Gertie's best interest, either. To think of her sister suffering the same fate as her own....

She must find a way to escape. But she wouldn't be foolish about it. No, she'd watch and wait, make a note of when the mail came, if the sailors left the boat unattended.

If only she could figure out how to do all that from *her* side of the island.

"MISS ATTA, DID YOU HEAR ME?" Nurse Edith stood at the corner of the pavilion, her words causing Atta's hands to quiver.

She hadn't bathed yet. She needed to bathe before seeing the new doctor. She'd have trouble enough on the exam table *with* a fresh appearance, never mind in her disheveled state.

She pushed a strand of hair behind her ear, willing her shaking hands to stop the fuss. "Nurse Edith, would it be possible for me to see Dr. Mayhew later?"

"I'm afraid not. Most of the other patients need to go to the dispensary before they see the doctor. You should go first, dear."

She lowered her voice, pleading with the nurse. "I'm in desperate need of a bath, you see..."

Nurse Edith's eyes widened. "Is it your monthly? We have sanitary towels here. You should have asked. I'll run and get you some."

Atta's face heated and she rubbed her thumb against her pointer finger. "No, Nurse Edith. I mean thank you. But that isn't the problem right now. I just...I *smell*."

The nurse smiled. "Who doesn't this time of year? That's not much to worry about. I met Dr. Mayhew last night, and he didn't say anything of being particularly offended by body odor."

Atta nearly gasped, wanting to scold the woman for speaking so boldly. Was this place such a prison that she could not take a bath when she chose?

Nurse Edith's gaze softened. "I'm sorry, dear. I didn't mean to offend. But we do have a schedule to keep. For what it's worth, I don't smell anything odious right now. I promise that your visit with Dr. Mayhew will not be long. As soon as he's finished, I'll help you with the bathing facilities. Does that sound all right?"

No, it didn't sound all right. Neither did the way this nurse spoke to her—as if she were a petulant child who required soothing. Atta had spoken to Gertie in similar tones more than once. But short of running for the ocean and diving in fully clothed, she seemed to be destined to meet the new doctor—the doctor who may hold her life in his hands—with this very *odious* smell sticking to her.

She allowed the woman to lead her back to the hospital and down the hall, conscious of the scent of roses floating behind the nurse. Of course Nurse Edith didn't smell anything odious. *She* smelled fresh as a spring flower.

The nurse gave a light knock on the half-opened door of the room Dr. Parker had examined her in yesterday.

"Yes, come in."

Nurse Edith opened the door, keeping her hand on the knob. "Miss Schaeffer's here, Doctor."

Dr. Mayhew turned from a pile of papers on a mahogany desk. Scant morning sunlight from the windows shone off his blonde hair and Atta's breath caught. Robert's hair was the same shade. It didn't curl at his neck as Dr. Mayhew's did, but how many times had she brushed it lovingly from his forehead? Too many times to count. She pushed the thought from her mind as she studied the new doctor who wore a mask over his face and medical gloves on his hands. The similarity to Robert fled her mind.

"Thank you, Miss Nason. If you'd prepare Miss Peterson, I'll be seeing her next." Dr. Mayhew's sea-blue eyes seemed to smile at the pretty nurse before he turned his gaze to Atta. The light in his eyes disappeared.

"I'm Dr. Mayhew." He didn't offer his gloved hand. "Nice to

meet you, Miss Schaeffer. No point in delaying. If you wouldn't mind hopping up onto the examination table, please."

Though her insides quaked and fingers twitched, she obeyed. Dr. Mayhew flipped through the paperwork on his desk, his motions fluid and smooth. It seemed the man held complete control over every lift of a finger, turn of the chair. No expenditure of energy wasted. Everything calculated.

His own perfection made her ten times more aware of the scent clinging to her body. At least the windows were wide open. She glimpsed the gray sea off in the distance, a small white cross in the foreground. The island cemetery. How many outcasts were buried beneath the hard earth, sharing eternity with the sound of waves crashing against their sides?

"I understand your symptoms are minor. Since Dr. Parker did a thorough exam yesterday, I'll abstain from doing so again. I would, however, like to take another sample from the infected area. It will help determine how severe your case may be."

She nodded and Dr. Mayhew slid an examination tray beside the table. He sat at a stool at the bottom of the exam table and for one brief, horrifying moment, their eyes met. She wanted to grasp at his hands and fall at his feet. Plead with him to do more than his best. He could save her. He was quite possibly her only hope off this island. Her only hope in saving Gertie, in having a life with Robert.

"You'll need to lift your skirt, Miss Schaeffer." He gestured to her bottom half, scalpel in hand. The shining steel glinted off the lamp nearby and all at once, she became terribly conscious of the horrible scents that went with a doctor's office. No amount of sea-breeze could diminish the smell of carbolic acid.

With trembling hands, she lifted her skirt to the area on her thigh. A breeze caressed her legs, wiping them free of the suffocation beneath her skirts. Still, dizziness overtook her, whether from the anticipation of the cold metal cutting her skin, or from this young doctor's hands upon her, she could not discern. Before this moment, she'd only known doctors old enough to be her grandfather. This man must be Robert's elder by only a few years. No young man had ever touched her bare skin in such places before. No matter the gloves, she became aware of every exposed inch of skin, every flaw along the inside of her leg.

"Why don't you go ahead and lie down, Miss Schaeffer."

She nearly fell back against the table, her midsection releasing visible tremors.

"You must relax. It will only make it more difficult to get what I need."

"And how do you suggest I do that?" she asked through clenched teeth. She turned her head to look at the small white cross on the horizon. Her stomach coiled and the sour taste of bile and eggs climbed her throat.

Those piercing eyes landed on her, his brow furrowed beneath close-cropped curls. Her body reacted in disobedience to his probing gaze. Father in heaven help her.

He turned his attention back to the task at hand.

No, she wouldn't be able to fool herself into thinking this one a sweet old sea captain.

"I don't know, Miss Schaeffer." His tone held a trace of annoyance. "Look out the window at the waves or something."

The waves. As if they would calm her nerves. No, they would only serve to remind her of the impossible barricade around this prison. And the single cross, standing tall before the sea, mocking her. She imagined those buried beneath it. The patient who had slept in her newly assigned bed...buried beneath it. Maybe his last breath had been taken on the pillow she laid her head on the night before.

Dr. Mayhew released a loud sigh and pushed his stool away from the table. "You may cover yourself. I'll never make a clean cut with all your shaking."

He was angry, and she didn't blame him. She must control her quivering body. Order it into submission.

"No please, Dr. Mayhew. I'll do better, I promise." She *must* do better. Maybe they could still find out this had all been a mistake. That Dr. Browne had been wrong.

She lay down again, lifting her skirt above the marks. This time, instead of trying to relax her defiant body, she held it rigid and tight, willing it not to tremble. She thought of Gertie...no, that wouldn't serve to soothe her. Robert. Yes, Robert. They were in Robert's one-horse shay, trotting down Main Street, greeting passersby, telling them of their engagement, going to the theatre. They were on their vacant lot of land, Robert's hands held up, drawing their house on the tablet of her mind. They were taking a walk through the woods, talking of serving the youth of St. Mary's Church.

Robert had spoken often of having children.

"I wouldn't mind a barnful, would you, Atta?"

"A barnful? Am I going to be having children or piglets?"

His deep laugh drew her in further. "Children, piglets, what does it matter? They'll be a part of you and a part of me."

A part of him, a part of her no longer. She'd never have children. Even if she was given the opportunity to conceive, she refused to share the burden of the cross she bore with an infected offspring.

"You may sit up, Miss Schaeffer. I was able to take the sample."

She covered herself, breathing easier as Dr. Mayhew walked to a small table at the wall, slide in hand.

"I'm still acquainting myself with the leprosy bacillus, but I've read quite a bit on the disease and Dr. Parker has shared his medical journals with me. For now, I concur with his treatment to start you on chaulmoogra oil injections twice weekly. Also, a few drops of the oil in capsules to be taken at mealtimes. If you have any ill side effects, we'll discontinue the doses."

She nodded, her mind grasping to remember the dozens of questions that had occupied it since the commissioner spoke those unutterable words.

If only Dr. Mayhew would take off his mask. Not only was she curious to see his features, but to talk to him person to person, instead of educated doctor to simple-minded...well, she knew what he thought of her. His every haughty gaze and authoritative word told her of his opinion.

"Roll up your sleeve, please."

She obeyed, her teeth chattering as he prepared the injection of brownish-yellow oil.

"It'll only hurt a moment. No need to be nervous."

That's right. She needed to be brave. If the oil helped others, it may help her too.

He came closer, so close she knew he could hear her teeth chatter. His breathing sounded hollow beneath the mask. For a moment, the scent of bay rum overpowered that of iodine.

The cuff of his white coat brushed her arm. He pinched the skin of her upper arm with his left hand while she looked away, eyes squeezed shut. The medical gloves pressed tight and sticky against her skin. She longed to wriggle free of his grip.

The nip of the needle wasn't as bad as the hot oil burning through her veins. It traveled up her arm and into her shoulder, where it finally spread and cooled.

He placed the needle in a basin of clear liquid and turned to her. "I'm studying the patients' histories and previous cases on the island before recommending further treatment. At that time, you will be part of certain...treatments that may not have been tried before." His words, muffled beneath the mask, were nevertheless pregnant with meaning.

Experiments, he meant. She'd vowed to go to any lengths to get better, but now, when the opportunity stood before her, fear gained a foothold on her heart. Images of Mami, pale and trembling with sweat, lying on her deathbed, taunted her mind's eye.

"And if I refuse?"

He released a small exhalation of breath. "With all due respect, Miss Schaeffer, it is my job to treat my patients the best way I see fit. You may refuse, but I suspect in the end it will not matter much. You are a ward of the state, in full custody of this hospital."

"In full custody of you, you mean." Of all the no-good, arrogant—

"I'd hate to put it so harshly, but yes, that's what it boils down to."

Oh, if she ever wished a curse upon anyone, it was this man before her.

"I am a citizen of America, Dr. Mayhew. Have I lost all my rights with this diagnosis?"

His right foot tapped out a rhythm on the hardwood floor— the first disorderly movement she'd seen from him. Good, so he was human after all.

"I'm certain your rights are still in place, Miss Schaeffer. But they will come second to the good of the general public, as you've already witnessed in your evacuation to this island."

He was right. He was right, and there was naught she could do about it.

Forgive me, Father, for I have sinned...

She had sinned. And this was her punishment. But she couldn't accept it. This lack of compassion. This fate he seemed willing to throw her to.

She'd asked God's forgiveness, and He hadn't heard her either, or rather chose to ignore her.

A fierce need to fight welled up within her. If she wanted to get well, she'd have to stand on her own two feet. She came from a long line of hardy German stock after all.

If she couldn't figure out an escape plan soon, she'd have no choice but to give herself to Dr. Mayhew's experiments. But not without questions and an intelligent mind. And not because he ordered her to do so, but because an innocent six-year-old sister waited for her—was counting on her—to get better and come home.

Chapter Thirteen

He should have stopped at the tavern. There was no reason to rush home to Gertie. Niklas hadn't seen so much as a blonde curl since Atta left. Gertie could take care of herself. She didn't need him or want him. Could he blame her?

Niklas dug out a skillet from the cupboard and placed it on the cast iron stove. Scrambled eggs. With Atta gone, he had better get used to simple cooking.

Oh, Atta. No good thinking of the girl now. He couldn't help her. The best thing he could have done for his family would have been to stay in Germany. But no, he'd insisted America would give them a better life.

Poor Katharina. She'd been up for any adventure as long as it was with him. But they shouldn't have come. *Ja*, maybe then Katharina wouldn't have had the consumption. Maybe if they'd stayed in the heart of his homeland, Atta would be spared the trials she now faced. At least there would be none of this business of being exiled. The girl was the picture of perfect health. How absurd to cast her off as if she were a lice-infested rat. The freedoms of America proved little benefit now.

He cracked eight eggs into the pan and stirred them. The sound of Gertie's voice wove itself down the staircase. Little girls and their imaginings. Atta used to pretend she owned a small pony. Niklas had bought her a hobby horse the Christmas she'd turned five. She rode the thing everywhere, begging Katharina to let her bring it to Mass.

One day, she'd come galloping out to the barn on the thing, giddy-upping and neighing up a storm. The ruckus had caused their skittish mare to rear up before little Atta. Niklas had lunged, pushing his daughter from harm. The mare landed on his forearm instead. Oh, the treatment he'd gotten from Katharina. She'd hailed him a hero back then. Laid up for weeks with her coddling had been the closest he'd get to heaven—even with a broken arm. He flexed it now. It felt good. Only bothered him when the heavy rains came. It had been worth it to spare his little girl hurt.

Too bad he couldn't save her from the mess she was in now just as easily.

More talking from Gertie. Niklas dished out two servings of eggs and placed them on the small table in the kitchen before heading up the stairs. He knocked hard on Gertie's door.

"Gertie, dinner."

She spoke again, her voice muffled.

"You got someone in there with you?" He tried the door but came up against something hard. Atta's hope chest. Guilt wormed its way into his heart at the thought of the six-year-old holing herself up in her room because of him. Guarding the door, because of him. Just as quick, anger took its place. This was his home, after all. He shouldn't be locked out of any rooms.

"Open the door, Gertrude. Come down and have your supper." Scuffling on the other side. The scrape of the chest. More talking. "Who's in there with you, girl?"

Gertie peered around the door, her porcelain cheeks flushed. "Kat's in here, Papi. We're coming down. She said she needed to be home in time for supper."

Kat. Had Gertie spoken of this friend before?

He pushed the door open several inches and glanced around the room. "Where is she?"

Gertie's gaze swept the bed and the braided rug, where her ragdoll sat. Her lips puckered. "She—she was right here." She ran to the open window and looked out, relief painted on her face. "There she is. Must have shimmied down the gutter again. I told her it was dangerous, but she said she did it all the time when she lived in England."

Niklas strode to the window but saw nothing except tiger lilies swaying their orange heads in the breeze. He spun and gripped Gertie's arms. "You lyin' to me, girl?"

Gertie shook her head, curls bouncing around her temples, pale blue eyes wide. "No—no, Papi. I swear it."

Ach, but she reminded him so much of Katharina. Too bad he couldn't see so much as a smidge of himself in her sweet face. He released her. "Go eat your dinner."

She scurried downstairs and he looked out the window again. A mere girl couldn't shimmy down two flights. And the gutter— the cast iron pipe—was five feet away. He would have trouble getting to it. More than likely, Gertie fed him a crock of horse manure. But she'd been so sincere.

Sighing, he started down the stairs, where Gertie inhaled her eggs.

"Slow down."

She obeyed, her knuckles white around the fork.

"You milk Gussie before you left for school this morning?"

"Yes, Papi." She shoveled in her last bite of eggs.

"Where's the milk, then?"

Her pale eyebrows knit themselves closer together. "I—I— thought I...."

"Spit it out, girl. *Wo ist die Milch?*"

"I think I left it...in—in the barn." Her voice skittered to a whisper.

Blast. He couldn't handle a scatterbrain little girl. He couldn't raise her by himself. Katharina shouldn't have left him. Atta shouldn't have left him. He couldn't be responsible for this child. This child who may not be his.

He slammed his eggs on the table. The top had congealed into a hard yellow lump. They'd be cold by now.

"Go dump it and clean out the bucket. You make the same mistake tomorrow, you'll be over my knee."

She ducked her head and scrunched her face up tight.

"You hear me, girl?"

She looked up at him, a thin sheen of wetness glazing her eyes. "Yes, Papi. I'll remember. I promise." She placed her dish in the sink and walked to the door. She stopped before turning the knob but didn't look at him. "I'm sorry, Papi. I know how much you like cold milk with your dinner."

Then she was gone, leaving him with a strange sense of longing in her absence. Quiet enveloped the house, and again he regretted not stopping at the tavern. He wouldn't make that mistake tomorrow.

Tires crunched over the drive. Niklas shoveled down the cold eggs and opened the door.

Wunderbar.

He left the door open and went to the sink. The knock came a moment later.

"Niklas? I came to see how you and Gertie are holding up."

Niklas scrubbed a piece of steel wool against the skillet. "I think you forgot something, Sheriff. Better run home and get your mask and gloves."

"For what it's worth I'm terribly sorry for what's happened. An awful thing, Niklas. An awful thing."

He continued with the dishes, feeling inadequate beneath Charles's gaze, but not willing to supply him with conversation.

"I've spoken with Mrs. Walker. With Amelia just married, she needs help around the boarding house. Says she'd be more than willing to take Gertie in. She'd be well taken care of there. I told her I'd speak with you regarding the matter."

Niklas scrubbed the pan harder, his insides bubbling and popping hotter than volcanic ash. "No."

"No?"

"No."

"You won't consider it? The girl needs a woman's touch, Niklas. You can't expect to raise a six-year-old girl without help. With work and..." Charles's face turned red beneath his black beard.

"Go ahead, *Sheriff*. Spit it out."

"We used to be friends, Niklas. I want to talk to you as such now."

"Talk then." He dried the pan and laid it none-too-gently on the counter.

Charles sighed. "I know you like your liquor—heck, what man doesn't, but frankly Niklas, I'm scared for Gertie. With no woman around to temper your irrational side when you drink—"

"And what woman tempers your irrational side when *you* drink, Charles?"

Satisfied with the sheriff's speechlessness, he put the pan away. Charles Lincoln had lost his wife six months before Katharina had died. He never married again, but rumor had it the churchgoing town sheriff frequented a brothel in the next town over.

"You seem to forget that Gertie's the only family I have left. *Meine Familie.* We both lost Atta. We need each other right now." That was true, wasn't it? Did Gertie need him?

"Think about what Katharina would want, Niklas. If she were here—"

The volcano flowed without restraint, erupting in a satisfying right hook to Charles's face. The sheriff fell flat on Niklas's kitchen floor, blood trickling from his nose.

And that was the last time Charles Lincoln would waltz into his kitchen, pretending to know Niklas's wife better than he had.

Chapter Fourteen

Harry bent over the papers before him, fountain pen uncapped, eyes burning. The need for fresh air—a breath without this confounded mask—overtook him.

He shoved the papers to the side and walked down the hall to a small changing room, where he'd brought a fresh change of clothes. He threw the pants and shirt he'd worn for the day in a laundry bin before walking down the quiet hospital corridors.

A patient sat reading in the amusement room, and Harry nodded acknowledgement to the silver-haired old man. He racked his brain for the man's name. Twelve patients. He'd seen them all today—a hodgepodge of festering limbs, ulcers, and mutilations in his mind. Yet, he'd tried hard to commit each one to memory, to study their cases, notice patterns that had developed during the course of their illnesses.

Goodman. That was his name. Seventy-two. Tubercular case. First noticed nine years ago. Ulcers on nose, forehead, legs, and feet. Pain in fingertips and legs, making it difficult to walk. Like many of the patients, the battle between the immune system and the bacteria had been going on for years in this man. The result was nerve damage and loss of feeling, which in turn caused more damage.

Harry left the building, spotting a ladder and three men on the side of it. Parker with a paintbrush. And yes, he was with two Chinese men. Patients. No mask or gloves for Parker. The man seemed determined to become a martyr. And yet he showed no sign of the disease. Could the older doctor be right about the low level of contagion?

Harry avoided the work crew and kept his mask on as he walked up the hill to the center of the island. Flattened grass marked a crude path alongside gull prints. He didn't remove his mask until he crossed the barbed wire. Only then did he allow himself a full, satisfying breath of salty sea air.

One of the Chinese men who worked with Parker, Goon Lee Dip, had been his last patient of the day. Another tubercular case. Ulcers. Eyes and feet inflamed and painful. He'd been on the island since its inception, longer than Dr. Parker. He held the sole paying job on the patient side of the island as a launderer. Besides the obvious problems associated with leprosy, he seemed healthy, both physically and mentally.

Which was more than Harry could say for the majority of the patients. The general lot of them struggled with depression, and no wonder. The reports stated two of the four women's mental conditions rapidly deteriorated. One had screamed at him when he'd tried to examine her. The other spoke in rapid Italian, none of which he understood. But she'd been distressed trying to explain something to him—what, he had no idea. Maybe he should have taken Dr. Parker up on his offer to accompany him the first day. But imagining the older doctor looking over his shoulder, criticizing his every move, prompted Harry's refusal.

He sighed and veered toward the farm buildings instead of the administration building. The sound of a grunting pig reached his ears, followed by the *baa* of a sheep. The list of patients continued to run through his mind.

Hallile, although one of the healthier patients, was practically in tears because he was not able to provide for his family back in Turkey. Miss Peterson's breathing difficulties and leonine face—the result of the cartilage in her nose becoming affected by the leprosy bacillus—were hideous. Yee Toy had long ago lost sensation in his hands. Manuel Baptiste complained of intense pain and fevers to go with his pigmented skin and swollen limbs. Wong Quong suffered mentally. Klein's ulcers blocked his nose and throat. Nicholas Cacoulaches bore a badly ulcerated mouth.

Harry shivered. It was more than enough to send him back to Boston, to leave his medical degree on this island, along with the grotesque images he'd seen this day. But he was a doctor. He would be nothing if not for his career. And his only hope of making up for past sins lay on this island. Like it or not, these patients were the key to his redemption.

He counted off the patients in his head, priding himself on remembering their names and histories all in the first day. But that was only eleven...there were twelve.

It came to him like a cold crashing wave slamming against the shore. Miss Schaeffer. He'd seen her first and with the lack of symptoms, he'd almost put her from his mind. But he couldn't. As strong as she was, she could prove a crucial part in the formula to his success.

Except for the slight hyperpigmentation on her upper thigh, she showed no trace of the fierce disease. Her skin was flawless. Her legs so smooth and pale he could see the thin veins running beneath her skin. Hard to believe the bacillus could hide beneath near perfection.

He'd questioned the diagnosis, and after she'd left, he'd heated and stained the smear before sliding it beneath the waiting microscope. But though there had not been many, the unmistakable pink rod-shaped bacilli marred the slide, dashing doubts that Miss Schaeffer was not a leper.

She'd been uneasy around him, and yet something about the

girl gnawed at a tender spot in his heart. Before the examination, she'd looked at him with wounded eyes—eyes as soft as a dove's feathers—as if he held the answers to all her problems. As if her world depended on him. And part of him longed to be her hero—to be the hero of each patient he'd seen today. Of Miss Ballentino, who struggled to be understood. Of Hallile, crying for his children. And of Miss Schaeffer, who no doubt had been torn from the life of an ordinary nineteen-year-old woman.

And another part wanted nothing to do with them and the responsibility that came with possible—likely—failure.

Casting them all from his mind, he stuck his head inside the barn, eager to see what manner of animals made their home here. He didn't expect the straw hat bobbing beside a spackled brown cow.

"Dr. Mayhew! Pleasure to see you here." Mrs. Parker continued squeezing the cow's udders. "Do you have an affinity for farm animals?"

Harry chuckled. "I've never been in a barn, actually, Mrs. Parker. Now that I'm here, I can honestly say I don't think I've missed much." He wrinkled his nose at the pungent smell of the livestock.

Mrs. Parker straightened on her stool and patted the cow's rump. "I was never much of a farm girl myself until I came to the island. It's quiet here. I do most of my thinking and praying on this stool, the Lord's creatures at my side." She slid the pail of milk out from beneath the cow's middle and gestured to it. "For our dinner party tonight. Have you reconsidered, Dr. Mayhew?"

Mrs. Parker had told him that every Friday night, the doctors and nurses ate with the patients. Though she insisted the cook, Betsy, would bake a cake in honor of Harry's arrival, Harry had brushed off the invitation. It was one thing to spend the day examining the patients, but to eat with them?

"I don't think so, but thank you, Mrs. Parker. It's been a long day—a bit of a shock too, if you understand."

"I most certainly do, although it's been some time since we've lived and worked on the mainland. I dare say going back would be a shock to us now."

Harry clasped his hands over the cow's stall door. "You're a fine woman to stay by your husband for the sake of his desires. It can't be easy being cut off from society like this...and for so long."

"I was quite the social butterfly back in Malden." Her gaze grew unfocused, somewhere far away.

"How is it...when you go back to visit, that is?"

She stood, and he opened the stall and grabbed the milk pail for her, careful not to spill it.

"Oh, I'm sure you can imagine. We're quite avoided. Being here, ministering to these patients, has fleshed out our true friends. Of course, Howard and Ralph—our two boys—they don't mind. That gives me great comfort."

Harry thought of his own family. His father, who had all but fed him to the lepers. And his mother, who sobbed in hysterics when she'd heard he'd been cast to Penikese. She hadn't so much as given him a proper goodbye, said it was too painful. Would they write him off as an outcast as easily as those in the Parkers' social circle?

He sighed. Maybe he'd miss his parents with time. And Carrie. Even if she'd take him back, would he want to count her as part of his family—as a wife?

They emerged into the hazy sunshine and walked toward the house.

"And how was your first day, Dr. Mayhew?"

"Please, ma'am. Call me Harry."

"Very well, then. How did you manage today, Harry?"

Something soft in her gaze wrestled his guard down. He exhaled a long breath and fought a tick starting in his cheek. "They seem so helpless."

"They are."

"But the majority of them don't seem to *want* to get better. That makes my job a bit harder."

Mrs. Parker stopped walking and he set down the milk pail. Her straw hat shaded her face. "They've lost hope, Harry. Maybe you can help them gain it back."

A tall order considering their circumstances. "What hope do they have? Is it right for me to give it to them falsely? To pretend I can cure them?"

A breeze came off the water and her silver hair danced at her temples. "Perhaps they need a better promise than a physical cure."

He tapped his foot on the dry grass, the scar on his leg tightening. "With all due respect, Mrs. Parker, I'm only a medical doctor. I can't give more than I have to offer."

"And what do you have to offer?"

She was trying to teach him something. Either that or annoy the socks off of him. He gestured toward the direction of the mainland. "My education, my training, my experience at the hospital. My ability to work hard and persevere."

"Those are all fine qualities, Harry. But you have much more to offer than that."

Nothing could be more important than what he'd listed. He'd worked his entire life to achieve that list.

She continued. "A chance to heal their hearts, dear. Heal their hearts before you heal their bodies. The patients...they need to be understood just as much as they need a cure. You have the power to give that to them. You *can* give them hope."

Harry picked up the pail and resumed walking, tempted to sweep the older woman's words aside. He refused to coddle the patients. To dote on them like an old grandfather. If that's what Dr. and Mrs. Parker felt led to do, so be it. But he hadn't fought his way through Harvard to excel in compassion.

That had never been his specialty. He supposed he took after his father in that regard.

Chapter Fifteen

Atta clutched her stomach and curled into a ball on her bed, riding the wave of nausea as it crested. The scent of kerosene wafted through the room, further sickening her. But she would not be without the lamp's cheery light—the only thing comforting these days.

How long would she be able to put up with the pain? It never entirely loosened its grip on her insides. A common side effect of the chaulmoogra oil, Dr. Mayhew had told her. He'd offered to stop administering it, saying he didn't put much stock in its healing qualities anyhow.

Yet, she'd insisted, and he'd acquiesced. It remained her only hope. If anything could possibly cure her, she would fight to the ends of the earth to make it so. And since the mail boat had only come once since her arrival and she'd been too sick to try to investigate a getaway, she relegated herself to the salvation of a cure, not an escape.

She blew out a shaky breath and laid the back of her hand on her sticky forehead. The tick of the windup clock on the table pounded alongside her head. She hadn't felt well enough to perform her daily check-up today. She supposed she could skip one day. The routine of searching every square inch of her body for more rose-colored spots had become a near obsession in the past days. As did pinching her earlobes to test them for the loss of feeling that so often came with Hansen's disease. Like a drug, she found solace in finding each inch of her skin clear, each of her two earlobes with perfect sensation.

The hissing of the gaslight echoed through the room, competing only with the lap of the waves on the not-so-distant shore, the ticking of the clock, and the lonely cry of a gull. Although just after lunchtime, the gloomy weather dictated the need for the light, which flickered beside two letters.

Gertie's had come at the same time as Robert's, for surely they had been sent together. Atta had long since memorized her sister's short letter, the words big and the punctuation helter-skelter.

DEAR ATTA
  I MISS YOU I AM GOOD. I MADE A NEW FRIEND HER NAME IS KAT. PLEASE COME HOME SOON. I LOVE YOU.
  LOVE GERTIE

Four sentences, but her sister sounded well. For now, that would have to be enough.

Robert's letter hadn't been much longer. She reached for it, imagining his calloused fingers upon the piece of paper.

Dearest Atta,

I received your letter today and immediately ensured Gertie received hers also. She is doing well. Your father seems to keep his distance, and although I've seen his car at the tavern often, a friend tells me he does not drink as heavily. Gertie is lonely but has solved that problem with an imaginary friend. I don't discourage it, although I believe your father is none too happy.

I'm glad to hear you're settled. I light a candle for you every
Sunday. Take care, dear Atta.
    Regards, Robert

And that was it.

Nothing too personal or overly comforting. No reassurances about their future. He hadn't mentioned her invitation to the island. She probably shouldn't have asked, but when she learned patients were allowed visitors during the warm months, she shoved aside all pride and asked Robert to come. Didn't he miss her as much as she missed him?

Apparently not.

Grief tore at her with piercing claws. Though she couldn't dredge up a true tear to cry, it didn't prevent her heart from doing so. Gertie had no one—how was she to grow without proper nurture and love? And now, the very medicine that was to cure Atta made her sicker than she'd ever been in her nineteen years.

What was she to do? Why had she been created? For a lifetime of misery and exile? Did God hear her prayers, or was she cut off from Him forever because of her past transgressions? If He'd cursed her, she might as well die now.

She regretted the thought the moment it entered her mind. Hadn't she vowed to either fight this thing or run from it? Admitting defeat would only give power to the curse inhabiting her body.

A knock sounded at her door and, willing strength to her weary limbs, she sat up, sweeping several loose strands of hair up into her chignon before opening the door.

"Mrs. Parker—hello."

"Hello, Atta dear. Are you feeling any better today?"

Atta left the cottage door open and sat on the oak chair in the main room, comfortable with Mrs. Parker's presence after so many visits. "Please sit, Mrs. Parker. I'm faring well enough."

Mrs. Parker closed the door, the velvet ribbon in her hat

flowing with her movements. The woman never ceased to amaze Atta with her fearlessness over catching the sickness.

"Maybe this will cheer you. I have the material Dr. Parker requested for you." She pulled out several yards of different colored fabrics from a burlap sack. "I can't wait to see what you can do with a needle."

Atta's fingers itched to stroke the fabric on top—a shade of green matching that of a fir tree. The cramps in her stomach loosened as she stroked the fabric. Still rough, the material would need washing before she could work with it. Gertie would love the color. "Thank you."

"I think a new quilt would certainly spruce up this cabin, don't you?"

"Yes, I suppose it would, but I was thinking to make it for my sister."

Mrs. Parker gave her a sad smile as Atta realized her mistake too late.

"But don't you fumigate the mail before it's sent out?"

"Yes, but the formaldehyde fumigator wouldn't fit such a large package. I'm so very sorry, dear."

Atta tucked her chin. "I understand." She recalled the quilt she'd made for little Peter. Robert said he'd cherished the gift above all others. She'd never been able to give much, but somehow a quilt seemed worthy—her time and talent and prayers stitched into each blanket. A part of herself. And now, she would be denied even that.

"Reverend Bailey has arrived. Would you care to join us for service?"

Atta rubbed the green fabric between her thumb and forefinger. Service on a Tuesday afternoon. Although she longed to sit in her cabin alone and wash the fabrics with her pitcher and bowl, she couldn't deny her curiosity over the kind of service such a ragtag group of individuals would make up.

"May I ask your favorite hymn, dear?"

Oh, but she needn't hesitate on that one. "Loving Shepherd of Thy Sheep." It had been one of her mother's favorites.

"Splendid. I love that one as well. Perhaps if I ask Reverend Bailey to begin service with it you might be persuaded to join us?"

Mrs. Parker's hopeful expression wore at Atta's will. Over the past three weeks, she'd learned one thing: the Parkers' compassion was not imagined but made of the most genuine fabric Atta had ever known. It was almost enough to give her hope where hope wasn't warranted.

"Yes, Mrs. Parker. I think I will join you." She rose, smoothed her black skirt, and scooped her rosary from the table, attempting to ignore another small wave of nausea.

"Wonderful." Mrs. Parker opened the door and Atta surveyed her fetching—but clearly aged—blue dress. The lace at the neck sagged. Not for the first time, she pondered the type of sacrifices this woman made for the patients on the island. Quite likely, Mrs. Parker was a sort of outcast herself. The notion comforted and shamed all at the same time.

She followed Mrs. Parker out the door.

"Looks like we're outside today. Maybe the sun will make an appearance." Mrs. Parker led her to the pavilion outside the hospital where the patients and staff gathered.

"Is the weather always so dreary?"

"Some months, yes. But we do have our share of nice days. I'm sure you'll see some yet."

"I'm sure I will too, seeing as I may have to spend the rest of my life upon this island."

It was an attempt at humor, but it came out shallow and reeking of bitterness. She hated herself for it and regretted the words more so when Mrs. Parker only gave her a kind, understanding smile and squeezed her arm. Atta didn't flinch. She'd taken such things for granted in her former life. A peck on the cheek from her sister, a goodnight squeeze. Robert lifting her hair to kiss the nape of her neck.

She remembered Dr. Mayhew's gloved fingers upon her body. Far from comforting or loving, his nearness served to rattle her for an entirely nonmedical purpose. Whether it was his brazen confidence—or the appalling notion that she was somehow attracted to him simply because of his mysterious good looks, she couldn't be sure.

Again, guilt assailed her. She was affianced, after all. How could she expect Robert to stand by her through this mess when she felt quite an ungodly attraction toward her doctor—a man whose full face she'd never seen up close?

Patients and staff sat on wooden chairs beneath the pavilion. Mrs. Parker led her to a gentleman with a dark beard and mustache who spoke to Lee Dip. When they drew near, he smiled, said something to Lee and stood.

"Reverend Bailey, I'd like to introduce you to Miss Schaeffer," Mrs. Parker said.

Reverend Bailey held out his hand and Atta stared at it, not making an effort to raise her own. Gloves and masks back at home, handshakes here. Incomprehensible.

"It's a pleasure to meet you, Reverend." She dipped a small curtsy, hoping to make amends for her social sin.

The Reverend dropped his hand. "Likewise, Miss Atta. I'm looking forward to getting to know you."

Mrs. Parker cleared her throat. "We were wondering if we might begin the service with 'Loving Shepherd of Thy Sheep?'"

Reverend Bailey's eyes lit up. "I think that can be arranged. A lovely hymn."

Mrs. Parker led Atta to a spot beside Lucy. The Parkers, the nurses, and the remaining staff sat in the back row—all except Dr. Mayhew. No surprise there. The man didn't leave the administration side of the island without his mask in place. She'd heard some of the patients poking fun at him in the dining hall. He certainly wouldn't stoop to share a service with the infected.

"I can't believe you." Lucy spoke to her, but looked straight ahead, as if preoccupied with watching Reverend Bailey flip through his hymnal.

"Can't believe what?"

"You know." Lucy's voice was still a hoarse whisper, but Atta had grown accustomed to it over the last couple weeks.

"No, I'm afraid I don't."

"You're looking for him." Her brown gaze turned to Atta's, a twinkle of mischief in their depths.

"Who?"

"That cocky doctor. The man behind the mask. You like him, don't you?"

Atta lowered her voice, horrified Lucy would voice such a suspicion, and right before a service no less. "I do not. You are being ridiculous. Are we in grade school, for heaven's sake?"

Lucy shrugged and smiled, and Atta realized she no longer defined her new friend by her flattened nose, but by her friendly eyes. "I have to get my fun where I can, don't I?"

"Some fun," Atta mumbled, focusing on Reverend Bailey as he greeted the misfit of congregants.

True to his word, they started their service by standing and singing her favorite hymn. Many of the patients didn't sing. Some swayed their heads, as if enjoying the music. Some looked to be humming. Lucy's whispered song struggled to Atta's ears, but her friend's eyes were closed and a look of peace adorned her face. Dr. Parker's strong baritone carried the song over the waves, and Atta joined in, fingers wound tight around the cool beads of her rosary as she found more joy in these precious few moments than she'd known in three weeks' time.

> "Loving shepherd of Thy sheep,
> keep me Lord in safety keep.
> Nothing can Thy power withstand,
> none can pluck me from Thy hand."

She let the words drench her wounded soul, having taken them for granted all the past times she'd sung the hymn. She questioned their truth. She'd thought she'd belonged to God yet had convinced herself otherwise the past few weeks. If nothing could pluck her from his hand, did that "nothing" include the feared malady inhabiting her body?

> "Loving shepherd Thou didst give,
> Thine own life that I might live.
> May I love Thee day by day,
> gladly Thy sweet Will obey."

God had given His life that she could live…but live for what—a life of exile? And what of His will? Was it God's will she be cast off from her family, from her fiancé?

After a few hymns, a gospel reading, and a short prayer, Reverend Bailey ended the simple service with "Alleluia! Alleluia!"

Soft murmurs rippled through the patients as they made their way to the hospital for an early dinner. Familiar, taunting laughter came from behind, and Atta's blood ran cold. Mary. As if possessed by the devil himself, she cackled like a hyena. Atta turned, hesitant.

"You, again." Mary pointed at Atta with a crooked, wobbling finger. Wisps of gray hair covered her crazed eyes. "See those beautiful hands? Not for long, I tell you, girlie. Wait…soon they'll look like mine!"

A shiver racked Atta's body as the woman held out trembling hands and began swatting at them, as was her habit.

"They'll be ugly soon—only a matter of time."

"Mary. That's enough, now." Lucy lay a hand upon Mary's shoulder. "I think Mrs. Parker was looking for you. Over here, dear."

Lucy led the wretched older woman away, leaving Atta with visions of Mary's claw-like hands in her mind. If ever she could hate a person, it would be that loathsome woman. Just because she didn't want to face reality didn't mean she should taunt Atta. She tried to imagine Robert still loving her with such deformed hands. She tried to imagine stroking Gertie's hair with nubby fingers but couldn't bear the thought.

Surely, there was something that *could* pluck her from God's hand. A thing so terrible, a thing embedded deep within her body, a thing she couldn't bring herself to speak of aloud. And like a dark, swelling raincloud over her spirit, any semblance of peace she'd captured in the last hour fled.

Chapter Sixteen

1993

When the priest concludes the service, the congregation stands and Gram flips open her hymnal.

"Loving shepherd of Thy sheep,
keep me Lord in safety keep.
Nothing can Thy power withstand,
none can pluck me from Thy hand."

Atta's hymn. I squint at Gram but she sings right along with the organ, not giving any indication that she recognizes the hymn from her story the night before. But she seems pretty tight with her church—I bet she requested it.

I softly sing the words, imagining my Aunt Atta singing them all those years ago on Penikese. In the core of my being, I understand her questions about God. Although I'm not religious like my great-aunt, something draws me to the words of this song—the insistence that nothing can take me out of God's care.

The idea is foreign, but for a millisecond of time, I entertain it. Just as quickly, I chastise myself. God's care isn't for someone like me. And what kind of care was it, anyway, to rip me from my school and friends and graduation, to force me to have a child I would have to give up as soon as it was born?

Not that the alternative was any better. Giving up my hopes and dreams for single motherhood at eighteen didn't sound appealing, either.

I sigh, my gaze straying to the familiar profile hunched in the front row alongside an older man—his grandfather, no doubt. Maybe Sam isn't the rebel boy I feared him to be if he goes to church with his grandfather.

As we sing the last verse, I make a decision to say hello to Sam after the service ends. He's been nothing but nice to me, and I've allowed my unwarranted fears about him to get in the way of befriending him.

After we finish singing and the priest speaks the benediction, Gram closes her hymnal. "I'll be happy to wait if you'd like to go with the youth group."

I bite my bottom lip. The priest had announced the youth would have a brief gathering after Mass to discuss a summer trip. "I don't think so." They wouldn't want me, surely.

"Come now, Emily. I know our games of pinochle have been quite rousing, but do you really want me as your only company the entire summer?"

I smile. "Okay, I'll go." If I can't find a nice friend at church, then chances are slim I could find one at all.

She pats my hand. "I'll be in the car. No rush."

I push back my shoulders at the same time that I tug the sides of my button-down shirt across my belly. The youth are gathering in the back. Three girls are off to the side chatting.

Here goes nothing. With my heart trembling, I start toward

the girl with long hair as black as Snow White's. When she turns and sees me, I catch her quick glance at my stomach before her eyebrows raise. She looks down her nose at me.

I halt. My gaze flies across the group, landing on another girl on the opposite side of the foyer who gives me a welcoming smile, but my feet are cemented to the floor.

This was a mistake—thinking I can fit in. Thinking these kids will accept me.

I back away as nonchalantly as possible. Maybe I can still catch up with Sam. But as I turn, an elderly couple blocks my view of the front of the church. When I get around them, I glimpse Sam walking toward the youth, straight for Snow White.

She gives him a radiant smile and bumps him with her shoulder when he stops at her side.

My stomach churns.

Of course Sam would want to hang with the pretty, popular girls. He was a red-blooded, American teenaged boy, after all. Boys —even nice boys—want only one thing, right?

And even if Sam was interested in more than that, he'd want to be with a girl he could be proud of. Not a charity case.

I whirl around before I can torture myself further.

In the parking lot, the wind cools my burning face as I seek out Gram's car. I slide into the passenger seat of the Volkswagen without looking at her.

"That was a short meeting," she says.

I inhale the now familiar scent of her Avon perfume. Funny how it comforts after such a short time.

"I just don't think I'd fit in. It was a nice idea, but let's go home."

She raises her eyebrows. "I'm assuming something happened to make you feel that way?"

I don't answer.

What does it matter anyway? I'll be gone by the end of the summer.

"I'm sorry, dear. But remember, you'll always fit in with God."

A sarcastic snort escapes me.

"I mean it, Emily Grace. You can't let one person—or even two or three—hinder you from living your life. People are going to talk. You can't stop them. But dear, you can choose to shrink beneath the weight of their condemnation or be stronger despite it."

I think of the snooty looks at school, and now here, at church of all places. I think of my parents. Though they're arranging for the adoption, they already believe I've thrown my life away.

I think of my Aunt Atta, and all she endured. I think of Gram as a little girl, so alone she made up an imaginary friend.

You know what? Gram is right. I can choose to shrink or I can choose to stand and be strong. This baby does not signal the end of my life. I would make it past this challenging time. I *would* graduate high school. I *would* go to college. And I *would* become a great teacher one day.

With a bit of hard work and tenacity, I would prove everyone —especially my parents—wrong.

Chapter Seventeen

1916

Harry held himself back from slamming the door of the examination room behind Mr. Yee. Instead, as soon as the door clicked, he hurled his fountain pen across the room. It broke against the window, leaving a stain of black ink trailing down the glass.

Confound it all! Making any progress on this God forsaken island proved impossible. The patients refused to cooperate. Language was an issue, of course, but so was their stubbornness. How Dr. Parker got along with them was beyond Harry. If only they could see that a bit of discomfort now may reap a harvest of benefits later on.

He'd seen eleven patients so far today, and not one of them had allowed him to remove pieces of tissue or glands. If he didn't secure the leprous tissue, he wouldn't be able to work on cultivating the bacterium. If he couldn't cultivate it, he couldn't begin experiments.

He ran his pointer finger along the inside edge of his mask.

The indentation from the mask had taken up permanent residence on his face. The thing irritated him to no end, as did the carbolic acid he scoured his skin with at the close of each day. More than once, he'd toyed with the idea of throwing the mask in the trash. Working so closely with the lepers, he could have already contracted the disease.

A knock echoed through the examination room and Harry glanced at the list of patients. Miss Schaeffer. His last patient. He hadn't planned on asking her for another tissue sample—he'd seen her slide, the numbers simply weren't enough. But maybe they'd have to do.

"Come in."

Harry started when Dr. Parker appeared instead of Miss Schaeffer.

"Dr. Mayhew—thought I'd check in, see how you're getting along." The older man's bushy eyebrows rose as he looked askance at the ink running down the glass pane of the window. The pen lay broken at the bottom. "Better than your pen, I hope."

Harry almost smiled. Something about Dr. Parker's presence grounded him, calmed him. Being a doctor was only a small part of Frank Parker's position on the island. A man of many hats, Harry often witnessed Dr. Parker shoeing horses, planting, gardening, and building. Teaching the patients to do the same. And now he stood, looking like a distinguished gentleman in his bowler hat and gray suit. Without a mask.

Harry sighed and removed his mask, rubbing at the lines along his face. A gust of salty wind swept through the large windows, replacing the smells of carbolic and alcohol. He breathed it in. "The patients won't allow me to take samples. I'm afraid I'll have to resort to force if they continue these shenanigans."

Dr. Parker cleared his throat and walked to the window with his hands behind his back. "Maybe a dinner party is in order."

"Excuse me?"

"You've been here for more than a month, Harry. You work in

this room all day long, come back to the other side for dinner, work in my lab until who knows when, *maybe* get some sleep, then repeat the day all over. Reverend Bailey's been here twice and you haven't bothered to attend service. Marion invites you to the dinner parties she throws for the patients each week, and you've declined each one."

Harry couldn't deny it, but surely his reasons were obvious.

"I realize this is a punishment of sorts for you. I also realize the height of your determination. But you still need to live a life. We all do."

"I don't wish to live *this* life." He ground out the words through clenched teeth.

Dr. Parker strode toward the window, hands clasped behind his back. Silence enveloped the room. Finally, he spoke. "The administration building is new. A fire in 1912 destroyed the old building. Marion and I lived here, with the patients while they rebuilt. Any psychological and physical barriers I tried to erect came down during that time. That fire was a blessing in disguise."

He turned to Harry. "You walk around here with your mask plastered to your face. The patients don't know what you look like. You make no effort to relate to them, yet you dare ask the world of them."

Harry grappled for a defense but came up short.

"Attending service wouldn't kill you, Harry. Neither would a dinner party. Marion's planning the usual tonight. It'll be an outside affair, beneath the pavilion. Plenty of fresh air. No one's asking you to share a fork with Lee. I'll expect to see you there." Dr. Parker made for the door but turned before Harry could stutter a protest. "And Dr. Mayhew? Leave the mask in the exam room."

ATTA LIFTED her face to the sun and allowed it to warm her. If only more days like this existed on the island. The temperature had warmed to a balmy eighty degrees. The sun, a brilliant saffron orb in the sky, reflected its radiant color against the paling green shrubbery surrounding the path to the cemetery.

Mrs. Parker's dinner party would take place within the hour, but right now Atta longed for a bit of solitude. She'd never visited the cemetery, but it was fast becoming a place she feared. The place in the distance with the little white cross—the place where, in all likelihood, all of the patients on the island would find their final resting place. Better to face it now, on the tails of a beautiful day, than at one of her peers' funeral services.

She neared the end of the island where the cemetery nestled on the top of a large cliff. She stopped short at the sight of a man, his back to her and hands tucked in the pockets of his suit pants. He stared at a headstone. Atta recognized the blonde curls and began to back away. It didn't matter whose side of the island they stood upon—Dr. Mayhew would not welcome her presence.

A slithering strip of dark brown blocked her next step, and she inhaled a sharp breath before almost stepping sideways into a patch of fresh gull waste. The glistening body slid from view.

Had the doctor heard her? Slowly, she looked up to see his broad shoulders turning. The wind blew a few short curls from his maskless face.

Though she'd seen him from a distance on the boat and her imagination had filled in what the mask covered, it had not done his features justice. A strong nose sat above a firm, full mouth and chiseled jaw. All at once, she ached for Robert's nearness, how she used to run a hand along his forehead, how he used to pull her close for a kiss with parted lips. Heat rushed to her cheeks as she realized her thoughts. She dipped her head. "Excuse me, Dr. Mayhew. I—I was just leaving." She turned and started away at a fast clip.

"Miss Schaeffer. Please, don't leave on my account."

The kind words almost sounded foreign. She waved her hand at the cemetery. "I haven't a real purpose in coming. I can take my constitutional elsewhere."

"Please stay, Miss Schaeffer. I'd like to speak with you."

"All right, then." She took a cautious step forward. "But I think you're forgetting something." She drew her pointer finger around her nose and mouth. Would he realize his blunder and run from her to the other end of the island?

An easy smile inched its way across his mouth, and he cleared his throat. "I'm—I'm trying to conform."

She supposed she could relate to that.

"Maybe you could help me," he said.

She took another step forward, struggling to hear him above the heavy crash of the waves against the shore below. "How so?"

He opened his mouth and scratched the hollow on his cheek above his jaw. "Perhaps speak with me a bit. Help me become accustomed to communicating with..."

"A leper," she finished, the word on her lips surprising and offending all at once, and every bit as sour on her tongue as she imagined. "You have to be the most tactless doctor I've ever met."

To her surprise, he didn't defend himself. Instead, a blotch of red dotted each of his cheeks. "I suppose I'm not off to a good start."

"I'd say not."

They stood far apart. Heavy silence coated the briny air between them. He looked out to the sea, slightly to the right, and pointed. "That's the closest point of mainland to the island. New Bedford." He nodded to the wooden marker with the initials *I.U.* at his feet. "Iwa Umezakia rowed there in '13. I read it in his records. Only patient on the island to escape. Thirteen miles to shore. Of course, he was apprehended. Went straight to Boston to plead his case. They say if he'd gone to New York he'd be a free man—no laws like here, I guess." He shot her an apologetic grin, and something pinched within her. His manner was different here, out of the examination room. "Forgive me, I'm rambling."

"On the contrary, you're doing rather well communicating with a—a..."

His smile disappeared, and she wished to snatch her words back. She should have encouraged him to continue instead of jabbing him with an insult.

Instead, she grasped onto what he'd just told her.

Someone had escaped from the island. Freedom was possible.

He took two steps forward, past a happy bunch of daffodils in an old jar next to a grave marked *I.B.* They were almost close enough to touch one another now. "I'm sorry I canceled your appointment today. Dr. Parker gave me a few things to think about."

"Please Dr. Mayhew, don't ever apologize for sparing me time in that dreadful room."

"You don't like being there—more so than the other patients."

Atta's throat closed as she thought of her mother. Of what she had done. Of what she hadn't.

"Have you been feeling better since we ceased the chaulmoogra oil?"

"Much."

He opened his mouth, then closed it. "Mrs. Parker's party should be starting any moment. Shall we?"

She knew proper etiquette dictated he offer his arm, but that was back in her former world—not this one. Of course, he didn't offer—she was foolish to imagine it. He extended his hand to the path, and she took the lead.

"A *C*, Dr. Mayhew."

"Pardon?"

"I have a feeling you do well when striving for the best grade, so I give you a *C* for your performance."

"I'm not performing, Miss Schaeffer. I'm trying to change."

"You haven't convinced me yet. That's why I gave you a *C*."

HE TRIED to hide his annoyance over being pegged so well. Had his time in the cemetery with Miss Schaeffer been a complete performance? Maybe, but as much as he hated to admit it, he'd almost enjoyed the female companionship.

Miss Schaeffer moved with dainty steps before him, and he found himself mesmerized by her small, graceful feet.

A *C. Humph.* And why should he care a straw what sort of a grade this outcast gave him?

You make no effort to relate to them, yet you dare to ask the world of them.

Maybe that's why the grade bothered him. Because his success or failure hinged upon how well he related to his patients. If he couldn't relate to Miss Schaeffer—the only one who could pass for a normal person—he would never be able to do so with the others.

And yet, it was a beginning. In an odd way, Dr. Parker had set him free in the exam room today. In ordering him to appear without a mask before the patients, he had given Harry the confidence and assurance he needed to do so without fear. Without a debilitating fear, that is.

The shrubbery made way for a view of the hospital. The setting sun cast orange streaks across the front windows of the building. Patients and staff mulled about the pavilion where several tables stood, china and silver gleaming. A lively strand of ragtime music drifted from the Victrola, set on a distant table.

For the first time in days, he thought of Carrie with a longing heart. She loved to dance. He'd turned her down too many times. What he wouldn't give for a jaunt with her about now. He'd written to her once, and she'd obliged him with a short, cursory note back, asking him to kindly not send her any more letters from "that cursed island."

Miss Schaeffer wandered off to speak with Miss Peterson. Even among outcasts, they seemed to form their own cliques. He watched as Goon Lee Dip parted from the other Chinamen and trudged his way over to Harry in his specially made shoes, lined with cotton.

"Eh, Doctor. No mask." The man smiled up at him through a mustache that bore an uncanny resemblance to Dr. Parker's. If he'd learned one thing about Lee Dip, he was ever the optimist. Ulcers and pustules plagued his body. His eyes constantly bothered him, yet he took pride in any work he did upon the island—especially running the laundry building beside the hospital.

Harry nodded, finding it more difficult to "perform" in front of the Chinaman. The mask had been more than protection from the diseases that inhabited the patients' bodies—it had established a patient-doctor relationship. Without it, the line blurred. He didn't take comfort in the lack of boundaries.

"No mask tonight, Mr. Goon."

"No, no. You call me Willie Goon."

The corner of Harry's mouth twitched as the little Chinaman tried to befriend him. Yet despite his amusement, he ordered his feet to remain in place. It appeared Dr. Parker was right. A dinner party, maybe service on Tuesday...by Wednesday the patients may willingly put their lives—and their glands—in his hands.

Chapter Eighteen

The funeral was as pathetic as its attendees. Reverend Bailey had said a few words over Solomon Goodman's body, which had been transported in the island's only conveyance, a dump cart, with as much dignity as could be mustered. Now the staff and patients—all with a fresh reminder of their own mortality—straggled back to the hospital building from the cemetery.

Harry almost hadn't attended. A death meant the opportunity for an autopsy and cultures, both of which he'd performed. He couldn't wait to return to the lab to begin experimentation, as none of the patients had yet agreed to allow it.

Miss Peterson and Miss Schaeffer walked in front of him, speaking in hushed tones. Miss Peterson had been the only one to shed a tear for Mr. Goodman. The Hebrew teacher's heart had failed him. Old age, Harry surmised. Strange enough, the death seemed to have little to do with leprosy, although certainly the pain and unfortunate circumstances of Mr. Goodman's body had worn down the elderly patient.

The small procession ended beneath the pavilion, where the hospital cook had arranged sandwiches and a vegetable platter.

Harry picked at a chicken sandwich on his plate, wary of eating food so close to the patients. He wondered how Miss Schaeffer would grade him on that.

Unhindered, thoughts of Carrie and the letter he'd received the day before—her first real letter since he'd arrived—came to him. In no uncertain terms, she'd begged Harry to come home. Finally missed him enough, he supposed. She said his father was having second thoughts about his time at Penikese. She urged Harry to beg his father to let him into the practice. The letter smelled of Carrie's rose-scented water, and crinkled watermarks dotted the ink—her tears?—as she wrote the desperate words.

Without shame, he sniffed the lovely scent on the stationery that symbolized Carrie—pure, clean, beautiful. He'd almost written his father then, but in the end, he'd abstained. It would be in Carrie's best interest to goad him into begging his father. How much of her letter was truth? If his father wanted him in the practice, he'd make it known. William Mayhew was anything but shy.

"Dr. Mayhew?"

Harry broke his vacant stare to find Reverend Bailey holding out a hand. "I don't believe we've met, Doctor. It's a pleasure."

Harry shook the man's hand in a firm grip. The Reverend wore a double-breasted straight-hanging jacket, oxford shoes, and a friendly expression.

"Call me Harry, Reverend. I attended your service here last week."

"Rather different from those on the mainland, eh?"

The corners of Harry's mouth tightened. "I understand why you simplify it here."

The Reverend swirled a glass of sweet tea in his right hand. The ice clinked against the sides of the glass. "Don't get me wrong, there are times I'd like to preach a good long sermon, but with the majority of patients unable to understand, it isn't practical. They enjoy the hymns, and I pray they know God's love through them."

Harry tapped his foot against the soft grass, uncertain what to say in response to the Reverend's comment. He was a man of medicine, not a man of God.

"How is your studying coming? Lots of firsthand experience here."

His lungs expanded at the change of conversation. "More than I'm ready for. Sometimes it seems I'm getting nowhere, but I suppose the patients need time to grow accustomed to me."

"And you to them."

Harry squinted at the older man. "Yes. And me to them."

Reverend Bailey took a swig of tea and looked toward the ocean. "Are you familiar with the island's history?"

Harry shook his head.

"The first owners of the island share your surname. Maybe you're related. That would certainly be a point of interest to break up your research."

Harry grunted. He remembered Dr. Parker mentioning something similar on his first night at Penikese. But what did it matter? The last thing he needed was a rabbit trail to derail him from his true venture.

Still, maybe a letter to his father wouldn't hurt. He could ask him what he knew of his ancestors—and feel out if there was any truth in what Carrie wrote.

ATTA TUGGED a piece of thread through a block of beeswax before threading it. Sitting beside Lucy, she worked the needle in and out of the two squares of fabric at her fingertips, her stitches flowing tiny and quick. The work served to calm her fidgety hands. Stitch or pray the rosary—the only two endeavors that provided comfort on the long days revolving around mail time.

"Do you ever forget what you're missing? Being here, I mean," she asked her new friend.

"Some of it." Lucy sipped the tea Betsy had made for her. Mrs.

Parker had ordered lemons, honey, and stick cinnamon in hopes the cook could make a brew that would soothe Lucy's sinuses. "At times, it seems I've been here forever—that this is where I'm meant to be and that the mainland is nothing more than a dream." She looked out the wide windows of the amusement room where the leaves of various shrubs sported drab shades of yellows, oranges, and reds beneath a rainy sky. "And then at other times I want, more than anything else, to hear the sound a dove makes when it takes flight."

Atta inhaled the scent of Betsy's apple pan dowdy, but instead imagined it one of her own making, one she had intended for Robert and Gertie in their little home. A pair of doves sat beneath their pine tree, cooing gently to one another.

Oo-wah-hooo, hoo-hoo.

In her mind's eye, a squirrel fell from a short limb, setting the pair of doves to the air with gentle whistling twitters.

She hadn't remembered such a small detail until now. How many others had she forgotten? She'd missed the peals of the great church bells of St. Mary's and the rich, wonderful scent and shade of a pine tree...but there was so much she'd never experience again. Simple things. Like the flight of a dove.

She glanced down at her sewing, envisioning a dove appliquéd on the front of the brown and green fabric she prepared. All at once, she knew who the quilt would be for. She may not be able to shower Gertie with gifts ever again, but she may be able to show her friend a bit of gratitude and love with a simple gift.

"Thank you for reminding me, Lucy."

A gentle smile curved Lucy's lips, but it disappeared as she massaged her throat, taking in short, wheezy breaths. Atta set her stitching aside. "Should I fetch Nurse Edith?"

Lucy shook her head and took another sip of tea. "I'll...be... fine. It comes and goes."

"Is it very painful?"

"Sometimes...but more...often than not, it's just a nuisance."

She gestured for Atta to continue quilting. "Tell me about...your life. Before this."

Atta stuck her tongue in her cheek. She didn't want to walk down this road now. Her former life seemed further and further away each morning she awoke on the island. The only evidence that it still existed were her letters from Gertie and every so often, from Robert.

The Victrola echoed out strains of a classical piece by Max Reger. Goon Lee Dip, Yee Toy, Manuel Baptiste, and Wong Quong played a rowdy game of cards. Funny how they found a way to break through their language barriers. The rest of the patients were either in their rooms or enjoying Betsy's apple dowdy.

"I was to be wed last month."

Lucy placed a reassuring hand on Atta's now limp fingers, lying in her lap. Cackling laughter erupted from the corner of the room, and Atta startled. Mary. The woman rocked back and forth, her vacant eyes on Atta, laughing as if she'd heard of her misfortune and was happy about it.

"Leper!" she yelled. Her gaze did not waver from Atta as she swatted at her own clawed hands. "Unclean! Unclean!"

Not for the first time, Atta longed to get up and slap the woman into sanity. She was the only patient that tended to disgust her, probably because Atta was the only patient Mary fixated on, mocked day by day.

She shivered as the yelling continued, only ceasing when Mrs. Tufts coaxed Mary to another room.

"Never mind her." Lucy said. "She's sicker than...all of us."

"I wish she'd leave me alone. I can't sleep well at night—not without a lock on my door."

"Mary's harmless...go on with your...story now. I want to hear."

Atta sighed, attempting to reconcile this life with her old one. With each new sunset, it proved harder and harder to convince herself she hadn't imagined her former existence. Even Robert's face took on a picturesque quality in her mind. Black-and-white, where once there had been color.

"My sister turned seven last week. We'd planned for her to come live with Robert and me. Papi...he drinks too much." Her throat closed with emotion and she took up her sewing again. "What about you, Lucy? What was your life like before Penikese?"

Rain dotted the windowpane and Atta looked to the filmy clouds, hoping it would downpour enough to fill the cistern that held their water. If not, there would be no baths for the next week.

"I left...my mother and sisters in Russia to work as a domestic in...Concord when I was twenty. My brothers and uncle lived in America. I couldn't wait to come here. It was...hard work, but I loved it. A fine gentleman...Thomas...courted me before I was sent to Penikese. We grew serious, but as soon as he heard the news.... I didn't have to blink and he was gone."

Atta stopped sewing. Apparently, unconditional love was not granted to those with Hansen's disease. They all likely shared similar stories.

"Do you know of Flavia and Mary? Did they have husbands? Families?"

"Flavia has a husband, although it's likely he's filed for divorce. I'm unsure of Mary—she lived with her married daughter before coming here. So many sad stories. My friend Isabelle...was the first woman patient on the island. They tore her away from her husband who had been caring for her, and two small children, who had to go into foster care. Her husband fought so hard...they sent him to a madhouse. She gave birth to... her third child on the island. She held him for twenty days before they took him away."

"I can't imagine." Atta pressed her lips together, her heart like a damp cloth being wrung out to dry as she thought of Gertie. Of Isabelle dying, not knowing what had happened to her children. Would Atta ever see her sister again? Gertie's letters spoke of a safe routine, yet if that were so, why did Gertie need an imaginary friend to get through her days?

Dr. Mayhew's words returned to her.

Iwa Umezakia. Escape. They say if he'd gone to New York he'd be a free man—no laws like here, I guess.

Soon winter would be upon them and her chance would be gone until spring. Atta envisioned herself making the thirteen-mile trip to the mainland in the open ocean under the cover of night, with dark, cold waters beneath her. If she could summon the courage to make the trip, perhaps she could catch a morning tram to Taunton. Robert would help her if she went to him. They could catch Gertie on her way to school, take a train to New York, start a new life together. The disease was nearly nonexistent. She could hardly believe she'd be putting others in danger. Look at the Parkers and the nurses. They lived among the outcasts—many of whom were sicker than her—and they were fine. The public was misinformed, or plain fearful. She could find a job as a domestic. Robert may not wish to go with them, but maybe when he saw with his own eyes how well she was....

"You're thinking too hard, Atta." Lucy drained the last of her tea. "Whatever it is you're dwelling on, you'd best not. Look, Mrs. Parker's here to read to us. Let's go sit."

Atta tucked away her sewing along with her rebellious thoughts and joined the other patients in a semi-circle around Mrs. Parker, who opened a black leather Bible and gave them a bit of background regarding the text, which she said was written by Saint Paul.

"...for I have learned, in whatever state I am, therewith to be content. I know both how to be abased, and I know how to abound: everywhere and in all things I am instructed both to be full and to be hungry, both to abound and to suffer need. I can do all things through Christ which strengtheneth me."

Mrs. Parker continued reading, and Atta pondered the words. Being content no matter what, Saint Paul had said. Yet, was that truly in all circumstances? Saint Paul didn't have a little sister locked in her bedroom with only a hope chest between her and death's door. Saint Paul wasn't proclaimed an outcast and exiled to a lonely island. Saint Paul hadn't been snubbed by the person he'd thought to love for the rest of his life.

But as she considered these things, painful memories kicked to the surface. Her thirteen-year-old self, sitting watch over her mother's death bed. Finding the questionable bottle. Seeing Mami worsen. Not telling a soul.

Of course, Saint Paul could take comfort in God. He had likely not committed such transgressions. For surely, Atta's sin of silence was enough for God to condemn her forever.

Chapter Nineteen

1993

This was a stupid idea. Why did I allow Gram to talk me into this?

I shift in my seat and glance at the circle of young people in the church's basement. I had come with Gram to bring some non-perishables to the church for a food drive, but when I found the basement filled with teens, I'd realized the full extent of Gram's craftiness.

"Let me introduce you to Mr. Kaminski. He's the youth group leader," she'd said breezily.

When I shook hands with the broad-shouldered middle-aged gentleman, he gave me a friendly smile. "Why don't you stay for our study? We're making ice cream sundaes afterward."

He was nice, I'd give him that. But something about the entire situation made me feel out of place and incredibly young. But I agreed to stay—partly to prove to Gram I wasn't absolutely pathetic and partly to prove to myself that I was serious about not letting others discourage me from living the life I wanted to live.

Now, I sit in one of the hard metal folding chairs. Would Sam come? And if he did, would he sit next to me or seek out Snow White who was across the room giggling with her friends?

A small, red-headed girl plops down on the seat beside me. "Hey. I'm Phoebe."

I smile. "Hey. I'm Emily."

"You're new here, right?"

I nod.

She pops her gum and I study her. She's incredibly young—probably in junior high.

"Mr. Kaminski is pretty cool and there's always a yummy snack before we go." She fidgets in her seat, as if ready to hop up and get the snack the second it's put out. "My mom makes me come, but I'm starting to like it. They're taking us to Rocky Point in June. My favorite ride's the Corkscrew, but the Freefall's pretty awesome, too. I wasn't tall enough for either of them until last summer. What's your favorite?"

Rollercoasters? Nausea climbs around my insides and somehow I'm dizzy. Though I haven't suffered much morning sickness, I have an inkling that even if I got on a rollercoaster, my baby would *not* be having it.

"I'm kind of boring when it comes to amusement parks. I guess the train's more my speed now," I say.

Her forehead bunches in genuine puzzlement. "I don't think Rocky Point has a train...."

My stomach gurgles. I'm going to be sick. "I'm sorry. I have to go. It was nice meeting you...Phoebe." I rush down the hall to the lone bathroom at the end and close the door. I lean against it and stare at the slightly brown toilet water in the bowl. I *really* do not want to puke.

I close my eyes and breathe deep, the nausea slowly settling.

Must I go back? Phoebe is nice, but she isn't Ashley.

I breathe out slowly, feeling the sickness lifting. Silly of me to expect some random girl to replace my best friend, especially someone as young and innocent as Phoebe.

And yet, perhaps I'm being too picky. Sometimes circumstance, more than choice, decided friendships. My mind wanders to my Aunt Atta and her new friend, Lucy. My aunt was abandoned by not only her friends and family, but practically the entire world. Who am I to complain about being alone? At least I'm not trapped on an island, surrounded by people who barely speak my language. These last few months of pregnancy might well be lonely, but after the baby is born I would go on to college. I'd have as many friends—and maybe boyfriends—as I wanted.

I clear my throat, surprised at the sudden emptiness that consumes me at the thought of my life post pregnancy. If I feel like an outcast now, how will my baby feel growing up knowing it wasn't wanted?

And yet, that's silly. There are plenty of happy, well-adjusted children who are adopted. The baby will be fine. Better than fine, even—with parents who are ready to care for it, able to afford all the things it'll need. I'm overthinking things. Gram's story is getting to me, is all. My own emotional, hormonal turmoil is making me doubt common sense. Making me question what my parents have already decided.

What I need is to stop thinking so deeply, stop letting emotions distract me from what must be done. The baby will inevitably come—it will only hurt more to dwell on how I might fail him or her, as I've already failed myself. I simply need to graduate high school, have this baby, and move on with my life.

And right now, that means getting back to the youth group and pretending I can't wait to eat an ice cream sundae.

Chapter Twenty

Dear Harry,

I trust everything is going well on the island and that you are learning much in your time spent there. I have corresponded with Dr. Parker on occasion, and he seems satisfied with the work you have completed. Take care with your patients, Harry. No matter what their afflictions, they put their lives in your hands. That responsibility should never be taken lightly. Remember where you come from and determine to carry on the Mayhew medical legacy in all you do.

Your mother still mourns your absence and cannot bring herself to write, delicate as her state is. She sends her love, though, and looks forward to the day when we can put this entire incident behind us, as do I.

As for your question, I am in fact familiar with the Mayhews that owned the Elizabeth Islands in the seventeenth century. I talked of it many times when you were a lad. While they were quite successful, they were also known as religious zealots. I think it was fortuitous *indeed when some of the Mayhews turned away from the pulpit and to medicine.*

Take care in all you do, Harry. Work hard and think intelligently.

Sincerely,
Dr. William Harvey Mayhew

HE WAS FAILING. Miserably.

Harry massaged his right shoulder and mentally summoned the work he'd completed the last three months. The patients had warmed to him, yet what did it matter?

Dozens of smears, urinalysis, blood counts. He'd spent hours examining sputum under the microscope for tuberculosis, and just as much time running Wassermann tests for syphilis—diseases patients with leprosy were more susceptible. But while he was more familiar with the disease of leprosy, none of it moved him toward a cultivation of the bacteria, which for some reason proved impossible. Even the blasted rats refused to contract the disease, never mind the expensive monkeys he'd ordered.

Same went for him. Harry leaned back in his chair, watching the much-needed rain tap on the window. He'd given up on the mask, as Dr. Parker had done long ago. Weekly, he turned scalpel to his own skin and scraped from his earlobe, a spot especially prone to leprosy. Weekly, he examined his own stained smear beneath a microscope. Weekly, it came back negative.

He had not contracted the disease though he'd gone weeks without a mask. Maybe the sickness really was a curse from God. It simply didn't make sense why some caught it and others appeared immune. And yet, if God dictated who contracted the illness, maybe there wasn't a cure to be found under the sun. Maybe cultivating the bacteria was impossible. Maybe he was wasting his time and talent on this chunk of desolate land.

Desperate, his mind raced to the age-old remedy he'd pondered the last several days. Hippocrates's words.

Give me the power to produce fever, and I will cure all disease.

All disease...including leprosy?

The idea held merit. But although the side-effects shouldn't be too severe, it would be better to enlist a strong patient. One whose skin smears showed little bacteria to begin with. Maybe a few hot baths would be enough to extinguish the stubborn disease from Miss Schaeffer. It was worth a try to save her from the stark, bitter future that was ahead for her.

Decided, Harry rose and walked down the corridors of the hospital building. The days had cooled, and the patients spent much of their time in the amusement room. He'd often seen Miss Schaeffer sewing by the window. She didn't disappoint today.

In a brown skirt and white blouse, she concentrated on each stitch, her fingers moving deftly over the fabric. Raindrops streaked across the window behind her and for the first time he imagined her as normal. In a fine house, stitching by the light of a window.

Unexpected compassion welled within him. If he couldn't cure her, she would live out all her days on this island. She would be buried in the same cemetery in which Solomon Goodman and Iwa Umezakia lay. Her fingers would go numb over time, her pretty face would grow distorted. She wouldn't be able to stitch. Walking would become difficult. Maybe she'd lose her eyesight, maybe her attractive nose. In all likelihood, her life would be meaningless.

Unless he did something.

"Miss Schaeffer?"

She jumped, jabbing her finger with the needle. "Dr. Mayhew. Good afternoon." She wiggled the finger she'd pricked.

"May I see you in the exam room, please?"

She blanched, and he wondered again what secrets she held. He wanted to know, and at the same time it irked him that he cared.

Tucking away her sewing, she stood and followed him.

"My mother embroiders. What are you stitching?" He needed her to relax. She'd never agree to anything if she felt pressured.

"A quilt."

"For someone back home? I'm sure that would make a lovely Christmas gift."

She sighed as they entered the room. "It would. Unfortunately sending such things from the island is forbidden. I have someone else in mind."

Strike one. Different tactic in order.

"I think it's about time for my weekly assessment, don't you? I'm hoping for some improvement over last week's low *B*."

The sweetness of her smile caught him off guard. She really was a sight to behold with those dark eyes and loose tendrils of matching hair framing her face. She may not be striking in the same way as Carrie, but something about her gave him hope. Why? Why would a leper give him, an Ivy league graduate, hope?

"You did share tea with Lee." She tapped her chin and glanced up at the ceiling. "I think I even recall a genuine laugh over something he said. That'll earn you a high *B*."

A smile came to his lips as he remembered the joke Willie Goon had told him in his heavy accent. Not a particularly clean joke, but a funny one nonetheless.

"I have doubts I'll ever earn an *A* with you, Miss Schaeffer."

"Best keep trying, then." Her cheeks reddened beneath her almost coy manner.

Harry cleared his throat. He needed to be more careful. Just because he didn't wear a mask didn't negate the need for a strict doctor-patient relationship.

"Have a seat. Please." He gestured to a spare chair and she lowered herself into it, giving him a wary look. And no wonder. She'd never sat anywhere in this room except the exam table. "I have an experiment I'm looking into. It's relatively safe—"

"Relatively?"

How much should he explain? Maybe another patient—one who didn't understand English perfectly—would be a better choice.

"I'm not trying to hide anything from you. It is an experiment, so nothing is guaranteed. But nothing is gained either, if we don't try."

"And what is it we're *trying*, Doctor?"

Confound it, the woman was difficult. He sat on the edge of his desk. "Fever therapy." Her blank stare prodded him onward. "I've spent the last week reading up on ways to create hyperthermia. Some thirty years ago, it was proven that one's body temperature could be raised more than five degrees by prolonged immersion in hot water. The body's natural inclination to fight disease is fever. Hot temperatures often kill disease. I haven't read of anyone trying this technique on lep—Hansen's disease—but I'm willing to give it a go if you are."

"What are the risks? The truth please, Dr. Mayhew." Her brown gaze sparked with defiance.

"I've always been honest with you, Miss Schaeffer. Sometimes to a fault."

"I'm not willing to subject myself to experimentation unless I have all the facts. The only reason I'm considering such a course is because of my—my circumstances."

She meant more than a life of exile. What—or who—had she left behind on the mainland?

"Fever therapy is fairly simple, and if monitored well, it's low risk. One of the nurses—whomever you're most comfortable—would prepare you a hot bath. The idea is to continue to add hot water until any more wouldn't be bearable. We'd monitor—"

"We? Of course, I'd only be comfortable with a nurse in my bathing chambers."

Heat worked from his neck to his face. For heaven's sake, he was a doctor.

"Of course, Miss Schaeffer. The *nurse* would monitor your

temperature. I'd like to raise it by three or four degrees, if possible. You'd then stay in the bath for an additional fifteen to twenty minutes, after which you will get out, wrap yourself in a thick robe and get into one of the beds here, where your body will slowly cool off on its own."

"That's it?"

"We'd have to do it at least twice a day. For how long, I'm uncertain."

"You said the risks are low."

He nodded and tapped out his energy with his right foot. "The greatest is the risk of dehydration. You would sweat greatly—which is the desired effect. Yet, we would need to be careful to replace your fluids. Nothing cool. It would defeat the purpose."

"Is there anything else I should know before I make my decision?"

Her decision. So much for his threat of three months ago. And yet, it wouldn't have been pleasant to force such experimentation upon the patients. Especially upon Miss Schaeffer, who quickly had become his favorite of the motley crew.

"I've never performed this procedure before. I'm not sure many would recommend it. I don't know if it'll work. I haven't been able to infect monkeys or rats with the disease, and so I have not been able to demonstrate that hot temperature will kill the bacteria while it lives in a host." He raised his eyebrows in her direction. "Have I convinced you yet?"

She stood, the corners of her mouth turned upward. "No. But I think your honesty has. When shall I expect treatment to begin?"

Chapter Twenty-One

"What art tha' doin? He'd be out with us for good if he got th' notion us was interferin'."

"I can't help it, Kat. Aren't you in the least bit curious what set Papi off?" Gertie picked up the crumpled piece of stationery in the corner of the sitting room. She and Kat had heard Papi come home. He didn't act like he'd been to the bad place. He even whistled when he walked in the house. She'd seen him from her bedroom window.

But in the time it took for her to braid Kat's dark hair, a loud explosion had traveled up the staircase. Gertie and Kat scurried beneath her bed and waited for the heavy footsteps, but they hadn't come. Instead, they'd only heard the crank of Papi's Tin Lizzie and his tires screeching down the drive.

Kat poked at the broken chair, which must have been where the big sound had come from. "Tha' think he could have been agreeable enough to spare th' poor chair."

"What made him so angry?" Gertie knew she shouldn't snoop. Disagreeable children snooped. But what if it had something to do with Atta? Did her sister have to stay away longer?

Gertie uncrinkled the letter. The writing on it was wobbly.

Papi's name was at the top, and it was signed by a *Tante* Lea. Some of the words were too hard to read, but she understood that Papi had written to this *Tante* asking for a wife. A wife! Gertie's breath caught in her throat. She wasn't sure she wanted another Mami. She'd never remembered having one. What she wanted was a sister. An Atta.

Before she could think about Atta too much and begin crying, she kept reading. The lady said there would be no wife for Papi. Said no lady in her right mind would betray her country and marry an American.

"Art tha' goin' to be tellin' me what it be sayin'?"

Gertie shook her head, balled up the letter, and placed it back where she found it. Kat knew a lot of her secrets, but right now, she didn't want to bring shame to her Papi. He might not be like other Pappies, but he was hers. "Let's go back upstairs and play."

"Aye. Checkers be soundin' good."

Gertie nodded.

They started up the stairs, but Gertie stopped. She'd forgotten to do something. Something important. But what?

Oh, the chair. Kat had moved it. She returned to right it so Papi wouldn't know she snooped, but the chair was in the same position they'd found it. Funny...she'd thought Kat had picked it up...

"Kat?"

No answer.

"Kat? Are you ready to play checkers?"

She ran up to her room, but it was empty.

Kat was gone. Again.

BEADS OF SWEAT poured down Atta's forehead into the bathwater. Dr. Mayhew said the water should be as hot as she could stand, but this was near the temperature of Hades.

"How are you, dear?" Nurse Edith entered the small chamber with a thermometer.

"Oh, pretty warm."

The nurse slid the thermometer into her mouth and Atta stared at the cracks on the wall. Nurse Edith's rosy scent threatened to suffocate her.

"Lucky for you, we've had all this rain the last few days. Without it, there wouldn't have been enough water in the cistern to fill a bathtub."

Atta tried to smile, but the thermometer poked the sensitive nerves beneath her tongue.

After a couple of minutes, the nurse slid the instrument out of her mouth and examined it under the light. "A hundred and one point four. That should do it for the first time. Dr. Mayhew wants you to stay in here for a bit now. I'll be in and out to check on you. Call if you need anything."

Nurse Edith left, leaving Atta alone with the steamy air and a tight hot kink in her chest. She laid her head back against the edge of the tub and tried to relax. Baths usually set her mind at ease. She usually loved them. But the pressure of this bathing was almost too much, as was the temperature in which to enjoy it. Her thoughts chased to the grand bathroom Robert was to build for her. He'd been so caring, so enthusiastic about their little home. She thought of him less and less with each day, his letters growing more and more scarce.

Father, forgive me...please. Don't punish Gertie for my past mistakes. Heal me, Father.

She stuck her arm out of the tub and felt for the cool beads of her rosary on a nearby chair. Beginning with the Apostles' Creed, she moved onto the Our Father followed by three Hail Marys.

Glory be to the Father, and to the Son, and to the Holy Spirit. As it was in the beginning, is now, and ever shall be, world without end. Amen.

The words had been etched in her memory long ago and she

could say them without thinking of their meaning. But now, she was questioning if God was pleased at her continuous petitions.

She moved along the circle alternating between Our Fathers and Hail Marys, trying to meditate on the mysteries of her faith.

She'd just finished the circle when Nurse Edith returned. Her skin boiled. Swells of dizziness rode over her as the nurse assisted her out of the tub. She wrapped a heavy robe around Atta's body, and then a thick towel around her hair before guiding her to one of the beds in the other room—beside the woodstove, no less.

"Let's get you tucked in. I'll bring you some apple cider, how's that sound? You mustn't take off any covers or towels, understood dear? You can fall asleep if you'd like. In a couple hours your temperature should be back to normal and you can change into your dressing gown."

Atta nodded, too woozy to acknowledge the nurse with words. When Nurse Edith came back, she made her drink the whole cup of warm cider, then left her alone.

Low voices echoed through the thin walls. Some of the patients stayed here, in the hospital, instead of cottages. Like Mary and Flavia. Atta thought of Lucy, of how pleased she would be with the quilt. In another week, the border of stitched vines would be complete, and she'd begin the binding. She'd done the blanket in shades of greens, reds, and browns. The middle block, where she'd appliqued two doves in flight, was larger than the others and offset with a cranberry border.

Cranberry. Just like the additional marks she'd found on her other thigh that morning.

Forgive me Father, for I have sinned...heal me, God....

Her body steamed beneath the heavy sheets, the fire of the woodstove burning her face. Her eyes grew heavy.

"And how's my patient doing?" Her eyes snapped open at the sound of Dr. Mayhew's voice above her. Why would he come now? And yet, he was her doctor. He'd seen plenty of women in their beds over the years. Just never...her.

"You don't look well." Concern etched his features. Her breath hitched as he lifted the back of his bare hand to her cheek. His skin was cool and welcome and she leaned into it.

"Atta? Talk to me, please."

Atta...he'd never called her that before. It sounded nice. Maybe the heat caused her to hallucinate.

She worked her tongue around in her dry mouth. "Perhaps a fan is in order, Doctor."

He removed his hand from her face, fished a thermometer from his pocket, and propped it beneath her tongue. "Glad to see your sense of humor wasn't washed down the drain."

"Oh, but it was. I'm demoting you to a *D* for having the nurse put me next to this cursed woodstove."

He leaned closer. "I'm sorry? I couldn't hear what grade you gave me with that thermometer stuck in your mouth."

She rolled her eyes but doubted he could see by the dim light of the stove. Another few seconds and he plucked the thermometer from between her lips and examined it. Deep grooves appeared on his forehead.

"Perhaps it would be best to move you to another bed."

He removed the covers, but she gathered enough of her senses to grasp them close to her body. "Doctor, I'm indecent. Please call Nurse Edith."

"You should have the robe on, I hope."

"Yes, I do. And as I said before, I'd appreciate Nurse Edith's assistance."

Dr. Mayhew sighed and shook his head. "Whatever pleases you, Miss Schaeffer. I'll check on you in the morning. Good night."

"Good night."

Moments later, the nurse appeared to help her switch beds. She also gave her a cup of water.

Then, once again, Atta was alone.

Soft, eerie crying echoed through the hospital walls. A log in the woodstove popped. She blew air from her mouth upward, an attempt to cool off her sweating body. The crying turned to sobbing, then yelling, and then ranting in Portuguese. Then more screaming, like an animal being butchered in a slaughterhouse.

Mary.

Atta was glad she couldn't understand the language. She didn't want a better picture of the demons haunting the troubled woman's mind.

She hunkered lower in her covers and wished for the light of morning.

"GERTIE. Gertie, where are ya, ya worthless girl?"

Gertie's eyes snapped open. She'd fallen asleep with her clothes on. Dark tree shadows and patches of moonlight fell on her bedspread from the window. Pain shot to her fingers, numb with cold, when she pushed herself up.

The hope chest. She hadn't placed it against the door. She'd left her bedroom door unguarded in hopes that Kat would come back to play checkers. Now, Gertie hopped down and struggled to drag the chest the few feet to the closed door. If only her fingers would work right...

"Gertie, you forgot the milk again, girl. What'd I tell ya about that?" Papi's words sounded like they did when he'd been at the bad place. A heavy thump on the steps followed by a word she'd never heard before.

"I'll find ya...you need to learn your lesson."

Gertie's heart beat so fast she thought it might fly clean out of her chest. She wished she could fly, then. Fly far away. Maybe find where Robert's father had taken Atta.

The chest budged an inch and then another. Footfalls came closer. One corner against the door. One more push and—

The doorknob rattled, the moonlight from her window

making the brass look prettier than it did in the daytime. Strange that she should notice such a thing in the middle of her terror.

Papi's fingers curled around the edge of the door and fear sent her scurrying past the braided rug to scoop up Rosie before shimmying beneath the bed.

"You ain't gonna get away this time, little girl. I told you I want the *milch* in the icebox every morning. Maybe last time's beatin' wasn't good enough."

A firm hand grabbed her ankle and dragged her out from beneath the bed, where hot fingers squeezed her shoulders.

Atta. Atta, how come you didn't take me with you? I would have been good. I would have!

She imagined herself a bird as the blows came, one after the other, each more painful than the last.

Maybe God would take her to heaven and then she really could fly.

Far, far away from here.

Chapter Twenty-Two

1993

My throat is clogged with emotion when Gram finishes. To think of her, alone and small, with no one but her imaginary friend...it shatters something inside me. Who am I to complain about my own father? Yes, he's embarrassed by me. Yes, he's hidden me away, and no, he's not the kind of father I wished him to be. But at least he didn't *beat* me.

"Gram..." But I don't know what to say. I think of the letter from the Cuttyhunk Historical Society and I vow not to pester Gram about going to Penikese. It's painful enough for her to tell me the story. She can deny it, she can claim it's one of hope, but I see it in her eyes.

It's taking a toll.

On the table before us is the picture I found in her nightstand drawer. She'd asked me to fetch it. It's a picture of my Aunt Atta, her friend Lucy Peterson, and Goon Lee Dip. It is different seeing it now, knowing a bit about the people staring back at me.

"It's not the end," she says. "It's important to remember that.

When life feels like it's going to suck every last breath out of you, remember that, child. It's not the end. You are *not* alone."

She's not talking about her young self anymore. She's not even talking about her sister. She's talking *to* me.

And for the first time, sitting here with my grandmother, I sense a kinship with another person on an entirely different dimension. Gram is opening herself up to me and I want to do the same.

"But I'm scared," I whisper. The back of my eyes burn and I wipe a hand across the bottom of my nose. The light above the kitchen is dim, splashing shadows on the faded linoleum floor. The clock on the oven reads 11:34 p.m. I should let Gram go to bed.

She places her hand atop mine. It's wrinkled and freckled with age spots, the skin as thin as paper. "What are you afraid of, child?"

I sniff. "Of having the baby. Of giving it up. Of not giving it up. Of what it all means for my future. Of going home to my parents and my friends. Everything."

What if I could stay here, even after the baby is born? After the child is placed with some perfect family with a mother and a father. With a swing set in the backyard and maybe a sandbox. Wanted...loved.

What did Maryland have for me anyway? Ashley hasn't called since I've arrived. I could just as easily attend college in Massachusetts. It's not as if I'd miss my parents...much.

But I'm pretty sure I've reached my rejection quota for the year, and I can't bear to ask more of my grandmother.

"There's an old, wise proverb for exactly this sort of moment," Gram says.

"There is?"

"I'm sure there is. I'm just not exactly sure what that proverb is."

I burst out in laughter. "Thanks a lot."

She smiles. "Seriously, honey, these are big questions. Questions only you can answer. Not me. Not your parents. This is your life. What would you do with it? How do you feel God guiding you?"

"That's just the thing. I don't feel Him guiding me at all."

Gram opens her mouth, then closes it. She runs a finger over the edge of the black-and-white picture, pats it slightly. "I think we should go to Penikese, after all."

"What? Why? Besides, I'm not even invited."

She winks at me. "I have a feeling I can pull a few strings."

"You said you didn't want to go, and I understand why you wouldn't. Don't force yourself for me. How will Penikese help me, anyway?"

"I'm not entirely sure it will, child. But I do know that once in a great while, miracles happen on that island. Perhaps it's your turn."

I can't get Gram's words out of my mind—the bit about the miracles—as I walk up the path to the library. What kind of a miracle does she expect for me? Ugh, the pressure. Maybe Penikese was a bad idea after all.

I think of Aunt Atta banished to the island seventy-seven years ago. It *would* be surreal to visit her grave. To see where she lived. To even see the school my grandfather built. Considering how much history our family has on the island, why *not* see it?

I walk into the library, but Sam is not behind the librarian's desk. I slide *Flowers in the Attic* and *Castaways*—Gram said I could borrow her copy anytime—in the book drop.

I head down the stairs and to the back of the library. I'm not looking for anything in particular, I simply like the long rows of books. They tower above me on either side like members of the Queen's Guard on duty at Buckingham Palace. I find a section of biographies on an end cap labeled *Women Who Dared to Change the World*, and I'm instantly intrigued. I grab a few at random—

Rachel Carson and Anne Hutchinson and Louisa May Alcott. I sink to the carpeted floor, enjoying the cozy privacy the sentinel of books creates.

Soon, I'm lost in the pages, reading of women who inspire. Women who many considered outcasts but who would have their stories told as long as libraries existed.

"Psst."

My head jerks up.

"Pssst." Louder this time.

I look in the direction of the sound. Through a row of books, I make out a pair of thick glasses, inquisitive ocean-blue eyes behind them. I smile.

"Psst, yourself," I whisper.

"Ten more days...."

I casually turn the page of my book. "Did you know Anne Hutchinson was like, the first woman preacher? Puritans got real skunky over that. She had a trial and everything."

"Skunky? Did you just make up that word? Because it's a pretty cool word."

"I did," I say with an air of superiority, as if making up cool words is all in a day's work. I return to my reading.

Sam sticks his head farther into the bookshelf. "Pssst." Still louder. "Ten more days."

The corners of my mouth twitch, but I keep my gaze on the printed words in my lap. "She was banished."

"What? Who?"

"Anne. Her charge said they 'cast her out and delivered her up to Satan.'" I shiver, wondering what my Puritan forefathers would have done to me in my own sinful state. I read the words that quote Hutchinson's sentence of condemnation. *I command you in the name of Christ Jesus and of this church as a Leper to withdraw yourself out of the Congregation.*

"She ended up going to Rhode Island to Roger Williams' settlement at Providence Plantations." I close the book, commiserating with Anne and my Aunt Atta—both lepers in their own way. Both cast off and alone.

"You know what I think?" Sam asks.

"What?"

"I think if Anne Hutchinson were here, she'd want you to read *Jurassic Park*."

I raise an eyebrow. "I don't know...I'm thinking she'd want me to read something a little more...meaningful."

"Like *Flowers in the Attic*, you mean?" His tone is mocking. He comes around the shelf and sits beside me like it's the most natural thing in the world.

I blush a little because the book was more than a little risqué. And yet, I couldn't stop reading it. "Probably not *Flowers in the Attic*. Maybe *The Handmaid's Tale*. Definitely *To Kill a Mockingbird*."

He slings his arms over his splayed knees. "You're really not going to read it, are you?"

"Nope."

He leans his head against the books behind us. "Fine. You win."

I did? Too bad it didn't give me an ounce of pleasure. "Are you working now?"

"On break."

"My grandmother's cleaning out her drawers. You still up for helping us move her furniture downstairs?"

"Oh, do you need..." He holds up an arm and flexes, points with his other hand to his bicep which, I have to admit, is really a nice bicep. "...these?"

I elbow him and he lets his arm fall. "We'll pay you, of course. You and your friend."

"I have a better idea. You read the book and I'll help free of charge."

I groan. "Seriously?"

"Seriously."

"Cash is worth way more than me torturing myself for ten hours."

"Your money's no good here." He said it like he was quoting someone again, but this time, I didn't know the movie.

"Why do you care so much that I read the stupid book?"

"I'm going to pretend you didn't just call the greatest science fiction book of our time stupid."

"Oh, please don't pretend."

A woman with silver hair passes our hiding spot and glares at us openly before passing.

"I want you to read it"—he says the words slow, enunciating them—"because then we can go see the movie."

"Who's to say I can't watch the movie without reading the book?"

His jaw falls open. "Because it's sacrilege. It's breaking the first cardinal rule of 'books made into movies.'"

"That being?"

"Thou shalt not watch a movie based off a book without first reading said book."

"Not sure you caught this or not, but I'm not exactly the rule-following type." Had he seriously not noticed my bulging belly? "Besides, why should I follow that rule? Just so I can leave the theatre saying, 'It was a pretty good movie, but the book was better?'"

"Yes!"

"But that's what everyone says!"

"And hence the reason for the cardinal rule. Books win. Books always win."

How could I argue with such logic? Books *should* always win.

I fling a hand in the air. "Fine. I'll start the stupid book tonight."

"And if you want my help, you will never refer to it as stupid again."

I muffle a giggle into my shoulder.

"Emily—what's your last name again?"

"Robertson."

"Robertson?" He seems distracted for half a second. "Hold up your right hand."

"This is so—"

"Do it for the sake of your grandmother's furniture."

I roll my eyes, hold up my hand.

"Emily Robertson, in the name of all that is good and right with science fiction, do you promise on your grandmother's furniture to *never*—ever—call *Jurassic Park*, or any other book by Michael Crichton, stupid ever again?"

My shoulders shake. I nod.

"I'm sorry. The jury didn't hear you."

"Yes! Yes, I promise!"

"Okay. Then may God have mercy on your grandmother's furniture when I move it down the stairs."

Our soft laughter dies out before I speak. "Why do you want to go to the movies with me, anyway? I mean, why hang out?"

"Why not?"

I place my hand on the babe rolling freely around in my belly. "If you haven't noticed, I have kind of a lot going on." I stare straight ahead, unwilling to meet his gaze.

"I know."

So he *had* noticed.

"Then what's the point?"

"Does there have to be a point to friendship? Can't it just...be?"

A smile softens my mouth. Sam was offering me a gift of friendship. I'd written him off—thought a friendship with a boy was not wise or not what I sought. But here he was—willing to come alongside me, be there for me, even. It didn't matter that he might not understand me fully, he wasn't running away.

And that was a gift.

Before he can ask any more questions about the baby or my

future or worse, the baby's father, I readjust my legs so I can prepare to stand—something that was a lot easier to do a couple weeks ago. "I should get back home. Gram's been telling me about when Penikese was a leper colony."

He stands first and holds out his hand to me. "No kidding."

I allow him to help me. "Yeah. Before my grandfather started the school. She seems to know a lot about it." I don't tell him my aunt was interned as a leper on the island. It feels so...personal. Yet, almost immediately, I'm ashamed. I am no better than my aunt's fiancé or any of the others who counted her an outcast.

Sam still holds my hand. We stand close, but his brow is scrunched beneath a shock of dark, messy hair.

I can't tear my gaze from his. "What's wrong?"

He shakes his head. "Nothing. So, can I come by next weekend to do the furniture?"

"Yeah, sure."

He releases my hand but stares at me again. "This was fun."

My insides warm. "Yeah. It was." I say goodbye and start upstairs. As much as I'm looking forward to hearing Gram's story tonight, a part of me wishes I didn't have to leave Sam quite so soon. Maybe reading the book won't be as bad as I'm expecting.

Chapter Twenty-Three

1916

No, it couldn't be true. She'd seemed fine yesterday. How could it be so? Her only friend.

Mrs. Parker draped an arm around Atta and led her to the table and chairs in the living area of her cottage. She didn't resist the older woman, but instead sunk into her warm, soft arms—the first true hug she'd received in more than three months. Emotion burst in her throat and behind her eyes, yet no tears came forth.

"I'm sorry, dear. We all loved her."

Atta lifted her head to Mrs. Parker's wet gaze. "How—what happened?"

"Lucy lost her breath, dear. It started off as her attacks often do, but quickly became worse. Dr. Parker and Dr. Mayhew tried everything. That's why it took so long for Nurse Edith to fetch you from the tub."

Atta had almost blacked out from being in the bath so long for her morning treatment. She would have left if she'd had clothes waiting for her. But all that paled in comparison to this devastating news.

Lucy...gone. It seemed like everything dear to her was destined to be taken away. Maybe that—and not the disease—was the true curse upon her. Maybe she would be alone. Forever.

"It's a wonder she lived as long as she did." Harry shook his head and wrote a few more notes on the autopsy report.

Dr. Parker nodded. "I agree. I can't believe the medication was of any help."

The autopsy revealed two small growths on Miss Peterson's thyroid, one on either side of her larynx. Now and then one of the growths dropped down and blocked the laryngeal opening. Dr. Parker assumed that both growths had dropped at once, causing Miss Peterson's airway to become completely blocked.

Again, Albin Zielinski's face flashed in Harry's mind. Another failure. Maybe he could have done something different for Miss Peterson. He could have tried to surgically remove the growths had he known. Yet, that could have proved fatal also. What's more, Miss Peterson likely wouldn't have consented to such a procedure.

A rapid knock on the door. "Dr. Mayhew, it's Miss Schaeffer. Come quick."

Scooping up his medical bag, Harry jogged out of the room. "Where is she?"

"In her cottage. She was with Mrs. Parker. She fainted—I think she's overheated."

"Set up a bed and an IV," he said to Edith.

He ran out the hospital door before realizing he didn't know which cottage was Atta's. He scanned the area for any clue when he saw Mrs. Parker beside a door, waving with frantic gestures. He sprinted toward the older woman, the cold ocean breeze stealing the little air left in his lungs.

When he entered the cottage, he caught Atta's scent—fresh

earth and sun and flowers. A copy of *Ethan Frome* sat on her table. All that was dashed from his mind, however, when he saw his favorite patient lying on the hardwood floor, her face the color of a fiery sunset.

"She's coming to, I think." Mrs. Parker propped a pillow beneath Atta's head.

"Did she bang her head?"

"No. I caught her."

He didn't waste time examining her. What she needed—fluids —he could only give at the hospital. Easing his arms beneath her slight body, he tucked her close to his chest and started out the door, the heat from her skin traveling straight through his shirtsleeves.

He glanced at her face only once during the long walk but knew it would forever be etched in his mind. He had done this. She lay small and vulnerable in his arms, her long lashes fanned over cheeks as red as cherries. If she died....

Just yesterday she'd been in the exam room, looking at him with so much hope it almost made him want to disown his medical degree. He hadn't told her the truth then, thought maybe one more round of therapy might kick those few pesky bacterium....

She stirred with the jolting he created and mumbled something.

"You're going to be all right, Atta. Stay with me."

"Don't...feel...well."

He broke into a run until he reached the hospital bed Nurse Edith had prepared, IV waiting.

"Nurse, undress her and cool her with a washcloth."

Edith did so, stripping Atta to her bloomers. Creamy skin alongside the undergarment shouted at him how inappropriate it was that this woman be named a leper.

With Atta's arm free of her blouse, he broke through her tight skin with the IV needle. She didn't wake. After the IV was secure, he prepared an injection of salicylic acid. Again, the needle didn't wake her. He ordered a cool cloth be placed over her head, neck, and beneath her arms, and then turned to Dr. and Mrs. Parker, who stood at the foot of the bed. "That's all that can be done for now. I'll monitor her through the night."

Mrs. Parker wrung her hands beneath her bosom. "Frank, don't you think you should take a look...?"

Dr. Parker shook his head. "It seems our Dr. Mayhew has things quite under control. Better than that, I'd say."

Harry's chest swelled. Strange how he longed for the older doctor's approval. If only his own father had shown him half the support as Dr. Parker.

He looked at Atta, her chest rising and falling in small spurts. "I won't leave her side until she's out of danger."

ATTA WOKE to a cramp in her stomach and bright sunshine streaming through a hospital window. The hospital. Why was she in the hospital?

All at once, it came rushing back to her in nauseating swells. Mrs. Parker...Lucy.

"Miss Schaeffer?"

To her left, in his office chair, sat Dr. Mayhew. His hair stood at unruly ends, his normally crisp shirt wrinkled and unbuttoned at the top collar.

"What—what happened?" She tried to prop herself up, but dizziness swooped upon her, along with an awareness of her indecent state. She lay back down, pulling the covers to her chin.

"You were severely dehydrated, but it looks like you're recovering. How do you feel?"

"Thirsty."

"Edith will bring your lunch soon."

"Lunch?" She'd been unconscious too long. "Have you been here awhile?"

He nodded. "We should have stopped the fever therapy by now. I—perhaps I should have known better."

"Do you think I might be cured?"

Silence blanketed the room, and with it, Atta had her answer.

"I'm sorry, Atta. The slide I made yesterday afternoon was positive."

Her bottom lip quivered. Dr. Mayhew shifted in his seat.

Was that it then?

She licked her lips. "Maybe a few more days of the baths—"

"No." His voice brooked no room for argument. "It's too risky at this point. And I didn't see any deterioration in the bacteria, no sign that the therapy was of any help at all."

She turned her head away from him and looked out the window. The little white cross stood boldly in the distance. Had she been unconscious for Lucy's burial?

"I found more marks. On my other leg this time." He'd find out sooner or later, anyhow.

His head and shoulders drooped.

"I'm certain showing dejection in front of a patient is not going to earn you any high grades." Despite the joke, her tone held little humor.

"Forgive me, Miss Schaeffer."

Back to Miss Schaeffer, then, was it?

For some reason, she couldn't bring herself to grant him clemency. No-good doctors thought they were so smart, thought they had all the answers. Until lives were lost. Then they were *sorry*.

Quiet hung like a thick black curtain between them until Nurse Edith's oxford shoes squeaked against the linoleum.

"I'll check in on you later." Dr. Mayhew left, leaving a thick, sticky void within her heart.

"Nice to see you awake, dear. Chicken fricassee for lunch. Eat as much as you can." She turned to go before tossing over her shoulder, "And enjoy your letter!"

Atta snatched up the white envelope on her lunch tray with greedy fingers. Gertie's writing. Thank God. It had been too long.

Pushing the fricassee aside, she ignored the steamy, moist scent and tore open the letter.

COME HOME ATTA. PAPI IS BAD. I CANT START FIRE. IT IS COLD. YOR CHEST IS TO HEAVY. NOT ENUF TIME. KAT DOESN'T COME. I WANT TO FLY. PRAY GOD WILL LET ME FLY.
GERTIE

Atta read the letter over and over again, dread squeezing her insides tighter than a vice. She searched the tray for more mail. Nothing. Nothing from Robert.

She pulled at her hair. What did Gertie mean she wanted to fly? Atta remembered how, as a little girl, she'd climbed up to the barn loft and stood at the very edge. She used to think if she believed enough, she'd be able to jump and grow wings.

She'd never tried. Surely, Gertie wouldn't do something so foolish?

But there was no denying her sister sounded unwell or...no. She refused to think of Gertie in the same way she thought of Mary. Unless Papi had indeed knocked her senseless.

The chicken fricassee grew cold as she contemplated all the possibilities hidden in Gertie's letter. No doubt Papi came home drunk every night. And poor Gertie hadn't been able to lock herself in her room.

Panic replaced fear, followed by an intense desire to do *something*. Enough of this. She was done with this place. With this hospital, with these nurses, with Dr. Mayhew...with this disease.

No one was taking care of Gertie well enough for her liking. Not Robert, and certainly not Papi.

A calm peace swept over her as she realized what she would do, what she needed to do, what she should have done long ago.

Reaching for her plate, she forced small bites of the moist fricassee down her dry throat. She'd need all her energy to enact her plan.

Thirteen miles of rowing would require every ounce of determination and strength she possessed.

Chapter Twenty-Four

Niklas leaned his elbows on the worn wood of the bar. He shouldn't be here, he knew that. And yet this place was like poison in his blood, calling to him all day long. Even Katharina had never been so addicting.

"What'll it be, Niklas?" Jimmy stood with both hands on the counter, ready to serve.

What'll it be?

A big kick in the pants...you sell tall glasses of those, Jimmy?

He'd had too much last night, been too upset over that letter. *Ja*, rotten coincidence. He was too German to be considered fully American, and too American to be fully German. There would be no wife for him. No German wife, anyway.

Last night lay like a thick fog swathing his mind. His anger at his *Tante* followed by his fury toward Katharina. Again. She'd left him when he needed her most. Had she been faithful? That line of questioning always veered his rage toward Gertie. She was the only one left to bear the brunt of his frustrations, and when the alcohol coated his brain, the justice made perfect sense.

But not now. And yet the call of the whiskey was too strong.

He'd told Gertie she could stay home from school today. Maybe for a few more days if she didn't heal quicker.

"Tough decision, Niklas? Tell ya what. I'll make you something special. On the house tonight. You look like you could use a treat."

"*Aye,* Jimmy. Much obliged."

He'd be a fool to refuse such an offer.

He chugged down one drink. Then two, all while those ladies from hell sang of redemption and God's love and forgiveness.

And the only way to drown out their voices was with another drink, and then another. Maybe he'd drink himself dead.

Now that would be true redemption.

HARRY WOKE TO A COLD CHILL. The fire in his room had gone out. Or maybe he'd never started it.

Shuffling to the small woodstove, he poked at the glowing embers and threw in a log.

If the bitter cold of November foretold Penikese winters, he didn't wish to think on January and February. A scraping sound from outside broke through the paned windows and he peered into the darkness. Moonlight glittered on the calm endless sea.

Once again, his thoughts turned to Atta. She was better when he'd last checked on her. No cramps, her color and temperature both normal. But maybe he should have stayed with her another night. It wasn't much trouble to look at her delicate face, lips parted in sleep, by the light of the fire.

Shaking his head, he rebuked himself. Nothing good could come from such thoughts. If anyone found out, he'd be ridiculed from here to Kingdom Come, and rightfully so.

The scraping started again and small movements by the shore caught his attention. What in tarnation? It couldn't be.

But there was no mistaking the petite figure struggling with the rowboat. She couldn't...could she?

His right foot tapped on the hardwood. His throat threatened to close. She meant to escape. He put his hands on the window and started to lift the painted wood. Then, he stopped.

Could she make it? He himself had given her the information. If she could make it to the mainland and then on to New York she'd be free to live her life. A beautiful young woman with opportunities instead of a cursed outcast feared by all humankind. She wasn't a danger to society, she would take precautions. And yet, the sea could be cold and unforgiving. A storm could come. She could lose direction or encounter a shark.

He swallowed down the fears and reminded himself of Atta's otherwise hopeless future on Penikese. If given the choice, he'd brave the elements also.

But he'd miss her. It was too bad she'd leave with hard feelings toward him. Perhaps someday she'd realize he'd only been trying to help.

Goodbye, Atta. I'm sorry I couldn't help you.

Yes, he would miss her far more than he'd have expected.

Chapter Twenty-Five

Atta's arms strained against the pressure of the water behind the oars. Her heart pounded a steady rhythm against her chest, but still she trembled with cold and fear. She refused to allow herself a moment's rest until the bright moonlight ceased to illuminate the faint outline of Penikese.

Her toes stung inside her shoes, still wet after casting the rowboat away from shore. Doubts nipped at her heart. She'd reduced herself to stealing. To breaking rules. Yet, someone would find the boat and return it, wouldn't they? As for the pitcher she'd taken from her cottage, she'd leave it in the boat and trust it would also be returned. It was the only thing she could find to hold drinking water.

Cold darkness draped over her in a blanket of loneliness. A cloud slid past the moon. A faint splash in the black sea startled her. Then another. What kind of big fish occupied these open waters? She'd seen drawings of whales and sharks and other such creatures, but couldn't fathom how big they were in actual life. And sea monsters. God might send one to swallow her up for her disobedience. Unlike Jonah, she doubted her Creator would give her a second chance.

Though she longed to lift a prayer to the starry sky, she abstained. She couldn't risk bringing attention to herself. If she rowed strong and steady all night, maybe no one—not even God—would notice she'd left.

Her heavy breaths puffed out visible air. She shrugged off the quilt she'd made for Lucy and tugged it over her numb fingers. It fell to the bottom of the boat with her next stroke. She should have pushed forward with this escape plan earlier. The beginning of November was hardly an ideal time for an all-night boat ride.

When she could no longer see the island, she rested the oar in the boat. Her fingers sliced with pain as she picked up the chilled pitcher of drinking water. Half of it had already spilled. It would have to do. She needed to stay hydrated, alert. Keep the moon to her right and she'd reach New Bedford by morning.

Thoughts of getting lost rivaled those of big ugly sea monsters beneath the water's surface. She pushed the demons away. She could not be immobilized with fear. She must continue on. Gertie depended on her.

She took up the oar once again. Her right shoulder cramped hard and the oar slipped. She screeched and grasped for it, but her hand hit icy water. Fishing around, she glimpsed its wooden surface glinting in the moonlight several feet away. With frigid fingers, she paddled toward it, but once again the moon ducked behind a thick cloud.

Trying not to imagine the creatures that dwelled beneath the black surface, Atta moved her fingers around. They struck something stringy and soft—certainly not an oar. She squeezed her eyes shut. Her fingers hit a smooth, hard object and she scooped it from the water, splattering her dress with salty sea.

She gazed up at the sky for a clue of her placement. A single, bright star winked down at her. Was it the north star? With the moon gone, she had no choice but to assume so.

Swallowing down her doubts and fears, she thought of Gertie as she rowed in the direction she hoped was north, one slow paddle at a time. When thoughts of turning back nipped at her, she fought them with thoughts of seeing Gertie again. Her head ached. Still, she rowed north, singing *Schlaf, Kindlein schlaf* as the loneliness and black cold threatened to suck her into a maelstrom of weariness.

Sleep, child, sleep.

In her mind, she sung the words to Gertie, hoping her sister did indeed own a peaceful slumber this night. Maybe she dreamt of flying.

With new resolve, Atta sliced the oar through the water, one side then the next.

Reach and pull. Reach and pull.

She had to get home to Gertie. Either that, or die trying.

"HARD TO TELL we received any rain last night."

Harry joined Dr. Parker in peering at the few inches of murky water in the bottom of the cistern. Secretly, he thanked God for Atta's sake that the rainfall hadn't been more substantial.

He'd spent the night thinking about her, doubting his decision not to stop her. Had she made it, or had the cold been too much for her weakened constitution?

"I'll have to write to the Board of Charity—ask them to send water."

Harry grunted.

"Something on your mind?"

Harry stepped back from the large hole in the ground. "No, sir. Just didn't sleep well last night."

Dr. Parker gestured toward the hospital and they walked down the hill toward "the other side" of the island. "Don't let Miss Atta's therapy get you down, my boy. No one expected you to find a cure in three months."

"I'm aware of that, Doctor."

"Why don't you call me Frank, son?"

Son. Humph. He didn't think he'd mind Dr. Parker for a father.

"Any success with the cultivations?"

The corner of Harry's mouth tightened. "A little since using the two percent neutral water agar instead of the peptone after the last filtrate, but the rats and even the monkeys won't take the disease. Nothing. You'd think something so horrific would be easily transmittable."

Dr. Parker leaned back as they descended the well-worn path. He sidestepped a patch of gull waste. "It is indeed a mystery."

"Do you think there's a cure to be found?"

The older man raised bushy eyebrows in Harry's direction. His curled mustache twitched. "The doctor in me is certain that for every sickness there's a cure to be found. But I suppose that may not be so." They walked a few more paces, the worn grass slippery from the dew of the cold night. "If I told you there wasn't a cure for leprosy, would you stop trying?"

A small smile inched up Harry's lips. "I'd probably try twice as hard to prove you wrong."

Dr. Parker let out a loud chortle. "You remind me of my oldest son, Howard. I'll wager you and your father had quite a few rows when you were growing up, too."

"You haven't a clue."

Whether or not they could be classified as "rows" was another question altogether. It normally took two people to create a row; his father's boisterous lectures were usually given to a withdrawn son.

"I just received a letter from him, you know."

"Howard?"

"No, your father." The older doctor clasped his hands behind his back. "He wanted to know how you were holding up, what kind of progress you were making."

A report card. His father wanted a report card after all these years. "And?"

"And I testified you are a gifted, determined doctor with whom I take pleasure working."

A foreign bubble of gratification formed at the base of Harry's throat. "Thank you, sir."

"Frank, son."

"Frank." Harry tried out the name, but it didn't fit well. "My father is none too happy with me. I was sent here for disregarding orders at Mass General. A patient's death resulted." He expelled a long breath but relished the release of the confession. "I still dream about his family—wonder how things could have been if I'd made different choices."

Dr. Parker stopped walking and dug his hands in his pockets. "The curse of the medical degree, Harry. We just never know. But we can learn from others and from our mistakes. We can strive forward, strive to serve the sick, not just cure them."

Dr. Parker didn't condemn him. Neither did he release him from responsibility. Harry savored the relief as they continued down the hill. A crazy notion that his father wasn't the ultimate judge on every issue teased the corners of his mind.

"Say, Dr. Parker—"

"Frank."

Harry shook his head, laughed. "Frank. Do you have any history books relating to the Elizabeth Islands? I've been curious about some things."

"There are a few in my office. Help yourself. Not everyone has such an interesting story behind their family name."

Harry doubted how interesting it could be if his father rarely talked of it. It was time he found out for himself.

Dr. Parker pulled the door of the hospital entrance open. Mrs. Tufts' white oxfords squeaked to a halt before them.

"Dr. Parker—we can't find her anywhere. There's not a trace of her."

Harry tried to mirror Dr. Parker's confused expression. "Who?"

"Miss Schaeffer. She's gone."

Chapter Twenty-Six

Freedom played a tune of victory across Atta's heart when she glimpsed the mainland, beautifully secure and anchored amidst the red glow of dawn. The sight strengthened her resolve and her burning muscles. She reached the dock more than an hour later.

She left the quilt in the boat, refusing to put anyone in danger's path—all she wanted was to reach Gertie.

Needles of pain shot through her fingers. Would they ever work again? She'd made it to the mainland, but the obstacles ahead wouldn't prove easier than rowing a boat all night. She'd hoped to arrive before dawn, but already the sun climbed higher in the sky, shining its bright light upon her for all to see.

A trolley. She simply needed to board a tram to Taunton without anyone asking questions. Atta dug in her skirt pocket for the change Robert had sent her some weeks back after she'd written of the little store Mrs. Parker ran for the patients. There, right beside her rosary. Sweet of Robert really. At least she'd put the coins to good use now.

She walked along the boardwalk, wiggling her toes to induce feeling in them. She searched for signs, hoping she'd landed in New

Bedford. Then, like a miracle, a trolley stop appeared across a vacant street. She hurried to the bench and collapsed onto it. Her limbs shook and she rubbed her thighs and arms to stop the shivering.

She'd made it, and she had a plan. She'd go to the Boys Club first to appeal to Robert. She couldn't expect to waltz into Gertie's school and dismiss her. She needed Robert for that.

He'd be surprised to see her of course, but surely, he'd be happy. She'd tell him a doctor on the island had told her she could be free in New York. Not a lie. He would see how well she remained. Maybe he would be so happy to see her he'd forget himself and tuck her in his strong arms. How she longed for those arms.

She allowed her daydream to carry her on warm wings. He'd realize he couldn't live without her, that it had been wrong to abandon her. She wasn't scary, after all. He'd insist on going to New York with her, make immediate plans to start a Boys Club in whatever town they settled. They'd marry, of course, and live in their love for as long as God gave them. Wasn't that what life was about? No one knew any one person's expiration date. Dr. Mayhew had speculated Atta could live with the disease until well into old age.

Dr. Mayhew...she should have forgiven him. His experiment hadn't been performed with malicious intent, she saw that now. Perhaps she'd post a letter to him one day. Yes, that would be the right thing to do. Forgive him. Thank him. She promised herself she'd do so once she was settled and the authorities stopped looking for her.

"Ma'am? Are you planning to board?"

Atta blinked at the trolley in front of her, the driver looking down from his high perch. His brow furrowed below his hat. "Say, you don't look too well. Do you need a doctor? I go by one of them hospitals founded by the Dominican Sisters."

Atta shook her head. "No—no, sir." She placed a weak foot on the first step of the trolley and deposited her five cents into the waiting bucket. "I'm right as rain, thank you."

She found an empty seat in the rear and crumpled onto it. A man who'd never set eyes on her thought she needed a doctor. Maybe Robert wouldn't see her as the picture of perfect health.

She should have never agreed to the fever therapy. Nasty doctors, the whole lot. Yet, even as she cast blame on Dr. Mayhew, she remembered how he hadn't left her side when she was sick. He'd cared.

And she'd withheld her forgiveness.

Sitting up straighter, she smoothed her hair with the palms of her hands and tried to pinch her cheeks. Her fingers refused to obey.

Each stop proved torturous. She breathed as lightly as she could and tried to smuggle her breath into her shawl without looking suspicious. She avoided the boarding passengers' gazes and took up most of the seat so no one would sit beside her. The ride was long. Too long. Had she landed farther east than she'd planned?

When the tram finally glided into Taunton, Atta eased the shawl over her hair. If someone recognized her, all her hard work would be for naught. They passed Olivia's Bakery and a burst of emotion welled in her chest. Though this town didn't want her, she loved it. Every cobblestone and streetlamp. Every building and every person. Even Jimmy's Tavern—dark as it now was—proved a welcome sight. She'd grown up here. It was hers, or at least had been at one time.

She picked her way down the steps of the trolley and onto the bustling streets. Women's skirts swished around toddlers in knee-high breeches and sailor dresses. Men with boaters and suits and ties strode by.

She walked down the street with her head down and her shawl pulled up to her eyes. Her numb fingers gripped the sliding cloth as it fell back from her face.

"Ma'am! Ma'am!"

She ignored the voice. If she stopped now, if she were caught, she'd never see Gertie again. Her heart pounded against her rib cage. She was so close!

"Ma'am!" A strong hand grabbed her arm, knocking her weak fingers from her shawl. It fell from her hair and she pushed it back up with her palms before looking toward the gentleman's feet.

"Y—yes?"

"You dropped this when you came off the tram." He held a coin out to her and she almost took it, relief bursting through her. But she couldn't risk brushing his fingers with her own. He could catch her curse.

"Keep it," she mumbled and continued on without a backward glance.

After what seemed like hours, she reached the edge of town and slipped onto a familiar wooden path. Her beloved pine trees awaited her, offering their protection and soft embrace. She slipped deeper into the forest and ran the back of her hands along their limbs, buried her nose in their piney depths. Wherever she and Gertie lived in New York, Atta would make sure there were pine trees. A whole mountain of them, if possible. The towering trees would hide them forever. From Papi. From the Board of Health. From all the doctors in the world.

Veering onto a side path, she ignored her weak legs and dry mouth. She passed the YMCA. When the brick building of the Boys Club came into view, Atta slowed and smoothed her skirts, trying to pretend this was a visit like any other. But of course, it wasn't. Everything hinged on how Robert received her.

She wrapped her hand with the corner of her shawl and pulled open the door by tucking her wrist through the handle slot. Loud shouts came from the back corner near the boxing area. Smells of sweat and worn boxing equipment reached her nostrils.

It only took a moment to spot him. Long and lean and powerful, he slung an arm over one of the ropes surrounding the ring. A slight smile played on his face as he coached a youngster. How could she consider herself worthy of such a man? Why would she think he'd escape with her—an outcast?

A wave of cool air swept in from behind her and a petite blond woman strode past Atta. She walked with a gentle sway to her shapely hips, as if she knew all eyes were on her. Robert's certainly were. She walked up to him, lay a familiar hand on his arm. His smile grew as he ducked his head to plant a kiss on her brow.

Every ounce of adrenaline seeped from Atta's body. Time stood still as the fuzzy image of the happy couple blurred before her. Her knees weakened and she stumbled against the cool wall, all the while staring at Robert. At Robert...and her replacement.

She didn't recognize the woman, but one thing was as clear as the glassy sea surrounding Penikese: Robert didn't miss her. And why would he with such a doe-eyed, healthy beauty on his arm? Even without this disease, she could never hope to compete. *Oh Robert, is our love so easily forgotten?*

She must leave. Of course she couldn't face him now. The situation was too awkward. He wouldn't escape with her. But Gertie... perhaps Robert would help her if for no other reason than Gertie's well-being.

Gathering her strength, she pulled the shawl over her nose and mouth and walked closer to the boxing ring, her feet heavy. She'd have to sacrifice every last shred of dignity she possessed, but she'd do it for her sister.

She cleared her throat. The woman glanced in Atta's direction with a miffed look upon her face. She tugged on Robert's arm. His smile disappeared when his gaze fell on her.

"Can I help you, ma'am?"

She realized then that she expected him to recognize her, if for no other reason than the closeness they once shared.

"Would—would it be at all possible to speak to you in your office, Mr. Lincoln?" She didn't attempt to disguise her voice, and his eyes widened.

"Cer—certainly. Excuse me, Betty."

She followed him to the corner office, and when he closed the door in his small, windowless room, she lowered her shawl and waited. Still, some part of her that didn't understand reason hoped for his embrace.

It didn't come.

"Atta." His strong voice was soft. "What are you doing here?"

Her planned story fell apart with her first word. She simply couldn't ignore the hurt. "She seems nice."

Robert backed away, as if remembering her disease. "I'm sorry you had to find out like this."

"Yes, much better a safe, distant letter, no?"

"What did you want me to do—pine for you forever?" He sucked in a sharp breath. "I'm sorry, that came out wrong."

Was it too much to ask that true love pine away forever?

"I'm doing this for Gertie, Atta."

She blinked. "Gertie?"

"Once Betty and I marry—"

"You're *marrying* her?" The words dripped with the blood of her wounded heart.

"Your father may let Gertie live with us once Betty and I are wed. I think he's beginning to understand how much Gertie needs a stable home. A mother to take care of her."

The corners of Atta's eyes stung. "Betty will *not* be Gertie's mother. She belongs with me."

His lips released a short laugh. "But that's impossible—"

"I'm going to New York, Robert. I'll be free there. I want to take Gertie, but I need your help."

"Take her? Steal her away, you mean?"

"She can't stay with Papi. I know how she suffers."

Robert pushed blond hair off his forehead. "Atta, this is ludicrous. You're a leper, for heaven's sake!"

She shivered at the name passing his lips with cruel, final judgment.

"Look at yourself—you can barely stand. Why did they release you?"

"I rowed here. That's why I'm in this condition—not because of the disease." As the words left her mouth, she wanted to grasp them back. She realized her mistake, stepped farther away as he practically pilfered air from the corner of the office.

"Please help me, Robert. I need you to dismiss Gertie from school for me. Please."

He rubbed the back of his neck and stared at his feet. When he brought his hand down, it slapped against his thigh. "They have you on that island for a reason, Atta. I don't mean to be callous but—maybe Gertie being with you isn't the safest thing."

"Papi is beating her, Robert. How is that safe?" Her voice rose and he shushed her.

"I'll take care of her. I told you I would."

"You aren't doing a fine enough job."

"I can't help you steal Gertie. I have my own future to think about. Betty, my father. Gertie. I'm sorry. My answer's no." He didn't even look at her.

A soft, desperate moan escaped her lips and she covered her mouth with her paralyzed fingers. "*Please*, Robert. He'll end up killing her."

"I think you should leave." His quiet tone belied his meaning. She was no longer welcome. Not at the club, not in his life.

Smashing the shawl to her head, she placed the corners on the doorknob and attempted to turn it using both her palms. The smooth yarn slid against the brass. Robert's gaze lay heavy upon her, but she wouldn't meet it, certain his eyes would be filled with pity or disgust.

Another moment of struggling.

"Atta..."

But the offer to help didn't come. Of course it didn't. He'd have to share the same foot of air as her, have to touch the contaminated knob.

Her eyes burned as she continued with the struggle, disbelieving that he could stand by with such indifference. Finally, she let the shawl drop and used her bare hands to gain traction. No doubt he'd have the entire place fumigated, anyhow.

She scurried out of the building, her head down. She turned in the direction of home, the gash in her heart raw and festering as she tried to focus on her next problem—how to get Gertie out of school.

If she waited until her sister was dismissed, she'd run the risk of being caught. Surely the nurses on Penikese discovered her missing by now. She and Gertie must board a train to New York by noon.

Her only chance lie in recess. She'd hide in the woods in the back of the school and beckon Gertie to her. Somehow. If only the sisters wouldn't notice.

Robert's accusing words bit at her conscience. *I can't help you steal Gertie.*

But she wasn't stealing her. She could hardly steal someone who belonged to her in the first place! Besides, she didn't care whether it was right or wrong. Protecting her sister trumped all moral obligations. She'd break any one of God's commandments if it meant keeping Gertie safe. It wasn't as if He could curse her any more than He already had.

Chapter Twenty-Seven

The island's auxiliary catboat sped off with Dr. Parker toward New Bedford. Ripples of water crested in its wake until the boat disappeared on the horizon.

His mission would not be a pleasant one. If he didn't find Atta's body floating in the cold Atlantic, he'd have to report her escape, which would no doubt make him and the island's staff look incompetent.

Harry stood on the shore, squinting beneath the hand above his brow. What if, by some miracle, Atta was on her way to New York, to freedom. The odds weren't on her side.

He turned from the gleaming sea and massaged a kink from his right shoulder. The wind reached beneath the collar of his crisp white shirt, licking his bare skin of any warmth. He shivered and started up the steps of the administration building.

The hospital could wait until the afternoon. Right now, he longed for something to get his mind off Atta, off the mysteries of the disease he couldn't piece together, off the reason he was here in the first place.

He placed kindling in the belly of the woodstove in Dr. Parker's office. Rubbing his hands together, he sought the books on the walnut shelf beside the window.

After he found several on the history of Massachusetts and one on Cape Cod, he settled at Dr. Parker's desk, bare except for a green-shaded double lamp.

Flipping open one of the books, he scanned the index for "Mayhew." Nothing. On to the next book. Again, nothing. In the last book, one lone page number was listed beside his surname. He turned to it and scanned the information.

Thomas Mayhew left England with his family in 1631. He and his son, Thomas Mayhew Junior, received the Elizabeth Islands as a proprietorship from agents of the King of England. Though the land belonged to the Mayhews beneath English law, Thomas Mayhew Sr. sought to purchase it fairly from the Native Americans. Both Mayhews learned the customs and language of the Native Americans and set up a court system which gave equal rights to the white settlers and the natives. They befriended the natives, hoping to spread their faith by creating relationships with those who first inhabited the islands. When King Philip's War broke out on the mainland, the settlers and the natives lived peacefully together on the islands.

In 1656, Thomas Mayhew Jr. set out for England to report to the Church's authorities regarding his missionary work. Neither he nor his ship were ever seen again.

Harry shifted his eyes from the book and stared out the window. His former ancestor had been shipwrecked. He'd had his entire life ahead of him. No children to carry on his name. For some reason, Harry found himself longing to be a direct descendent of this man. But that was near impossible, wasn't it?

Thomas Mayhew Sr. continued his work as a missionary for another fourteen years before he began to sell some of the islands.

There wasn't much more. What were Thomas Mayhew Sr.'s other two sons like? Had they shared their father's passion for serving God? For the first time in his life, Harry ached for something other than a concrete medical degree. He ached for something other than success.

What drove these men to work so hard for something so intangible? What passion did they possess that Harry didn't?

ATTA limped through the forest without stopping until her home came into view. Besides the dead weeds in the garden, the white farmhouse looked the same. Intense homesickness wrung her insides dry. She hobbled up the dirt walkway on numb toes.

She'd pack Gertie's things. Retrieve a pair of dry socks for herself. Then she'd go to Gertie's school and make the quickest getaway possible. She stuffed her hand in her skirt pocket and searched out the cool beads of her rosary, but her fingers registered nothing. They'd been reduced to lumps of useless bone and blue skin.

She entered the house like an intruder. Without the sun's rays, it was colder inside than out. Dishes sat in the sink, stinking up the kitchen. A lowing reached her ears. Gussie—she must need milking. But Atta didn't have the time to relieve her or any strength left in her fingers.

She tiptoed up the stairs and reached for the bedroom doorknob. When she finally turned and pushed, it didn't budge. Was it her fingers or...

"Gertie?" she whispered. "Gertie, are you in there?"

Nothing.

She spoke louder this time. "Gertie, please open the door."

"I don't want to play today, Kat. Especially after you left me all alone."

Atta's heart leapt. Gertie hadn't gone to school. She fell to her knees in gratitude, pressing her face to the corner of the door.

"Gertie, it's not Kat. It's me, Atta. I've come home."

A split second of silence and then an excited gasp and a loud thump, as if her sister had rolled off the bed. "Atta?"

The sound of her name threatened to undo Atta, so filled with hope and disbelief and longing, it twisted inside her chest. "Yes, dear. I've come to take you with me. You must move the hope chest, though."

Eager, quick sobs traveled under the door as the chest protested the shift. Slowly. Then it stopped. Atta tried the door again. "Gertie, can you move it farther?"

Silence.

"Gertie?"

"How do I know it's really Atta?"

The poor child had lost trust in anybody and anything. Atta could sympathize.

She'd have to be patient with her sister, work to gain back her trust. Surely, there was something that would break down the walls around her sister's heart. Then it came to her. Atta began to sing, her voice raw from the cold night on the water.

> "Schlaf, Kindlein, schlaf.
> Draußen steht ein Schaf,
> Stößt sich an ein em Steinelein,
> that ihm weh das Beinelein."

A silly song really, about a sheep getting a boo-boo on its leg.

Gertie still didn't answer so Atta continued, ignoring her numb fingers and the hardwood biting her knees.

> "Schlaf, Kindlein, schlaf.
> Schlaf, Kindlein, schlaf."

The chest commenced its squeaking. When Gertie threw open the door, she collapsed onto Atta's lap. A shallow cry erupted from her sister's body, like that of an injured kitten. Atta picked her up, but Gertie cried out again.

"What—what is it, dear?"

"My belly hurts." For the first time, Gertie looked up. Her face puckered with ugly black-and-blue marks.

Atta gasped. "Gertie—oh no. I'm so sorry." Oh, but she wouldn't think twice about shooting Papi right now. But no, they needed escape, not retaliation. Atta stood and lifted her sister, who bent over, protecting her belly. "Show me where it hurts, Gertie."

She pointed to a spot to the right of her breastbone. Her rib. Papi had probably broken it. Atta knelt down and peered into her sister's wounded eyes. "We're leaving together, Gertie. We're going to go away from here, to a place with lots of pine trees where no one will ever hurt us again...doesn't that sound nice?"

"Are we going to fly, Atta? That's what I prayed for. For God to make me a bird, so I could fly to you."

"Oh, if only we could, Gertie. But we'll find another way. We will. And we'll get you a doctor to fix you up right good when we get there, you hear?" Again, her sister nodded. "Sit on the bed now while I pack our things."

Gertie obeyed. Atta dug out dry socks, undergarments, a few of Gertie's dresses, a shawl, hats, and two pairs each of mittens and scarves. "We must wear these while we travel. People may be looking for us. We need to be quiet and try to hide our—our injuries." She looked down at her own blue fingers.

"Atta, what happened?"

"Don't you worry. You just put that hat on your head and that scarf around your face to ward off the chill, you hear?"

Gertie draped the articles of clothing around herself with slow, rigid movements. "Like this?"

"That's perfect." Atta grabbed the pillowcase she'd stuffed everything into and ushered her sister to the door. "We'll need to walk a ways. Did you eat your breakfast?"

She shook her head.

"Never mind, I saw some apples on the counter. We'll take one with us. Come, now."

A hammer thumped within her chest. She should eat, too, but there wasn't time. Besides, pure adrenaline would keep her going.

She didn't look back at the house, but practically dragged Gertie down the drive. They hadn't reached the end when Gertie stopped. "I forgot Rosie. I can't leave her."

Atta couldn't argue. Rosie was likely the one stable thing in her sister's life. "Hide in the trees. I'll run and get her." Atta did so as fast as she could. How good it was to take action, to decide her own future. If only they could board the train without drawing attention to themselves.

She made good time but slowed once Gertie walked in her wake. Her sister moved at a snail's pace, and her face wrinkled as she fought back tears. They still had so far to go.

"Here, get on my back, dear."

Gertie clutched at Atta's neck. "It ...it hurts too much. I'm sorry." She slid from Atta's back—probably a beneficial thing since Atta didn't have enough strength to carry her.

Atta studied the sun, almost overhead. They hadn't a moment to lose.

Her conscience bucked at the notion entering her mind, but she had little choice. Desperate times called for drastic action. Taking Gertie's hand, she pulled her up the road.

"Come now, Gertie. We're going to get ourselves a horse."

Chapter Twenty-Eight

"But will Robert's father mind?" Gertie stood beside a large oak behind Robert's house.

The sheriff's Ford wasn't in sight, and with Robert cozy at the club with Betty, no one would be the wiser. "He'll get it back, Gertie."

"How?"

"You're asking too many questions. Follow me."

Gentle whinnies and the smell of fresh straw greeted them as they entered the barn. Atta cooed softly to Goliath as she placed the saddle on the horse and struggled to cinch it tight. Once she'd slipped on the bridle, she helped Gertie up and slid behind her, the pillowcase between them.

She nudged the old stallion's sides and tested his speed, minding how Gertie handled the ride. Her sister didn't complain, but her little body tensed beneath her arms. Atta tugged gently on the reins.

She didn't regret taking him. She didn't. Goliath would find his way back.

They kept to the paths in the woods around the main part of town. When buildings broke into the sky ahead, she pulled on the reins and slid off, helping Gertie. She gave the horse a slap on the rump. "Go home!"

"Will he get lost?" Gertie's pale blue eyes widened.

"No, horses have a sense about these things." Didn't they? "Now, we must walk like we're not hurt. The train station is right up the way." She adjusted Gertie's navy-blue scarf around her neck so that it nearly covered her mouth.

The train station lay across Dean Street, one of the busiest roads in town. When a policeman on a horse allowed them to cross, she waved a thank you and avoided eye contact, trembling beneath the officer's gaze.

"Almost there, dear. Keep a lively pace, now."

Gertie didn't answer, but matched Atta's stride. The brick station with its large front gable loomed ahead. They climbed the steps and slipped inside.

Few people milled about and before long the clerk called her in front of the barred window. "Two to New York, please."

"There's one changeover to New York. All together that will be six dollars, miss."

Six dollars? *Please, Lord...*

She didn't come this far for nothing.

She fished in her pocket, scooping out the coins and fistful of bills and laying them flat on the shiny counter with her palm. She counted them with her eyes. Two...four, five. Five dollars and eighty cents. Ninety cents...ninety-two, ninety-three, ninety-four, ninety-five. She was short five cents.

Trying to keep her frantic gaze off the clerk, she pushed the money toward him. "I'm short five cents. Is there anything you can do to make the trip less expensive?" She'd ride in the cargo car if she must.

He pushed the money back toward her. "No, I'm sorry ma'am. Good day."

She slid the change and paper money into her other palm, but the coins clattered on the wood floor. "Gertie—help me pick these up, dear."

If only she'd taken the nickel from the man who'd found her coin earlier. Five measly cents. She searched the station, spotting an old woman sitting by the window. The lady was dressed in all manner of finery—surely she could spare five cents.

"Excuse me, ma'am?"

The woman looked up, her gaze raking over Atta's unkempt clothes. Her lips curled into a grimace. "Yes?"

"My sister and I are short a nickel for the train. Do you suppose..."

She hated begging. Hated the haughty look the woman gave her. Hated how everyone treated her as if she were nothing. Perhaps that was her worth. Five cents. Practically nothing.

"I'm sorry. I can't spare that amount."

The woman turned her head. Atta led Gertie away. What could she do? Would someone buy a scarf or a hat for five cents? Oh, but she should have brought her quilt. It was worth at least as much as a train ticket. But she couldn't sell her clothes or the quilt, even if she had it. She wouldn't be able to live with herself knowing she endangered another person.

A desperate prayer bubbled up within her, though she doubted it would do any good.

"Ma'am?"

She swirled around to see a young man in a crisp starched shirt akin to those Dr. Mayhew wore. His skin was the color of chocolate. He held out a five-cent piece to her.

"I heard you were in need of this."

Atta restrained herself from kissing his feet. She let him drop the coin into her palm. "Thank you, sir. Thank you so much. You have no idea what this means to me and my sister."

He smiled and something about it looked familiar. And then he was gone.

"Come now, Gertie. We have a train to catch."

ATTA DIDN'T BREATHE easy until the churning of wheels against track propelled them into a whirring countryside. She leaned back in her seat and closed her eyes.

Thank you, Father.

She hadn't a cent to her name, but as long as she and Gertie could get to New York, she'd find a way to make money. She could work at a boardinghouse in exchange for room and board. If her fingers healed, that is. When Gertie healed, she could help too. No, a little girl needed to go to school. A little girl needed to be a little girl.

Her eyes weighed heavy as she attempted to untangle the knot of problems before her. Still, they would make it. Anything was better than that island, than Gertie living with Papi. Her sister leaned into her and she pulled her warm little body close. This is what mattered—she and her sister, together.

She fell asleep with that last joyous thought brilliant in her mind.

ATTA WOKE to the screech of iron wheels against the track and pain in her fingers—hopefully a sign they thawed out. This must be the changeover in Springfield. She'd take a quick glance at the map on the station wall before they boarded the new train to see how close they were to New York.

She nudged Gertie awake. Her sister smiled and snuggled closer.

"Atta. I was afraid it was a dream. But you really came. You really came."

"Of course I did, you goose. Things may not be easy, but we'll have one another, won't we?"

They gathered their things and squeezed down the aisle.

Should they make up new names to go with their new lives? Dr. Mayhew said patients with Hansen's disease were free in New York, but did that include her, someone diagnosed in Massachusetts?

Yes, they'd have to decide on new names. She'd talk it over with Gertie during the last stretch of the ride.

The days had grown shorter and already the sun loomed low in the sky. She imagined Dr. Parker reporting her to the authorities. She didn't mean to trouble the older man. Hopefully, he'd delay. For even if he reported her, the authorities had no way of knowing where she was or where she was going.

Clammy dread uncoiled within as she saw the uniformed officers waiting on the platform, rubber gloves tight on their hands, masks secure on their faces.

Robert. She'd told Robert she was going to New York. He wouldn't have betrayed her....was it Dr. Mayhew, then? He himself had given her the advice to go to New York.

But it was Robert's words that stood out in her mind.

What did you want me to do—pine for you forever?

You're a leper, for heaven's sake!

But Robert wasn't so heartless. He may not want to be with her, but to ruin her and Gertie's chance of a life together? He wouldn't.

Still, the harsh truth crippled her as the officers gestured her off to the side. She tried to grab Gertie and run but firm hands came down hard upon her.

"Atta!" Gertie's scream curdled the air. "Atta!"

"Gertie—no, please don't take her away. Please! Please..." Atta's body jerked in spasms and the officers didn't bother to hold her steady. An inhumane sound erupted from her body.

Gertie! Her sister's screams punctuated every coherent thought, every hope and dream she'd ever wished for her. Then, everything went black.

Chapter Twenty-Nine

1993

I inhale the scent of the sea and push my feet against the porch floorboards to move the rocking chair. My hands are on my slight belly, and the child within—whom I have taken to calling Little Nugget—moves beneath my fingers. The rocking chair, the fluttering within my womb—it all feels very maternal.

"He's late." Gram sips her glass of iced tea. Cubes of ice tinkle against the glass, sounding along with the wind chimes. The day hangs like a thick warm blanket around us and I question the wisdom of Sam and his friend moving heavy furniture down a flight of stairs on such a hot day.

"He'll be here. He had to pick up his friend."

We're silent for a moment and I ponder where Gram left off in her story last night—dragged off a train, so close to freedom. I can't fathom how any of it will lead to the hope Gram claims.

"I can understand why you wouldn't want to go back to Penikese," I say. "Aunt Atta made such an effort trying to leave it behind."

"I've already RSVP'd for both of us. I think it will be good for me to see the island one last time."

I open my mouth to say something—what, I don't know. That surely, she had many years left? That she could see the island as often as she wished?

A small, black truck, more than a little worn around the edges, turns into Gram's driveway. A moment later Sam hops out of the driver's seat. My heart speeds up and I hate myself for it. Nothing good can come from such nonsense.

The boy who gets out of the passenger seat looks vaguely familiar. Likely, I've seen him around school. He's short and wiry and I hope the two of them can manage to move Gram's furniture without injury.

If I'm reading that God-forsaken book for nothing, I'll never forgive him.

"Sorry we're late," Sam calls as they come up the stairs. "My grandfather fell and I had to take him in to get checked out."

"Oh my goodness, is he okay?" I ask.

"Doc says he's the picture of health. Swears Gramps is a Bumble—you know, like in *Rudolph*? He simply bounces." He shakes his head, holds out his hand to Gram. "Sorry, ma'am. I'm Sam. This is Peter."

Gram smiles and grasps Sam's hand, and then Peter's. "I'm Emily's grandmother. You can call me Gertie if you'd like. Are you certain your grandfather is okay while you're here? I'd hate to take you away from him."

"Are you kidding? He practically pushed me out the door. He likes watching the Saturday morning cartoons alone." Sam laughs good-naturedly and a warm surge of affection rushes through my insides.

What is wrong with me? Is it the hormones again? Why does this boy with his thick glasses, messy hair, and love of science fiction seem like the sexiest man on the planet in that moment? I tamp down whatever's stirring inside. I am eighteen and nearly seven months pregnant. I don't need any more issues to complicate my life. I need to redeem myself—not get my heart broken by another boy.

I blink, realizing the awkward silence that has overtaken the porch. Gram is tapping her chin, staring at Sam. "Do I know you, Sam? You look so familiar..."

Sam's gaze slides to me, then back to my grandmother. Without warning, a snatch of our conversation from that first day in the library comes back to me.

"You don't exactly seem the type to give your parents grief."

"You'd be surprised."

Did Sam lead a double life? Did he go around, stealing from *Fancy's Market* and making mischief in town? Is that how Gram recognizes him?

I've been duped by a boy who says one thing while he's alone with me and acts completely different while in public. Could I have an unhealthy habit of gravitating to such guys?

"I don't think so, ma'am," Sam says. But he shifts from one foot to the other in an uncharacteristic, nervous move. "What do you say we get started on that furniture?"

"I'll show you the rooms." I start for the door, my stomach still unsettled.

Two hours later, Gram's bedroom furniture is downstairs and the twin bed that was in the guest room is in Gram's old room upstairs. I can't honestly say that watching Sam maneuver the furniture expertly up and down the stairs, droplets of sweat meandering down his face, did anything to calm the simmering flame within. It had to be pregnancy hormones. Or pregnancy brain. Either way, none of my emotions could be trusted.

Friends. We were friends, and friends alone. And with my renewed doubts about Sam's character, what business did I have entertaining romantic thoughts?

Gram pours the boys iced tea and presses a fifty-dollar bill into each hand.

Sam refuses it. "I can't take this actually, Miss Gertie."

"Why ever not? You certainly earned it."

"I have a deal with your granddaughter, ma'am."

Her face tightens. "And what kind of deal is that?"

"I told her I'd only help with the furniture if she reads *Jurassic Park* and lets me take her to see the movie."

Gram raises her brow. "Is that so?"

"Yes, ma'am."

Gram turns to me. "And are you holding up your end of the bargain, Emily Grace?"

I roll my eyes. Now Gram's on Sam's side. The kid is brilliant. "Though I'm hating every minute of it, I am."

Sam winces. "*Hate* is such a strong word, Emily Grace."

I fold my arms across my chest and shake my head at him, the earlier doubts about his character already melting away.

Peter holds up his fifty. "Well, I didn't make any deals, so am I good to take this?"

"You certainly are." Gram pushes the fifty back toward Sam. "For the movie."

"With all due respect, Miss Gertie. You know what will happen if I take this money, don't you?"

"No, I'm afraid I don't."

"Your granddaughter won't read the book. Then we can't go to the movie."

"You can't go to the movie without reading the book because—"

"Because books will lose," I interrupt, grabbing the fifty and placing it on Gram's counter amidst Sam's laughter. "I'll show you guys out. Thanks so much for your help today."

"Thank you, boys!" Gram calls.

Sam turns to me before opening his truck door. He looks adorable with his hair sticking up from sweat. He smells great, too. Like spice and leather. Must be his deodorant working overtime. How does a guy sweat and smell that good?

"So, will you finish by next weekend?"

"I can make sure that I do." My words are flirty and once they are out, I become ten times more aware of my bulging stomach. Do I really want to fool myself into thinking Sam finds me attractive?

He grins, and I notice his two front bottom teeth are slightly crooked. It suits him. "Sounds like a plan. Thanks, Emily Grace."

"I hope your grandfather feels better." I wave to Peter. "Bye!"

When I go back into the house, Gram is standing in the middle of her new bedroom, staring at the wall.

"You okay, Gram?"

She startles. "Oh yes. Just thinking how different it will be down here. Your grandfather and I shared the room upstairs for more than forty years." She sighs, starts pulling a fitted sheet onto the mattress. I take the other side. "But this is good, I suppose. No more hassle going up and down those stairs."

Again, I don't know what to say.

"Sam seems like a nice young man." She takes the last bottom corner of the bed and slips the sheet beneath the mattress.

"He is."

"You like him."

"I do, but don't worry. I'm under no false illusions we can be together."

She flings the next bed sheet over the fitted one. "Sometimes love finds us in unusual places."

Chapter Thirty

He couldn't believe she'd made it. Not only to the mainland, but more than halfway to New York.

Harry took Atta's limp hand and set it in the bowl of lukewarm water at the side of the hospital bed. Her frostbitten fingers hung lifeless and blue.

The Board of Charity had reported Atta's escape to the law enforcement in Taunton. The sheriff had been conducting his investigation when a man named Robert Lincoln stepped forward, reporting Atta's plan. Robert Lincoln, her former fiancé. Atta had been about to be married. The man had failed her.

And so had Atta's father, from the sounds of it. Atta had been found trying to escape with her younger sister—one who bore the ugly marks of a man who beat her.

No wonder Atta had gone to such lengths to escape the island. She hadn't been simply trying to save herself.

He studied her sleeping face, selfishly glad he could see her again. Today, he was proud to be her doctor. While Nurse Edith had offered to handle Atta's constant frostbite care, Harry rejected the idea. He felt entirely too responsible for the woman before him. For both her desperation in her escape, and for allowing her to get on the boat when he knew the risks full well. Not to mention the fact that he himself had given her the idea of going to New York.

Atta stirred and her eyes fluttered open. Her hands jerked in the water, creating slight ripples. Her gaze skittered about, and then—slowly—she closed her eyes in undeniable defeat.

"I'm sorry you didn't get away, Atta."

The corners of her mouth tightened but her eyes remained closed.

He continued. "Dr. Parker told me about Gertie."

Her vivid brown gaze found his. Still, she didn't speak.

"They're taking her away from him, Atta. They're finding a new family for her, one that will love her. Dr. Parker said he'll see to it himself."

Quivering breaths forced their way from her pale lips. She looked so helpless. So broken.

"Are you going to talk to me?"

She didn't acknowledge him, and he plunged his hands in the bowl of water alongside hers, massaging her rough, swollen fingers. If he could coax the nerves to life...

Her eyes widened at his touch. She tore her hand from his and put the lifeless fingers to her chest.

"It'll help the blood circulate. You must keep your hands in the water if you wish to get better."

After a moment, she obeyed and once again he stroked her fingers. If she lost feeling in them, life would be ten times more difficult for her. She would need help eating, dressing herself, stitching. He rubbed harder, trying to analyze her vacant stare before giving up and wrestling with himself instead.

Everything he thought he knew fell before him like a long trail of dominoes. He'd been so obsessed with his career he hadn't seen the people inside the skin of his patients. Now, he gazed at Atta again, dark eyelashes fanning closed lids. If there were a loving God, why had he condemned her to such a bleak future?

"YOU MUST EAT NOW, Miss Atta. It's the only way you'll get your strength back, dear. Now, open up wide."

Obeying would mean further degradation. Atta set her jaw and turned her head away from Mrs. Tufts. The nurse set the bowl aside.

"Fine then, dear, but sulking will not change the course of things. I'll leave you alone for a bit."

The woman's footsteps echoed down the hall, leaving Atta with a loneliness drier than her mouth. She moved her hand around in the bowl of water and thought she felt the slight swish of wetness against her skin. A good sign—why then, did she hardly care?

But she knew.

She wanted to die. She wasn't getting better. She'd failed at escape. She'd failed Gertie, who now lived with strangers.

Her future stood before her like a long, hard, endless road in the scorching sun. No shade. No shelter. No escape.

No hope.

"She's right in there, Reverend. Take your time." Mrs. Tufts's voice wafted to Atta's bed a moment before Reverend Bailey entered the room.

He approached her without pretense, but she refused to acknowledge him. Not speaking was easier. So was not eating. Not drinking. Maybe then, God would end her life.

"Hello, Miss Schaeffer." He settled in the seat beside her and although Atta felt rude snubbing a man of God, she closed her eyes.

"I've heard you've suffered quite the ordeal. I came as soon as I could get away."

Why? Why had he come? What could a single man do to make her better?

"I thought you might like someone to talk to." A log popped in the fire. "I'm told I'm a good listener."

She turned away and closed her eyes.

"Perhaps you are a better listener than I. Can I talk to you? Tell you more about myself?"

She let the room stink with the silence she created.

"I have a wonderful wife of twenty years and three children—Mary's ten, Nathan's nine, and Clarissa is six."

The Reverend rambled on and on for what must have been an hour. Sometimes she listened, sometimes she didn't. He spoke of his pastoral position at North Baptist Church in New Bedford, of his church—his "flock," he called them, and of his son's mischievous ways and his older daughter's fearful streak.

"Mary's always been a frightened child. Scared to walk in the woods, scared to prick herself with a needle, scared of the dark. We talk often of how we build walls around ourselves out of fear, and how we must tear them down out of faith. She's come a long way. To tell you the truth, I thank God for each one of my children's weaknesses, for I know the Lord can and will use them to show His strength."

God using weakness to display his strength. Absurd. Atta was weaker than ever, and she didn't see God showcasing His power through her. Didn't expect Him to, either.

The Reverend went on to read from his Bible, skipping around and reading entire pages at a time. She wished he'd save himself the trouble.

She gazed out the window to the little white cross on the cliff. Lucy was now buried there. Oh, how convenient it would be to fling the darkness that embodied her own soul into the bottom of the deep sea, to watch it sink to an endless murky bottom. Exiled from her life. Banished.

If she jumped from that cliff—hurled her body against the rocks, would she be spared the same burial as her friend? Would the deep, black sea steal her away into its never-ending depths?

The fact that she contemplated suicide while sitting beside the Reverend drove fresh misery deep within her bones. Words nudged up her throat and onto her tongue, suddenly anxious to break free, for fear if they didn't, she would lose herself to the sea.

"Has God cursed me, Reverend?" Her throaty whisper sounded strange to her own ears.

The startled Reverend sat up straighter. "Pardon?"

She spoke slower, louder, clearer. "Is the curse of God upon every patient here?"

"You mean because you have Hansen's."

She nodded, fast.

"Oh my dear, Miss Schaeffer. I never thought—I mean it's never been much of an issue with the other patients."

The comment made her feel stupid.

"I'm sorry, you've caught me off guard. What I mean to say is no. I can say with full conviction that God has not cursed you."

A small shaft of sunlight crept to the darkened corners of her heart. Could it be true?

He must have seen her puzzled expression. He sat back in his chair, pressed his lips together before speaking. "I wonder if we as the church get ourselves a bit mixed up every now and then."

"What do you mean?"

"Why do you think I come to the island every week?"

"I—I don't know."

"Because I believe, if Jesus resided today in Massachusetts, that Penikese would be one of His favorite places."

Atta raised her eyebrow. "Perhaps someone should take *your* temperature, Reverend."

The older man released a hearty laugh. "I'm serious, Miss Atta.

Time and time again, Christ admonished the religious leaders—
the men who thought they had all the answers. Men, I'm ashamed
to admit, who remind me of *me* all too often."

She blinked at the Reverend's admonition.

He continued. "Jesus sought out the poor, the ostracized and
oppressed, the sick and downtrodden. The outcasts. And they
were always the first to respond to Him. His Kingdom truly is an
upside-down one, and I quite like that."

The wedge of sunlight grew as the Reverend flipped through
his well-worn Bible, one that never left his side. "In Exodus, God
first gives Moses leprosy to demonstrate his power. It is given after
that to show us the human condition of sin."

Atta's head swirled, and the streak of sunlight threatened
to dim.

"Bear with me now, Miss Schaeffer. For soon Jesus comes to
free us of that sin. And what does the Son of God do? He heals
leprosy. And not just once. There are three accounts in the gospels
of Him performing the miracle, once to ten men."

"B—but he has refused to cure me. I'm getting worse," Atta
croaked.

"I wish I knew why. I wish I had answers for you, Miss Atta.
All I know is that God is good. That He has a special spot in His
heart for the outcast. That He came to give us a glimpse of what
the kingdom of God is like, which is what He did when He cured
the diseased. Christ touched the untouchable when He touched
our sin. When Jesus comes again and the full glory of His kingdom
is revealed, Miss Schaeffer, He *will* heal you."

A soft peace lapped at the outskirts of her soul. Could she have
been wrong? Did God still love her?

All too soon, doubts sailed in to snatch her momentary peace
away. If it weren't for her, Gertie would still have a mother. So
would she. All because of her transgressions.

She met Reverend Bailey's gaze. When he spoke, his voice was
intimate. "In a sense, Miss Schaeffer, we are all people with leprosy

—a bad case of it, too. Every one of us has been deformed by our transgressions. Every one of us fights our Creator. But God *has* rescued us. He sent his Son to touch the most dreadful corners of our hearts. Christ gives us the opportunity to be healed where it counts most." He tapped his chest. "In here."

Her breath wobbled. "But Reverend, I've done such terrible—"

"None of us can measure up. That's why He had to come. Run to Him, Miss Schaeffer. He will accept you as you are. As His daughter."

All her life, Atta longed for a loving father. If God was willing to forgive her.... But it seemed too much to hope for.

Reservations overran the prospect of hope. They pressed harder and harder, whispering suspicious accusations. For a moment, she allowed them access to her heart. But so bleak and black were they, she couldn't bear to further entertain them.

If there was hope, it was here, with God. She may not be free of her uncertainties—maybe she never would be—but if she chose to cling to them, they'd be her death. Even now, she knew the only way to fight her doubt was to reach out and grasp the hand God offered.

She closed her eyes and whispered words to her Creator. She poured her heart out to Him. Slowly, an otherworldly calm caressed the hard edges of her spirit. The chasm between her and God closed. When she was finished, two tears rolled down her cheeks, the foreign dampness a cleansing—a release.

"Thank you so much, Reverend."

The man's face glowed. "It is entirely my pleasure, Miss Schaeffer."

She smiled through her wet lashes when he laid a hand on her arm.

"I will continue to pray for you."

"Thank you for coming. You've given me hope."

"I am only a messenger."

A knock echoed at her open door.

"Dr. Mayhew, pleasure to see you." Reverend Bailey patted the doctor on the back. "I'll leave you to your patient. Good day, Miss Schaeffer."

"Good day."

Dr. Mayhew walked into her line of vision, holding—

"My quilt. You found it."

"And you found your tongue, I see. It seems the Reverend can indeed work miracles."

She lifted one hand from the bowl of water, dried it on a nearby towel, and reached for the blanket. "Thank you for bringing it to me."

"Don't think you're off the hook so easily. You stole island property, Atta. The patients' privileges on the rowboat have been restricted. The men are none too happy with you."

She avoided his probing gaze and ran her fingers over the outline of a dove. They dragged, but she felt the unmistakable pleasure of the rough, appliquéd brown stitches. "I—I am sorry for them, but I had to do what I did. If given another chance, I would do nothing different." Except see Robert. She would have done that differently. And yet, after her talk with the Reverend something unnamed had been freed within her. To think that God was not against her…it just might be worth all the troubles of the last two days.

"Why doves?" Dr. Mayhew stood with his hands in his pocket, an uncharacteristic look of unease on his handsome face. Dark shadows resided beneath his eyes.

"It was for Lucy—Miss Peterson. We spoke of things we missed, things we may never experience again. She missed the sound of a dove. I wish I had finished it one day earlier," she whispered.

His Adam's apple bobbed, a strong, decisive motion throughout the muscles of his neck. "And what is it that you miss, Atta?"

She squirmed beneath his gaze, beneath the warmth with which he spoke her name. It seemed none of what he said was a performance any longer. The cocky, self-assured doctor she'd met that long ago day in the examination room was fast morphing into someone else altogether.

"I miss Gertie the most." And Robert. The old Robert, the one who loved her. "But as far as smaller things...pine trees. I can't imagine living on a treeless island forever." She bit the inside of her cheek. "But I suppose I'll have to manage, won't I?" She attempted a sunny smile, but knew it fell short.

He removed his hands from his pockets and brought the chair closer to the bed. "Your fingers look better." He scooped her hand up and ran his large thumbs over each one. A wooziness swept over her when one of his thumbs brushed the pulse inside her wrist.

"Yes. Much better. Can you feel this?" He gently stroked each finger, then pressed on the tips of each one.

"I—I think I can." If only she could concentrate with his nearness. The smell of bay rum mingled in the air. Her skin grew hot and black spots jumped in front of her eyes.

"Close your eyes. Tell me when you feel pressure."

His pinkies grazed her palms as he probed her wounded fingers. No. No, it was wrong to have such feelings for her doctor. A doctor! When had she lost her fear of them? And what of Robert? She shouldn't forget their love even if he did.

"Nothing?" Disappointment edged the word.

"No, wait. I'm sorry, I wasn't concentrating." Down the hall, Mary's screams disrupted the quiet. "There. Something on my index finger."

She opened her eyes to Dr. Mayhew's smiling face. Her heart stilled when he squeezed her hand with his own. "I think you may not lose your fingers, after all." He placed them in the water, holding her hand for a moment longer than necessary. "You'll have to continue to soak them, and I'll check for further improvement tomorrow. Do you need anything else?"

She shook her head.

"Very well, then. Rest easy."

"Doctor?"

He turned, his full attention upon her. For the first time, she questioned how he truly saw her. The unkempt leper with the limp fingers in the hospital bed.

"I don't blame you for the failure of the fever therapy."

One corner of his mouth lifted. "Thank you. That means a lot to me."

"And I think you deserve an *A* today. A high one."

His deep baritone laugh reverberated off the walls. It sounded wonderful. "You, dear Atta, are one in a million." He walked out of the room still laughing, leaving her stomach jittery and her brain fuzzy.

Dear Atta. But she mustn't dwell on it too much. She'd only be hurt again. She was an outcast. She'd never enjoy the love of a man.

Especially one who was her doctor.

Chapter Thirty-One

The patients chattered like excited children as a strain of *Oh Holy Night* wound down on the Victrola. The amusement room glistened with shiny decorations and the beautiful tabletop tree managed to transform the room into a merry Yuletide gathering. Betsy had arranged a variety of cakes and molasses cookies on the table. Their freshly-baked scent made Atta's mouth water.

She laughed as Willie Goon, in his excitement, danced an awkward jig on his cotton-wrapped feet. Yes, they were all sick. But with the revelation of God's love, Atta found herself growing in love toward each of them. She tucked the package she'd brought beneath her chair. If only she could have sent Gertie a Christmas present.

Thoughts of Gertie threatened to snuff out her serenity. Though her sister's new family thought it best Gertie cease communication with Atta, Dr. Parker had written the family to ease Atta's mind. By all accounts, it seemed her sister had gone to a loving family, a family that had longed for a little girl of their own for nearly ten years. They spoke with fondness of Gertie, saying she was everything their hearts imagined a daughter to be. She went to school and helped her "mother" in the kitchen, all while getting the very best doctor's care.

Gertie had a new mother. Atta was happy for her. Truly. How could she begrudge her sister a second chance, a better life? Certainly better than one in New York, scraping for survival. And, most important of all, Gertie was away from Papi.

Someday, Gertie would forget about Atta, forget how much she loved her. But even that was a blessing, for if Gertie were safe and happy, Atta could limp along in life, do her best with what the Lord bestowed.

Dr. Parker released a shrill whistle from the front of the room. He looked on with mock disapproval at Willie Goon's antics, which died down with the strident shriek. Mrs. Parker stood beside her husband in a stunning suffragette suit of deep green, a smile on her lips. Dr. Mayhew, in a brocade evening coat and bow tie watched from the side wall. Tonight, he looked every bit the educated, Ivy-league doctor, and the chasm seemed to widen between them—the chasm that had always been there, yet of late seemed to grow smaller and smaller.

"Your attention please, ladies and gentleman. It is with great pleasure that I wish you a Merry Christmas!"

The patients and nurses clapped. Cheers filled the room. "Now, Mrs. Parker will read the Christmas story to us."

As Mrs. Parker read of the shepherds and the angels from the book of Luke, Atta ran her fingers over the cool beads of her rosary in her skirt pocket. God had indeed given her much that long ago Christmas. She'd finally unwrapped the greatest gift He'd given her —freedom from the chains that had bound so tightly since her mother's death.

When Mrs. Parker finished, Dr. Parker stepped forward. "Now that we've all been reminded what this season is about, we have some gifts for you all." Again, the patients let out loud whoops and cheers. "I'd like to thank the Board of Charity for the privilege to play Old Saint Nick and pass out presents. They've provided these grand decorations and this tree. At the suggestion of Dr. Mayhew, we purchased a potted tree this year in hopes you will all help us tend it for the remainder of the winter. If she survives, we'll plant her near the hospital and see how she fares. With any luck, you'll all have a beautiful tree to sit under a few summers from now."

Atta struggled to take her next breath. A pine tree, on the island. Maybe it would never become a forest in her lifetime, but it was something. More than something. She'd told Dr. Mayhew of her longing, yet surely that wasn't why he'd suggested...

Scared, but unable to help herself, she looked at the younger doctor, standing at attention. Those deep blue eyes, the color of the sea on a cloudless day, met hers. He winked, and her gaze flew back to Dr. Parker as a furious blush worked up her neck. That one wink was enough to tell her all she needed to know. And all she feared. Why would he go through so much trouble for her?

Her stomach churned, and she ran a crease of her cotton skirt between her fingers. She must put distance between them. He was her doctor. He could leave the island whenever he wished. She, on the other hand, was bound to this island—maybe forever. She would be alone always. No, not alone. God would be there for her.

As the presents circulated, "oohs" and "aahhhs" rippled around the room, Atta not excluded. Ruffle-trimmed drawers, flannelette gowns, stockings, castile soap, a new shirtwaist of light blue, and best of all, an abundant supply of fabric and sewing novelties. Atta looked up from her packages to see Mrs. Parker watching her. Atta mouthed a "thank you." It may have been the board that donated the money for the gifts, but only Mrs. Parker could have matched them so perfectly to each patient.

Beside her, Flavia opened her drawers and a new Ralph Vaughan Williams record. Toy opened two sweaters, some flannel overshirts, black socks, and seeds for spring.

And so it went with each of the patients until the amusement room was a mess of new gifts and brown paper wrappings. Atta only wished she'd thought of something for Mrs. Parker. She and Dr. Parker were the ones who deserved to be showered with presents. But she had only one gift to give this Christmas.

After arranging her packages, she scooped up the bundle beneath her chair and walked to Mary. The older woman snarled with frustration as she tried to unwrap a small gift, her clawed hands fumbling over the brown paper.

"Here, let me help you." Atta reached for the present, but Mary snatched it away and held it to her chest, teeth bared.

"Leper! Go away. Get away from me!"

This time, Atta refused to be dissuaded. "I only wish to help, Mary." She held out her hands.

Hooded eyes stared up at her, seeming to vacillate. At last, she allowed Atta to hold a corner of the package while she clamped her deformed fingers over the rest. Atta tore it open and Mary shrieked, grabbing the present and hugging it to her chest.

A ragdoll. One similar to Gertie's Rosie. Had her sister lost her stuffed friend in their separation? She prayed not.

Mary snuggled the doll against her cheek and patted its back, rocking on her knees and whispering shushing sounds, sounds that sounded almost normal. As if she were a young mother again. The older woman stood and sought the rocking chair in the corner of the amusement room.

Atta sniffed, not wishing to interrupt the moment, but not wanting this fragile nonaggressive time to pass, either. She approached the corner of the room, the package tight beneath her fingers. She opened her mouth. Stopped.

Often fast and frantic, Mary's rocking was slow and steady, her eyes closed in peace. A soft hum vibrated from her wrinkled mouth. Atta couldn't bring herself to break the moment.

She sighed and worked the package she held from beneath the paper. Lucy's quilt, the one with the doves. She'd wanted to offer it to Mary as a token of friendship, a token of peace. But the older woman might not even remember where it had come from.

Atta stepped forward and tentatively draped the blanket over Mary and the ragdoll, tucking it behind her free shoulder to keep it in place. Mary's eyes opened. A gentle smile crossed her lips before she slipped one arm on top of the blanket to tuck it around the ragdoll. Then—in the best Christmas present Atta could have received—Mary met her gaze, her brown eyes almost friendly. "Thank you," she whispered, the soft, throaty words caught in her throat.

Goosebumps traveled over Atta's skin. *Thank you, Father, for this tiny Christmas miracle.*

Anxious to leave before Mary changed her mind and began spewing curses upon her, Atta turned and ran straight into Dr. Mayhew.

HARRY PLACED his hands on Atta's arms. "Whoa there. Where are you running off to?"

Atta crossed her arms over her stomach. "Good evening, Dr. Mayhew. Merry Christmas."

"Merry Christmas to you."

They stood in awkward silence and Harry questioned his decision to approach her. He should have sought out Edith. Yes, Edith would have been the better choice. But when he'd seen what Atta intended to do with all her hard work, he'd wanted to stop her. Turned out he was too late.

"May I speak with you a moment?" He gestured to an empty spot beside the billiard table.

"Certainly, Doctor." She tucked her chin, the color of her cheeks matching her skirt. She looked radiant tonight. Happy. Could he take any credit for that happiness?

"Please, Atta. It's a Christmas celebration. Let's forego the doctor-patient relationship for one night. Call me Harry."

She ran her healthy fingers over her skirt. "I—I don't think that would be at all proper."

"Surely you see me as more than your doctor by now..."

She blinked fast and he cleared his throat.

He hadn't meant— "Your friend, Atta. Have I not earned your friendship?"

Her lower jaw trembled. "Whether you have or have not is irrelevant. You are my doctor. Our relationship should exist as such."

Anger bubbled in his chest. She—the outcast—would dare shun him? "Have it your way then, *Miss Schaeffer*. I'll go speak with my peers."

The hurt on her delicate features caused something unpleasant to twist his gut, but well enough. Maybe her pain would cause her to open up to him.

But no. She sat in stony silence, her head bowed as if in prayer, and he felt every bit the ungracious gentleman. He couldn't claim to want her friendship and then sputter hateful words in the next breath.

He exhaled, his foot tapping of its own accord on the linoleum. "Forgive me. That was uncalled for."

She lifted her gaze to his and a sudden, fierce longing overtook him, scared him. Why couldn't they have met at a different time, a different place? On the streets of Boston or a boardwalk in Taunton? Anywhere but on this cursed island, where even a friendship would be hard to maintain.

"Forgive me, also. Perhaps friendship is not a terrible thing after all. And I believe I owe you a thank you. The tree—well, I couldn't imagine a better present."

So she realized he'd meant it for her. Good. He'd try like the dickens to keep it alive until spring. Come April, maybe he'd send for a few more pine saplings and pray the salty sea air wouldn't destroy them.

Upbeat bells rang out from the Victrola and soon *Jingle Bells* echoed through the amusement room. Willie Goon bowed to a blushing Flavia and offered his hand. The two started prancing around the room, Willie with scarce a limp. From the corner, Dr. Parker clapped. "I think Lee has the right idea." He led Mrs. Parker to the middle of the room, where they joined Lee Dip and Flavia. One of the orderlies asked Nurse Edith to dance, and soon Hyman Klein—the youngest patient besides Atta—rose and started in Atta's direction. Harry tapped his foot against the floor before making a quick decision.

He presented his hand to Atta. "May I have this dance, Miss Schaeffer?"

She pressed fingertips to her flushed cheek. "Oh, but I don't think—"

"Come now. One dance. Christmas is a celebration, after all." He led her toward the middle of the floor, ignoring her protests, which stopped when they began dancing along to the music. He placed a hand on her tiny waist and led her around the floor, conscious that he had no business dancing. Despised it, even. That's what he told Carrie on countless occasions. But now, with Atta's hand loose in his own and the warm soft padding of her fingers like a smooth blanket against the back of his hand, he thought he could get used to this social necessity. She exuded grace with each step and tried to keep from laughing at his own missteps.

"Go ahead. You have my permission to laugh. I do indeed have two left feet."

She smiled, revealing straight white teeth. "I don't think you're exaggerating, Doctor."

They laughed more and danced straight through *Deck the Halls.* Her soft breaths played against his throat, where his pulse pounded hard. He faintly wondered if Dr. and Mrs. Parker saw who he danced with, wondered if they disapproved. Yet, he'd seen Toy dancing with Edith. This wasn't any different....

His speeding pulse, hot as oil in his veins, told him it was. He should leave. Atta was right. They shouldn't be friends. He shouldn't even be her doctor with such wretched emotions coursing through him. He shouldn't have allowed himself to be so cavalier, to care this much for one of his patients. And not any patient. A leper. What on God's green earth had gotten into him?

Yet none of it seemed to matter with Atta in his arms. She would get better. Somehow. He'd see to it. Then she'd be released from the island, and so would he.

"May I, Doctor?"

Hyman, cutting in. Harry wanted to deny the man the pleasure of dancing with Atta, but social etiquette wouldn't allow it.

"Of course. It's been a pleasure, Miss Schaeffer." He fought the urge to stoop and kiss her hand, to claim her as his own before everyone, but of course he'd be declared insane on the spot. Maybe he should declare *himself* mad.

He turned and walked out the door, striding down the corridor and out into the cold air. Winter's hand rushed over his warm skin, sending reality sweeping in to replace fantasy. Atta was a leper. He'd gotten too comfortable with her, allowed loneliness to make him vulnerable to dangerous emotions.

He walked beneath the pavilion and leaned against one of its great posts. The stars shone clear in the sky, reflecting a million lights on the water. He must go back in soon. His fingertips grew numb from the cold. Yet, he didn't want to see Atta dancing with Hyman. For pity's sake, why did it bother him so much?

"Son?"

Harry started at Dr. Parker's voice. "Hi, Dr. Parker. Nice night."

"It is. A bit warmer in the hospital, though."

"Just taking a breather."

Dr. Parker came beside him, abundant starlight glinting off his white mustache. "Harry, you're walking on thin ice."

"Pardon, sir?"

"With Miss Schaeffer, son."

"But I haven't—"

"I know. But you feel strongly toward her. It's obvious. To everyone, I think."

The fact that everyone saw what he hadn't seen until moments earlier embarrassed him. But they were wrong. He did not feel strongly toward—toward a leper. A German leper, of all people! Her ancestors were probably the very reason war raged overseas.

"I realize you can't control all your inclinations. You work closely with Miss Schaeffer. She is attractive, with or without Hansen's."

"Dr. Parker, please. I must ask you to stop with this line of thinking. I have no inappropriate feelings for Miss Schaeffer. You have nothing to worry about."

The older man stood silent a moment before speaking. "I hope that's true. Because my duties as superintendent of this island would force me to release you from further obligation here if I suspected the opposite to be the case."

His ticket to getting off this cursed island. Admit, or rather pretend, he was in love with Atta. Dr. Parker laid it out before him, his to grasp at any moment. He'd wanted it so badly months earlier. Now...now, he wanted something else more. He wanted to find a cure for leprosy.

He wanted to find a cure for Atta.

"HERE YOU ARE, Gert. A fresh bowl for us to string." Mother, as Gertie was told to call her, put a heaping bowl of popcorn on the floor between them. The room smelled of pine trees and whispered of secrets to be unwrapped the next morning. Gertie had helped Mother arrange apples and nuts around the sitting room. Dried cranberries and princess pine hung on the grand veranda outside.

"Don't be afraid to steal a few now, dear." Mother popped a

kernel into her mouth and smiled at Gertie. She was happy. Gertie didn't understand why, but she made Mother very happy. It was nice to please her, but it also made her feel strange—like the time a rock had been stuck at the bottom of her shoe at recess and Sister Agatha wouldn't let her take it out. Like something wasn't quite right. As if one day, Mother would wake and see the bad in her that Papi saw.

Gertie liked Mother well enough. She was pretty and smelled like flowers. She never got angry and she let Gertie help with dinner.

But she didn't know how to sing *Schlaf, Kindlein schlaf.* Mother had asked Gertie to teach it to her and she'd tried to sing it once, but it didn't sound right. Not like when Atta sang it.

"Is she snatching more popcorn, Gert? I'm telling you, she can't be trusted." Father looked at Mother with a smile on his face. Gertie watched, mesmerized as he leaned down and planted a kiss on Mother's head.

So this was what it was like to have a real family. A father and a mother and a—

A blur of wet coat and snow boots flew past them. "Hold up, now. Save some for me, will you?"

And an older brother.

"George Matthew, you march back into the foyer and take those wet things off right this minute." Mother used her firmest voice and Gertie cowered near the pillows.

Father nudged Mother in the shoulder and gestured toward Gertie.

George smuggled a kernel before walking toward the foyer with a laugh. "Nice to have *her* around, I suppose. I never get yelled at much anymore."

"Albert, please discipline the boy. He's getting worse and worse."

"He's being a boy, dear. Nothing to fret over."

Did Mother want Father to get the rolling pin and hit George, like Papi used to do to her? She hugged Rosie to her chest. It still ached sometimes where Papi had hit her.

A loud pounding started at the door.

"Who do you suppose?"

"I'll get it," George yelled.

Gertie heard the door open and then some loud voices. It sounded like...she scooted closer to Mother as Father strode to the foyer. Mother picked her up and knelt behind the couch, Gertie tucked in her arms.

"Where is she? She—she's mine ya know. Belongs to me!" Papi's voice filled the room and Gertie covered her ears. It didn't stop the angry voice, the voice that came when Papi had been at the bad place. "I come a long way for her, had a heck of a time finding her, and I ain't leavin' till I get her back!"

Mother clutched Gertie tighter.

Father's voice came from the foyer. "Mr. Schaeffer, you know what the judge said. You are not allowed to come here. If you don't leave this moment, I'm calling the police."

"Gertie? Where are ya, my girl? Gertie. Gertie!"

She saw Father at the edge of the couch, speaking into the mouthpiece of the phone. "The police will be here any minute, Mr. Schaeffer. I suggest you leave my house."

"What are ya goin' to do? Make me, college boy?"

A loud thump. Gertie knew that thump all too well. Papi had hit Father. She wiggled from Mother's arms. She couldn't let Papi hurt Father like he'd hurt her. It was all her fault. None of this would ever have happened if—

"Gert!" Mother snatched at her dress, but she slid from behind the couch. Her hand scraped painfully against the metal poker sitting near the fireplace. It had been propped up on a piece of wood, and in her haste, she'd ran right into it.

Papi's hard gaze landed on her. "There ya are, girl. Come on home with me now. Ya don't belong with these here rich folks, now do ya?"

"You lay a hand on her and I swear to St. Pete I'll—" Father didn't finish his words, for something hit the back of Papi's head with a bang. He fell to the ground. George stood over him with Mother's cast iron pan clutched in his hands. A wild look carved his face. At that moment, George scared her more than Papi did.

"George!" Mother rushed to scoop the pan from his hands. More loud voices, then an argument, but all Gertie could do was stare at Papi's still body, unable to make herself feel sorry for him. She knew she should feel sorry for him, but she couldn't.

Later that night, long after the policemen had taken Papi away and Mother had bandaged up Gertie's hand and the family had finished decorating the tree, Gertie lay in bed, questioning if Jesus saw her heart, saw that she was almost glad when George hit Papi.

"There ya be."

Gertie sat up. "Kat! I was worried you wouldn't come again after last time."

George had barged into Gertie's room on Kat's last visit and told her to quit talking to herself.

"Aye, he'd be out with us for good again if he got th' notion I be in here."

"It's not you, Kat. It's me. George doesn't like me much." Gertie clutched Rosie's stuffed feet.

"An' what is it tha's got to tell me?" Kat knew when to come. She knew when Gertie wanted to talk.

"Papi came tonight. He—"

"Blast it all, Gert." George shoved her bedroom door open. The moonlight glinted over his white thermal pajamas. "Knock off that talking, will ya?"

Gertie pulled the covers over her knees. "I'm sorry, George. Kat just wanted to—"

George looked around the room, his dark eyes angry. "I don't care what Mother and Father say, you're as loony as a Betsy bug. Keep quiet, you hear? Tomorrow's Christmas and I want first dibs on the presents."

George left and Gertie huddled deeper into her warm sheets. "Kat?" she whispered.

No answer. George had scared her friend away again.

Gertie clutched Rosie to her chest with her bandaged hand and closed her eyes. She thought about Atta. Then about Papi. She tried to make her heart happy, but no amount of wishing would do it. Instead, it felt like someone dug a big hole inside her. The ache moved through her body and then into her legs where it throbbed with a very real force.

She counted the chimes on the clock echoing from downstairs.

*One, two, three...*all the way up to twelve. The ache in her legs didn't go away. Neither did the one in her heart.

It was Christmas, a time to be merry and full of joy. But would that ever be possible again?

Chapter Thirty-Two

"There you are, Missy. I knew these would fit you perfectly." Atta tucked the dress snugly around Mary's doll and fastened the button she'd sewn in the back. She handed the doll to Mary, who smiled, adoration in her gaze.

"It fits."

"I'd say it does."

Mary snuggled the doll to her shoulder and arranged the dove quilt over Missy and herself. "Thank you."

Atta swallowed the emotion climbing her throat. The simple gift had served to clear the hazy insanity that haunted Mary, replacing it with calm contentment. True, she believed the doll to be her real baby, but Atta didn't see the harm in that if it served to quell her demons.

She turned and crossed the empty amusement room to take the flatiron off the woodstove. The pine tree, now naked of ornaments, still filled the room with cheer and a comforting scent.

She sensed, rather than saw, a form darkening the far threshold. Dr. Mayhew. He stood gazing at her with such intensity, she thought her insides would burn from the sear of his blue eyes. He'd avoided her since Christmas Eve—nearly a week now. He'd canceled two of her appointments also, saying they weren't necessary.

Now, she pretended not to see him but continued to clean her scraps.

Gertie was safe and happy. Atta must find contentment in God alone. Nothing else would satisfy—not getting well, not escaping back to the mainland, not Robert, and certainly not the fickle attentions of her doctor.

Footsteps drew closer. She hated the way her pulse knocked against her throat, hated the way her body betrayed her will.

"Why are you encouraging her?"

She hadn't expected the harsh tone, the stern look. "Pardon?"

"Miss Martin. Need you encourage such foolishness?"

"Hush. Not so loud." She refused to let Dr. Mayhew ruin Mary's illusion with his callousness.

"Do not tell me how to speak, Miss Schaeffer. Miss Martin is my patient and I think I know what's best for her."

An abrupt shift from across the room caught Atta's attention. Mary gathered Missy and the quilt, giving Atta a shaky smile before leaving. Almost as if she knew her peaceful world was being threatened.

"Do you, now?" Atta raised her chin, daring to look at those piercing eyes. "And can you tell me Mary isn't better since Christmas Eve?"

"Of course she's better. She's living in a dream world!"

"She wasn't living in the real world before." She folded her arms across her chest. "I think it bothers you that *you* weren't the one to make her better. I think it irks you that she finds comfort in a simple gift. I think her illusion makes you uncomfortable, and so you wish to upset it."

His jaw worked back and forth, and his right foot tapped out endless energy on the floor. She shouldn't have been so bold. If she wished to maintain the doctor-patient relationship, she must stop treating him as her equal. She needed to step down, to show him respect.

"I'm sorry, Dr. Mayhew. Please excuse me." She gathered up her belongings and started for the door.

"Seems we can't have a conversation lately without one of us begging forgiveness of the other."

She should keep moving, keep leaving. It was dangerous for them to open up to one another. She knew better. So did he. But she couldn't make her feet move forward.

"I suppose that might take me down a mark or two?"

She couldn't help the smile that crossed her lips. "I'd say you're teetering dangerously toward a low B." She turned. "But I am sorry for thinking I know better than you. I don't. All I know is Mary is peaceful now. I only wish to show her the love that..."

His brow puckered. "Continue, please."

She hadn't talked about her newfound freedom much to anyone besides Reverend Bailey. "I only wish to show Mary the love God has shown me."

He snorted and looked out the window. She followed his gaze over the white landscape, the ice forming over the jagged rocks on the small beach. "And what love has God shown you, Atta? To cast you off onto this barren wasteland, to forbid you a normal life, to deny you your family, deny you the warmth of a husband's arms?"

Heat rose to her face at the intimate portrayal. She'd asked the same questions of her Creator time and time again. But she couldn't be so quick to forget the biggest gift he'd given her.

"The Lord saved me, Harry."

She couldn't deny the pleasure of his Christian name on her lips. And yet, it was appropriate. For she wasn't talking to him as her doctor, but as a friend.

The hard lines of his mouth softened and he stepped closer to her, raising a hand to her cheek. "How has God saved you? How can you call your fate salvation?"

She closed her eyes, her body fighting to relinquish itself to his tender touch. Her stomach swirled and a strange but wonderful dizziness swept through her at the sensation of his thumb traveling down her neck.

But no. This wasn't in Harry's best interest. She stepped back and his arm dropped against his gray trousers.

"If it weren't for this disease, I wouldn't have been broken. Fully broken. Don't you see? I've relied on myself all these years. I've relied on myself to protect Gertie, to change Papi, to marry well. When it was all taken away from me and I had nowhere to turn, that's where God found me. Where I could finally lean on him."

A storm cloud rolled past the sea-blue of Harry's eyes. "If you've given your life to God, then it's only right He give it back to you. He should make you clean, Atta. Whole. Why doesn't He heal you?"

His voice cracked. He cared for her. Perhaps more than a doctor should.

"I—I don't know. Perhaps I must cling to the promise that I am 'fearfully and wonderfully made,' with or without leprosy."

He looked at her as if she were mad. She fought to maintain her composure, to not crumple beneath his cynical look, for surely he did not think her wonderfully made.

"He may not heal me physically, but inside I am whole again," she said.

"A healing God, eh?"

He mocked her. She shouldn't have opened her mouth at all. "What do you live for, Harry?"

He smiled. "I like it when you say my name."

Oh, but he could get her off track with such little effort. She smoothed her skirt. "What do you live for, Dr. Mayhew?"

He sighed, plowed a hand through his short curls. "Success. Prestige. Recognition. There, you've evaluated me and found me shallow. Are you happy?"

Well, at least he was honest. "Why?"

"Why what?"

"Why do you live for those things?"

He shook his head, his gaze skidding when it landed on the billiard table. "How about a game?"

"I beg your—"

"Oh, come now, Miss Schaeffer. I've seen women play billiards before."

"And where was that, pray tell?"

He shrugged, an impish grin on his face. "Around."

"You've changed the subject."

"Billiards serves to loosen my lips. Come now. No harm will be done." He gathered the balls and placed all but the white one in the wooden triangular frame, alternating between stripes and solids.

"Dr. and Mrs. Parker wouldn't—"

"I've seen Mrs. Parker play myself."

"Truly?" She tried to picture the stout, respectable woman bending over a billiard table.

"No. But what does that say about what you live for? Only trying new things if someone else has done them first?"

She fought the urge to growl at him. "I haven't a clue how to play."

"I'll teach you." He picked up a billiard stick and bent low, aiming at a white ball. His tie hung loose at his neck and she tried to veer her gaze away from the few chest hairs poking out. She thought of Robert then. Had he married Betty yet? Did they sleep in the house that had been meant for her?

The snap of the balls cracked the air. Four balls found a home in pockets. He looked at her with a smug grin.

"Is that good? Should I applaud you or something?"

He crooked a finger at her, beckoning her to him. She grabbed a stick on her way.

"You can only hit the white ball, called the cue ball, with your stick. Don't hit it in a pocket though, you'll lose your turn. I'll take solids, you have stripes. Try to get the striped balls in the pockets."

She tried to imitate his stance, ignoring the foolishness of sticking her backside so far out. She hit the white ball, allowing a striped, yellow ball to move about two inches closer to a pocket.

"Good try."

He took aim at the white ball and with an effortless snap, sent two more solid balls in corner pockets. "My father is Dr. William Mayhew." He glanced at Atta, as if expecting a reaction. "Back in Boston, that means something. He's one of the most respected physicians in the city. Chairman of the Board at Mass General. Has saved more than his fair share of lives."

He gestured for her to take her turn, and she did so, not wanting to ruin the moment.

"Dr. William Mayhew always gets his way. Whether it's saving a patient's life...or running his son's." Atta drank in every word he shared, knowing it cost him something he didn't easily give away. The white ball knocked into one of her red striped ones, budging it into the black one.

Harry leaned down and allowed the stick to slide through the cavity he made with the fingers of his left hand. The balls snapped. "It didn't matter much to me. I was drawn to the medical profession since I was old enough to hold a stethoscope. Runs in the blood, maybe. All I really wanted to do was make my father proud of me. I can still remember receiving my report card upon finishing my third year of grammar school. All *A*'s. My teacher brought me aside after school and told me I received the highest marks in the class. I was jumping out of my trousers, I was so excited, high-tailed it straight to my father's office to show him."

They'd stopped playing billiards, now. Harry stared at the coarse green of the table and Atta held her breath, hoping he'd forget she was there, hoping he didn't end his story.

"Mrs. Cranshaw was his secretary—still is. She never allows anyone past my father's exam room door if he's with a patient. My father often performed minor surgeries in his office, tried to save his patients the expense of the hospital"—Harry's brows lowered —"or maybe make some extra money for himself, I don't know. Anyway, I barged into his office when I didn't see Mrs. Cranshaw at her desk. I had that report card in my hand. I could practically hear the long-withheld praise.

"Instead, I ran straight into my father's surgical instruments on his portable table. I fell, cut my leg on something sharp. He cursed. I'd never heard such words from his mouth. He didn't look up, just started barking orders at his intern who scooped up the instruments to disinfect them. Blood was everywhere. Saints alive, I still don't know what he was operating on that could have caused that much blood." He licked his lips, bent to take his turn at the billiards table. With one snap, he sent the cue ball into the last solid red one. "The patient died. Father hurled a roll of catgut at me, told me to stitch my leg up myself. Took me the longest time to find a needle to disinfect, and it hurt like the dickens." He aimed for the black eight ball. "Needless to say, Father never saw my report card that day, nor anything else worthy of praise. All he sees in me is failure." The eight ball bounced off a striped ball and rolled to the middle of the table. "So that, Miss Atta, is why I depend on success for happiness."

Atta worked her tongue around her dry mouth. "You're still looking for his approval."

Harry shrugged. "What does it matter?" He flicked his stick at her. "Your turn."

She didn't move. "I'm sorry. And...I think I understand." She swallowed. "Perhaps there's a better kind of approval out there, though. One that can't be measured by earthly means."

He smacked his stick against the table. Atta jumped. "How can you stand there, spouting things of faith at me? For heaven's sake, look at all the good God has done you." He walked away from her, then turned back. "I don't think like you. I can't. I'd shrivel up and die from lack of purpose if I lived for something immeasurable, something so abstract."

She stepped closer, laying a hand on his wrist. "How do you know unless you try? Perhaps you'd find yourself more alive than ever."

His stick dropped to the ground and he grabbed both of her shoulders. His fingers dug into her arms, and she thrilled at their possession of her skin. "Do you want to know what would make me alive?" His gaze traveled down to her lips and he moved his own mouth closer to hers.

His warm, excited breath danced along her face, the scent of bay rum intoxicating, tempting. But he couldn't. He wouldn't. Would he? As much as she wanted him to, she couldn't let him. She scrunched back, squeezing her eyes shut. "Please, don't."

He held her tightly for another moment before releasing her suddenly. "I think the game's over. Maybe your precious God can keep you company."

She watched him walk from the room, a whirlwind of anger and hurt. The man was a volatile explosion waiting to happen. Just like...but she couldn't compare Harry to Papi, they were nothing alike.

Still, she shivered, his absence leaving the large room cold. Best they stay away from one another—as well as a patient with a deadly disease could stay away from her doctor.

Chapter Thirty-Three

"Schaeffer!"

Niklas jerked to attention at the rough use of his name, the sound of metal against metal.

"You have a visitor." The guard sneered and walked away, his boots scraping against the cement floor of the jail.

Charles Lincoln appeared in his place, his sheriff's badge shiny on the lapel of his coat. Shiny and blasted annoying, especially in this place.

"Come to gloat, Sheriff?" Niklas rubbed his neck, wishing for a drink. The last seven days of sobriety was the closest thing to hell he'd ever known. And still, the craving wasn't knocked.

"No, Niklas. Came to tell you that Robert's looking after your place."

"Mighty sweet of the boy."

Charles ignored his sarcasm. "Came to talk to the judge, too. See if he can go easy on you."

The words failed to comfort. No one needed him. All he had was work, and who knew if Reed and Barton would grant him his job back after he'd landed himself in this place.

He stared at the cracks in the cement wall, one deeper and

longer than the rest. Its ragged grooves traced a pattern to the floor. "You and the boy have a nice Christmas, Charles?"

The sheriff nodded. "Betty came over, made us a fine dinner."

"Betty?"

"The girl Robert's marrying come spring."

A need to defend Atta rose within him. "You come to my prison cell to tell me your boy's forgotten about my daughter, eh?"

"Niklas, I didn't come here to argue with you. Atta's gone, as good as dead. What she has is nothing but a holy horror. It's best Robert moves on. You, too."

Niklas gritted his teeth and looked up at the man's blue gaze. "Atta ain't dead."

Charles sighed. "The judge tells me Gertie's with a real good family. You shouldn't worry about her none. This is all for the best."

"Have you been to see her, Charles?"

"Yes. She's well taken care of. She has a mother and a father."

A father. He hated the man after only laying eyes on him once. Boy, it'd felt good when his fist had connected with that clean-shaven face.

"Niklas, I know you think Katharina and I—that we were improper toward one another, but—"

"I don't want to hear it!" Niklas stood and shook the bars in front of Charles.

The sheriff backed away and held up his hands. "There was nothing between us, Niklas. I swear. Yes, I was in love with her. Even as a married man, I'm ashamed to admit she caught my eye. More ashamed to admit I acted on my feelings. But she refused me, Niklas. Said she loved you."

The man's words swirled in his head. Could they be true?

Charles inhaled a shaky breath. "I'm here because of Katharina. God knows what she saw in you, but it was something. I want to help you, Niklas. I shouldn't have loved her, but I couldn't help myself. I'm asking your forgiveness. I'm asking that you let me help you."

Niklas swallowed, his throat dry. A prisoner down the hall banged on the bars of his cell. A guard yelled back.

"Is Gertie mine?" He whispered, unable to bring himself to look Charles in the eye.

The sheriff stepped forward, placed a hand on a black bar. "Yes. Katharina and I—we never—for heaven's sake, Niklas, she barely allowed me to help her down from a wagon. Gertie is yours through and through. Maybe it's time you start acting like it."

A part of Niklas wanted to reach through the bars and strangle Charles Lincoln for putting him in his place. But another, greater part wanted to throw his arms around him in a bear hug. Maybe he should have never doubted Katharina's love. He may not have been happy with himself, but that wasn't reason to assume his wife would look elsewhere for love.

Gertie was his...could it be possible?

Gertie was his.

And he had lost her.

A stinging sensation crept to his eyes, and without the numbing effect of alcohol, it wouldn't go away. A warm tear ran down his cheek and splattered onto the dusty floor. He'd let Katharina down. He'd let Atta down. He'd let Gertie down. He'd lost everything that was dear to him. Now, it was too late. There was nothing he could do to get any of them back.

A black pit of nothingness stretched before him. Dark. Foreboding. Compelling. He wanted to drop all his pain into it and watch it disappear. Charles spoke again, saying something about the judge, something about the animals at the house, but his words were nonsense to Niklas.

The black pit called to him, and more than anything, he wished to succumb to it.

HARRY SQUINTED out the darkened window, a medical journal held tight in his hand, his thoughts running wild. Icicles trickled methodically, like an IV drip, onto the ledge of the outdoor windowsill. Moonlight shone off the patches of green dotting the landscape. Spring couldn't come soon enough.

Again, Harry read the article before him, written by Dr. William Park of New York City. The man wrote of a diphtheria toxin he'd produced to create active immunity in both animals and humans.

Harry squinted at the words on the page. The diphtheria bacteria and the Hansen's bacteria shared many similarities. They attacked the body in similar ways, often by the skin and respiratory tracts. The bacteria even shared the same structure.

What he wouldn't give to administer the toxin to one of the patients, to observe if any positive results came about. But he didn't know enough yet. If only one of the animals would contract the disease. It was so much easier playing with a rat's life than a human's—than Atta's.

Absurd how he should miss her when they shared the same small space of land. Yet, except for one necessary exam, they'd avoided one another for three long months, ever since that blasted day at the billiards table. His face burned thinking about it now.

He'd almost kissed her. If only she'd leave his mind, his very soul. He watched her every evening before he left the hospital. She went outside and stood at the shore, the wind tugging her hair from its combs. Sometimes she'd raise her thin arms to the star-studded sky, no doubt praising her God. What was it about Him she found so fulfilling?

He gazed down at the journal, where William Park's stern photograph stared back at him. Park's immunization hadn't been proven effective. But here on the island, where Harry had little to work with, he was all too willing to grasp at anything that might hold promise.

Maybe one of the patients would be willing to try it. The

island's newest patient, Adskhan Kaya, perhaps. Although the man was only six years older than Harry, he looked ancient. Craters marked his entire body. Fluent in English, the Turkish Hebrew spoke little, except when his temper got the better of him, which was quite often. Dr. Parker himself admitted the man had added a disturbing element to the island. Would he—or any of the men for that matter—be desperate enough to try the diphtheria toxin?

The sound of a door shutting down the hall resonated through the building. Harry glanced at his watch. Eight o'clock. Time to head home. Since he never took his meal with the others, Mrs. Parker kept it warm until he arrived at the administration building, usually about eight-fifteen, after his work was done. After he'd seen with his own eyes that Atta had finished praying and was safely in her cottage for the night.

ATTA's boots crunched against old snow and she leaned back on her heels as she picked her way down the rocky shoreline. The cold air bit her cheeks and she huddled farther into her coat and scarf, her hands buried alongside the rosary beads in her pocket.

No matter the frozen air, she wouldn't give up this precious time. Only her and the endless stars, the ocean breeze licking her skin, illogical peace whispering to her soul.

This is where she prayed for Gertie. Each night, she prayed first for her sister, that she would forget her old life and embrace her new one. She prayed for Dr. and Mrs. Parker, for the nurses, and for all the patients. Sometimes she prayed for Papi. She always prayed for Harry.

She lifted her hands to the sky, the distant clouds luminescent beside the moon. *Father, make my soul as beautiful as your creation. May it sing—*

A combination of screaming and sobbing cut through the night air. Atta couldn't mistake the voice.

Mary's. Her heart leapt in her throat.

"No! Leper! Miiissssy!"

The moonlight shone along the length of the beach where a darkened form ran toward the shoreline. Mary hobbled after...Atta couldn't make out the figure. The shadow stopped at the ocean's edge. The moonlight caught him as he looked back over his shoulder—the new patient, Adskhan. In one powerful motion, he hurled something into the black ocean and wiped his hands against one another.

Mary shrieked and limped after him, all while Adskhan rained down curses upon her. When Mary reached him, she didn't attack him as Atta expected, but instead plunged herself into the ocean, arms flailing with wild strokes.

"Mary!" Atta's blood froze. She pushed her legs forward, running as fast as they could carry her. "Dr. Parker! Nurse Edith!" Someone must hear her. She'd seen Dr. Mayhew's lamp on. "Harry!"

Adskhan had disappeared by the time Atta reached the scene. Mary struggled to stay above the water. "Mary! Mary! Stand up, dear!"

She couldn't be sure, but she didn't think the water could be deep so quick. But the older woman didn't acknowledge her and continued her struggle.

Atta started into the water, the coldness crawling up her legs and stealing her breath. The water reached her thighs when Mary slipped completely beneath the surface.

"Mary!" Atta's breath hitched when the water reached her midsection. Her skirts and coat dragged her down and she paddled her palms through the water to give her extra momentum. Mary, oh Mary. Where was she?

When she'd reached the spot where Mary had gone under, she pressed her hand into the black water, searching for a scrap of clothing, hair, anything. Instead, her next step failed to hit bottom and she plunged into the biting water.

Panic gripped her like a vice and she fought to drag in a breath. A hard, claw-like hand grabbed her skirts, hauling her beneath the water's cold surface. She pushed her hands, her arms, her feet against the water, but again the hands pulled her beneath the icy black needles of the abyss. Her chest squeezed. Her lungs refused to hold.

Atta inhaled the salty seawater.

HARRY HAD NEVER KNOWN true fear until the moment Atta's body disappeared beneath the water's surface. Throwing off his shoes and coat as he ran, he hurled himself into the unforgiving sea, hardly noticing its chill, swimming with powerful strokes to where he'd last seen Atta. He dove beneath the surface, unable to see any sign of her in its bleak depths.

The frigid water froze his head, his lungs. He came up for air and then went down again, vowing not to come up until he'd found her.

His outstretched hands hit nothing but cold blackness. She should have let Mary drown. God only knew why the batty woman chose the month of March to take a swim. Blast that crooked woman, and blast Atta for being so blamed kind!

He lost his sense of direction, but then—there, something. He grasped hold of it at the same moment he caught a glimpse of the moon. Kicking upward, he brought Atta's head above water. Mary's head bobbed to the surface too, and he pried her hand from Atta's hair as his foot made contact with blessed sand.

More shouts from the shore—others coming to help. Dr. Parker waded into the water to carry a hysterical Mary to shore, rag doll tight in her grip. When the water reached his waist, Harry did the same for Atta. By the moonlight, her lips shone blue, her eyelids dark with death. He lowered her to the pebbled shoreline.

God, make her live!

It wasn't a request. It was a command. If Atta's God existed, He'd save her now. Surely, He'd recognize her loyalty and come to her rescue in this dark hour.

He rolled her onto her stomach and pressed hard on her back. Again and again until he wondered if he were breaking bones. When neither a cough nor sputter shook her body, he wiggled her shoulders none too gently, knocking her nose against the ground.

He couldn't imagine this island without her, couldn't imagine his life without her. She must live.

God!

A gust of water spewed from her mouth and nose and Harry sat back, shocked that his prayer had been answered. She coughed and gagged, finally taking in a single, large gasping breath. Harry stared at her, his mouth falling open, his hands clutching her shoulders as he rolled her over. A wheezy laugh echoed from his constricted lungs, and he squeezed her to his wet chest, pressing his lips to her soaked hair, not caring what the others thought. None of it mattered. None of them mattered.

They could go ahead and think what they liked, for he could no longer deny it. Was no longer even ashamed of it. For yes, he, Dr. Harry Mayhew, was in love with an outcast.

Chapter Thirty-Four

1993

I roll onto my side, trying to get comfortable, but a burning sensation sits above my belly and Little Nugget seems intent on not letting me sleep.

Heartburn.

I sit up, propping pillows behind me, and glance at the clock. 4:37 a.m. Gram and I stayed up late, and after she'd finished telling me more of Atta's story, I couldn't have gone to sleep if I tried.

What would it be like to be loved like Harry loved Atta? Loved through the most repulsive social stigma? Loved without reserve?

I stare into the dark, remembering Bryan's touch that hazy night. I thought he loved me. I was already planning how our relationship would grow over the spring and summer, how we would stay connected when we parted for college. I remember the feel of his lips on my neck, his persistent hands.

"I love you, Emily," he'd whispered into my hair. "God, I love you so much."

And I'd believed him.

When he lay above me and we were about to do what I'd never done before, he even asked me if it was okay.

I'd nodded. I'd wanted to be together, to please him. To give him this part of myself. In my naiveté, I believed it would make him mine forever.

He dumped me ten days later for the Homecoming Queen. I realized I was pregnant six weeks after that. The morning after I'd taken the pregnancy test, I'd approached him in the hall when he was alone at his locker.

"Hey," I said.

He had the decency to falter. "Oh, hey, Emily. How's it going?"

The familiar scent of his body spray wafted toward me and my heart ached.

"Could we talk sometime?"

"I've been pretty busy with baseball starting. Coach says a scout from Roberts Hopkins is coming by today."

"That's great." Great. He had no idea I was about to ruin his life. Maybe I shouldn't even tell him.

He closed his locker. The hall emptied, most of the kids already in their third period class.

"So, what do you need to talk to me about?"

I almost told him "nothing." But I hadn't been alone in the back seat of that car.

"I'm pregnant," I said.

He stopped walking, his backpack sliding off his shoulder. "What?"

"I—I'm pregnant. I found out yesterday. Bryan..."

I'm scared.

I'm alone.

I don't know what to do.

"That's crazy." He glanced at me. "What? Don't look at me like that. It's not mine."

My mouth hung open. I worked my tongue around, tried to say something, but no words came out.

"I said don't look at me like that, Em. You can't get pregnant with what we did. We used a condom."

The words flowed with such brazen confidence that I questioned myself. Had he used a condom? I wasn't exactly experienced in these things. And it had been fast—only a few minutes. All I knew was that I'd taken two tests—both positive. I hadn't gotten my period for sixty-three days. I *was* pregnant.

He rested a hand on my arm. "I'm sorry you're going through this, but don't try to drag me down too, okay? I know the breakup was hard on you, but we both have to move on."

My ears rang. I blinked. "This is *not* just my problem."

He tapped my chin gently with his knuckles. "Sure it is. But don't worry. You're a smart girl, you'll figure it out."

And then he was gone. So much for loving without reserve.

Two months later, when my parents demanded to know who the father was, I didn't tell them. They were already deep into plans for hiding me and calling adoption agencies, anyway. What did it matter?

I NEARLY JUMP out of my seat when the life-sized T-Rex on the movie screen releases a mighty roar above the car that Tim and Lex occupy.

Sam leans toward me. "Are you okay?"

I place a hand over my chest and nod but jump again—this time clear out of my seat—as the dinosaur crashes its massive head into the glass roof of the car.

"Come on." Sam tugs my hand and stands in a crouching position so as not to block the view of the screen for the theatre-goers behind us.

"What? What are you doing?" I whisper.

He pulls me down the side stairs of the theatre until we're standing in the dimly lit hall of the cinema.

"What's wrong?" I ask. "We're missing it!"

He licks his lips, looks back toward the door we've just exited. A gigantic roar reaches our ears even out here.

"It's just..." He glances at my stomach. "It's pretty suspenseful. I don't know a lot about this stuff but is that okay with"—he looks at my belly again—"you know, is it okay for you?"

My insides melt. I rest a hand on Sam's bare forearm. "You are super sweet, you know that?" I want to kiss him on the cheek but hold myself back. "I'm sure a little suspense won't hurt me or the baby, but thanks for thinking of us."

We return to our seats to watch the rest of the movie, which I'm not ashamed to admit I thoroughly enjoy. We've finished recapping the most memorable scenes when Sam opens the passenger door of his truck for me in the theatre parking lot. "So, we have to talk about it. We can't avoid it any longer."

I freeze while reaching for my seatbelt. He's going to ask what I plan to do with the baby. He's going to ask about the father. He's going to make me face a future I would give anything to delay.

"What?" I ground out.

"Which one wins—book or movie?" He walks around to the driver's side.

I let out a long breath in a great whoosh. "You're not going to like it."

He winces.

"As much as I'm for books—"

"No. Don't say it, Emily Grace. Don't."

"That movie was definitely better than the book."

He flops against the seat, shakes his head dramatically. "How dare you let movies strip books of their power."

I giggle. "Oh, come on. The book was good, I'll give you that. But there was so much science in it. That movie made me care about the characters. And don't even get me started on Ian Malcolm."

Beneath the parking light glow, Sam's face turns grim. "May God rest his soul."

"But only in the book. I like that Spielberg lets him live. Score one for movies."

He starts the truck. "This conversation is not over."

"Did you seriously think the book was better?"

He shrugs. "It was a good book."

"It was a good movie," I counter. "Why can't they both win?"

"Because life has taught me that there's only one winner. Ever."

His comment is filled with a gravity I can't digest. Is he right? Maybe. My parents have certainly won in hiding me away. Bryan has certainly won in evading responsibility for our child. I'm the one who's stuck with the whale-sized body and aching back and uncertain future. The guilt of giving up my baby or the guilt of keeping it. Either way, I lose.

"What have you lost at?" I ask as Sam pulls out of the parking lot.

"I lose at poker with Gramps. Every time."

I smile and decide not to press him.

"So, where to next, my lady, or should I take you home to get your rest?"

"I could really go for some ice cream."

"Spot on. Four Seas it is. What's your favorite flavor?"

"Used to be Rocky Road, but Little Nugget here has been craving Pistachio."

"Little Nugget, huh?" He turns west toward Centerville and I'm glad we're driving to the next town over. I'm glad I get to spend more time with him.

"You think it's stupid I don't want to know if it's a boy or a girl?" That fact might form more of an attachment between me and the child. It might make it all the more real.

"Not at all. But everyone should have a name, even if it resembles something on the McDonald's menu more than a tiny human."

I bump him with my elbow. "What about you? Favorite ice cream?"

"Vanilla."

"You're joking."

"What?"

"I guess I just thought with all your...quirks you'd go for something less ordinary."

"Ouch. I'll have you know vanilla can be downright quirky. Especially with gummy bears on top."

I wrinkle my nose. "You win. Definitely quirky."

He grins. "I *love* winning."

Forty minutes later we walk down a sandy path to Long Beach with our ice cream—his with colored gummy bears on top.

We find a patch of sand and sit. Moonlight splashes down on the waves. They crest to the shore with fierce speed before cowering to a gentle, bubbling whimper. I savor the smooth coldness of my nutty ice cream, breathe in the scent of wet sand and cool salt. "Mmm, that's good ice cream."

We sit for several long moments in silence, but it doesn't feel awkward. Sam rests his forearms on his knees, hangs his ice cream dish over them as if he's taking a break. "Do you miss Maryland?"

What a loaded question. I'm tempted to lie and say "no," but then I wonder if that's really a lie. In the dark, with the waves cocooning our words, it feels safe to be truthful.

"I hated that my parents sent me away. I didn't want to leave my friends, my home. So yeah, I guess I do miss my own room, talking on the telephone to my best friend about everything and anything. The way Mom hums when she's making breakfast. How my dad stands in my bedroom door at night when he's finally come home, even though he thinks I'm asleep." I press my lips together. I still don't believe my parents should have sent me here, but the distance has allowed me to realize that Maryland—even my parents—weren't all bad. "But I love being here too, getting to know Gram. Getting to know you. I don't love school, but in a few days that will be over."

Graduation is next week. The beginning of the rest of my life. Ready or not.

Sam scrapes the bottom of his cup with his plastic spoon. "Will you go back after...?"

"I don't know. I guess it all depends on the baby."

"You'll be a great mother," he says with confidence.

I place my empty ice cream cup in the sand by my side, twisting it so it has an anchor and won't blow away in the breeze. "I don't know that I'm keeping it. My parents have contacted an adoption agency. It's all planned."

He nods. "I don't blame you. Being a parent is hard work."

"You sound as if you have experience."

He snorts. "My dad left when I was too little to remember him. My mom turned to drugs. The state took us away when I was six. Parenting must be hard if grown adults can't find the strength to stay with their own children."

My hackles rise. "It's not that I don't have the strength, I want what's best—"

"Whoa, easy there, Emily. I didn't mean it like that." He places his hand on mine. "What I mean is, it's wrong to call yourself a parent but neglect your kids. That's not you."

I stare at our connected hands, shadows and light in the moonlit sky playing across them. I turn my hand so our palms face one another. The movement becomes ten times more intimate, and he curls his fingers around mine. The gesture pulls at something broken inside of me, threatening to release a deluge of tears. I pull away.

"I—I don't want to hurt you, Sam. I don't want to get hurt. I don't know what September will bring. I might be going to college or figuring out how to be a mother. I don't know."

"I'm not asking for anything, Emily. Just your friendship." He glances down at his empty hands. "As far as the baby...what do *you* want?"

He is the first to ask me that question. No one—not even the adoption specialist we'd been working with. Mom and Dad dove into the adoption process as soon as they found out. It wasn't just that my parents didn't want me and the trouble I brought upon them—they didn't want my opinion on the matter, either.

"I wish I knew," I whispered. What did I want?

The waves are puddles of swirling moonlight, the sky and stars a brilliant backdrop for their dance against a bruised sky.

"Do you believe in God?" I ask.

"I think so. He just seems far away most of the time."

"Gram's telling me this story about when she was younger. It's about my Aunt Atta. She was—" I can't bring myself to finish.

"What?"

I shake my head. "It's not like it matters anymore. But it's a family secret, apparently. One my father never told me."

"And you don't know if you want to share family secrets with a quirky kid like me?"

I smile. "I've had trouble opening up to anyone since..."

"He's not worth thinking about." Sam says under his breath, reading my mind about Bryan. "You told him?"

I nod.

"And he doesn't want in?"

I close my eyes. "No."

"Then he doesn't deserve you." He says it like it's gospel-truth. "So what's the big family secret?"

It doesn't matter, does it? No one around here cares about Maryland elections. Besides, Sam won't tell anyone—I'm sure of it.

"What if I tell you one of my family secrets?" he asks.

I raise my eyebrows. "Besides the one about your parents?"

"Yeah."

"Okay," I agree, taking a deep breath. "But I'll go first. My great-aunt was a leper on Penikese." I exhale, unable to look at him. Sure, leprosy is an age-old disease. Nothing that anyone truly has to worry about today. But it still carries a stigma.

"Oh, wow. *Wow.*"

I've scrunched my shoulders up, trying to hide away like a turtle, neck muscles tight. "I shouldn't have told you. It's horrible, I know."

"Are you kidding? It's amazing. If it were my family, I'd want to know all about it."

I laugh. I like the way he thinks of being a leper as something unique and interesting. "I don't know, but it is quite a story. Unfortunately, I think my father's political career has taken front seat. I think he's ashamed of our family history."

Sam seems to mull over my words.

"Gram's taking me to Penikese at the end of July for a ceremony honoring the doctor who spent most of his life—and his career—ministering to the lepers. She wasn't going to go, but I kind of convinced her to change her mind."

"That's awesome." But Sam's voice sounds far away now, distracted.

"Your turn," I say. "I'm ready for your deep, dark family secret."

"I have a brother. *Had* a brother."

"Oh." It's a pitiful response, but I'm surprised by the word *had.* "Is—was—he older or younger?"

"Older. By three years."

"What happened?"

"You know how I said before that there's only one winner?"

I nod.

"After we went to live with Gramps, Ronny started going downhill. Hanging out with a rough crowd. He got arrested for arson. I think he knew your grandfather, actually. Maybe your grandmother. That's why I looked familiar to her. He was sent to Penikese when he was sixteen."

My breath catches. So Sam knew of Penikese more than he'd let on the day we met.

I remember Gram's words about the small percentage of boys who turned their lives around after Penikese. "Did it help him?"

Sam shakes his head. "Ronny vowed to change his ways. His intentions seemed good for a while. My folks set him up for a part-time job at an auto collision place in New Bedford. On his last night at Penikese, he just couldn't believe life could get better, I guess. He was a failure. Expected to continue being a failure. He hung himself. One of the teachers found him."

My throat clenches and I place my hand on Sam's arm, wanting to soak up his hurt, take it away. "Sam, I'm so sorry."

"So I guess out of me and my brother, I'm the winner. Because I'm at least alive and on track to graduate, you know? But it's funny how many times I feel like the biggest loser in this life."

We're quiet for several moments. It's my turn to say something, but I can't think of anything worth saying. Nothing will bring back Sam's brother. Nothing can reverse the past.

I swallow, grasping for words. Sam deserves so much more than *nothing*. Unlike my situation, he didn't do anything stupid or wrong. It simply...happened.

"It's not your fault. There's nothing you could have done differently."

He looks at me, and his glasses reflect the stars. "Wasn't there? How do you really know, right? Maybe I could have asked him to play baseball with me more or insisted on tagging along with him at night. Maybe having his little brother around would've stopped him from making stupid choices."

"You were a kid, Sam. You weren't responsible for Ronny's decisions."

His Adam's apple bobs, and he nods.

A short time later, he stands and reaches a hand out to me. "Ready?"

I allow him to pull me up. When I stand, his face is so close I can smell the musky scent of him, the faintness of gummies on his breath.

He pushes a strand of hair away from my eyes. "I'm glad you came to Osterville. I'm glad we're friends."

Yet the tangle of emotions coursing through me feel like anything but friendship.

We start for the truck and I want to tell Sam Gram's story. Or, better yet, I want *her* to tell him. Will she allow Sam to join us for the rest of my aunt's story?

Penikese has taken something away from him, too. Is it possible the hope Gram says is there could be something we both could cling to?

Chapter Thirty-Five

1917

Atta hugged herself to ward off the chill of the April evening. She breathed in deeply of the sea air, the hollowness of it vibrating and tightening within her. Unlike the disease lurking within her body, Harry said her lungs would heal with time.

She thought of the Christmas tree, its needles supple and green. It had made it through the winter. Soon Dr. Parker and Willie Goon would plant it outdoors.

Atta leaned against the post of the pavilion and studied the blue sea, smooth as glass. News came yesterday that America was at war. Out past Cuttyhunk, past the vast ocean, battles were fought, lives lost. Yet here on Penikese, with the patients and staff cut off from the rest of the world, the idea of war didn't appear real. In a strange twist, Penikese was a haven of sorts. A place of security.

Except when she was with Harry—then, all refuge vanished. His intensity toward her, his possessiveness, unnerved her. He held feelings for her, that much was clear. But why? How? How could a man who made a god out of success, fall in love with someone who had the potential to ruin his life?

And yet, he'd risked his life for hers. In a sense, she owed him everything. She owed it to him to stay as far away as possible.

Unless...she thought of her clear legs. The spots had vanished in the last few weeks, though she refused to get her hopes up. Any day now, they could creep back as easily as they first appeared.

"Atta! There you are."

She turned to see the object of her thoughts racing down the hill toward her. His face glowed. This must be how he'd looked racing to his father's office with his report card in hand that long ago day. When he reached her, he grasped her elbows and she couldn't help but smile at his good mood. She'd only just seen him for her appointment. What could have possibly happened, unless...

"Your slide. I—I can't believe it myself. But under the scope—there wasn't a bacillus to be found. Not one. It was negative, Atta."

Her hand flew to her mouth. It couldn't be. Impossible. Negative? It couldn't possibly mean... "I'm—I'm not cured, am I?"

Harry gripped her arms tighter and smacked a quick kiss on her forehead. She stood frozen, stunned.

"I want to run a few more tests. Would you come to the exam room with me? Now?"

Of course! But she'd go anywhere with him to unlock the chains that bound her these past ten months. She nodded, and he grasped her hand to drag her up the hill to the hospital. Despite the good news, she wrested her fingers from his. He shouldn't be so unmindful to how such a gesture appeared to anyone watching —especially the Parkers.

They entered Harry's office and he closed the door. "I want to take three more scrapings—one from each lobe of your ear, and another from the region where the marks used to be."

She nodded, and sat on the table, not thrilled to have the scalpel once again turned to her skin, but willing to go through anything for the sake of more negative tests. Obviously eager, he picked up the instrument and made the small cut on her ear. "Did you feel that?"

"Yes."

"A good sign. And now for your leg."

She hiked up her skirts, and while normally Harry looked away or pretended to be busy elsewhere, he forgot his good bedside manners in his excitement. She trembled beneath his scrutiny, but he appeared oblivious, eager to obtain the slide.

"I'd noticed your marks had faded, but I assumed they'd reappear elsewhere as they tend to with Hansen's patients." He made the incisions.

She watched as he heated the slide in order to stain it. She adjusted her petticoats, sending up countless prayers.

"Shall I—shall I wait?"

"If you wish. It will take a half-hour."

She wrung her fingers together, trying not to imagine the possibilities. If she were cured, she'd have to make some decisions. She couldn't live with Papi again. Would the state allow Gertie to come home? Thoughts of Robert with his new wife sitting in a front pew at St. Mary's made her stomach churn.

And then, of course, there was Harry. Her heart ached. What if she never saw him again? The potential problems of a new life circled in her head until she wanted nothing more than to go back to her cottage and bury her head beneath the pillow.

Seconds ticked by. Then minutes.

"Atta?"

Harry gazed at her with those piercing eyes. "They're negative. Every one of them."

"Negative?" she whispered the words. "But how—"

"Maybe the shock of the cold water last month zapped it from your body. Maybe—"

"But then maybe Mary is better too."

He ignored her, walked to where she sat on the exam table, and grasped her hands. He ran his thumbs over the insides of her palms. "I'll need to retest you for the next couple of months, but as of today, as of right now, you no longer have Hansen's."

She stopped herself from throwing her arms around his neck. She was healed, cured. She bowed her head, thanking the Lord for not only healing her heart, but her body as well.

A touch at her cheek interrupted her thanksgiving and she looked up to see Harry closer than he'd stood before, his fingers stroking her cheek. His thigh pressed against her knee. She might have to lie back on the table to save herself from swooning.

"You are so beautiful. Inside and out."

She didn't pull away when his lips brushed lightly over her cheek, then traveled to her ear, his breath plucking warm notes on her skin.

"Atta, I need to tell you something. Something I couldn't tell you before. But now—maybe this is a second chance not only for you, but for me as well."

No, her heart should not leap as it did. Things must remain the way they were, the way they were meant to be. She'd stay here a couple more months, garner the proper amount of negative tests. Then she needed to go home. Find Gertie. She needed to forget the last ten months. She needed to forget Harry Mayhew.

"Atta, I've fallen in love with—"

She scrunched away. "Don't, Harry."

"And why shouldn't I? I've never wanted anything as much as I want you. Even before the negative tests. But now, now there could be a future for us."

He lowered his head to hers, grazed his eager lips against her own trembling ones. She tensed, but couldn't resist for long. Sinking into his embrace, she allowed herself to be carried away on waves of ecstasy, emotions that surpassed anything she'd ever known—being with Robert, even being with God.

She pressed flat palms against his chest, pushing him away. "No."

He grabbed her up again, more forceful this time and for a moment, fear ran tight in her veins. She couldn't trust him, and she couldn't trust herself around him. He pressed his mouth to hers, hunger on his tongue. She allowed herself to taste him for a moment, to satisfy the want that plowed through her, despite the inner battle waging in her spirit.

She forced her lips from his. "No. We can't have a future together, don't you see?"

He backed off, his breaths heavy. He plowed a hand through his blond curls. "No. No I don't see at all. You're cured. No one ever has to know. You can live a normal life. I can take you back to Boston with me, you'll never want for anything." He grasped her hand with his own. "I'll take care of you, Atta."

She tried to picture herself sharing Harry's social circles, living in constant fear that someone would discover her history.

"I don't want to hide myself. I want to show the world what miracles God can do. How He used this to draw me to Him." She ran her fingers over the collar of her shirtwaist. "Harry, people are afraid of this disease because it represents what they are—what we all are—on the inside. Rotting away like the living dead, being eaten alive by misery of our own contriving. If it weren't for the grace of God—"

"God," he sneered. "Maybe God had nothing to do with your cure. Maybe it was all a fluke. Maybe you should spend your time thanking Adskhan for throwing Mary's doll in the ocean. Maybe you should thank *me* for saving you!"

"I am grateful—"

"Then show me. Marry me, Atta."

"What?" She exhaled the word in a short, hard breath over quivering lips.

"My dove, I promise—I promise to care for you forever, to be faithful until the day I die. No matter what."

His words made her dizzy. They were wonderful. Wonderful, but impossible. He didn't understand the things of which she spoke. He didn't understand her. "You'd live in fear that I would tarnish your reputation. And I would live with a man who mocks my faith. I'm too weak. You'd suffocate me, and I'd willingly surrender."

His jaw worked overtime, his anger churning beneath the surface. "So you're choosing an invisible...*being* over me, is that it?"

"Harry, please—"

"People won't understand, Atta. If you're honest with them, they'll shun you. I know, I was one of them."

She swallowed, folded her hands in her lap. "That's a chance I'm willing to take." She looked into eyes that could have swallowed her whole if she let them. "I want to live for God, Harry. I wouldn't be able to do that with you."

He snorted and paced the room. "I can't believe it. I'm being rejected by an outcast."

His hoarse words failed to deliver the sting they intended, for she understood the hurt behind them. She slid off the table, placed a hand on the bare skin of his arm. "I do care for you, Harry." More than he could ever know.

"But you care for God more." His words had lost their fight. She couldn't bring herself to affirm them, unsure if they were true, which scared her all the more.

He cleared his throat. "I have to get over to the administration building. We have a new patient arriving tomorrow. I have to go over some things with Dr. Parker, do some paper—"

"Harry—"

He put a finger to her lips. "Don't. You'll only make it worse." He dropped his hand and opened the door. "I am a fool for falling in love with you, Atta Schaeffer."

And then he was gone, leaving Atta with the all-too poignant memory of his kiss—a kiss that would never again be hers.

ATTA FINISHED the chorus of *Be Thou My Vision* and stood from the small garden plot behind her cottage. She brushed the dirt from her hands and skirt. She'd never been much of a gardener, but this year, the idea of growing something beautiful or good to eat from a tiny seed fascinated her.

Gray clouds loomed upon the horizon. She'd woken with a heavy sense of dread this morning. Not at all how one freed from bondage should feel. In some twisted way, she missed her sickness. Missed the way it brought her to her knees every minute of every day. In her weakness, she knew the strength of her Heavenly Father. Now, He felt farther away, like she'd lost Him. Like she'd lost Harry.

Several forms took shape at the top of the hill. She recognized Harry's and Mrs. Parker's. The third was Dr. Parker, and next to him a smaller form. A child—yes, it had to be a child. The new patient. A child?

A girl from the looks of it. Atta's heart clenched at the thought of a youth being taken away from her family to live with strangers. The poor dear.

As the group drew closer, Dr. Parker pointed at Atta and spoke to the little girl beside him. A little girl who bore a striking resemblance to—

Atta gasped. Her legs gave out and she fell onto the patch of freshly turned earth. No! Her mind screamed along with her heart. Gertie. It couldn't be. Emotion clamped down on her throat, making her breaths come in short gasps. Had she given Gertie the disease? She hadn't been careful enough when she'd escaped, she'd been too careless with her hugs, she hadn't disinfected things properly.

But no. No. It couldn't be Gertie. Just someone who looked like her.

As the group walked closer though, her fears ebbed true. She forced her gaze from the child's face, but it landed on the doll the girl clutched in the crook of her elbow.

Rosie.

Lord, what have I done?

She hadn't the strength to get up, to envelop her sister in her arms as she so wished to do. Outside the garden plot, the four of them stood. Gertie stared at her, face expressionless as stone.

Dr. Parker stepped into the soil and helped Atta stand and walk to Gertie. Atta fell to her knees again, this time to clutch her little sister to her chest. Gertie remained stiff. Didn't bring her small arms around Atta's neck as she used to. Didn't register a smile, a tear, anything.

Atta held her back a space. "Gertie. I'm so sorry, dear. I'm so sorry. But now—now we can be together. And Dr. Parker and Dr. Mayhew are splendid physicians." She looked into Harry's eyes, pleading with him to forget their history for the sake of her little sister. "He'll have you fixed up in no time, dear. And you can tell me all you've been up to and what you've done. How school is."

Gertie stared past Atta's shoulder to the pale blue horizon.

Harry knelt down. "That's right, Gertie. And summer's upon us. Soon you'll be able to go swimming. And fishing, if you like. Have you ever fished before?"

Atta chewed on her bottom lip as the ocean's waves ate up Gertie's silence. Why wouldn't her sister speak?

She stood, holding Gertie to her. "She'll stay with me in my cottage, of course." The strength of her words belied the trembling within.

"Of course, dear," Mrs. Parker said.

Atta inhaled a long breath. Didn't release it. "I want full charge of her. I wish to accompany her to every appointment, every meal, every service and event. No procedure will be done without my approval." She looked at Harry, knowing she exercised rights outside of her authority, but hoping they would agree if for no other reason than to give Gertie security.

"Granted." Dr. Parker nudged his wife.

"Gertie, how would you like to see our amusement room? We

have a Victrola where I can play you music. And some new jigsaw puzzles. Does that sound nice?" Mrs. Parker took Gertie's hand and tugged her gently toward the hospital. The child didn't look back, didn't acknowledge Atta with so much as a glance.

When they were out of earshot, Atta buried her face in her hands. Harry rubbed her arm with awkward movements.

"Why won't she speak? What's happened to her?"

Dr. Parker's expression turned tight, pained. The wrinkles around his eyes plowed deep lines through his ruddy skin. "The family she was placed with last November seemed to have little trouble releasing her once the diagnosis was made."

Atta's insides twisted and churned. Sour bile filled the back of her throat. If only she and Gertie had made it to New York. But then Gertie would still have contracted the disease. Her sister needed a doctor, the very best of medical care. She needed Penikese. She needed Harry.

"I expect time will heal her. Let her know she's loved, Miss Schaeffer. Let her know she's safe, wanted. Have fun with her. Don't make a fuss of her inability to talk. She will come back to you."

Dr. Parker squeezed her elbow, and then set off after his wife.

"Dr. Parker?"

The older man turned.

"Has Dr. Mayhew told you the results of my recent slides?"

"Yes, dear. I'm quite happy for you."

Aside from the fact that she could better care for her sister, the good news meant nothing now.

"If I should collect the appropriate number of negatives over the next couple of months...that is to say, if Gertie is still unwell, would you be able to arrange it so that I may stay here with her?" Unshed tears burned her eyes.

"Of course, Miss Schaeffer. I would see to it myself."

Her jaw quivered. "Thank you."

❧ ❧

THE SCENTS of corn cake and bacon drifted to the breakfast table as Harry sat down for his morning meal. Usually, such a feast would set his mouth watering. Not today.

The sight of Atta's little sister grasping her old rag doll played in his mind's eye like a repetitive moving picture, interrupted only by the look of horror on Atta's face as she realized the identity of the new patient. It left him unable to sleep, unable to eat. Something must be done.

Before yesterday, his thoughts had been consumed with curing Atta, with paving a way for them to be together. Now, they were consumed with Atta's pain—with Gertie's. He'd been foolish to allow himself to get emotionally involved with his patients. It made him weak, unable to serve them in an appropriate manner. He needed to rein himself in, to maintain his status as doctor, not friend.

One of the maids placed the moist yellow cake before him alongside bacon, still dripping with grease. Mrs. Parker and the two nurses were already at the hospital, but Harry and Dr. Parker had slept in.

"I think you should take the day off, Harry. It's Saturday, after all." Dr. Parker took a swig of his coffee and studied him.

Though he normally worked Saturdays, the thought of facing either Atta or her sick little sister threatened to undo him. Maybe for today, he'd stay holed up on his side of the island.

"I might just do that, Dr. Parker."

"Frank."

"Excuse me?"

"You need to call me Frank." Dr. Parker lifted a piece of cake to his mouth and flipped through a newspaper the tugboat had brought the day before with Gertie's arrival.

Dr. Parker skimmed the paper. "General Archibald Murray's been dismissed."

"General...?"

"The commander of the Eastern Expeditionary Force. He was in charge of getting the British into that mess in Gaza last month."

Harry racked his brain for something to contribute to the conversation. "I'm sorry, Dr. Parker. I haven't been attuned to world affairs of late."

Dr. Parker closed his newspaper and looked at Harry above his reading spectacles. "You do know we're at war, don't you, son?"

"Yes, of course."

"I think you've become too involved in your work. It's eating you alive. That's why"—he pulled an envelope from his pocket—"Well, I think this may be a good thing for you."

Harry took the envelope, his insides quaking at the sight of Massachusetts General Hospital's logo on the top left. He ran his fingers over it. "It's addressed to you."

Dr. Parker chewed his bacon with care. "It's concerning you. Seems the hospital wants you back. It appears your father was rather insistent that your time on the island be cut short. Congratulations. You're expected home at the end of the month."

Chapter Thirty-Six

The black pit never left Niklas. After he'd gotten home from prison, it lingered, lucid and alluring. It followed him to work. To the tavern. Home. It gained power after Charles informed him of Gertie's diagnosis.

Where had his girls caught such a foul disease? When had he begun to steer his family wrong?

He had rope in the barn. He'd make a noose, string himself up from the loft. Go on down to the tavern first, get good and drunk. No better way to go.

In a daze, he walked past those no-good Temperance women, singing their lungs out with their no-good hymns—in the rain even. He resisted the urge to spit on their polished shoes as he walked by. He sat at the bar. Called Jimmy over.

Jimmy glanced skittishly from side to side.

"*Ach*, Jim. Still no Weizenbock? How about your next best thing?"

The bar grew quiet. Too quiet. "I'm sorry, Niklas. I don't have anything for you today."

He laughed. "What do ya mean?"

"It—it seems it's in the best interest of my business to stop serving you. Again, I'm real sorry."

Only then did Niklas notice how the men shrank back from him. How even Jimmy kept his distance. Someone from the corner spoke. The dim lighting and crowd obscured Niklas's view. "Rumor has it both your girls are at Penikese. They're lepers. That story you tell us about your oldest sent away with TB was just a hoax. We don't want to be drinkin' with no leper. Much less a German-lovin' one."

Niklas stood, anger rippling through each cord of muscle in his body. "I am an American! *Jah*, that should mean something. But it doesn't." He pounded the bar with his fist. "I've half a mind to go back to Germany, take up arms, and fight against you imbeciles." He was losing control, felt as if he'd already had several drinks. If he would end his life tonight, why not let loose all his anger before he died?

"America—America is a joke. It takes everything. My Katharina. My girls. Then it belches out half-wits like all of you. Well, I'll tell you what, I hope—no, I pray—Germany whips your *Leider Hintern* from here to Hamburg!"

He shoved his hat on his head, caught sight of that hoity-toity Temperance woman peering at him with her pert little nose pressed against the window, and shoved open the door. He ran straight into a sheriff's big-barreled chest. It wasn't Charles.

Cold, familiar cuffs clasped around his wrists. "Mr. Schaeffer, is it? You're under arrest, sir. This will be easier for both of us if you cooperate."

"Arrested?" Niklas let a German curse tear through the air. "For what?"

"Treason."

ATTA BRUSHED Gertie's long blonde hair until it gleamed. Then she separated it into three sections to braid. "It's warm today. I've been looking forward to spring all winter. These cottages are so drafty I had to put on three layers of socks and close to five quilts to keep warm."

Gertie sat as motionless as a rag doll. Atta worried her bottom lip between her teeth. Perhaps she'd veered the conversation in the wrong direction.

She tried again. "Would you like to help me in the garden after breakfast? The flies are a nuisance, but I've learned to get along with them. And in a few months' time, we'll be eating our own tomatoes. We can make sauce, like we used to." Her voice sounded forced, fake. "And later we can go down to the beach and look for sea glass. I love to imagine where they've all come from. Milk of magnesia bottles, bits of crockery and cobalt, perhaps some as far away as England. We can make up stories and tell them to each other."

Except it would only be Atta telling them. And Gertie listening. Or not listening. Lately, Atta questioned if her sister even knew who she was. Would she become as disturbed as Mary at such a young age? She shivered, grabbing a blue ribbon to tie in Gertie's hair.

She spun her sister around, looked deep into her hollow eyes. "I love you, Gertrude Schaeffer. I am so, so sorry for all you've gone through. I wish I had the power to prevent all of this. But we're together now, Gertie. All I can do is promise to take care of you from this day on."

For a moment, Gertie's gaze flickered. Then, like the foam in a wave after it crashes, the vacant hollowness returned. Atta drew Gertie closer. Her sister flinched, but Atta held her tight and began singing *Schlaf, Kindlein schlaf.* When she'd exhausted that, she turned to *Jesus Loves Me.*

She didn't stop singing for a long time, hoping the words and her voice, would pry open the lock on Gertie's heart. When she finally separated from Gertie, the front of her shirt clung to her with wetness.

And while her sister's gaze showed no spark, her tears indicated that her heart was still very much alive.

"THERE. THAT SHOULD DO IT." Harry brushed his hands of dirt and watched Gertie pour a small bucketful of water around the base of the pine tree. When she finished, he tugged her braid. "You can decide where we plant the next tree. Sound good, Gertie?"

The little girl blinked and swiped at a fly buzzing around her golden head. Was that a nod?

"That would be lovely, Dr. Mayhew. Thank you." Atta stepped back from the tree to admire it. "It's perfect."

"I'd say it is, Miss Schaeffer." Her gaze flickered to his. Did she dislike the formality? Yet, it was appropriate. Now, more than ever. "I'm looking forward to our appointment later. I hope to discuss Gertie's treatment with you."

"Yes. We'll see you later, then. Thank you." She looked behind his shoulder. "I think Mrs. Parker is hoping to catch your attention."

He turned to see Mrs. Parker waving a hand at him at the top of the hill, where the barbed wire separated one side of the island from the other. "I guess I better be going. Would you mind bringing some of the sea glass you collected the other day to your appointment, Gertie? We can look at it under my microscope."

Gertie's expression remained blank, but Atta's warmed. "Thank you, Harry," she whispered, squeezing his arm.

He tried not to thrill at the sound of his name upon her lips, at the tender touch she bestowed on him. Her second batch of tests had again returned negative. A future for them was possible. He couldn't relinquish the idea.

Turning, he jogged to the top of the hill, where three figures stood. His heart pounded against his chest with the force of a wave crashing on the rocks. What in tarnation was Father doing here? And for heaven's sake, why did he think it suitable to bring Carrie along?

"HARRY, DARLING." Carrie surprised him by rushing into his arms and placing a warm kiss on his cheek. "Father and I have been ever so worried about you!"

Father? Oh, his father. Yes, but she'd barely written to him over the winter.

"Father. Good to see you, sir." He cleared his throat, conscious of the dirt on his hands. He looked toward the hospital, where Gertie and Atta admired the tree. Atta placed an arm around Gertie's shoulders, spoke something to her.

Carrie let out a small cough. "This island is absolutely darling, isn't it, Father?" she gushed. "No wonder Harry wishes to stay. I'm tempted to vacation here myself."

Mrs. Parker cleared her throat. "Perhaps a spot of tea, Miss Gerard? I'm sure Harry and his father have a bit of catching up to do."

Carrie looked annoyed, but she agreed. "And after you're done with him, Father, I would like to do some catching up as well." Without a hint of shame, she winked at Harry and flounced down the hill after Mrs. Parker.

The two men stood silent, unmoving. Finally, Harry's father dragged in a long breath, pulling himself up to his full height—three inches over six feet—an inch taller than Harry. "I've come to talk some sense into you, Harry."

"Father, we agreed at the start that I would serve out my time and regain my reputation. I am only honoring my commitments." No need to delve further into explanations than necessary. How

Dr. and Mrs. Parker, the nurses, the patients, Atta—how they were all more family to him than his father had ever been.

"I've gone through a lot of trouble to save your skin, Harry. The least you can do is—"

"Why the change of heart? And why bring Carrie along? How did you ever get her to agree to the trip? Last time I saw her, she vowed to have nothing to do with me if I came to Penikese. Now you both come?"

"I simply explained to her that it was perfectly safe as long as she had no direct contact with the patients—which she won't." His father clasped his hands behind his back, stood on the balls of his feet and then rolled down, the soft earth molding to his polished shoes. "Carrie's mother had a stroke."

Oh, man. "How bad?"

"Bad."

He gazed down the hill toward the administration building. Carrie must be devastated. And yet, he'd not have known it from her performance earlier. Trained to play the part—whichever part suited her needs best. Atta had once accused him of doing the same. And she'd been right. But somewhere along the way, the performance had melded with reality. His heart had changed.

"I'm sorry for her, I am. But what does this have to do with me?"

"I misdiagnosed Mrs. Gerard's symptoms. Carrie's father is threatening me with a lawsuit. Malpractice, of all the ridiculous hogwash. Blackmailing me, of all people."

"Blackmailing?"

"He wants you to wed Carrie. He's always wanted to have a part of our name, our family. Our social standing. Now he's found his chance."

Harry shook his head. "That's ludicrous. You did nothing wrong." But as he spoke, he remembered the patient his father had operated on all those years ago. In his office. The one whose blood lay on eight-year-old Harry's hands. Had it been Harry's fault or his father's? Could he have laid the blame on his son to avoid the repercussions? "Father?"

"Of course I've done nothing wrong!"

"Then we don't need to succumb to Mr. Gerard's wishes, do we?"

"It's not as simple as all that. Finer doctors than I have been ruined by illegitimate claims." His eyes grew dark beneath the shade of his Panama hat.

"So you want me to flee my obligations here—my patients—to rush home and wed Carrie?"

Father expelled a blast of breath. "Yes. I thought you'd be happy to get off this cursed piece of land, get back to Mass General."

"No. I won't do it."

"Excuse me? Boy, I think you've forgotten who you're talking to."

"I'm not forgetting, sir. I simply won't do it."

The elder Mayhew took off his hat and crumpled it in his hands—a desperate gesture full of frustration. A gesture Harry had never seen. "Fine. We'll wait until July. You can fulfill your commitment, then come home. Your mother has always been fond of summer weddings."

Harry pressed his fingers against his tense right shoulder. His forthcoming words wouldn't make things easier. "I don't wish to take Carrie for a wife. Even to save you, Father."

His father's face turned red. "It's not a matter of what you want, boy. It's a matter of our family's honor."

Honor. Looking at his father now, at the man whose approval he'd tried so hard to earn all these years, he couldn't dredge up a speck of admiration. What honor was there in bending to blackmail? Especially one that had no grounds.

"I won't marry her, Father."

"You must. She's everything a wife should be. Attractive, well-bred. She takes part in all the proper social clubs. Her family's wealth is not something to dismiss so quickly."

Harry had once thought like that. The fact disgusted him.

"I've already decided what I'll do after my time here is through. I intend to continue on if Dr. Parker agrees. The work here —"

"You will do no such thing!"

The fact that he was able to stay calm in the face of his father's wrath empowered Harry. "I may have cured a patient, Father." He inwardly winced at the credit he gave himself, but in a sense it was true. Atta had become well under his care. He could rightfully take recognition for the accomplishment. "I want to continue my research."

"Then do it at Harvard. I'll speak with Dr. Bradford myself. I'm certain he'll comply. You can't remain here. You'll be soiled, ruined. The hospital won't want you. Just look at how they shun Parker when he visits the mainland. Why do you think he vacations so little? There's nothing left for him back home."

Was that true? Quite possibly—Dr. Parker had been shunned from society. No American wished to be treated by a doctor who had come into contact with lepers. A doctor like himself. And yet, Harry couldn't shake the notion that Dr. Parker possessed ten times more honor than the man standing before him.

He shook his head. "I will remain here." He braced himself for the crashing wave of ire to wash over him. It didn't.

Instead, his father studied him, a sardonic grin inching up the corners of his mustached mouth. "Who is she, son? A nurse here perhaps? A maid? None the matter. We'll take her with us. You can carry on with her after the wedding. All involved parties will be happy."

Harry's ears rang. He grasped for something suitable to say, but the ability to construct sentences fled.

"Now, don't look at me like that. You're a man. Start acting like one. It's done quite often, really."

Harry's stomach churned. He shared the same blood as this

man. And the frightening part was he wouldn't have scorned the idea a year ago. Before Penikese. Before Atta.

He clenched his fists. "And is that the honor you wish for our family? Is that the honorable way in which you've treated Mother?"

"Leave her out of this," Father growled. "I've never been unfaithful to your mother. Although if I'd taken up a mistress, that may have increased my chances of having at least one decent son."

The words didn't hit as hard as they should have. Instead, in them, Harry found the power to utter his final decision.

"I have no desire to save your *honor*, Father. As I said before, I will continue my work here."

HARRY WOKE to a soft knock on his bedroom door. Maybe he'd imagined it—his sleep had been fitful. Flashbacks of his conversation with his father. Of a tense dinner with Carrie and the Parkers—one for which he had rescheduled his appointments.

Was abandoning his family his only alternative? And yet, why was Carrie determined to marry him, anyhow? Why had she risked herself to come to the island?

The knock came again, followed by his creaking door. He couldn't see a blasted thing. "Who's there?"

No answer, but he knew by the tantalizing scent of jasmine and gardenias. She moved aside the covers and he couldn't voice the order for her to leave.

But nothing good could come from her presence. Still, his mouth froze—weak as he was—when Carrie slid in beside him, her warm, soft body scantily clad, her curves soon pressed against him. She found his mouth and against every logical thought, he responded to it. Her hands roamed his body with freedom. Boldness. Possessiveness. Every inch of him came alive with fire as he melted into her tempting presence.

It annoyed him when Atta's face flew into his thoughts. She had rejected him. Even when a plausible future lay before them, she hadn't wanted him. He had told himself that no good could come from Carrie's presence, but already she created ecstasy within him simply by being here.

But the reason she was here hit him hard. He'd have to marry her after this. He'd have no choice but to leave the island, make an honest woman of her. Especially if a child were conceived. He'd never work with the patients here again. Never have the opportunity to help little Gertie. Never see Atta.

Before he could change his mind, he leapt from the bed, paced the chilly room to expel the passion tingling within. "Leave."

The springs in the bed creaked, but he didn't hear the door open. Instead, he sensed her presence closer, the heat radiating from her body onto his.

"Who is she, Harry? Your father told me about her, you know." She tasted his lips with her own. Trailed his face and neck with her mouth. "Whoever she is, she doesn't know you like I do. Can she please you like this, Harry?"

Carrie's hands once again possessed his body, ruling his skin. His flesh warred against his mind, and for a moment he thought his senses would lose. *God help me.*

The prayer, however short, was heartfelt, and in the next moment he pushed Carrie away. She fell on the bed. Sobs echoed in the darkness. "I thought you loved me. Harry, I didn't realize it until you were gone, but I love you. I love you so much. I miss you so much."

He gritted his teeth. Could this possibly be the reason for all her trouble to come here? Had she convinced her father to finagle a marriage? Did it all stem from a warped view of love?

She sniffed. "You'll never get a decent wife after working here, you know. You should be the one begging *me* to take you back."

As the words rolled off her tongue, his resolve deepened, his body cooling with each syllable. This was not the woman he wished to spend his life with. Even if it meant saving his family.

"Leave, Carrie. Now. Or I'll have Dr. Parker escort you to the other side of the island for the night."

He meant it, and she must have sensed it, for she scurried off the bed and out of the room, the scent of gardenias on her heels. Harry lay back in bed. It was still warm from their bodies. He threw the covers off and searched for the clothes he'd worn the night before.

He'd take a walk. Maybe end up at the lab. He had more important things to think about than Carrie's hands upon his skin.

Chapter Thirty-Seven

"But are you certain this is the best course of action?" Atta placed her fingers on Gertie's shoulders, wanting to protect her from all of this. The island, the hospital, the exam room. Harry.

He rubbed his eyes—eyes that lacked their usual fire. "No. I'm not certain, Atta. All I have to go on is guesses—is that what you want to hear?"

"Hush." She glared at him, jerking her head toward her sister. "Gertie, why don't you go outside and water the pine tree. It looked a bit droopy this morning."

Gertie nodded and left the exam room, sending Harry a wide-eyed glance before she left.

The room grew quiet, the calling of a seagull annoying outside the window. "You must be careful what you say around her. I'd appreciate it if you exuded more confidence in her presence."

His jaw tightened. "I thought you wished for my honesty."

"Of course I do. But I don't want Gertie to feel like—like one of your experimental mice."

"I'm doing my best, Atta. Truthfully, I don't know the best course of treatment. Something cured you. Maybe the cold annihilated the bacillus. It stands to reason it may work for Gertie, too. Your cases are mirror images. The others may be too far advanced in their illness." He walked to the window, waved his arms at the squawking seagull. It flew off toward the beach. "Winter's grip doesn't release this island easily. Still, if we wait much longer it may not have the desired effect."

"First you want to heat the disease. Now you want to freeze it." Her tone came out harsher than she intended. "What are the risks?"

"None too great. She's a healthy girl overall. We'll have to watch her carefully for signs of pneumonia. I'd say that's my biggest concern."

Atta put her palm to her forehead. Pneumonia. People died from pneumonia. "She could live a long time with the disease, couldn't she?"

Harry nodded. "Years. But she'd be here. No one her age. No real life. Her best chance of combating the disease is now, in its early stages."

"Are you working on any other...alternatives?"

He looked at his desk, at a stack of journals that looked as foreign to Atta as some of the patients first had to her. "There's a diphtheria toxin out that's fairly new. It's had good results. I'd love to see if the Hansen bacillus would respond to it. But not with Gertie. I was leaning toward asking Adskhan."

"I take it the idea doesn't hold much promise if you're willing to sacrifice your least pleasant patient."

For a moment his eyes lit up. Butterfly wings fluttered in her stomach at the sight of those piercing blue orbs.

"In fact, I believe it holds much promise." His gaze darkened again. "But as I said before, I'm uncertain about any experiment and I'm unwilling to try such a drastic one on a seven-year-old girl."

"What do you think we should do, Harry?" No doubt, he saw her fear, saw her heart, how dread had overtaken her faith.

She didn't resist when he squeezed her hand. "I think we should try the cold water."

"Fine, then. But I wish to go in with her."

"That's not necessary, Atta. I intend to accompany her. Your condition may still be weakened by the slightest—"

"We do it my way or we don't do it at all." She lifted her chin.

His shoulders slumped. "Fine then. But I would pray to that God of yours that all will go well."

"I plan to." She turned to leave but couldn't resist a look back at him. His head drooped, his eyes closed. How different was this posture than the arrogant, self-assured stance of that long-ago first appointment. She much preferred this Harry—the one who had every patient's best at heart.

"Harry?"

When he looked at her, those blue pools seemed to be in another world.

"Do you think I—do you think I gave it to her?"

Pure sympathy bathed his face. "No. I don't. Likely you were both infected at the same time. It could have been years ago."

She took comfort in his words, though she assumed he'd hide the truth to protect her.

"Would you pray for Gertie?"

His shoulders slumped farther, as if she'd asked him to bear the weight of the world on them.

"Yes. I'll pray for her."

GERTIE STEPPED INTO THE SEAWATER, its chill biting at her ankles, her feet slippery against the algae-covered rocks. Atta had explained why she must do this, but Gertie didn't know if she trusted Atta.

Atta had left her.

Atta had promised to come back.

Atta was the reason she'd been alone with Papi.

Atta was the reason Mother and Father abandoned her to the health man.

Atta shouldn't have left. She should have fought harder.

Gertie squeezed her eyes shut and clung tight to Dr. Mayhew's hand. Atta held snug to her other one. Their petticoats swirled around them and Gertie imagined a fish with large biting jaws swimming beneath her and nipping at her legs. She wanted to tell Atta and Dr. Mayhew that she didn't want to do this, but then she'd have to talk. They would ask her about Mother and Father. About her life with her new parents. About how they mustn't have wanted her that badly to let the health man take her away without a fight.

She gasped when the water reached her belly, biting her skin.

The group of patients standing at the shore cheered her on. Even Miss Mary and Missy. Gertie liked Miss Mary. She and Gertie and Rosie and Missy often had pretend tea parties together. At first, Miss Mary's hands scared her. But when she saw how Miss Mary's ugly hands could tend to her doll, they didn't seem so scary anymore. None of the patients seemed as scary as they first did. They were all just people, like her. People with big boo-boos that Dr. Mayhew was trying to fix.

"There now, you're doing right fine," Dr. Mayhew said. He smiled at her and she decided then that she liked him. He had shiny blue jewels for eyes, like Robert. Like Kat. Where was her friend now? Had she gone back to England? Wherever she was, Gertie missed her.

Gertie's breathing quickened when the water came up to her chest. It reached Atta's waist and the top of Dr. Mayhew's legs.

"Tha' doin' right fine."

Gertie wasn't sure when Kat appeared beside her, but she chose not to acknowledge her presence. George had told her she was imaginary. Was he right? Neither Atta nor Dr. Mayhew seemed to notice the pretty dark-haired girl with the accent.

Gertie blinked, but still saw Kat's dark hair out of the corner of her eye. Maybe she *was* loony. Maybe that was why Mother and Father hadn't fought the health man when he said he had to take her away.

She remembered Mother's silent tears and trembling hands as she handed the health man Gertie's suitcase. She had tried to hug Gertie, but Father held her back with strong arms and persistent, whispered pleas.

"It's so cold," Atta said, teeth chattering. Her gaze fell on Gertie, as if she were a poor bird with a broken wing.

Gertie pulled her hand away from her sister.

"The colder the better," Dr. Mayhew said.

Dr. Mayhew believes this will make you better, Gertie. There's a little thing inside of you that isn't good for your body. It used to live in me, too. But I went in the cold water, and now I'm better. Do you think you can be brave enough to get better?

Gertie had nodded because she knew it was what Atta expected. Now though, she was scared. Her breaths came faster and faster. She clung to Dr. Mayhew's warm hand.

"Now, I want you to hold your nose and close your mouth, Gertie. Pretend you're a fish and dunk yourself under the water. Stay under as long as you can and then come up for a nice breath of air. We'll do that ten times. Does that sound all right?"

Gertie wondered if pretending she was a fish was an important part of getting better. She'd never much liked fish. But she nodded, pinched her nose, and slid beneath the water. Dr. Mayhew's big, strong hand held her arm, and she was glad.

The cold rushed beneath her hair and in her ears. She imagined a hungry fish swimming up to her face and biting off her nose. She clutched Dr. Mayhew's hand tighter as she began to shiver, sure she'd never been so cold in her life—even when there was no fire back at Papi's house. She held her breath as long as she could before popping up into the sunshine.

"That was magnificent, Gertie. When you've caught your breath, we'll do it again."

She filled her lungs with air as quickly as she could in order to get out of the water and into some dry clothes. She still closed her eyes, but this time she pretended she was a fish and another friendly fish came to talk to her and ask if she wanted to play. Eight more times she played with the fish. They jumped above the water and splashed down. They wiggled their bodies to race around the island. They visited the other side of the island, where Gertie wasn't supposed to go.

When Atta and Dr. Mayhew helped her to shore, she trembled so violently she couldn't keep her fingers around either of their hands. Her breaths sounded as if air bubbles were in her chest.

In the hospital, Atta helped her into dry clothes before tending to herself. Though her body still trembled, with dry clothes and having been tucked beneath layers of blankets beside the wood-stove, she felt snug and cozy.

When Atta left to change, Mrs. Parker walked in with a big black book. "Would you like me to read you a story, dear?"

Gertie nodded, sinking deeper into the blankets. As Mrs. Parker began to read a story about a man named Jonah, Gertie listened to the older lady's soft voice. It sounded like a set of jingle bells during Christmas. Like how a grandmother's voice should sound. Yes, if Gertie had a grandmother, she'd want one like Mrs. Parker.

The woman read of Jonah and how he ran away from God. How God saved him by allowing a big fish to swallow him up. How he stayed in the fish's belly for three days and three nights. How God gave him a second chance, but Jonah stayed angry even though God helped him.

Gertie listened with careful ears. She was glad Mrs. Parker hadn't told her the story before she had to go under the water. She might have had trouble pretending she were a fish if she was scared a bigger fish would swallow her up.

Mrs. Parker closed the big book. "Did you like that story?"

Gertie smiled.

"Good. I like it too. It reminds me that sometimes God sends us places we don't want to go. But in the end, He always has our good at heart."

Gertie wanted to tell Mrs. Parker that she wasn't sure if God had *her* good at heart. If He did, why did Papi hate her? Why did the health man take her away from Mother?

"I like to think of the fish that swallowed Jonah as a type of hospital for Jonah's soul. Like God sent you and Atta to this hospital to help you."

Quiet filled the room.

"Atta didn't want to leave you, Gertie. You know that, don't you?"

Gertie pressed her lips together real tight to keep the tears from spilling.

"She had no choice, dear. They made her leave. You should have seen how she worried over you."

Gertie studied the flames in the belly of the woodstove. They blurred in front of her eyes.

"I can say for certain she loves you more than anything in the world. You know, I had a sister once. A long, long time ago. She took ill when I was about your age. Went to be in heaven. I always thought one of the greatest presents God can give a girl is a sister. I still believe that."

They sat quiet and Mrs. Parker handed Gertie a hankie to dry her eyes.

"I'll warrant Mrs. Parker has a passel o' grandchildren." Kat sat on the edge of her bed.

Gertie blinked. Mrs. Parker didn't respond to her friend and Gertie faced the terrible truth that Kat wasn't real at all. The sorrow was too big, and she grasped at anything—even talking—to snuff out the loneliness.

"Do you have grandkids, Mrs. Parker?" Her voice sounded funny from not being used.

Mrs. Parker sat up straighter, her mouth turned into a perfect *O*. Then she smiled. A big one. "Not yet, my dear. But I hope to soon. One of my sons is planning a wedding."

"You'd make a good Grandma."

"Thank you. That means a lot coming from a sweet little girl like you." Mrs. Parker stood and tucked the blankets tight around Gertie like Atta used to do at night. "Oh, you almost forgot someone very important." Mrs. Parker held up Rosie. "I'll stick her right here to keep you company."

"Thank you." Gertie closed her heavy eyes as Mrs. Parker brushed damp hair from her face. When Atta came back, Gertie was in that funny place between sleep and awake. Mrs. Parker and Atta spoke in quiet voices outside her room. Then her sister walked in, the bed shifting when she sat on it.

She planted a kiss on Gertie's forehead and stroked her hair. "I love you, Gertie."

Gertie's eyelids fluttered open. "I love you too, Atta. I'm sorry I was angry at you. I know you didn't want to go away. Like Jonah. He didn't want to go to Nineveh, either."

Her sister raised a shaky hand to her mouth. Her eyes looked wetter than Gertie had ever seen them. "That's right, dear. He didn't."

"Mrs. Parker said the big fish was a hospital for Jonah. It's how he got saved. Maybe this is the place God will save us, too. Do you think He will?"

Atta's eyes darted around the room faster than a kitten chasing a toad. "He will take care of us forever, that I'm sure of."

Gertie drifted off to sleep, not sure if she liked Atta's answer. She supposed it was good to have God take care of you, but why hadn't Atta told her everything would be all right?

Chapter Thirty-Eight

The deep, hollow echo of a bugle woke Niklas from a bottomless sleep. He rolled over on the top bunk and smashed the flat pillow to his ears, trying to block out the sound, trying to forget his new home.

An internment camp. Fort Oglethorpe, Georgia. Hundreds of miles from Massachusetts.

After two months in prison, he'd been sent to Georgia after the government passed some sort of high-falutin' Espionage Act. A spy of all things! Him, who made an honest day's pay as a silversmith. Him, who'd wanted peace for as long as he could remember. He'd come to America to find it. Could still remember the smoothness of Katharina's hand in his as they stood beneath the sails of the great ship that would take them to freedom. He'd whispered promises in her ear. Promises that never materialized.

Maybe he *should* have become a German spy. His home country had been ten times more loyal to him than America, who, like a thief in the night, had snatched away all that was precious to him.

Charles warned him to be on his best behavior, admitted he was probably being sent away not just for his careless words in the tavern, but because the county was scared of him. If both his daughters had contracted leprosy, they worried Niklas might contaminate the town.

The bugle wound down its tune, and groans sounded from the length of the barracks. He'd been one of the first inmates here, along with another few hundred. He avoided the other men but listened to his home tongue eagerly when they spoke to one another.

Pushing himself up, Niklas let his legs dangle over the sides of the bed. A German curse lit the air as he struck his bunkmate with his heel.

"*Traurig.*" Niklas lifted his feet and set to work making his bed, readying the area for inspection and then roll call before breakfast. When he lifted his pillow, he saw the scrap of paper. The one Charles had given him with the name of that doctor from Penikese.

Harry Mayhew. Did Dr. Mayhew treat his daughters with care? How did one go about treating leprosy in the first place?

With all their circumstances so bleak, he found himself bonded to his daughters in an unusual way. He wouldn't write them, of course. Not after all this time of silence. But he could write their doctor. They would be none the wiser, and he could satisfy the need to know how well—or poorly—his daughters fared.

FEAR STITCHED tiny holes across Atta's heart as she listened to Dr. Parker's words, her worst terror realized.

"It's not a death sentence, dear, so don't look like that. There are simple treatments for pneumonia."

Harry didn't look so confident.

"And—and the disease? What did her latest test show, Dr. Mayhew?" Would Gertie's body be able to fight both Hansen's and pneumonia?

"The bacillus is still present, I'm afraid. More than last time. I'm so sorry, Atta."

So his theory had been wrong. Again. As much as she tried not to cast blame, her emotions sought a place for release, a victim. "We should have never done it. I shouldn't have listened to you."

Dr. Parker lifted a hand to the cotton fabric at her elbow. "Dear, you mustn't blame Dr. Mayhew. He outlined his plan to me before going ahead with the experiment. I agreed that the cold water treatment was a sound theory. Unfortunately, we never can tell. Not with Hansen's."

Atta's lower lip trembled. "And now Gertie will be the one to pay for your research, is that it? All for the sake of medicine! But let me tell you right now, your medicine can't have her. I won't let it. From now on, I will care for Gertie. You—you both stay away from her!" She fled the room, her world falling apart. Again. And she couldn't pretend she wasn't partly to blame.

She could imagine how Dr. Parker and Harry viewed her. Broken Atta. Crazy Atta. The faith she'd clung to so tenaciously the last several months was nothing but a farce. Where was her belief now when she needed it? Would she only trust God as long as Gertie was safe, but grab back the reins of control when her sister was in harm's way? Gertie...the most precious piece of Atta's existence. How could she let anything happen to her sister?

Atta crept past Gertie's hospital room, seeking the solace of her cottage. There, she grabbed her Bible—the one Reverend Bailey had given to her—and lay on her bed. She closed her eyes and allowed the familiar lap of waves to flow through her. Ever-constant. Never-changing. Their presence had come to be one of comfort.

She flipped to Proverbs three, to a verse the Reverend had often quoted to her. "Trust in the Lord with all thine heart: and lean not unto thine own understanding. In all thy ways acknowledge him, and he shall direct thy paths." She said the verse aloud, drawing what peace she could from each syllable, each word, each sentence.

Sliding off her bed, she knelt and prayed that God would go with her into the belly of the fish.

"THEY'VE CHANGED." Harry squinted at the spots upon Atta's thigh. His mouth tightened. The marks had almost disappeared with her negative tests. Now though, they were noticeably darker and more numerous than last month. "Why didn't you tell me?"

"And what would you have done? I knew you'd see for yourself soon enough."

"When did you notice the change?" Harry made a small incision with his scalpel, trying to keep a steady hand. Dreading what his microscope would tell him.

"A few days after Dr. Parker diagnosed Gertie with pneumonia."

Another heavy weight pressed upon his chest at the notion of the little girl suffering because of him. Maybe Father had been right. He wasn't cut out for such a life. Much easier to treat patients back in Boston. Where he possessed the knowledge to save an individual and could swoop in to treat them appropriately. Here, his identity was one marked by helplessness and incompetence.

While Atta adjusted her skirts, he trudged to his microscope. Took his time heating the smear with carbol fuchsin before sliding it beneath the telling machine. He peered into it. As he feared, the enemy jumped out at him. Pink and rod-like. He hated the way it moved along the smear, hated the way it once more possessed Atta's body. He sat at the microscope longer than necessary, knowing that once he lifted his head he'd have to report the bad news.

"It's positive, isn't it, Harry?"

For once, he wished she'd called him by his professional name. The way she said his Christian name threatened to break his heart in half. He moved back from the microscope, leaned his elbows on widespread legs, and put his head in his hands. "I'm so sorry. I—I wonder if it ever truly left your body. I should have waited longer before recommending the cold water treatment to Gertie."

When he looked up, her chest rose and fell with measured precision. She sat straighter. "I wish to try the diphtheria toxin you spoke of earlier. Would that be possible?"

He blinked, fast. "No. No, it would not be possible, for I refuse to administer it. There's too much at risk, too much I don't know. You've seen how well my theories have worked so far. I don't trust myself anymore, Atta, don't you see?"

"Please. Let me try."

He ignored her words, slammed his fist on the desk beside his microscope. "If only the blasted mice would take to the disease." How much easier to risk a mouse's life.

"Dr. Parker says Gertie is making small improvements. It's a miracle, really. She's no longer spitting up that horrid rust-colored stuff. Her night sweats have decreased. She's out of the pneumonia jacket. If—if she recovers, I want you to treat her for Hansen's."

So that was it. She wished to be the experimental mouse for the sake of her sister. He should have guessed her motivation would have nothing to do with herself.

"No. I cannot recommend the toxin for you or any of my patients."

She hopped off the exam table. "What happened to the doctor I met when I first came here? The man who would risk anything for the sake of medicine?"

"Everything's changed. I've changed." He thought that had been a good thing. Maybe though, he'd lost one of the attributes that made him a good doctor. His edge. But being on this island, sharing meals and services with these people, it made him realize who they were—hurting people. All of them. Willie Goon, with his boundless optimism and good-natured jokes. Mary, with her tenacity in caring for the doll she believed her daughter. Atta, who had completely and wholly captured his heart—the woman he'd come to love.

Atta's life was in his hands. Again.

He didn't want the responsibility, not when chance stood that the bacteria would inhabit her body forever, that she would likely suffer for the remainder of her days.

He wanted to run. To leave the island, forget everyone on it. Go back to his safe life in Boston. Forget Gertie, forget the Parkers, forget Atta.

If it didn't mean leaving half his heart on the island, he might do just that.

Chapter Thirty-Nine

"Atta? What's wrong?"

Atta stared in horror at her sister's legs, hidden from Gertie's view beneath the sheets. Like unyielding metal cloaking her heart, the sudden doom dragged her soul to dark depths.

When one of Gertie's toes had turned a deep purple a week earlier, she thought it due to inactivity as her sister recovered from the pneumonia. Light violet spots on her ankles had appeared two days earlier.

And then, this morning.

Deep purple sores sprouted the length of her sister's tiny legs. One looked as if it would break down into the dreaded ulcers she saw in the other patients.

She tucked the blankets around Gertie. "Nothing, dear. You get some more rest and I'll ask Nurse Edith to bring you your breakfast."

She hurried away, but not to find a nurse.

She ran outside into the warm air and down to the rocky beach, where she sank onto a flat rock. Waves lapped at her feet, the ebb and flow of them numbing her to reality. All she could dredge from the depths of her despair was prayer. Jonah's prayer.

"'Out of the belly of hell cried I, and thou heardest my voice.' God, hear me!"

Did He? She'd been so sure of His love this past winter, so sure He had not cursed her as she first thought. Now, though...

She recited the remainder of the prayer, resting in the swell and recession of the verses. Her agony, God's response. Her distress, God's deliverance. Until finally, the last verse.

"Salvation is of the Lord."

He was her only hope. Even her own weak faith, her own fragile trust wouldn't carry her through. But He would.

Atta stood and shut her eyes tight to quell the burning. She must find Harry.

HARRY PRESSED his tongue against closed teeth to keep his frustration in check.

"I'm sicker, aren't I, Dr. Mayhew?"

"We've hit a small bump in the road, Miss Gertie. Nothing we haven't faced before, eh?" He patted her arm and looked up. "Ah, I think Nurse Edith has a real treat for you today. French toast. Eat up so you have energy to beat me in checkers again later. How does that sound?"

Gertie smiled, accepting the tray of food the nurse put before her.

"Edith, please don't bring Mr. Ali in yet." Hamed Ali. A new patient. Another hurting man that Harry hadn't a clue how to help.

Atta kissed Gertie on the forehead before following him to the exam room. He shut the door.

"It is the Hansen's. The pneumonia must have weakened her resistance. I am so sorry, Atta." He was like a broken gramophone.

He was tired of apologizing, tired of his inadequacy. If only he could do something! But while a dozen possibilities of experimentation lay before him, each held its own dangers.

"We mustn't sit idle when something can be done." Atta's fingers fluttered over the skirt of her dress, worn from wear and the salty air.

"I don't know of anything that can be done."

"Is there not a possibility the toxin will work?"

"Of course it's a possibility. Probability is another matter."

She stepped forward, placed a hand on his arm. "You're aware that my own condition is worsening."

Yes. The red marks on her legs had increased, spreading out in both directions to the rest of her body.

"I want to save you so badly," he whispered.

Her fingers tightened on his arm. "Please, Harry."

"You're willing to throw yourself into an experiment that I can't guarantee in the slightest?"

"If it means the possibility of healing Gertie, also. Then yes."

"I've asked both Willie and Toy if they'd be willing to try the toxin, and they've refused." The two men shared worse cases than the other patients. If any would be desperate, it should be them. "I think they have more sense than you."

"Maybe. But I can't sit by and do nothing. The way Gertie's progressing...what if it eats up her whole body? I won't be able to stand it. I won't be able to stand losing her." Her bottom lip trembled, eyes wide.

He reached out a thumb to stroke the side of her face. "My dove. How would I stand losing you?"

She pulled away. "You mustn't speak like that. It's improper, especially when—when..." She lifted her skirts up to her knees, where angry red marks punctured her skin. "Look at me, Harry!"

She'd never hinted to any frustration when it came to the disease, at least regarding herself. Always, it had been for the sake of others. But this time, her words proved she cared. Perhaps she even cared for him.

But that didn't change anything. They could never be together. The law wouldn't allow it. No doctor would recommend it. Their only hope was in her healing.

"I will administer the toxin to you. Only in small doses at first. If you can tolerate those amounts, I'll consider increasing it. It will take at least two weeks to secure—if I can get the funding." He worried his bottom lip between his teeth. "Atta?"

Those brown eyes, as soft as a dove's, focused fully on him.

"Even if your body responds favorably to the toxin, it will take a couple months to know. By then—well, I'm uncertain how progressive Gertie's case is."

"Please, Harry. Order it at once."

June 16, 1917

DEAR MR. SCHAEFFER,

There is no easy way for me to write this letter. You wish to know how your daughters fare, and I wish I had more palatable news to share. While both your daughters' spirits remain high, their conditions worsen. Your youngest, Gertie, suffered a case of pneumonia this past spring which did not bode well for her condition. Atta has stoically taken on the role of guinea pig and risked an experimental toxin in hopes of finding it suitable for her sister. Unfortunately, the need to discontinue the toxin was apparent, for her case worsened considerably upon its administration.

I am disheartened to inform you of this unpleasant news. Please keep in mind that although their disease worsens, it does not mean they will not live many more years. Many patients find fulfilling lives on the island and learn to live with the complexities of the disease.

I plan to honor your wish and not inform your daughters of my communication with you. If you are a praying man, please send up fervent petitions for your daughters, as I also have taken habit of doing.

Sincerely,

Dr. Harvey Mayhew

Penikese Island, MA

HARRY FOUND Atta lying in the warm sun on the beach in a pale green dress, her eyes closed. Her wide-brimmed straw hat lay halfway over her face. Many of the patients claimed the warmth made the lesions less painful. Perhaps the same were true for Atta.

The diphtheria toxin had weakened her immune system, resulting in more bumpy marks and sores along her legs and arms. He looked at her face, so far unmarked by the disease. Beautiful. And yet he couldn't imagine ever thinking her ugly.

He longed to scoop her up and hold her close, breathe his own health and strength into her wounded body. If only it were that easy.

He gripped the letter in his hand and swallowed down the emotion in his throat. "Hard to believe we've been here a year."

She bolted into a sitting position and adjusted her hat. "I didn't hear you."

He folded the letter with the Medical Corps stamp on the front, tucked it in his pocket, and sat beside her. She inched away. He supposed that distance, more than anything, was the curse upon them. "Where's Gertie?"

"Taking a nap. Resting up for the corn-roast later." Once a week, the patients pooled the corn they'd grown in their gardens. They'd light a bonfire and smother the corn with butter, salt, and pepper. "I promised to take her wading afterwards."

Gertie's condition had reached a stagnant stage. Although

ulcers on her legs needed to be cleaned and bandaged daily, they weren't growing worse. "She's handled things well for one so little."

"Yes, she has," she said.

"So have you."

Atta tucked her arms around her knees and gazed at the hazy shore of New Bedford far off on the horizon. "I've been thinking—about our purpose in life."

"Such deep thoughts."

She smiled. "What do you think your purpose is, Doctor?"

"To heal as many as I can. To relieve those who suffer. To make the world better one patient at a time." He winced. "I suppose I'm not doing very well."

"You've relieved much of my suffering."

"I've made you worse."

She lifted her hand as if to touch his face. Just short of his lips, she retracted her fingers. "No, you haven't. My real suffering came from being misunderstood. From being treated like someone who was less than human. You, Dr. and Mrs. Parker, the nurses, Reverend Bailey...you all took away pieces of my suffering. Thank you."

He shook his head. Only she would twist her curse into a blessing. "And what is your purpose?"

She raised her eyebrows at him, a smile tilting her mouth. "You may not like it."

"I'll hold my tongue, I promise."

"I think it's to love others. To mirror God's grace." She gazed at Harry, hope in her eyes. "Have I shown you any of that, Harry?"

A breath quivered up his throat. If he said yes, she'd ask why he didn't share her love for a heavenly Creator. If he said no, she'd think she'd failed at her purpose in life. He couldn't win.

"I see something different in you, Atta. It's why I fell in love with you." He inched his hand along the rough sand until it grazed hers. Slipping her small fingers into his own, he ran his thumb along the inside of her wrist. She didn't resist. "I've been praying, you know. Praying like the dickens. For both you and Gertie, for all the patients. I don't see that it's done a bit of good. And now…"

"He hears you, Harry. I believe that with all my heart." She looked down at their joined hands. "I'm learning to be content whatever the circumstances. I have joy, Harry. In here." She placed her other hand over her heart. "Though my body betrays me, I do know an otherworldly peace."

Harry tried to fight the jealousy welling up within him, that Atta's invisible God, who refused to heal her, had wheedled a place in her heart while she couldn't spare him so much as a corner. He fought down the urge to grab her, press his mouth to hers, dig his fingers through her hair, press his face to her neck—make her want him as much as she wanted her God—make her want him as much as he did her.

"Then why hasn't He healed you?" She carried her leprosy like a divine blessing instead of the curse it was. It frustrated him to no end.

"I don't know."

She looked out at the water, a peacefulness etched on her beautiful face. How had he ever thought her plain? Now, her eyes spoke of calm. Gertie seemed to feed off this peace her sister possessed. There was no question those eyes were the life of the island.

She continued. "But I think He sent me this storm to draw me to Him. Perhaps…perhaps that is the best gift of all."

He tapped his foot against the rocky pebbles. He wanted to undo her as she had him. Would his news accomplish that feat?

"I've received orders from the Medical Corps."

God forgive him, he enjoyed the shock on her face. The wounded look in those soft, feathery eyes. There. He did mean something to her after all.

"The—for war?"

He nodded. "I volunteered for the Reserve Corps before coming to Penikese. A last ditch effort to shirk my duties here." He released her hand, snorted. "Now, the last thing I wish to do is leave you, especially when I'm responsible for your worsening." He ignored the wetness at his eyes, surprised he was capable of shedding unmanly tears.

He hated himself, hated who he'd become. Hated himself for having to leave Atta, hated himself for being relieved he wouldn't have to see her grow weaker day by day, month by month. And all because of his irresponsibility. His father was right.

He *was* irresponsible.

"I should have never tried the diphtheria toxin on you. I should have refused."

"And what then? We'll have forever wondered if we had the power to cure the disease at our fingertips. No, Harry. I don't regret it."

He sure did.

She coughed an unfamiliar, throaty sound. "When do you leave?" He heard the whispered words above the breeze that caressed their faces, draping itself behind and before them with invisible hands.

"Three days."

"Oh, Harry."

He slid both arms around her in a firm embrace, rejoicing when she let the sobs that racked her body wet his shirt, when she allowed him to rest his chin on her soft hair. He inhaled the scent of the sea and her shampoo, stamping it in his mind for as long as necessary. A few months, a few years, a lifetime.

"Please, Atta. Tell me you love me. It's all I ask."

She lifted her head to his, didn't back away when he swiped a thumb below her eyes to dry the wetness. "What good would it do? What—"

He dropped his finger to her lips. "If it's true, tell me, my dove. I know you, sweet Atta. You wouldn't lie to me. So if it's true, please. I long to hear it from your lips just this once." He knew he was selfish. Coming into her life, making everything worse for both her and her sister, and now demanding a vow of love before he left to travel across the vast ocean.

Her jaw trembled. She opened her mouth, ever so slowly. The wind chased away his doubts, and he knew in an instant what she would say. "I do. I love you, Harry."

With tender restraint, he lowered his lips to hers in a gentle kiss that stole time and space from the air they shared. Nothing else mattered. Only her. Only him. Together.

When she broke away, he crushed her against his chest, suddenly ten times more protective of her. No matter if they never exchanged wedding rings. No matter if he'd never claim her body with his own. Atta was his. And he would live out as many days as they had completely devoted to her and her alone.

Chapter Forty

I don't bother hiding my tears as Gram's words paint a picture of Harry and Atta embracing on the beach.

It's no use—we've shared too much. We're both open and vulnerable in this moment. Even Gram's eyes are wet.

"Did he come back? Did he see Atta again?"

A smile softens Gram's mouth. "A proper story is a proper story, my dear. With a beginning, a middle, and an end. It mustn't be rushed."

I have so many questions. And not just about Harry and Atta.

Gram had been a leper. She *had* known what it was to be an outcast.

"You got better," I say. "That means Harry found a cure?" And if so, why hadn't it worked on my great-aunt? A terrible fear seizes me that Harry doesn't make it home from the war—that the hope Gram intends for this story is a spiritual one. Sure, it's nice to think of Harry and Atta together in heaven, but I am longing for something else entirely. I'm longing for more.

"Emily Grace, all I can tell you is the story must unfold in its time, and unfortunately, for me, that time is not tonight. I need my beauty sleep."

I want to demand she sacrifice her beauty for the sake of story. How dare she leave me in this spot! But it's already past ten and I have an English final the next day. If I want to keep my *A*, I'd have to study.

Strange how such a thought seemed petty in light of Atta and Harry's parting.

I sigh, kiss Gram goodnight, and head up to my empty room where I lay in my bed and tuck my feet beneath the covers just as a cramp wracks my middle. I place my hands on my babe and breathe deeply, waiting for another cramp, praying it's nothing. The babe wouldn't survive if it came this early, would it?

Minutes pass without any discomfort, but that doesn't stop a sudden panic from creeping over me, threatening me with its blackness. I switch on my bedside light and my gaze lands on a letter from Bryan that came yesterday. I pick it up, knowing it will only cause more pain, but like passing a car wreck on the highway, I'm unable to look away.

Emily,

I really don't want to mess around, so I'll make this short. You need to tell Ashley to keep her trap shut. I am not your bastard's father, and I'd appreciate it if you'd stop spreading lies that I am. Do whatever needs to be done so your drama doesn't affect me.

Bryan

Ugh. I run my hands over my stomach. "Your father's a real gem, isn't he? Pretty poetic, too," I whisper to disguise the hurt. If I held any illusions Bryan would step up and help me with this baby, his letter swept them away. I crumple it up and hurl it across the room.

How could I have ever believed he loved me?

Real love endured. Real love—the kind that Harry and Atta had for one another—stuck it out even in the inconvenient.

I swallow my despair, facing the terrible truth that I may never know a love like that. Though Atta had been a leper, at least she'd had the greatest gift of all—the gift of unconditional love.

THE NEXT DAY, I rummage around the kitchen in an attempt to gather what I need to make a cheesecake. Gram let it slip one day that it was her favorite dessert, so Sam brought me to *Fancy's Market* after school to pick up fresh berries and cream for a topping. Since Gram helps at the church's thrift shop on Wednesday afternoons, I hope to surprise her. She's done so much for me when others haven't even bothered to show they care with a simple note or phone call.

Oh man, I'm starting to sound like a bitter old lady.

The phone rings and I shut off the electric mixer.

"Hello?"

"Emily! How are you, darling?"

I lean against the counter, tension leaving my body. Maybe someone besides Gram does care. "Mom—hi. It's great to hear your voice."

"Of course, honey. I've been trying to give you your space. But you do know you can call us anytime."

My space? Why would I need space?

"How are you guys?" I ask instead.

"Well. Very well! Your father is gearing up for the next election, of course. Busy times, lots of connections to make."

For the first time, I am consciously thankful to be at Gram's where I am near the beauty of the ocean and away from the swell and press of people, politics, and parties. "That's good."

"How are you feeling?" Mom's voice lowers an octave, as if the neighbors might hear her and figure out the unfortunate circumstance that has fallen upon the daughter of Maryland's most illustrious governor.

"Big." I can't help the smile that tugs at my mouth. "This child likes to move around a lot." I imagine another time, another life, where I might be talking to my mother about my baby under circumstances of joy. Preparing a room, maybe planning a baby shower. Anticipating that newborn smell I hear about so often.

"It must be quite obvious by now." Mom's sharp words slash through my happy musings.

"Yes, it is. I guess it's good I'm so far away," I say coldly. I stare into the mixing bowl where clumps of cream cheese and sugar coat the sides of the stainless steel.

"It'll all work out for the best, honey. You'll see. Oh, did I tell you about the big rally your father's campaign staff is planning? It's going to be huge. You'll never guess who's going to make an appearance."

"Who?"

"Goldie Hawn! Can you believe it?"

"Wow. That's great, Mom."

"We're so excited. I just wish we had more than three months to prepare!"

Three months.

I clear my throat. "When is it?"

"August twentieth."

A fuzzy crackling overtakes my brain as she rambles on about the benefit of holding a rally before Labor Day.

I grip the phone harder as I wait for her to take a breath so I can interrupt. "Mom...I'm due August twentieth. You're—you're going to be here, right?"

Mom and I might be at odds, but I can't imagine going through the most frightening day of my life without her. Bad enough I suffer nightmares about childbirth. I'll need support as I grieve the loss of the child—a child I will have carried for nine months.

"Oh, *Emily*." She draws out the three syllables of my name, and I've never wished for her to call me "Em" more than I do in this moment. "If you actually deliver on your due date—which hardly anyone does—then of course I can't be there. This rally means everything for your father. It's too important. If I'm not there, it will invite questions—it could ruin the very reason we've sent you to be with Gram."

The *rally* was too important. More important, obviously, than me.

I swallow my pride. Good thing I don't have much left. When I open my mouth to speak, my voice trembles. "First babies are usually late, right? So you'll come after the rally, won't you?"

I sounded pathetic. I sounded pathetic, and I didn't care a whit.

Mom lets out a dainty cough. "Why don't we see how things play out, okay? No sense worrying about something that's still so far away."

As opposed to worrying about a political rally occurring three months down the road.

She seems to realize her mistake and speaks again. "Well, anyway, if I can't be there, your grandmother certainly will. And she has nursing experience, so you couldn't be in better hands."

Of course Gram would be there, but while I appreciated Gram's care over the last several weeks, she wasn't who I imagined with me in the delivery room.

Mom wouldn't be there. Ashley wouldn't be there. Bryan certainly wouldn't be there.

I think of Sam, can almost imagine him feeding me ice chips during labor. In some ways, Sam would be a perfect helper. But obviously, that would be entirely inappropriate. And I would rather die than ask him such a thing.

As I make an excuse to hang up with my mother and turn back to my clumpy cream cheese, a dark sadness once again overtakes me. For the millionth time, I wish I'd made a different decision in

the back seat of that Dodge. Giving birth should be a joyful celebration—a beautiful experience where those I love surround me in
support and offer their congratulations. But I'd robbed myself of
that when I'd said "yes" to Bryan that night.

Someday in the future, after I graduate and have a steady job
and find the love of my life, perhaps I will have another baby. I
remember Gram's insistence that Atta's story is one of hope. It's
what I'm clinging to, what I'm trusting in. And that leads me to
one conclusion: if hope is there for my Aunt Atta—a woman who
knew true misery and despair—then it's possible it can be there for
me as well.

Chapter Forty-One

1917

"That looks beautiful, dear. You've chosen very complimentary colors." Atta patted Gertie's shoulder as she admired the quilt her sister worked on. "You are becoming quite a little gardener and a very handy quilter."

Gertie smiled up at Atta. "Can I tell you something?"

"Of course." Atta sat on the chair beside Gertie. While their summer mornings were spent in the garden outside their cottage, their afternoons were spent here, beneath the shade of the pavilion, inhaling the sweet salty scent of the sea.

"It's a secret."

"I promise, I won't tell a soul."

Gertie pressed her lips together so tightly that the skin beneath her nose stretched flat. "I like being here, on the island."

Atta paused. "Do you?"

"Yes. I spend all day with you doing fun things. Working in the garden, quilting, schoolwork, taking walks, collecting sea glass and shells. We never got to spend so much time together at home.

There was always school and Robert...and Papi." Gertie brought her needle through the three layers of fabric and poked it down again. "Am I naughty for not missing him?"

"No, dear. It's hard to miss people who've hurt us. But I think both you and I should work on forgiving Papi."

"For all the mean things he did to us?"

The wind carried men's voices onto shore from the new boat Dr. Parker had given the patients. They'd have mackerel or flounder tonight, to be sure. The men would entertain them with a plethora of fish tales that, as Dr. Parker liked to say, proved them all descendants of Izaak Walton. Mary wasn't the only one who relished a life of fantasy—though hers had nothing to do with angling.

Atta marveled at the willingness of the patients to get behind the war effort, behind a country that cast them from her bosom, though most of them did not share in its citizenship. But support they did. They ate fish most nights, conserving wheat, red meat, and sugar to feed the troops abroad. Even Atta, who felt her country's betrayal more intimately than the rest, did her part to conserve. To forgive.

She sighed, knowing she had avoided Gertie's question. So easy to do with anything concerning Papi.

"It's hardest to forgive those who've hurt you. But the strange thing is that they keep on hurting you in here"—she pointed at her heart—"if you don't forgive them."

She was a hypocrite reciting such righteous words. Though she knew their truth, putting them into practice was an insurmountable feat. Something deep inside her wanted Papi to hurt as badly as he'd hurt his daughters.

Gertie let the quilt drop to her lap. For a moment she watched the seagulls soar along the coastline. "It's hard, isn't it?"

"Yes," Atta breathed. "But I think it's the only way to set ourselves free."

Oh, it sounded too simple. She shouldn't have so much trouble forgiving Papi. Or herself for Mami's death. Some things were so much easier said than done.

"I'll try, Atta. Promise I will."

"I will too, dear. We'll ask God for help when we say our prayers tonight."

Out of the corner of her eye, she saw a figure, and for an instant her heart leapt.

Then she remembered. Harry was gone to help the soldiers at war. He'd find satisfaction in helping the sick, in curing them. Then, he'd forget all about Penikese. All about her.

With Harry gone, loneliness swallowed her whole. Contentment fled. She missed him so much it frightened her.

"Hello." The lone greeting pulled Atta from her reverie.

"Mary. Is it time for tea already?" Every afternoon she and Gertie took tea with Mary and Missy.

Mary shook her head and pointed to Atta's sewing novelties. "Can you teach Missy and me?" As usual, her words poured out in a nervous gush.

"Of course." Her voice showed confidence, but in truth, she questioned how someone with hands as deformed as Mary's could handle a needle.

"Miss Mary, you can sew a blanket for Missy like I'm sewing one for Rosie." Gertie beamed at Mary, clearly not seeing how the disease had marked her body, how it had stolen her mind.

Atta reached for a piece of square fabric and a needle. The needle dropped from her hands onto a flat rock. She reached for it, trying to grasp it between her thumb and index finger. Her fingers bumped the rock, but no sensation registered in their tips. Again she tried, refusing to believe her senses. And again. But she couldn't grasp the needle.

No...if she lost feeling in her hands, how would she be able to create beauty in fabric, to dress herself, to tuck Gertie in at night?

She glanced at Mary's nubby fingers. Would her own hands soon bear the same fate?

Would there be anything left of her by the time Harry returned?

NIKLAS WALKED from the mess hall with one of his bunkmates. The man, Gernot, had been a sailor on the *SS Kronprinz Wilhelm*, an auxiliary warship for the German navy. He did not speak English and so he and Niklas conversed in German.

"They don't treat us too bad here, eh?" Gernot folded up his mail and shoved it in his pocket.

"No, but it's still a prison. Nothing will change that." Niklas looked past a set of barracks to the two barbed-wire fences, ten-feet tall. A guard stood in one of the watchtowers outside of the fence, his ever-ready eyes on possible escapees or problem prisoners.

"You have family, Niklas?"

"I did. You?"

"A wife. Makes the best Black Forest cake a man ever could eat. My son's in the Imperial Navy, too. At least I hope he still is. Haven't heard from him in some time. Children?"

"Two daughters." Niklas thought of Dr. Mayhew's letter, of Atta and Gertie getting sicker. Dr. Mayhew hadn't hinted at any hope for either of them. They seemed destined to spend the rest of their lives exiled. Maybe Charles was right. Maybe he should consider them dead.

"They married?"

"*Nicht*. Too young." He didn't flinch at the lie. Easier to avoid conversation.

Gernot tapped his arm. "I'm going to enjoy these letters. See you at that biology lecture later?"

"*Ja*." Right. Letters. He'd received one today from someone back in Massachusetts. A Miss Florence Whalen. Probably some letter from Charles's secretary. He went to the back of one of the bunkhouses. A gust of wind caught up the dusty ground in a whirlwind and spiraled at his feet. He sat on the dry dirt, leaned his back against the wall of the barracks, and slid his finger beneath the edge of the envelope.

July 17, 1917

Dear Mr. Schaeffer,

I have procrastinated long enough in sending this correspondence and although it may be awkward, the good Lord will not give me peace until it is off in the post. You may not remember me, or you may very well remember me. I saw you most often at the saloon. We had a run-in nearly a year ago. Do you recall? I refused to let you get in your motorcar before sobering up.

I saw them arrest you. Heard what you said. Since then, I've come to find out about your daughters. My heart aches for both you and them.

Mr. Schaeffer, I am writing to request your forgiveness. I've been quick to sing of God's abounding grace outside that saloon of yours, yet I fear I've also been quick to judge—to fail to show the grace we all need, including me.

I am praying for you, Mr. Schaeffer, and for your daughters. Know that not a day will go by where I will not plead with the Father for the well-being of your family. God bless.

Yours Truly,

Florence Whalen

Niklas stared at the letter. Read it again. Imagined the scent of lilacs he knew belonged to the woman who'd penned the words. That she had thought of him at all was enough to send his mind into a spin. That she had asked his forgiveness was something he was utterly unworthy to grant. That she was praying for him, Atta, and Gertie...that sent a wedge of sunlight to his shadowed heart.

❧ ❧

"Atta, must I go? It hurts when Nurse Edith takes the dressings off."

"I'm afraid so, dear. Your legs could become infected if they aren't taken care of. Besides, this time I'm to go to the dispensary as well."

A look of alarm passed over Gertie's face. "Must you be bandaged also?"

Atta placed her brush beside the bowl and pitcher she and Gertie used to wash. The marks had spread over most of her body. They terrified her, but never more so than when the spots on her legs started erupting into itchy, feverish sores. Small blood stains marked her underskirts. They would need to be bandaged. She'd thought she'd accepted her condition, but looking at the grotesque skin inhabiting her once smooth legs, she hated her body. It was ugly. Beyond ugly. She'd once proclaimed to Harry that even with leprosy, God had made her wonderfully, simply because she was His creation. As her body continued to betray her, however, God's truth seemed further and further away. Or worse yet, maybe God's truth wasn't true at all.

"I have some marks on my legs, too. I want Nurse Edith to look at them. That's all, dear. Now hurry along. If we leave now, we may not have to wait."

They finished up their toilettes and walked into the heavy fog of the island. When they entered the hospital, they walked to the infirmary hand-in-hand. Nurse Edith bustled around the room preparing supplies. "I have some early birds today, I see."

"Atta needs bandages, too." Gertie trudged into the room and sat on a wooden chair. Would Atta ever see her little sister run again? Not jog or skip, but run. With hopeless abandon. Not worried to fall. Not frightened to bump a chair that would send needles of pain to her legs.

When she looked up, Nurse Edith stared at her. "Is that so, Atta?"

She brushed off the concern. "I'd like you to take a look. They may not need bandaging. Please, go ahead with Gertie."

Her sister clutched the sides of the chair and scrunched her face up in pain when Nurse Edith unwound the bandages on her legs. Then the disinfecting, which was nearly as bad. Atta looked away.

Nurse Edith brought a large bucket of warm water over and Gertie placed her legs in it. Foot care was essential because of the nerve damage caused by leprosy. The destruction could leave a patient unable to lift the front of their foot, resulting in a walk in which one would have to lift the leg high to flop the foot forward. Atta shivered at the thought of Gertie walking in such a way.

About fifteen minutes later, Nurse Edith patted Gertie's red legs with a towel and applied petroleum jelly to her sores. Then the bandages. When the nurse completed the task, she squeezed Gertie's arm. "You're a brave little girl." She slipped something from her pocket and held it out.

"Licorice!"

The nurse smiled. "I bought some from Mrs. Parker's store just for you."

Gertie's grin widened. "Thanks, Nurse Edith."

"You're very welcome."

"Atta, can I go back to the cottage to share my licorice with Rosie?"

Atta clucked her tongue. "Licorice before breakfast?"

"Please Atta. Pleeeeaaase."

"I suppose. Just this once."

"Thank you!" Gertie skipped off with awkward jounces. Atta refrained from yelling warnings to slow down or be careful.

She sighed and sat in the chair.

"Breaks my heart to see one so young." Nurse Edith set out a new tray of bandages and iodine. Although the scent was far from pleasant, Atta had grown accustomed to it. No longer did it remind her of the events surrounding her mother's death. Now, it reminded her of Harry. "She's such a dear part of our small community."

"She's strong." Atta didn't want to talk about Gertie or the state of her body. The hopelessness of it all. Even now, Toy's bleak funeral two days ago hung in her mind like a thick black curtain. She'd miss seeing the uncomplaining little Chinaman around the hospital grounds.

"Now, let's take a look, shall we?"

Atta lifted her skirts to reveal the red sores, resembling blemishes. They shouted up at her, shamed her before the nurse.

"Now that isn't all that bad, Miss Atta. But you're right. We best bandage them."

Nurse Edith cleaned the sores, which did not sting as terribly as Atta feared. Then the nurse began to wrap her legs with clean white bandages, starting from her thigh and ending at her ankles.

Atta's breathing quickened. She hadn't expected to have such a reaction to the white bandages. She'd seen them on the other patients, and on Gertie. Now though, looking upon her own legs, the haunting image of lepers crying out "Unclean!" bled through her mind.

Soiled. Ruined. Without value. She closed her eyes, searching for something, anything to grasp onto, to keep her from sliding off this shaky ledge of fear.

The Lord will perfect that which concerneth me: thy mercy, O Lord, endureth forever...

Nurse Edith finished up the bandaging. "Dr. Briggs arrived last night. He'll see all the patients after breakfast."

Atta's blood ran cold, replacing the warmth she'd just basked in. "Dr. Briggs?"

"Yes. The man who's to replace Dr. Mayhew while he's away."

Dr. Briggs. It had been seven years since she'd set eyes on a Dr. Briggs. It couldn't be the same man.

Atta's thoughts returned to her thirteenth year. Dr. Briggs. The man who slowly killed her mother. The man who was too eager to try experimental medications. The man she feared more than any other.

Chapter Forty-Two

The November wind rattled the sides of the hospital tent, two miles behind the front lines—behind no-man's-land. Safe and dry, Harry lifted the flaps of the tent and let the wind wash away the smells of the sick and dying, of the gassed men. The numbers coming in showed close to one-hundred and forty thousand deaths for the sake of five miles of captured German territory.

One life for two inches of muddy ground.

He let the tent flap fall and made his way toward the other end of the hospital.

Holding a medical degree did little good when the enemy took life before he had a chance to heal it. Amidst the murky trenches, those fortunate enough to escape the bullets, mustard gas, and shell fragments were left to fight their own private battles of influenza and dysentery.

He no longer flinched at amputations. No longer paused at death. Whatever compassion stirred his heart on Penikese had been stolen by the Western Front.

Thoughts of Atta came to him in dreams and occasional vague letters. His own correspondence only touched the surface of the turmoil hidden within his heart, and hers seemed to do the same. She didn't tell him how badly the disease ravaged her sick body, and he couldn't bear to ask. God forgive him, he prayed she didn't volunteer the answer.

"Doctor?" A hoarse voice at his waist. A tug at his shirtsleeve. His mind numbed. He didn't have time to stop for a chat. He was needed elsewhere. Still, something nudged him to take a moment, to look into the eyes of the soldier on the cot. "Not feelin' too swell. You think—you think I'm gonna die?"

Harry looked at the man's glazed eyes, down past his feverish chest, and to the quivering stumps of his legless torso. He lifted the bandages above the man's thighs to check for signs of infection.

Just as he'd feared. The amputation of his legs had not stopped the angry spread of gangrene. In all likelihood, the man would die.

But what could he say at a time like this? For heaven's sake, he was a doctor, not a priest.

He thought of Atta. How she would have the right words for this man. How she would speak of her Jesus and how precious He was to her.

Harry rubbed the bridge of his nose. "I'm sorry, soldier. It's not looking too good down there." He signaled for a passing nurse to bring the man a tin cup of water.

He started to walk away, to let the man process his thoughts in peace, but the soldier clutched at Harry's hand with sweaty palms. "Please, Doc. Don't leave."

Harry paused. "I'll send the chaplain over if you'd like."

"Naw. I never been too comfortable around religious folk."

Harry lowered himself onto a packing crate, his father's stethoscope knocking against his chest. "That makes two of us." Another nurse rushed past. The cries of the wounded rang out, haunting and hollow. Maybe speaking with the man would relax his fears. He'd be dead before sunset. Harry could give him this much.

"You think St. Pete will let a guy like me past them pearly gates?"

Oh boy. Not his territory. He should have called for the chaplain. What might Atta say to this fellow?

But what did *he* believe? He'd been too filled with jealousy over the attention Atta gave her God that he'd never stopped to evaluate his own faith. Sure, going to church had been a convenient way for his family to look devout, but church aside, what about the realities of God, creation, the afterlife...everything?

"I'm afraid I don't know the answer to that one, Lieutenant. I'm sure St. Pete will be pleased with your efforts here on the front."

But it seemed an inadequate answer, and the man's demeanor seemed to deflate further. He gazed off into the space opposite from Harry where ambulances and flat wagons brought in more wounded. "Guess I can hope for the best, then."

Hope. With a warm gush, an idea came to Harry. He dug in his back pocket for Atta's latest letter and opened it. Skimmed past the part where she spoke of a new patient from Florida, past the mention of Willie Goon's recovery from a heart attack, past the words where she lamented Mrs. Parker's mother's sudden death upon the island during a visit. Then, near the end, she'd written something that hadn't helped him, but it spoke of hope.

He cleared his throat. "I know a woman of great faith. She's— she's amazing."

"Good looking?"

"Beautiful." He wouldn't share the details of Atta's sickness with this man, but he told the truth. No matter if the leprosy ate up her entire body, festered it into puss-filled sores and ulcers, Atta could never be anything but beautiful to him. "She wrote me something in her last letter that might give you peace. May I read it?"

The man nodded, his eyes less glassy than before, his shivers subsiding. There wasn't much time.

"'I pray, dearest, that the God of hope fill you with all joy and peace in believing, that ye may abound in hope through the power of the Holy Ghost.' Yes, I am quoting scripture to you again. Forgive me, but I have faith that someday we may share a greater bond than that which we already possess...one in Christ."

The man stared with unseeing eyes at his missing legs. "Can you read it again?"

The man closed his eyes, and Harry read Atta's words again, and again. The man's breathing slowed. Is this how he'd meet eternity?

The lieutenant let out a wispy breath, causing the sheet on his pillowcase to move. "I must believe, then. Trust in God for my life." A tremble worked up his throat. "Trust Him for whatever's next."

How had the man put it together so simply when Harry still struggled with the notion? "Yes. I think that's it."

Silence stole through the medical tent and the man opened his eyes. "Thanks, Doc. You listen to that girl of yours. I think she has it."

The man slipped away moments later, his words ringing in Harry's mind. *I think she has it.* What was "it"? And why was it so easy for Atta to grasp onto, so easy for the dying soldier to understand...yet so hard for Harry to make his own?

It was him.

It was him, and he didn't recognize her.

But of course he didn't recognize her. She was older, now. An outcast where once a blossoming thirteen-year-old girl had been.

The doctor didn't look at Atta. "We'll try the chaulmoosan, Miss Schaeffer. I'll be giving it to half of the patients here to test the effects it has on the disease."

He hadn't asked. He'd told.

"I—I've already tried the chaulmoogra oil. It made me very

sick and I showed no signs of improvement." She wouldn't allow him to intimidate her like he'd done when she was a girl.

"This is chaulmoosan, a proprietary preparation of the ethyl esters of chaulmoogra oil." He spoke to her with his lofty words, as if she were a small child. His tone brooked no room for argument. His smudged spectacles slid down his long nose as he prepared the injection.

She hated him. Hated him for all he had done to her—for all he had done to Gertie.

"You don't recognize me."

He started, and for the first time gave her his entire attention. "Pardon, should I?"

"My mother was Katharina. Katharina Schaeffer. She had tuberculosis. You killed her." Her calm words belied the turmoil within. She watched as, ever so slowly, recognition dawned in Dr. Briggs's dark, beady eyes. Then, it changed to something she enjoyed all too much.

Fear.

So, he did remember her after all.

"Forgive me for not recognizing you, my dear." Every syllable leaving his mouth dripped with false honey, like poison. "Your mother's death was most unfortunate, but I'm afraid you're mistaken. There is nothing I could have done to save her."

Atta stood. She refused to be the patient any longer. "You slipped her something—I saw you. You didn't want anyone to know. Your hands shook when you gave it to her and you dropped the bottle beneath her bed. I found it later. Sulfur something."

"Your mother did not die from the drug, but from the disease. I understand how a little girl's panic can cloud her judgment."

Her jaw trembled. That couldn't have been it. All these years she'd been so certain, so sure that something hadn't been right that day in Mami's bedroom. But doubt had kept her from saying anything. And after Mami's passing, she'd turned the guilt upon herself. Month after month passed as she laid the blame at her own feet. She should have questioned Dr. Briggs when she'd seen him, should have asked another doctor if sulfur was a normal treatment for tuberculosis. Yet, who would pay any attention to a girl?

And in the recesses of her mind, it felt safer. Safer not to know if she could have prevented her mother's death. Safer to fool herself into thinking she couldn't have done anything.

She didn't trust Dr. Briggs. She never would. He held the ability to swipe the Lord's peace from beneath her feet, from where she could stand with surety. Whether he committed an irresponsible act as a doctor or not, she needed to forgive him.

But not right now.

"Excuse me, Dr. Briggs, will that be all for today?"

He nodded, his gaze skidding over the room. "I'll give you your first injection of the chaulmoosan tomorrow."

She wouldn't fight him on that. Not unless...

"My sister, Gertie. I have charge of her. I don't wish for her to be subjected to this chaulmoosan until it's proven safe."

"Many leprosariums around the world have proven it safe, Miss Schaeffer. I will administer it as I see fit."

"And if you attempt to administer it to my sister, I will be forced to speak to Dr. Parker of the concerns I have regarding the past."

His silence confirmed her fears—Dr. Briggs hid something.

But she wasn't any better. Had God sent him here to confront Atta into confessing her fault in Mami's death? Suddenly, God's healing grace seemed to dwindle beneath the fresh guilt before her.

No one could change the fact that she could have prevented her mother's death. Not even God.

"Niklas, are you enjoying my lectures?"

Niklas approached Professor Hoffmeyer with caution. Though he didn't know why the professor was imprisoned, the inmates enjoyed the entertainment he offered in the form of university lectures.

Not one to hold interest in the sciences, Niklas had come at the invitation of Gernot. Better than staring at the ceiling, anyway. But today, Professor Hoffmeyer mentioned something that caught his attention.

"*Ja*, sir. I am. I was hoping to hear more about your experiences in Norway."

The professor raised bushy eyebrows to the ceiling of the mess hall. "You wish to know more of my studies of leprosy?"

Niklas nodded. While going over his biography, the professor mentioned he'd taken part in the Second International Leprosy Congress in Bergen, Norway.

"Do you believe yourself to be a victim of the disease?"

"*Ach, nicht*, sir! My daughters, Professor. They are exiled in Massachusetts. I—I've had contact with their doctor. I was wondering if you could help them." *Ach*, but he was a *Schwachkopf*. No matter if the Professor could help, no American doctor would accept assistance from a German intern. Still, with his mind fully, painfully sober, Niklas struggled with helplessness. This, at least, was an attempt at aiding his daughters.

The professor tucked a large book into a worn bag. "I'm not sure what assistance I can be. I don't have any cure for the disease that plagues your daughters."

"There is no hope then? Nothing you learned at your time in Bergen?"

Professor Hoffmeyer laid his bag on the steel table before him. "There were many possible treatments discussed in Bergen. Many more ruled out. Better doctors than I have tested their theories, but I'm afraid it's often been at the expense of the patients."

Niklas stepped forward, his hat clutched in his hands. "Do you believe any one of those treatments could help my daughters?"

"I'm afraid what I think does not matter, Mr. Schaeffer."

"But you could write to their doctor—suggest a treatment, *ja?* With your experience, maybe he will listen to you."

"And maybe the guards will take down that fence of barbed wire tomorrow, *ja?*" The older man laughed, and familiar anger bubbled in Niklas's veins.

With much effort, he reined it in. Now was not the time to let his emotions best him.

He thought of Florence Whalen, praying for him and Atta and Gertie. Somewhere in the world, someone cared enough to think of him, to write him a letter. The idea made him want to be a better man, even if it was in this sad camp.

He loosened his gritted teeth. "I don't mean to be a bother, Professor. I thought if you could find the time to help out a fellow *nativen...*"

Professor Hoffmeyer expelled a loud blast of air from his mouth. "Get me the address of your daughters' doctor. Not that it will be much use. But *ja*, I will write him."

GERTIE'S BREATHS wheezed in and out. She tried to move her legs into a comfy position, but the pressure of the thin sheets made her wince. It hurt. Every day, it hurt worse and worse.

She tried to be a brave girl, to keep her tears in so Atta wouldn't see, but they squeezed out of her eyes anyway. She couldn't keep them back.

And it was making her sister very, very sad.

Atta ran her wrist beneath Gertie's eyes to wipe away the tears. Her older sister had given up sewing months ago. Nurse Edith had to tie a fork to two fingers so Atta could eat by herself.

"There, there, dear. It's going to be all right. You're going to be fine."

No. She wasn't. The doctors couldn't find a way to make any of them better. Every day the pain bit at Gertie's legs, worsening with the arrival of winter. She'd cried enough tears for an entire bathtub by now.

"Atta?"

"Yes?" Her sister craned her neck so her face was above Gertie's. Red marks climbed her throat. She didn't want to see Atta's pretty face covered with them.

"Are you still asking God to make me better?"

Atta shifted in her chair. The harsh winter wind rattled the windows, the ocean a thick sheet of ice for miles beyond the shore.

"Of course. Every hour, every day."

"Could you stop?"

Atta stood still as a statue. "What?"

"I want it to be over. I want to go with Jesus and live with Mami in heaven."

Atta shook her head with force. She blinked fast.

"It hurts so much. Please, Atta. Please pray for Jesus to take me home. There isn't no leprosy in heaven."

Chapter Forty-Three

I shake my head through my tears and bite my lip to keep from cursing. "Why in the world are you telling me this story, Gram? I can't take it anymore."

At my feet, leaning against the porch rail with one arm casually slung over a propped knee, Sam sits stiffly, staring at a pot of white impatiens.

When I'd told Gram about Sam's brother and asked if Sam might join us for her story, she had surprised me by agreeing. If there was hope in our family's history—and right now I was having trouble seeing it—I'd wanted Sam to be in on it.

But now, I regret dragging him into this.

Gram reaches out a thin hand to me. "Dear, did you forget I'm sitting right here with you? I didn't die."

I breathe deep, and sniff, try to brush off my concern. "Of course. Of course, you didn't. Please, go on."

"Miss Gertie," Sam interrupts. "Since you *are* alive, and you *did* live through all that, how are you not writing books and talking to Oprah and telling your story around the country?"

I smile. I like the way he thinks of being a leper as a battle Gram has conquered, something to proudly shout out to the world.

"Oh, I've always been a bit of a private person. I haven't spoken much about it all until now."

I hear what she isn't saying—that my father's political career made that impossible. He's ashamed of her history as much as he's ashamed of my pregnancy.

I clear my throat. "Anyway, please go on, Gram. I'm sorry I interrupted—I was a little emotional is all. I'm ready to hear more now."

"Are you sure, Emily Grace?" Gram looks down her glasses at me, her voice a bit odd sounding. "You know, you're very pregnant, and you may be taking this story a little too hard. Maybe we ought to stop for the night."

I blink, trying to place the funny inflections she'd just used. I shake my head a little. "Are you quoting *The Princess Bride* at me?"

She grins. "A wonderful movie. I have it on Beta. Would you like to watch it?"

She had the tape? "Are you kidding me? That's one of my favorite movies of all time!"

"Then why don't we take a break and watch it? Send some good vibes to that baby of yours to make up for me putting you through all those emotions?"

I could be like Fred Savage in the movie and insist on continuing with the story, but maybe Gram's the one who needs a break —I'd noted how her voice had roughened, how she'd often swallowed back emotion the past half hour.

"Wait, wait, wait," Sam says. "*The Princess Bride*? I don't watch girly movies."

I tap my chin. "I think it's only fair since you dragged me to *Jurassic Park*—"

"—which you loved!"

"And you'll love *The Princess Bride*." I exchange a look with

Gram, both of us grinning. "Even though it's totally a kissing movie."

Sam groans and Gram and I laugh. Gram stands. "I'll dig out the tape if you'll pop the corn."

Sam doesn't look convinced. He's probably looking for an excuse to bolt though he'd said he was free all evening. I lean over and place a hand on his arm. "You'll like it. I promise."

He lets out a dramatic sigh and stands, offering his hand to me. "Let's find the popcorn."

It strikes me then how much I can count on Sam to stick with me even when he's not sure it's to his advantage. Maybe trusting a boy wouldn't be as hard as I'd thought—if the boy proved himself first, which Sam was certainly doing.

As we sit on Gram's couch and Savage's video game pops up on the screen, I think that maybe my parents haven't truly done me wrong after all. When was the last time I was this happy? I *wasn't* friendless. And perhaps, I was exactly where I needed to be. In the midst of the turmoil, in the midst of Gram and Atta's story, I was beginning to feel as if God were close by. Maybe even orchestrating things for my good. Surely, He'd been there for my Aunt Atta and my grandmother all those years ago when they'd faced complete and utter despair.

Because here my Gram was, more than seventy-five years later, watching one of my favorite movies with me.

God hadn't abandoned my grandmother. And maybe, just maybe, He hadn't abandoned me.

Chapter Forty-Four

March 8, 1918

Dear Professor Hoffmeyer,

I apologize for the delay in my response. You see, I am no longer at Penikese but serving overseas in the Medical Corps, so even with air mail it took some time to receive your letter. I'm certain Mr. Schaeffer was unaware of my current location. Nevertheless, I am still deeply invested in the patients living on Penikese and hope to return to them soon.

Your research on Hansen's piques my interest, as do your notes from the Congress in Norway. You mentioned dapsone as a possible cure. Unfortunately, I must agree with your colleagues in labeling it a drug too toxic for human use, even in small doses. Perhaps there were other possible treatments discussed? I would be very interested in hearing of them and of more of your theories. Kindly, give my regards to Mr. Schaeffer.

Sincerely,

Dr. Harvey Mayhew

"The chaulmoosan is not working. I wish to discontinue it." Atta crossed her arms over her body, the fatigue of the day and her earlier conversation with Gertie—the one in which she'd asked Atta to stop praying for her so she could go home to heaven—gnawing at her weary bones.

"I'm afraid that's not possible, Miss Schaeffer."

She hated the man. More and more each day, she hated him for all he'd done, for all he continued to do.

"I'm getting worse. I can't even properly care for my sister!"

"It takes some time. You must be patient."

"It's been months, Dr. Briggs. It's wearing on me, wearing me down. It's in my airways." Shortness of breath, sudden coughs. "I refuse to continue the treatment." She took hold of the doorknob and yanked it open.

"I'm afraid I must insist—"

Without a backwards glance, she strode from the office, down the hall past Gertie's room, and out into the cold without her wrap. She walked on numb toes. The wind licked the bare skin at her face and hands, forced itself beneath her clothes to bite at her delicate skin. She slid on a patch of ice.

If only Harry were here. If only the board had sent any other doctor besides Dr. Briggs. If only she'd saved Mami. If only she and Gertie had never caught the disease. If only her faith were deeper. If only God would heal them! If only, if only, if only...

She ran up the hill to the barbed wire where two stone columns guarded the path. She rang the bell mounted on the right one. The sound echoed to the icy ocean, frozen solid all the way to Cuttyhunk and beyond. She didn't stop ringing until she spotted Dr. Parker, bundled in a trench coat, hat, and gloves.

"Miss Atta, whatever is the matter? And where is your coat, dear?"

She shook her head, unable to form the necessary words. Would Dr. Parker understand?

"Come into the workshop."

She followed him down the path and into a small building. Heat enveloped her and Dr. Parker invited her to sit beside the woodstove.

"Thank you," she said, suddenly wary of intruding upon his private space, upon his side of the island.

"Before the hospital was built, I used this as an infirmary."

"It's...cozy."

"But I'm sure you didn't cross the island in subzero temperatures to talk of the island's history. Tell me, what's troubling you?"

She felt like a third-grade tattletale. But this wasn't a minor dispute over an erased slate of homework, this was her life. Gertie's life.

"I'm afraid I'm not relating well to Dr. Briggs."

Dr. Parker's kind eyes reminded her of how she had first thought of him as a sea captain. Strange how, now, it should comfort her to know him as a fine doctor. "You usually get along with everyone so well."

"You see, Dr. Briggs and I have a—a history. He treated my mother for tuberculosis seven years ago."

The older man's eyebrows rose to the brim of his hat. "Is that so?"

"She died under Dr. Briggs' care."

A log in the woodstove popped and Atta jumped.

"I'm terribly sorry to hear of that, Miss Atta. Unfortunately, these things happen. It's a sad part of the medical profession. I've lost more than my fair share of patients too, I'm afraid."

She must tell him. No matter if she looked foolish. Her sister's safety may depend on it.

"I've reason to believe he experimented on my mother without permission from my father, sir. I found a bottle—sulfur something. When I confronted Dr. Briggs, he seemed to be hiding something. You see, I'm afraid he's treating the patients on the island with the same lack of care."

Dr. Parker looked above his spectacles at her. "That's a serious accusation. What cause do you have to make it?"

"I've been on the chaulmoosan for near five months with no improvements. I've rapidly declined, and still Dr. Briggs insists on the treatment. He ignores my say in the matter and refuses to hear me out."

Dr. Parker paced the room. "I will be certain to speak with him, dear. Perhaps he is not fully aware of the rights we bestow upon our patients here."

That was it? Did Dr. Parker not care about Dr. Briggs's past? About what he did to Mami?

"Dr. Parker, is sulfur used to treat tuberculosis?"

The older man scratched the left side of his face, beneath his curled mustache. "I'll admit, it does sound like an experimental treatment. But I'm afraid I don't have the facts. Do you know for certain your father did not approve such a measure?"

Papi had been protective of Mami. He wouldn't put her life in the hands of an overeager doctor, would he? Had he been desperate? As desperate as she'd been when trying the cold water treatment with Gertie?

"No, I suppose not."

"Put your mind at ease, Miss Atta. I will speak to Dr. Briggs. You will no longer have to take the chaulmoosan if you do not choose to do so. Rest assured I will also make the board aware of your suspicions regarding your mother and Dr. Briggs. They alone have the right to do anything about his position here."

His words were said with care, and yet they held an underlying message. For what member on the board would heed the warnings of a leper—would put her word before an educated doctor's?

And once again, her faith floundered. It seemed all the joy had been stolen from her with Harry's departure. She could manage to write the proper words of faith in her letters to Harry, could manage to spout them to Gertie, but in her heart of hearts, fear and doubt and guilt threatened to diminish all God had done for her.

"Dr. Parker, could a treatment of sulfur have killed my mother?"

"Dear, tuberculosis is a deadly disease. Most likely, that was the cause of your mother's death. But to answer your question, yes. Sulfur is quite dangerous, especially when handled in experimentation."

His words cemented her fears. She'd played a part in killing Mami. She'd never said anything. Even if God could forgive her for so big a transgression, she didn't deserve that forgiveness—neither from Him or herself. Worse yet, she'd failed in caring for Gertie— the one precious thing Mami had left in her charge.

Chapter Forty-Five

Boston survived without his father.

Harry didn't believe it possible. For so long, he considered the city and his father as one, but with the exception of the numerous placards in windows—many draped in black—and the woman driver of the tram, everything about his childhood home seemed the same.

News of his father's death had come to him overseas. The influenza epidemic had taken not only half of William Mayhew's patients' lives, but his as well.

Harry had shed his tears in Germany and vowed to leave them there. With so much death surrounding him, it had been easy to harden himself. But his father...the man he'd revered, worshipped. Harry had never earned his approval. They'd still been at odds when he died.

Harry removed the mask over his nose before climbing the stairs to his family's verandah.

"Dr. Mayhew? Is that you?"

He turned at the sound of the familiar voice, music to his ears.

"Timmy, my boy!" He scooped the boy up in a hug, surprised at how good it was to see him, how much he'd grown in two years.

The child hung limp in his arms but snuggled his head against his neck. Loud sobs quaked his small body.

Compassion climbed Harry's chest. He was still human, after all. Good to know.

"What is it, Tim?" He gestured for the lad to sit on the top step of the verandah and sat beside him. The sight of his old stethoscope at the boy's neck pulled at his heartstrings.

"I—I tried to save them, Dr. Mayhew. But there was nothing I could do. Dr. Phillips said to cool them with a cold compress, and I did, I swear it. I didn't fall asleep last night or the night before, but —but they died this morning." Shiny tears magnified the boy's freckles.

"Who died, Tim?"

"Mother and Father." Timmy hiccupped back a sob. "I couldn't save them. If only you'd been there."

Harry put an arm around the boy, his throat welling with emotion. Timmy thought he could save the world, just as he'd thought his father could save the world. But none of them could.

"Tim, I wouldn't have been able to save your parents."

His wet gaze lifted. "You—you wouldn't have?"

Harry shook his head. "No. The influenza...there's nothing we can do. You did what any good doctor would have done, Tim. I am so sorry about your parents, though."

Timmy sniffed and studied his scuffed shoes. "Me too."

The steady clip-clop of a horse's shoes sounded against the cobbles of the street—a carriage to take away bodies. A loud, methodic voice rang out. "Bring out your dead!"

Harry shivered. Maybe Boston wasn't the same after all.

"Don't you have an aunt close by?"

Timmy shook his head. "The influenza took her last month, too."

The boy had nobody?

Harry's mother had nobody.

"Why don't you come in, Tim? We'll see about getting you something to eat."

The boy's eyes widened. "I don't know, sir. The last time your father saw me out here—"

"Father won't be hassling you any longer, little man."

Was it wrong to enjoy the relief in Timmy's eyes, the relief in his own heart?

He herded Timmy to the kitchen, fetched some milk from the icebox and a few Hydrox cookies from the cookie jar. "I'll be back. Make yourself at home."

Timmy lifted a cookie in a sort of toast. "Thanks, Dr. Mayhew," he said, his mouth full.

Harry placed his bag at the bottom of the stairs and started up the long, grand flight to the second floor. The house lay empty, quiet without his father's foreboding presence.

He knocked on the walnut door of his parents' bedroom. No answer. He knocked again before trying the knob.

Darkness cloaked the room, allowing only a thin shaft of sunlight from the center of the drapes. The faint scent of laudanum laced the air. Who, if anyone, was looking after his mother?

"Mom?"

A form shifted on the bed as he drew closer.

"Harry? Is it really you?"

"Yes, Mother. I've come home." He sat on the edge of the bed. Her frail arms inched around his neck and he held her quaking body close. She was so fragile. Strange how he had always been the one to take care of her. He couldn't remember a time when their roles had been reversed.

"He's gone, Harry. Gone..."

"I know." He held her for a bit longer before breaking away to open the drapes.

Amid the bright sunlight, his mother appeared shriveled and

small within the grand bed and its luxurious satin sheets. "He loved you, dear. You know that, don't you?"

Harry sniffed quick and hard. "He had a funny way of showing it." So did she—never answering his letters all this time. Was she also disappointed he hadn't married Carrie? Had her father gone through with the lawsuit?

"I know at times he was controlling and appeared cold, but he only wanted what was best for you, Harry. Please believe that."

"Yes, Mother." He hadn't come home to argue.

He looked out the window to the street below, where two men carried a body wrapped in a sheet toward the priest's horse-drawn carriage. They placed it alongside two other corpses. Harry turned away.

"Is it better out there?"

"I'm afraid not."

His mother laid back against the fluffy pillows. "At least you're home now, dear."

Should he tell her so soon? Blast, it wouldn't get easier if he waited. "I'm only home for a week. Then I'll be going back."

She sat up again, put a thin hand to her head in the dramatic fashion he knew too well. "To Europe? But I heard a report that the war will soon be over."

"Not to Europe, Mother. To Penikese."

"That wretched island? Harry—"

"The patients need me. I've been gone more than a year as it is." He hadn't received a letter from Atta in months. He'd spent countless sleepless nights contemplating her future and the disease that separated them. His worst fear lay exposed before him. Was Atta still alive? And what of Gertie?

He hadn't written Dr. Parker for fear of the answers.

"They are not your patients, Harry. They may have been, for a short while. But no longer. Your father left you his practice, dear. You have patients here who need you. They have no one else."

"Father's wealthy patients have their pick of doctors in this city. It is the patients on that island who have no one."

She shrank back as if he'd slapped her. "You would desert everything your father worked for? Leave it all to the wolves?"

"He's left you well-provided for, has he not? Or was Mr. Gerard successful in his suit?"

"You talk so callously, Harry."

Hadn't he a right? He wanted to tell his mother of the advice his father had given him that day on Penikese, reveal to her the ugly side of the man she'd married. But such information wouldn't help her. She needed to remember William Mayhew as a man of integrity and power. Fine, then. But he didn't have to stay around to satisfy her fantasy.

"The suit didn't hold up in court, thank God," she said.

Harry's mouth pulled into a firm line. Thank God. He remembered Atta thanking God for far simpler things, for the sunrise and the moon that ruled the stars. Atta thanked God for giving her the disease so that, through it, she would come to know Him. How petty his mother sounded compared to his Atta, an outcast.

He gazed out the window, past the tall buildings to the sun setting on the horizon.

"You've changed." Her gaze drilled into him, searing the back of his neck.

"Yes, I have."

They'd run out of words to say to one another. Then he remembered. "There's a boy downstairs. I used to speak to him often, a neighbor of ours. Timmy. He's lost both his parents just this morning."

His mother's hand flew to her mouth. "Oh my. Is he sick?"

"His heart is sick. He's having a hard time, Mother. I was hoping he could stay here for the next couple of days until he can get back on his feet."

"Is he contagious? I mean, I've been drinking that awful black draught tea your father recommended, but..."

He squeezed his eyes shut. The woman didn't possess an ounce of compassion. "I don't believe Timmy's contagious. It would only be for the week. I'll find other arrangements for him before I leave."

"Whatever you wish, Harry." She stood, pulled her robe tighter, and sat at her vanity.

"I'm glad to see you're getting up."

"Of course I am. We have a guest in the house. I want to make sure he's treated as such."

Harry left the room to allow his mother privacy. Maybe, just maybe, his mother and Timmy would help each other during this difficult time.

ATTA PRESSED her lips together to keep from crying out. Mrs. Parker shuffled into the hospital room, lay a hand first on Gertie's forehead and then on Atta's bumpy one. "My poor dears. Would you like me to read to you?"

Gertie nodded, but Atta lay limp in the bed. She didn't bother getting up anymore. She was too weak.

The arrival of summer had brought some relief to both of them, and at first Atta gave the credit to ceasing the chaulmoosan, but soon fall's bitterness swept in to steal her respite. Most of the time she couldn't feel her arms and legs, but her upper and lower extremities would often burn with pain at the slightest touch. Even a light sheet felt like heavy metal searing her skin. It grew harder and harder to blink, which caused her eyes to become dry and she feared, soon, ulcerated or blind. Every breath was blocked, congestion overtaking her insides. Just like Lucy.

But that wasn't the worst of it. The worst was the faint odor drifting up from her rotting skin. The last time she'd looked in a mirror—nearly a month ago—she'd been so disgusted by her blotchy face and puffy eyes, she'd vowed never to look at herself again.

Her reaction to her appearance, to her pain, caused her more distress. She was a child of God! Such nominal things as the way she looked should not depress her. But every time she looked at Gertie, a deep sadness exploded in her soul. Now, she understood Gertie's prayer that Jesus take her home.

She tuned in to Mrs. Parker's words, seeking comfort.

"Nay, in all these things we are more than conquerors through Him that loved us. For I am persuaded, that neither death, nor life, nor angels, nor principalities, nor powers, nor things present, nor things to come, nor height, nor depth, nor any other creature, shall be able to separate us from the love of God, which is in Christ Jesus our Lord."

Nothing could separate her from God's love. Nothing. Maybe not even her own weak faith.

A knock sounded at the door after Mrs. Parker had finished reading the passage. Atta didn't look up but heard Mrs. Parker's soft gasp. "Dr. Mayhew! What a fine surprise this is."

Atta's heart leapt at Harry's name. He'd come back. Harry... here. It had been more than a year since she'd seen him, yet all her insecurities snuffed out her excitement. He shouldn't have come. Oh, how he shouldn't have come. To see her like this...he'd claimed he'd loved her once, but that was before the disease left her skin swollen and festering.

She crouched farther down into the sheets, wincing against the pain along her back. She watched Gertie raise a weak hand in greeting. "Dr. Mayhew."

Harry walked to her sister, but his gaze rested on Atta. She refused to meet it, her heart strumming with irregularity like a broken banjo, heat rushing to her blotchy face.

"Gertie, how are you, dear?" Her sister didn't answer. "There now, don't cry. I have something for you."

Harry pulled a brown bag from his pocket and popped a ruby

red spice drop from the package. Gertie smiled when he offered it to her. Harry winked and placed the bag beside her bed. "Maybe you'll share some with your sister."

Atta avoided his gaze as he walked with slow steps toward her. "Hello, Atta."

She swallowed, her eyes darting around the room, landing anywhere but on him. "Hello."

"I heard you folks obtained some sort of moving picture outfit. I figured I'd come and check out Charlie Chaplin myself."

So this is how it would be. Jokes. Jokes to avoid the horrid truth. Jokes to avoid the fact that time in the real world had certainly awakened him to the fact that he couldn't possibly love a leper, that he couldn't possibly love her.

He lowered himself to the bed, first checking to see if Mrs. Parker had left the room. Atta tried to hide how the slight shift on the bed pained her.

"I'm—I'm sorry. I didn't realize—" He jumped up, grabbed Mrs. Parker's vacant chair and brought it by the bed.

"It's fine, Dr. Mayhew. Please, it's fine." She was scared he would leave, scared he would stay. Scared she disgusted him. Her skin, her voice which came out croaky and hoarse. Like Lucy's in the last months of her life.

"So we're back to this doctor business again, are we, Miss Schaeffer?"

She couldn't help the smile that cracked her lips. How she'd longed for him, and now, when he was finally here, she couldn't reach out a numb, blotchy hand to touch him. Oh, to know his arms around her once more...but it was impossible. He must be disgusted by her. Not to mention that the pain of an embrace would prove excruciating.

"I missed you, Atta. I'm sorry—so sorry I wasn't here for you."

He felt guilty. That was the reason for his visit.

"Please, Harry. You should leave. It's too, too—"

"Too what?"

"Painful to see you." Surely, it was as painful for him.

"Atta?"

The room filled with silence and she knew he wouldn't speak until she brought her gaze to his. He'd never looked more handsome, his eyes never a clearer blue. Beside her own disfigurement, he appeared perfect. Shining. Like a dream.

He placed a light, tentative hand on her upper arm, covered with the bed sheet. "I'm not going anywhere."

A sob rose in her throat as relief flooded her veins, instant and satisfying. She shook her head back and forth against the pillow. She was so undeserving of this man. "You'll only regret it."

"My dove, I'm quite positive I won't."

HARRY SAT with Atta for the rest of the afternoon. In between their small snatches of conversation, his mind searched for a way to fix her, to fix Gertie. Her breaths haunted him, each labored struggle spurring his desperation.

There must be something they hadn't tried. He could inject the leprosy bacillus into himself, maybe. If he could acquire the disease, he'd be able to experiment freely on himself without risking another's life. But it'd been tried—and failed—more times than one could count.

Dusk settled over the island and Gertie slept. His heart clenched with such intense pain he thought he might die from the hurt.

Atta would leave him.

She would go be with God and leave him alone. But no, he was too selfish to let God have her yet. There had to be a way.

Shadows from the fire bounced off the white walls, off Atta's face, where the marks of disease lay evident. Her ears were swollen and her nose looked as if it would soon collapse. How painful to see the face of a loved one change.

"I'm sorry about your father. How is your mother doing?" She seemed more willing to speak in the dim light.

"She's stronger than she thinks. She's taking care of a neighborhood orphan. I think they're helping one another cope."

"That's nice."

Silence.

"Thank you for your letters. I hope it's all right that I used them—parts of them, anyway."

Gertie's soft snores rattled through the room, and Atta craned her neck to check on her sister. "How so?"

"I read some to the men who were dying. You wrote once of hope. It helped them a great deal."

"I'm glad."

"Maybe I should read it to you?"

She laughed, a humorless, dry sound. "That obvious, is it?"

"You've lost your fire, my dove. Where has it gone?" He'd loved that calm fire. Still loved her without it, but it was as if only half of her existed. He longed to help her find the other half.

"Will Dr. Briggs be leaving now that you're here?"

She'd ignored his question, but he chose not to press.

"That's what I'm told."

"Good." Her hard tone fell like a brick.

"Has he mistreated you? Tell me and I'll make certain—"

"No, no, it's nothing, Harry. Please. I don't wish to speak of him anymore." She shifted in the bed. He stood to light the lamp. "No, don't. I'd rather we stay in the dark."

He ignored her, lighting the lamp with a nearby match, but kept the flame low. When he sat down again, he pulled himself closer until he could clearly see every mar on her pretty face, until he could take in her beautiful eyes. "You don't scare me."

"I scare myself," she whispered.

He raised his fingers to her temple, ran a gentle hand along her face. "Atta Schaeffer, you are still beautiful to me. Your spirit is what captured my heart in the first place. And I am certain that God considers you one of his best creations."

She licked her lips, sadness etching her features. "And what do you know of God, Dr. Mayhew?"

"I know that He's a part of you." He swallowed, suddenly realizing the truth. "I know that His light was what drew me to you in the first place." He hadn't been able to see past his own ego, his own stubbornness. But now, seeing his beloved again, the truth lay exposed. He'd missed her so much, had been angry at God for her fate. Now, being in her presence again, he knew everything she'd once believed was truer than anything he'd ever trusted. God had never left her. God had never left him.

He thought of Albin Zielinski, of Harry's own poor choices, of his stubborn pride. And still, God would forgive him, for everything. The realization was a sweet breath of freedom to his soul.

"Atta, I think I'm beginning to see why you love your God so much. He pursues us, doesn't he? Each of us are rebels, but he pursues us with His love. No matter the cost. He died and lives still for us. For me."

Atta looked at him in wonder. He ran his fingers along her cheekbones and felt her soft breath pass her lips. True love. God had shown him in a heartbeat what Atta had been trying to show him for months. God was the loving Father Harry had wished for all his life.

Real love.

Real love sacrificed. Not out of guilt or a desire to succeed, but out of love.

With that knowledge, Harry realized the only possible way to save Atta from the disease eating at her body, at her life.

The only way lay open before him, and he would do it gladly. He'd pursue her with the fullness of his passion, as God had pursued him.

And if his Heavenly Father saw fit to take his life in the process, then that was a risk Harry was willing to take.

Chapter Forty-Six

November 21, 1918

Dear Professor Hoffmeyer,

   While in a former letter I had discarded the notion of using dapsone in the treatment of Hansen's disease, circumstances have changed and I am now most interested in researching this treatment.

   The only thing I have found on my own is that the drug has a history of being used to treat cows with breast infections resulting in sour milk. Do you know of the dosages given to the cows? If this mammal has the ability to cope with the medication, it gives me hope that it might be used on my patients. Would you recommend beginning with a small dose? Please forward your reply quickly, as I am anxious to test the results. As always, please send my regards to Mr. Schaeffer, if you are still in contact with him.

   Sincerely,

   Dr. Harvey Mayhew

Niklas placed Florence's letter beneath his pillow and stared into the darkness, imagining the paper before him, her neat hand evident with each swirl of ink. He looked forward to receiving her letters, surprised each time he saw his name in her flowing script. She hadn't given up on him. She spoke of her faith most often and at first, it bothered him. Then he realized this was the same God she prayed to concerning him and his daughters.

And so, hesitant, he'd listened. Listened until his sober soul ached with knowing. And now this last letter seemed to pry at his heart with warm pliers, longing to open it up to something better, something bigger.

Florence had written of forgiveness. Niklas knew he wasn't perfect, but if things had been different—if his Katharina hadn't been taken from him—then, maybe he would have made better choices. But when he read Florence's letters, they had a strange way of making him accountable. He didn't know how she did it. Her words were innocent enough, most times she didn't point to his life as the failure, but to hers.

What would it be like to be forgiven? That's what he wanted most from his daughters, however impossible—their forgiveness.

An invisible voice called to him, and he couldn't find the strength to ignore it. For the first time, he opened himself up to it. Allowed himself to be vulnerable. Allowed himself to ask for forgiveness from Florence's God.

A swift, warm peace enveloped his being and with it a sureness. A light freedom. A knowing that the God of hope who'd sent His Son for sinners, of which Niklas had a leg-up on most, was not just Florence's God, but his also.

A foreign tear crept down his cheek at the undeserved mercy, and he didn't bother swiping it away.

If God could grant him such favors, was it unrealistic to hope his daughters might also?

~

ATTA CRUMPLED the letter with her palms, grateful Gertie was off to use the water closet so she wouldn't ask questions. She flung the piece of paper across the room, ignoring the prickling pain surfacing on her skin with the forceful action.

Forgive him? Forgive him! If it weren't for him, she and Gertie would have grown up beneath a loving household. If it weren't for him, Gertie wouldn't have gone to live with foster parents. If it weren't for him, she'd know the love of a father.

Her father—a Christian. The notion should have made her happy, but instead it revealed the ugly nature of her heart. She wanted the forgiveness and grace for herself, for Gertie, for Harry and even for all the patients. But she wanted her father out of the circle of mercy.

A commotion outside her room brought her attention back to the present. Dr. Parker barged in. "Miss Atta, if I could please impose on you to speak some sense to Dr. Mayhew."

Atta blinked. Dr. Parker had never acknowledged her relationship with Harry outside that of a doctor and his patient. But surely, he saw more than they cared to admit. "That appears to be a tall order, Dr. Parker."

The older man grunted. "Indeed."

Harry appeared behind him. "I don't see that this involves Miss Schaeffer in any way. If you please, Dr. Parker, let's resume our conversation in the confines of the examination room."

Dr. Parker raised his hands to the sides of his head in a rare show of frustration. "How you managed to secure the drug with government money is beyond me."

"All perfectly legal, sir."

Dr. Parker ignored Harry and sat on the chair beside Atta's bed. "Dear, Harry's got it in his head to try out a sulfur drug on himself before administering it to any patients for the treatment of leprosy."

Atta's brain froze. Sulfur drug. Mami's killer. Why would Harry—

"He's pulling this foolish feat for you, my dear. You must talk some sense into him." Dr. Parker stood. "And for the record and as superintendent of this island, let it be shown that I do not condone this practice."

Harry shoved his hands in his pockets, a quirky grin on his face. "Duly noted, sir."

"So help me, Harry, if I have to write the board of this—this irresponsibility—I will."

"Have not many doctors sacrificed their own well-being for the sake of medicine, Dr. Parker? Have you not sacrificed your own career, if not your health, here on Penikese? I don't see how this is any different."

Dr. Parker stared at Harry for a moment before turning his attention to Atta. "I leave him to you, my dear." He left, closing the door behind him.

"Harry, I don't understand. Why would you—"

"I'm unsure of the effects the drug can have on the human body. It only makes sense to try it on a healthy individual first. I'm not even sure it will cure Hansen's, but the first step is to locate a proper dosage."

"But—but sulfur drugs can be deadly."

He squinted at her. "What do you know of them, my dove?"

"My mother died after being administered sulfur."

Harry rubbed his forehead. "Your mother was sick, didn't you say? I'm healthy. I'm certain my body can take it."

She shook her head and sat up as best she could, shrugged him off when he came to help her. "Administer it to me instead."

"No."

"I can't get any worse, Harry. You'll be able to test the drug's effect on both the human body and Hansen's."

"No." The stubborn set in his jaw, the storminess in those ocean-blue eyes was all too familiar. He had made up his mind.

"Why not?"

"Your condition is too weak. An improper dose of the drug will kill you."

What did it matter? What merit was her life? She couldn't attend to her sister. A useless lump on a hospital bed, half her body wrapped in bandages, the outside air and the pine tree all out of touch.

"Please, Harry. My life is worth so much less than yours."

He gritted his teeth. Without warning, he strode to her side and flipped back the covers despite her protests. Carefully, he slid his hands beneath her body and lifted her to his chest. The pressure of his arms should have been excruciating, but the pleasure she found in his grip numbed the pain. With feeble attempts, she tried to hide her bandaged ankles, but he pushed her hands away and started out the door.

"Where are you taking me?"

"I have to show you something."

Arguing failed to change the mind of a man so stubborn. She laid her head beneath his neck, enjoying the security of his embrace, how steady he walked, how certain he was of his hold on her.

A cold breeze wrapped around them, lifting loose tendrils of hair from her face. He didn't stop walking until they'd reached the shore. "Look around you, my dove."

She opened her eyes, saw the endless ocean, pink streaks painting the sky rosy hues. A seagull's cry pierced the air. The pine tree, bright and green and alive. The scent of chilled salt teased her nostrils.

"What am I looking for?"

"Not what are you looking for. *Who* are you looking for. A very special young woman once told me that His thumbprint is on every aspect of creation, His worth embedded in everything He's made. In you, Atta."

She stared off at the pink orb setting in the sky. "I used to believe that."

"I still do. I can't tell you how precious you are to me." He squeezed her tighter and she bore the pain for the sake of feeling his arms close. "I love you, Atta. And as much as I love you, I'm certain that God must care for you more. He's about to do a wondrous work. Whether or not it turns out as we wish is yet to be determined."

She snuggled against him, the scent of bay rum playing chords of pleasure on the strings of her heart. "You shouldn't have come back."

His chin dug into her head, his lips played against her hair. "I would have been lost forever if I hadn't."

Chapter Forty-Seven

Harry injected the drug in the vein of his left arm, sore from the repeated injections. Two fifty-milligram injections per day, on Professor Hoffmeyer's recommendation. He'd worked it out to the last detail, had begun to experience the effects of the drug two days ago. Slight nausea and fever, tension in his muscles, nervousness in his thoughts. His eyes were sensitive to the sun, his ears to any type of noise. He avoided Atta, refusing to give her reason to fear for him more than necessary.

A knock sounded at the door as Harry finished off the injection. Dr. Parker strode in, set his medical bag on the table, and looked down at Harry. "I'm relieving you of your duties here, Harry."

Harry stood, steadying himself on the exam table. "Sir, you can't—"

"I'm not intending to interfere in this experiment of yours, but I think it best you keep yourself at the administration building. The patients are talking about how ill you look. I agree. You're in no condition to be their doctor at this time."

If only Dr. Parker spoke quieter, Harry would be able to think.

"I will tend the patients myself, Harry. I will also be checking in on you three times daily. Is that understood?"

He should refuse, but the thought of his own cool bed on the other side of the island quieted any arguments. "Yes, sir."

"Frank."

Harry managed a weak smile. "Yes, Frank." He scooped up his medical bag and turned to leave.

"Harry? Have you thought of decreasing the doses? Maybe three twenty-five milligram doses instead of two fifties?"

He had. But that would take too long. Already, Atta struggled significantly more with breathing than she had a week earlier.

"I don't have enough time. If I can be certain that a healthy human body can take the hundred milligrams, I plan to start a lower dose on Atta."

Dr. Parker sighed, seeming to accept that Harry would continue on. "I'll take good care of her. I promise."

"I know. There's no one I trust more."

"ARE the teas helping your breathing at all?" Dr. Parker tucked his stethoscope back in his bag, his mouth in a grim line.

"A bit." Atta hated the hoarseness of her voice, hated how she couldn't lift her head off the pillow without extreme effort. "How's Harry?"

"He's holding on. A will of steel, that one has."

"But—but is he well?"

Dr. Parker stood. "You needn't worry about Dr. Mayhew, Atta. He just received a letter from that Professor—Hoffmeyer, I think his name is—at the internment camp, suggesting he lower the doses, as I have done repeatedly. If he refuses, I plan to confiscate the drug from him."

Harry couldn't be doing well if Dr. Parker considered such

measures. "Internment camp? But why is Harry taking direction from a doctor there?"

Dr. Parker glanced up, licked his lips. "The friend of your father's—I thought you knew."

"My father? What does he have to do with any of this?" Her ragged voice caught, frustrating her further.

Dr. Parker's knuckles turned white against his black bag. "Atta, I didn't mean for you to find out this way. I thought Harry told you."

"Told me what?"

"Your father and Harry have been communicating, along with a friend of your father's who has studied Hansen's. This professor developed the idea of the sulfur drug."

It didn't surprise her when she'd found out Papi had landed himself in prison. It didn't even surprise her that he'd made an effort to communicate with Harry. But that he still had the power to reach halfway across the country to destroy everything dear to her shook her to the core.

Everything Papi touched, withered. First Gertie, now Harry. A hatred so pure and frightening gripped her and with it, an all-consuming desperation.

She needed to speak to Harry. Somehow, she needed to get to the other side of the island.

EVERY STEP, every roll of her foot, singed the soles of her feet. First her toes, then the ball of her foot, and finally her heel, crackling over frozen ground. Atta walked with halting steps beneath the sharp, cold moonlight. She remembered the night long ago when she'd tried to escape. How would things have been different if she and Gertie had made it to New York?

The white stucco of the administration building glowed beneath the white light. She hadn't a clue which room was his, or how she'd find him. She checked the gas lamp hanging from her wrist and prayed no one would see its light.

The sound of waves rushing the distant shore roared in her ears and she picked up her pace. It felt odd to climb the stairs to the administration building—like a distant neighbor's house one saw from the road, but never went near. Using the sleeve of her night-gown, she tried the handle by pushing both of her palms together. The door creaked open.

Her heart pounded against her ribcage. The Parkers had been nothing but kind to her, and here she brazenly broke one of the basic rules of the island—again. But if she didn't speak with Harry, he'd continue this nonsense. Nonsense nurtured by her fool of a father.

She started up the stairs, wincing at the whine beneath her light steps.

"Atta."

She froze at Dr. Parker's stern voice.

Her plans were ruined. Dr. Parker would send her back. While kind, he couldn't ignore the rule.

"Sir, I'm sorry. But I have to see him. Please." Her voice sounded sicker on this side of the island. The good side. The healthy side.

She didn't face the doctor, but closed her eyes against his silence, braced herself for his chastisement.

"Second door on the left."

She blew out a long breath. "Thank you."

"I have to warn you. I was a bit light on the truth earlier today. Harry is not well, Atta. I'm taking him to the mainland tomorrow. He needs more help than I can give him here."

She wound her arm around the rail of the staircase, unable to grip with her fingers. No, no. Her Harry. What had he done to himself? What had she done to him?

As fast as she could, she scurried up the stairs, pulling her body with the little strength left in her arms, no longer caring if she touched the fine wood with her own tainted skin.

When she reached the designated door, she didn't knock, but hobbled in and placed the lamp on a table by Harry's bed. He didn't awaken at first and she gazed at him beneath the dim light of the gas lamp. Beads of sweat laced his brow. He moaned, tossed his head back and forth. She placed her limp fingers on his forehead and whispered his name.

When his eyes opened, the dazed cloud over them frightened her. Minutes passed before it lifted. "Atta? What—what are you—"

"I needed to talk to you. I can't let you...please. Please stop taking the sulfur. I beg you." She kneeled down on the hardwood. It dug into her skin with fierce, driving precision.

"I won't be taking anymore. Dr. Parker has seen...to that."

Good. "I can't believe my father could do this. I can't believe—"

"Your father only wanted to help. This...is not his fault."

The devil it wasn't. "You don't know him. Papi's never gone out of his way for either Gertie or me, or anyone. He is to blame for all of this."

"My dove." Harry whispered the words, then shook his head again as if battling some inner demon. Wetness fell from his blond curls and Atta dug her rosary from her pocket, remembering how the cold beads had often comforted her. Now, they barely registered in her numb fingers. She placed the cool metal of the crucifix over Harry's forehead and he stilled. "My dove, such fire. Forgive, and ye shall be forgiven."

She struggled against the burning behind her eyes. Jesus's words from her beloved's mouth. She'd never heard anything so beautiful. Anything so convicting. If possible, she loved him all the more.

Forgive, and ye shall be forgiven.

Was that what had robbed her of God's peace? Her unforgiving spirit? Yet, how could she forgive her father for all he'd done? How could she forgive Dr. Briggs for his own actions? How could she forgive herself?

"I've found freedom, Atta. Freedom in forgiveness. In forgiving my own father. Join me."

She wanted to. Oh, but she wanted to be free.

Harry's Adam's apple bobbed and he ran his tongue along his lips. When he began to sing, his normally strong voice, weakened by the experimental drugs, caused her tears to spill forth onto their joined hands.

> "I hear the Savior say,
> thy strength indeed is small,
> child of weakness...watch and pray,
> find in me...thine all in all."

His voice broke off, the sound of his chattering teeth taking their place. Atta pressed her hand harder into his, the song's words caressing her burdened soul as she joined in with her own raspy voice.

> "Jesus paid it all,
> all to Him I owe.
> Sin hath left a crimson stain,
> He washed it white as snow."

Though their voices were nothing pleasant to the ears, the words were a balm to Atta's soul. Jesus paid it all. There was nothing she could or couldn't do to add to it. What right did she have to begrudge forgiveness on others? Her head understood the senselessness, but her heart bucked at the notion of bestowing grace.

But she couldn't ignore the miracle he'd performed in Harry's life. The love she saw. The perfect love that only God could give, which Harry imitated so very well, here in this dark, dank room.

Their voices melded into one, filling the bittersweet moment. Harry put his hand to her cheek and she rested against it as she sang out raspy words.

> "Lord, now indeed I find
> Thy power and Thine alone,
> can change the leper's spots,
> and melt the heart of stone."

God's mighty wings hovered over them, blanketing them in security. She petitioned Him for His hand upon Harry's life. Did He hear her, or did her unforgiving spirit block the way to the path of peace?

> "Jesus paid it all,
> all to Him I owe.
> Sin hath left a crimson stain,
> He washed it white as snow."

Chapter Forty-Eight

Atta inwardly pleaded with the skeptical faces of the patients. It had taken every bit of effort to drag herself to the breakfast table this morning, but a driving need to help Harry pushed her limping form down the hall and to the dining room.

"We should wait for Reverend." Willie Goon nodded his answer, enlisting the support of Quong and several others.

"We don't need a reverend in order to pray. Reverend Bailey isn't scheduled to come for several more days. Dr. Mayhew is very sick. He's sacrificed his own health to help us. Please, help. We're bound by a common sickness, but let's bind ourselves together with something more significant."

She remembered when she'd first glimpsed them all, how scary they'd been to her. Now, they were her brothers and sisters. She no longer saw their deformities, but their spirit to live.

She looked at their faces, at the many who did not worship Christ after many years of listening to Reverend Bailey's simple sermons. Had she been wrong to include them? No. God had created each one, and He could use anything, especially prayer, to draw them and help Harry.

"I want to pray with you, Atta." Gertie shuffled over to Atta's side, supported herself with the arm of the chair.

Mary stood next, a worn Missy clutched in her hands. Then Flavia by her side. Then the newest patient, Julia. Atta smiled appreciation at each of them, thankful that they were willing to take this step of faith with her.

But the men stayed in their seats. It may only take one. She looked at Willie Goon, willing him to look at her, to stand. Silence filled the large room, but finally the Chinaman stood. The rest of the men trickled behind and Atta breathed through her blocked airways, a smile stretching her face.

"Thank you. Thank you, all. Let's start straight away."

"IT'S QUITE a sight over at the hospital."

Harry opened his eyes beneath the blinding sunlight, beneath the pounding noise of Dr. Parker's words. The older man swabbed his arm with cold gauze and pierced his skin with a needle. He wanted to ask Dr. Parker if the injection was more glucose and saline but hadn't the strength.

"Every last patient is in the amusement room—on their knees no less—praying for their doctor. Atta rallied them all."

Atta? The words moved over his brain in a haze. They didn't make sense. Had Atta truly come to him last night, or had he dreamed her presence?

Around him, shadows moved. His own body jerked as he was lifted off the bed. Words were lost at his throat. He needed to help Atta. The dapsone. It would work, he was sure of it. They needed to start in small doses. He only needed to get Dr. Parker's attention...

A cool breeze wafted over his burning flesh. The sun's blinding brightness. Then, complete darkness.

❧ ❧

A LETTER NEVER CAME.

Of course not. He couldn't expect his daughters to forgive such great transgressions. Niklas had been so sure he'd been forgiven. But as each new day passed without a response to his letter, doubt nipped at his heart.

He approached Professor Hoffmeyer, his only hope in gaining contact with Atta and Gertie. The older man looked at him, his spectacles sliding down his nose. "Niklas."

"Professor."

"I'm sorry. I have no news for you."

Niklas tried to keep his head up, but an inner weight pulled it down.

"These things take time, of course. When Dr. Mayhew wrote me last, he said he was ordering the dapsone. It will take some time before he will be able to tell..."

Niklas's heart skidded at the Professor's uncertain tone. "Tell what?"

"I didn't see a need to mention it last time, but Dr. Mayhew was not comfortable testing the drug on his patients. He's decided to administer it to himself to make certain of its viability in the human body."

Niklas swallowed down a thick lump in his throat. He'd never heard of a doctor doing such a thing. Why would Dr. Mayhew risk his own health?

The Professor's mouth tightened. "I'm perplexed as you. All I can gather is that Dr. Mayhew is an extremely conscientious individual. I would say your daughters are in the best of hands."

"*Ja...ja*, I suppose so. Did he say he'd write soon?"

"He did." The older man coughed. "Unfortunately, I won't be here."

"You're going back to Germany." Now that the war had ended,

many of the civilian internees were given a choice of repatriation or remaining at the fort.

"Yes. It might be wise for you to consider the same."

He had considered it. He could start over in Germany. No one would know anything about his past, about his daughters being exiled, that he'd been arrested twice. The idea held appeal. Atta hadn't answered him, probably wanted nothing to do with him. His daughters were better off without him, anyway.

But there it was again. That niggling urge to make things right. Maybe he wouldn't be forgiven. Maybe he'd have to live with this black chain around his soul for the remainder of his days. But at least he would have tried.

"I can't leave my daughters, Professor."

The educated man nodded. "I understand." He scribbled something on a piece of paper and held it out to Niklas. "That's my mother's address. Send her an address where I can contact you. I'll pass along any information about your daughters that I receive."

"Thank you for your help." Niklas held out his hand.

"Good luck."

The two men parted ways, and Niklas walked into the moonlight, its gleam glinting off the barbed wire.

ATTA'S prayer hugged Gertie in a warm blanket. At first, her legs had hurt so much she couldn't think about kneeling, but when she'd seen Willie Goon with his big bandaged feet on his knees, Gertie somehow found the strength to ignore the hurt. Kat knelt beside her.

"I won't be comin' anymore."

Gertie nodded her head, had sensed some time ago that Kat would be leaving her.

"Tha's got a more fittin' friend, I'll warrant."

Gertie sniffed. She'd neglected Kat for some time now, had turned to Jesus instead of her friend from Yorkshire.

"Goodbye Kat," she whispered. "Thank you."

Gertie sunk into the warmth of the prayers as Kat disappeared. Then, a strange thing happened. The pain in her legs went away. Almost like it melted from her body into the floor. As the patients prayed, it continued to melt until at last, for the first time in a year, it was no longer there.

Atta stopped praying and coughed. When she didn't stop hacking, Gertie opened her eyes. Atta clutched at her throat, her eyes bigger than Miss Betsy's pancakes. Gertie's heart tripped. She reached for her sister, her heart racing faster than a wild horse. Atta drew in a thin breath. Shook her head.

Atta's eyes rolled back in her head. Then, Gertie's sister collapsed.

Chapter Forty-Nine

1993

Gram's voice wobbles as she speaks of my Aunt Atta's approaching demise. My own throat thickens. Even another rewatch of *The Princess Bride* won't cheer me up now.

I touch the arm of Gram's rocking chair and seek out her bony fingers. I squeeze.

Sam stares at the planks of the porch floorboards, eerily silent. He has been as much a fixture around here lately as the hummingbirds visiting Gram's feeder.

June had danced its way onto the shores of Cape Cod. Sam and I had graduated. He came over a few times a week when he wasn't working or busy with his grandfather. We ate lunch or dinner together, then sat on the porch and allowed Gram to whisk us away to another time, to an island just past the sea we faced.

I loved these moments. Each of us knew what it was like to be outside of social norms. Gram, with her label of leper, me hiding my pregnancy to protect my father's political aspirations, and Sam, an orphan who would forever feel the consequences of his brother's actions. Strange, but amidst Gram and Sam's companionship, I didn't miss the graduation parties back home; senior prom or the beach trip I was to take with a group of my friends. It all seemed so far away. Another life away, even. I wanted time to pause right here, with hot, lazy July days, walks on the beach with Gram, ice cream at night with Sam.

"Your healing," I say, "was it a miracle, then? Did it have nothing to do with Harry's experiments?"

Gram nods. "God healed me completely and fully. I never found another mark upon me."

"That's totally awesome." I rub my hands over my large belly. Little Nugget twirls somersaults within. On Monday, my OB/GYN said that I am measuring larger than expected. I pray the baby will stay snug within my womb for as long as possible. While I realize an adoption will be in the child's best interest, I also fear the departure from the tiny human growing inside.

"And Atta died," Sam says, stripping the moment of its awe. He sounds bitter, and I can only imagine him thinking of his brother's death on the same island.

I hold my breath, waiting for Gram to set Sam straight. But she swallows. "My sister considered herself healed in the way that matters most."

No...no, Atta couldn't die. I mean, of course she died. But not here, not now, in this terrible way, without seeing Harry one more time and leaving my grandmother all alone. And what was Gram thinking, touting this as some "hopeful" story? Where was the hope? Was Gram going to claim it was this hazy, otherworldly hope I couldn't quite grasp?

Anger stirs in my belly, but I keep it from bursting into the open. I was the one who had asked Gram to tell me about Penikese, after all. I was the one showing up on her doorstep with nothing to offer but mushy cheesecakes and inadequate dinner help.

I try to reconcile my anger with the type of healing Gram insists Atta had.

My sister considered herself healed in the way that matters most.

What would it be like to consider my circumstances secondary to a greater plan? Even riddled with leprosy, my aunt believed that God was good, that He loved her.

What if I could believe the same?

The thought splits me open, but I don't dwell on it. It's too unpredictable, too foreign. Too frightening.

"I've never visited Atta's grave on Penikese. Tomorrow will be the first time," Gram says.

"You've been on the island many times with the school and all. Why didn't you visit?"

"I suppose I liked to think of my sister as alive with the Lord, not buried within the cold ground. But I think I'm ready. Burial spots don't always have to be a reminder of death. In some ways, Atta found life more abundantly than ever on Penikese. That's what I will choose to remember about her."

Sam's jaw remains hard. Gram must see it too. "Are you all right, Sam?" she asks.

Sam sniffs and stands. "I'm okay. Just tired, I guess. I should head home. See you both on Monday?"

That's right. Since Gram and I are traveling to Penikese this weekend, I won't see Sam for an entire three days.

I push myself off the rocking chair and consider asking Sam if he'd like to walk on the beach. I hate the thought of leaving him. Something about the way he's curling into himself right now tells me I might be rebuffed—and yet, he probably needs someone right now.

Gram opens her mouth. "Sam, how would you feel about escorting us to Penikese this weekend?"

Sam blinks, stares at my grandmother. I'm just as shocked as he is. "Um...I don't know. I work Saturday mornings at the library."

"You could ask for it off, couldn't you?" My voice intensifies at the prospect of Sam joining us.

"Maybe. I just—" His gaze tangles with mine before moving to Gram's.

"Emily told me about your brother, Sam. I'm so sorry."

Sam gazes down the length of the porch where a swing is perched in the corner. "Yeah, well..."

"If you don't want to, we will respect your decision." Gram looks deep into Sam's eyes. "Penikese has seen a lot of hardship. But it's seen a lot of healing, too. Maybe it's time for yours."

"With all due respect, ma'am, I'm not certain if one visit to an island is going to erase what my brother did."

"Nor is it going to make losing my sister and my husband any easier," Gram counters. "But it's something I feel called to do. Perhaps your path is not the same. That's okay."

Sam bites his bottom lip. "Can I sleep on it?"

"Of course, dear. Emily and I are catching the boat at nine tomorrow. If you'd like to come, we leave the house at eight."

"Okay. Thanks." He looks at me, one corner of his mouth hitching up in a forced smile. "Either way, see you soon, Emily Grace."

My insides warm. "Bye, Sam."

AT 8:01 a.m. the next morning, Gram and I sit in her Volkswagen, ready to depart.

Sam is not here.

I shift in my seat, slightly crampy from a restless night's sleep. I thought for sure Sam would come with us. But perhaps it was too much, too fast. Perhaps it was even a silly notion—thinking that visiting the island could play a part in healing the sadness inside of Sam.

"We should go," I whisper. "We don't want to miss the boat."

Gram nods and puts the Volkswagen in drive, but she doesn't hide her disappointment. She'd hoped Sam would come, too. She's grown fond of him the last two months. I wonder if my grandfather battled demons over the boys he tried to help. The boys who chose death over life.

Just as Gram presses the gas, a black truck turns into our drive. A flushed Sam spills out of the door. He slings a bag over his shoulder and waves, jogging toward us.

Gram squeezes my hand.

With some effort, I climb out of the passenger's seat to allow Sam in the back.

"Sorry I'm late," he says, huffing slightly from the jog to the car.

I straighten, taking in his messy hair and tanned face. I love this boy, I realize, though I will never tell him. I care for him too much to saddle him with all that I am right now. Maybe some day... "I'm just glad you're here."

Sam ducks into the back of the car. "Ma'am," he says to Gram.

"Sam." She smiles. "Are we ready?"

Yes. I'm ready to experience the end of my aunt's story.

THE BOAT RIDE is choppy and I don't find my sea legs well. The captain hands me a sleeve of saltines, and I nibble on them until he points out a smudge of land that grows into a drab, brown lump of earth in the vast ocean. "There it is."

As we move closer, I make out a long, thin strip of earth that curves around part of the island, bulking at the end like a large comma in the sea. The captain steers the boat to the left of this strip and pulls up alongside a wharf.

When my feet meet land, I breathe in a gusty gulp of air. A man Gram knows greets us and I extend my hand and smile, though my stomach is still uneasy and I can't concentrate on what Gram is saying.

We walk up a crude path toward a large clapboard building with many windows. My grandfather's school.

"This used to be the doctors' residence, right?" Sam asks.

Gram nods. "Dr. and Mrs. Parker and Harry stayed here, on this side of the island. The patients were on the other side. We'll visit in a bit, I'm sure. The cemetery is there as well."

The gravity and wonder of history and my aunt's story surround me, making me forget about my nausea. These people— Gram, Atta, Harry, Dr. and Mrs. Parker—they lived an entire story on this small plot of land. They experienced all that humanity had to offer—love, despair, sadness, fear, happiness, hope.

We're shown the school, which is more of a crude camp with beat-up wooden tables and shelves, simple bedrooms, and a rustic kitchen containing a large woodstove and a long table with benches on either side. A separate room is lined with bookshelves and chairs and couches as well as an additional woodstove.

This building is where the boys lived and learned. This is where Ronny gave up on life.

The school is between sessions now, so no students inhabit the island. That disappoints me a bit, though I understand why the historical society thought it better to conduct the ceremony without the students around. There are only so many accommodations on the island—hence the need for the RSVP. I wonder if Gram was able to get in touch with someone on short notice to let them know Sam was coming.

I share a room with Gram, and Sam is directed to another across the hall. After we put our things away, Mrs. Simmons, a wife of one of the school board members, invites us for lemonade in the shade of the building. Another set of guests will arrive later in the day. The remaining will come tomorrow for the ceremony.

We are finishing our lemonade when Mr. Simmons comes up

the path from the wharf with a spry old man who looks slightly familiar. Gram inhales a sharp intake of breath. "Oh my."

"What is it, Gram?"

"Why, it's your Uncle Harry."

"Uncle Harry? I don't have a—" But I stop. I have an Uncle *Harvey.* I've never met him—my parents didn't think it necessary, but he sends birthday and Christmas cards that my parents always take out of the envelope before giving to me. Now I know why. I buy books with the money he sends and write him thank-you notes. I haven't given him much thought. A distant great-uncle... doesn't everyone have one of those?

Harvey. *Harry.*

Harry Mayhew? My parents don't believe in nicknames—is that why I only know him as Uncle Harvey?

I wet my lips, still trying to piece it all together. "Uncle Harvey is Harry? Aunt Atta's Harry?"

Gram nods, but her attention isn't on me. It's on the man with the white tuft of hair coming toward us. She stands.

But Dr. Harry Mayhew couldn't be my real uncle if my aunt died. Perhaps it was more a title of endearment because of the role Harry played in ministering to my aunt and grandmother upon Penikese? But he'd have to be...

"I haven't seen him since Atta passed on. I was invited to his hundredth birthday last year, but I couldn't bring myself to go." Gram speaks, but it seems she's talking more to herself than to me and Sam. "I should have known he'd come this weekend."

So Harry had survived his experimentation. He had lived on without his love. Without my aunt. And yet, he'd remained invested in what mattered most to my aunt—her little sister. Even going as far as staying in touch with Gram's grandchild.

Pieces of the puzzle come to me slowly, and then all at once. The realization causes my breaths to come faster. Sam leans toward me. "Are you okay?"

I nod. But I'm not okay. My parents shouldn't have kept this from me. I had a right to know about Penikese, about Uncle Harvey—Uncle Harry. But they'd hid it all out of shame or maybe fear. Fear that the stain of Penikese—the stain of Gram's time as a leper—would mar my father's political aspirations. All these years, they'd hidden me away from the truth. And now, when their own daughter threatened to deface their carefully-arranged life, they hid me away as well.

The two men approach and the older man takes Gram's hands. "Gertie," he says, and I can imagine him as Gram's doctor all those years ago, taking care of her, trying with everything within him to heal her.

"My favorite doctor." Gram seems to tease him, years falling off of her in his presence.

"And your favorite brother, I should hope."

"My only brother," she says with warmth as Harry wraps her in an embrace.

My mind jumbles with the onslaught of information.

Gram sniffs. "I miss them both so much." She means Atta, of course. But...

Seeming to remember herself, Gram turns to me, her face glowing. "Harry, this is my granddaughter, Emily." If I didn't know better, I'd say she is *proud* of me.

I hold out my hand. "Uncle...Harvey?"

He smiles, and in it I see a glimmer of youth—the handsome man my aunt fell in love with. He wraps both of his hands around mine. "Emily. It is so good to finally meet you." He turns to my grandmother. "I see Tim in her."

My grandfather...Tim.

"Thank you for all the cards. I'm glad to finally meet you," I manage.

He wraps frail arms around me, surprising me with a firm strength in his embrace. I squeeze back, feeling I know him on an intimate level thanks to Gram's story.

When we release one another, I introduce him to Sam. They

share a handshake. "Sir," Sam says. Though my uncle is respectful, I have an inkling he thinks Sam is the father of my baby. I will have to clear that up later.

"What do you say, Gertie? Are you up for a walk to the other side?"

"Only if these two can come along. I promised to finish my story before the ceremony tomorrow. And I'd like their company when I visit my sister."

Harry cocks his head. A strand of white hair blows upward in the breeze. "Story?"

"Atta's story, of course. Your story. My story. Will you help me finish telling it?"

My uncle's gaze searches out the ocean, and suddenly he is far away. "It has been a long time."

"We'll fill in the pieces for one another," Gram says.

Uncle Harry swallows. "I still miss her with every breath I take."

"Me too," whispers Gram.

My uncle straightens and offers his arm to my grandmother, though I'm certain she will be the one supporting him across the rocky grounds of the island. "Shall we, then?" They start up the hill and my uncle turns around. "Kids?"

Sam offers his arm gallantly to me. "You ready?"

I anchor myself to his side. "I'm not sure I am. But this is why I came."

We catch up to my grandmother and my uncle as Gram fills him in on all she's told us. When Uncle Harry begins to speak, it's as if the pause in Gram's story never existed.

Chapter Fifty

1919

"Ah, so you've come to join the land of the living, have you, Harry?"

Harry blinked. Once. Twice. The voice sounded familiar. The lights above him shone in his eyes. The scent of iodine hung thick in the air.

He licked his lips, worked his tongue around in his mouth. "Where—what's happened?"

The man who belonged to the voice came into view. Dr. Wright. A mask snug over his face, a white lab coat crisp and clean. "You're in Boston, Harry. You became quite ill on Penikese."

He sat up, fast. His head pounded. Too fast. He lay back down. "Atta...how is Atta?"

Dr. Wright's white eyebrows pinched together. "I'm afraid I don't know. There now, rest. You're on the road to recovery, son."

"Is Dr. Parker here?"

"He returned to the island. News of a patient's death came yesterday. He's promised to be back within the week."

A patient's death? His mind scrambled through the list of

patients, making mental check marks on those whose condition could cause imminent death. Wong Quong, Adskhan, Nicholas Cacoulaches, Willie Goon...his thoughts stalled, as he knew who was most likely near death.

Atta.

His body jerked up. "I need to speak with Dr. Parker."

Dr. Wright cleared his throat. "I'm afraid he will not return for a week. And you're in no condition to be out of bed yet."

Harry scratched his stubbled jaw as Dr. Wright pulled a chair to the hospital bed.

"When I sent you to Penikese, I never thought I'd have to coax you to return to Boston."

He didn't answer, his thoughts still miles away on a patch of land in the middle of the ocean.

"Harry, you pulled quite a trick over there. If your father were —" His gaze darted to the foot of the bed. "Sorry."

"For the record, Doctor, I'm aware of what my father would say about my recent experiment."

"I've been wrong about you, son."

Harry squinted at the man, longing to be free of the confining white sheets. "How so?"

"An act of such bravery and self-sacrifice is the mark of a true doctor. Though your experiment may have failed—"

"It did not fail, sir."

"Beg your pardon?"

"I'm here, aren't I?" Harry propped himself up on his elbows.

"Surely, you wouldn't advise putting your patients through such trauma. They will surely die."

"Not with a decreased dosage they won't. I know it, Dr. Wright. I'm certain the dapsone will work."

Dr. Wright sighed, his breath fogging up his spectacles. "Seeing as I have no say in the treatment of your patients on Penikese, I will not further insert my opinion. But as I've done before, I encourage you to practice restraint. Think about what your father would have you do."

His father. If only things had been different between them.

The older man stood. "I'll be leaving now. Unfortunately, I have the unpleasant task of informing you that this room is quarantined. You are not to leave it under any circumstance."

"Quarantined? For what reason? My illness was due to the dapsone, not to any contagious disease."

Dr. Wright's eyes looked sad. "Harry, you've been on and off a leper colony for the last two years. With your recent sickness, we must be sure you are recovered. I myself have ordered the quarantine."

"MR. SCHAEFFER, A WORD PLEASE."

Niklas walked out of the empty barracks into the December sun. The weather in the south sure was agreeable, though he couldn't say the same of the prison.

Niklas followed the soldier to the camp's headquarters. He'd had his monthly evaluation two weeks back. He figured they'd try to convince him to return to Germany again. With so few prisoners, it must be costly for the government to keep the camp running.

The major led him into his office and asked him to take a seat. A picture of a blond girl sat behind his desk. The major's daughter? She looked a bit like Gertie.

What had he been thinking to jeopardize such an innocent life? Once again, he questioned God and the power Florence claimed He held. If God were so powerful, wouldn't He have kept him from ever hurting his daughter?

The major cleared his throat and Niklas brought his attention back to the soldier.

"Mr. Schaeffer, I've been reviewing your case and it seems I no longer have grounds to keep you here."

Niklas's heart did a leap at the thought of returning home, of seeking out Atta and Gertie, if they'd accept him.

"I've done some investigating concerning your arrest and have spoken with your local sheriff, who seems to think you were sent here for a reason other than threats made in anger."

Charles. Another man with whom he needed to make amends.

The officer glanced at a second picture on his desk. A smiling major with a pretty woman and the same little girl. "I'm sorry to hear about the fate of your daughters, Mr. Schaeffer."

Niklas coughed into his elbow. "Have you news of them, sir?"

The man shook his head. "No, I'm sorry." He stood, signaling the end of the meeting. "Best of luck to you, Mr. Schaeffer. You are free to leave now or stay another night. Be sure to check out with headquarters before you go."

"Thank you, sir." The man didn't offer his hand; so Niklas left the building and walked back to his barracks to pack.

He looked at the tower outside of the barbed wire. Freedom. For the first time, he saw the reality of a reunion with Atta and Gertie. How were they? Would he be able to see them...and if so, would he have the courage to face them and ask their forgiveness? Would they possibly grant him that favor?

HARRY CLUTCHED at the hospital bed sheets, frustration surging through every nerve of his body. He hadn't given in to such anger in a long time. Now though, the rage consumed him right along with his helplessness.

The scrape of a chair outside his door echoed beneath the threshold. A new guard. Probably the third shift. Ridiculous. How could Dr. Wright quarantine him? Especially when so many were still sick with influenza. He showed no signs of either leprosy or the flu. How ignorant could one be?

The fact that he'd been none the wiser when he'd first been sent to Penikese jabbed at his conscience.

His anger cooled as he racked his mind for a way to get to the island. Dr. Parker wouldn't be back for a week. At the rate Atta's disease progressed, he couldn't afford a week. If she were alive at all...

Still, breaking hospital protocol was no light matter. He'd be punished. Maybe banned from working at the hospital altogether. Then, what kind of life could he bring Atta back to if he healed her? Unless...but he couldn't finish the thought, the notion plucking notes of dread across his heart.

He sat up, knowing what must be done. He wasn't accountable to Dr. Wright or the board or his father's memory. If he had the knowledge to help Atta and Gertie and all the other patients on the island, it was his responsibility to get there.

Ignoring the thumping in his head, Harry searched for clothes, shoes, anything to pull over the hospital gown. But there was nothing. Was the night enough to cloak him? Probably not beneath Boston's street lamps. He'd be caught for sure. His mother's house lay only ten blocks from the hospital. If he made it there unseen, he'd find clothes and money for the tram.

He removed the IV from his arm and slipped from the warm bed to the open window, the cold December air blasting him in the face and chilling his skin. Looking down at the three-floor drop made him dizzy, but he slipped a leg over the icy ledge and placed a bare foot onto the metal fire escape. Its steel coldness sent needles of painful ice gushing through every nerve in his body.

He descended the three sets of stairs. His hospital gown whipped in the breeze and he prayed no passerby chanced to glance up. The last drop was higher than the rest, at least eight feet to the street. Harry looked up the alley and down, saw no one coming, and hung from the bar before dropping to the stony sidewalk.

The cobblestones stung his feet and the sensation traveled up his legs. He fell to his knees, his body testifying to his recent bout of illness. The street swayed as he stood with arms splayed out to the side to gain his balance. His stomach churned, leaving sour bile in the back of his throat.

"Hey, you!" Someone shouted from behind him.

Adrenaline gushed through Harry's veins and he took off running, the road still swinging in front of him. Heavy footsteps pounded behind. Closer. Closer. If he were caught now, he'd never get to Atta. No one would listen to him. He pushed his feet forward against the harsh tingle of the frozen cobbles and prayed a frantic, hazy prayer that God would somehow give him wings.

In the next moment, the electric lamps gave up their light, enveloping the street in blackness.

Not wings, but a big help. He veered into another sharp alley, behind a trash can. His breaths rattled hoarse and wheezy in the cold air, and he choked. He crouched down, burrowing his legs beneath the hospital gown. The footsteps paused by the alley before continuing.

Harry waited in the dark, praying the lights would stay dead. The scent of trash filled his nostrils, adding to his nausea. He vomited on the pavement beside him, and then laid down on the freezing cobbles, his energy spent.

He could die here. He'd be frozen within the hour. If someone found him, they'd never guess he'd graduated top of his class at Harvard. They'd never guess his father had been one of the most successful doctors in all of Boston. They'd never know he wasn't more than a hospital patient who'd escaped his quarantine, died beside the stench of trash and his own vomit.

He was an outcast.

Harry almost laughed at the notion. No one would accept him here any longer. Just as Dr. Parker had become an outcast, so had he. Was it the fact that he'd been on Penikese, or the fact that he *wanted* to minister to the Hansen patients that made him a pariah to society?

His body grew numb, and again he contemplated surrendering to the elements. Atta may not even be alive. He could die right here tonight, be with her in heaven this very day. But if she were still alive, she needed him. All the patients did. If he held a cure, he must fight harder to get it in their hands.

Summoning every ounce of strength from his deadened, weary muscles, Harry pulled himself to his feet. His head spun. He steadied himself against the brick building.

Seven more blocks to go. He peered out the alley and crept around the corner, walking as fast as his legs would allow. There was no sign of the man—he assumed it to be a policeman—who had chased him earlier.

He turned onto his mother's well-lit street. The sound of carriage wheels approached and he ducked behind a bush. A moment later he did the same when a Model T sputtered past. Things would go much better once he found himself some clothes.

His mother's veranda had never looked so welcoming. He slid inside, pleasant warmth rushing around his legs and feet. The scent of cinnamon laced the air, reminding him of Christmases past. Collapsing near the fireplace, he lay on the Oriental rug, soaking in its furry heat. He wasn't sure how long he lay there, dozing lightly, listening to the steady tick of the grandfather clock in the corner of the room before a young voice spoke.

"Don't move, Mister. I got a weapon and I ain't afraid to use it. The police are on their way so I would stay put."

Harry's eyes flew open. "Timmy?"

"Yeah…"

"It's me, Dr. Mayhew."

"Dr. Mayhew…what are you doing in that girlie gown?"

Harry managed a laugh and sat up. His temples pounded and the room swayed. "I was in the hospital, Tim. Did you really call the police?"

"I'm sorry, Dr. Mayhew. Honest I am. I thought you were some crazy man going to rob Mrs. Mayhew. Why were you in the hospital?"

Footsteps sounded outside the door and Harry crawled toward the broom closet. "Timmy, I'll answer all your questions later. But for now, they can't know I'm here. Do you understand? I'll explain everything to you later."

"But Dr. Mayhew—you want me to lie?"

"You're a smart boy. Improvise." He shut the door and held his breath as Timmy's steps echoed across the floor.

"Good evening there, young man. We received a call about a disturbance at this address. Is your mother or father home?"

Timmy cleared his throat. Harry's pulse ran rapid. "I'm sorry, officer. I think there's been a mistake. You see, I thought a stranger was in the house, but I was wrong."

"I see. Who was in the house if not a stranger, then?"

"My big brother. He was dressed a little different than usual, you see. I didn't recognize him. Guess my imagination gets carried away sometimes."

Heavy steps echoed off the hardwood, closing in on where Harry hid. If he didn't release his pent-up breath soon, he'd faint against the door and give himself away.

Finally, the steps retreated to the front door. No one spoke for a moment, and Harry prayed the policeman would leave without further questions. "You sure everything is all right? Maybe you should wake your father."

Timmy sniffed. "My father died from the influenza, sir. I'm the man of the house now—me and my big brother. Everything's fine. But it was sure good of you to come. Not every day I see a real policeman up close."

The officer laughed and Harry finally released his breath in one long, even exhalation. "All right then, son. If you're sure."

"I am. Again, sorry for the trouble."

"Take care now."

After a moment, Harry opened the closet. "All clear?" he whispered.

"I think so, Dr. Mayhew."

Harry laid a hand on Timmy's pajama-clad shoulder. "Sorry for asking you to lie, son."

The boy's eyes widened. "Oh, I didn't lie at all, Dr. Mayhew."

Harry smiled. "You told them I was your brother. That isn't exactly true, Tim."

Timmy grinned, his freckles stretching across his face. "Yes it is. Mrs. Mayhew said she's gonna adopt me. So I guess that'll make you and me brothers, won't it, Dr. Mayhew?"

Of all things. A smile tickled the corners of his mouth. Maybe he wasn't the only Mayhew that was changing.

He ruffled the boy's hair. "I guess that means you'll have to stop calling me, Dr. Mayhew, now doesn't it?"

The boy grinned. "Sure thing."

"I'm proud of you, you know that?"

Timmy ducked his head. "Thanks...Harry. That means an awful lot."

"Don't let it mean too much, you hear? Take some advice from your big brother"—he winked—"don't ever worry about pleasing me or Mrs. Mayhew or your teachers or your employers more than you worry about pleasing God. You can't go wrong that way. Understand what I'm saying?"

Timmy stared off into the darkness of the kitchen. "I think so. My Dad, he used to tell me the same thing."

Harry wished his father had told him the same thing. But enough regrets. "I have to get some clothes from upstairs. Help your big brother up?"

Chapter Fifty-One

After Harry bid Timmy farewell, he slipped back onto the frozen streets, this time with a coat, bowler hat, and a handful of cash he'd taken from his father's study. He'd left his mother a note and a quick explanation, promising to visit soon.

After two blocks of brisk walking, Harry's legs weakened. His stomach twisted in a hard knot. If he could make it to the trolley stop, he'd be able to rest awhile. He'd reach the New Bedford docks before morning, find someone who would take him straight to Penikese. The amount of cash in his pocket was certain to be enough motivation.

Again, he wondered what he would find upon his arrival. Visions of a solemn funeral procession marching toward the island cemetery filled his mind. In the front, little Gertie, tears streaming down shiny cheeks.

"No." The spoken word vanquished the images. Atta was still alive. She had to be. For the first time, he let himself ponder the possibility that the dapsone may not be able to heal her. Was it only some crazy hope?

He was not in control.

A quivering sigh shuttered through his body as he placed the person he loved more than any other into hands far more capable than his own.

ON WOBBLY LEGS, Harry stepped off the trolley as the first shimmering light of dawn cast red hues over the landscape. His breaths came out in visible puffs as he panned the water's edge for a seaman and a boat. The first one he spotted boasted huge sails and elegant woodwork. He stood at the edge of the wharf and called to the man near the bow.

"Excuse me, my good man."

The older gentleman removed his pipe from his mouth and came closer to the rail. "Yes? How can I help you?"

"I was wondering about a ride to Penikese Island. Tell me a reasonable price and I will double it if you're willing to take me there."

The man laughed, his stocky frame jiggling. "Penikese, eh? You couldn't pay me ten thousand dollars to travel to that place. Especially in this weather. Getting ready to store her, anyhow. We've been fortunate so far, but winter's upon us." His bushy eyebrows scrunched, suspicion written on his face. "What business have you there?"

Harry waved him off and walked farther down the wharf. The gray ocean swirled beneath him and he fought off another wave of nausea.

His gaze fell on a fishing boat. Small and simple, white with *The Great Escape* painted in red. Such a grand name for a tiny boat, and yet it fit Harry's purpose perfectly. If only the man on the boat, who exuded an energy Harry envied, would agree.

"Sailor!"

The man snapped to attention. "Yes, sir?"

"I'm looking for passage to Penikese. I'll pay you more than a fair amount if you'll take me there."

The seaman scratched his stubbly jaw. "What's a fair amount?"

Harry fingered the wad of bills in his coat pocket. He couldn't afford the sailor's refusal. "One thousand dollars." It was everything he had.

The man reeled back. He grabbed up a rope and pulled the boat closer to the wharf. "Climb aboard." He helped Harry onto the ship but eyed him skeptically. "You ain't one of them lepers now, are you?"

"Hansen's patients," Harry corrected.

"Excuse me?"

"The proper and less offensive name for the disease for which you refer is Hansen's disease. And no, I am not a patient, but a doctor."

The sailor shrugged. "We'll be underway in ten minutes. But so I know you won't try to pull anything on me, why don't you give me half up front?"

Harry counted out five one-hundred-dollar bills and handed them to the scruffy man who ran his fingers over the green paper. "Guess all that praying my Evelyn's been doin' worked."

"And how's that?"

"The fish—they ain't treated me well this year. I'm getting desperate—was ready to take *The Great Escape* out for the last time...was gonna try and sell her afterward for enough money to save my family from the cold. But now, well, maybe God was listening after all."

Harry put a hand on the seaman's shoulder, sudden strength surging through his core. "God *is* listening, my good man. Always."

The sailor's eyes narrowed. "Thought you said you was a doctor. Sounds like you some preacher man to me."

Harry smiled. Maybe the Mayhews hadn't completely abandoned the pulpit after all. "We'll talk on the way to Penikese. If you please, I'm anxious to get underway."

He looked out at the brightening horizon in the direction of the island, where all he held dear lay waiting.

A few hours later, Harry clasped the sailor's hand, his gaze raking over the shore of Penikese. "Thank you, Peter."

"I'm the one who should be thankin' you. Guess it was God's providence that I met you this day."

Harry nodded but couldn't manage a smile with his worries clouding Peter's words. "Give my best to your family. Maybe we'll meet again. If not in this life, then the next."

He climbed onto the wharf and hurried over the frozen land-scape as quickly as he could, his heart knocking so heavy in his chest that spots of black hovered before him.

What would he find on the other side of the island?

He passed the administration building. Wet snow seeped into his shoes, stealing the little warmth his socks provided. When he reached the barbed wire, Harry looked down at the hospital. The snow on its roof gave way to patches of black shingles. Puffs of smoke from the cottage chimneys rose to mingle with the clouds in the sky.

No smoke ascended from Atta and Gertie's cottage. But of course, they'd be in the hospital, they'd been too sick to live away from the nurses for some time now.

The thought of Dr. Parker performing an autopsy on Atta's body stole his breath away. He ran forward, wanting to stop him from cutting into her.

A small form came running out of the hospital, closer and closer. Harry jogged toward it, dizzy from where his thoughts had been. Gertie. Gertie...running?

"Dr. Mayhew! Dr. Mayhew!"

He picked up his pace. When they reached one another, Gertie launched herself into his arms. Harry clung to her, frightened of the news she would tell him.

"Dr. Mayhew, I knew you'd come!"

"Gertie, you're—you seem so—"

"We were praying, and just like that, God healed me. But He didn't make Atta better. She's still really sick."

Atta. Sick.

Sick, but alive.

WARM LIQUID DRIBBLED down Atta's swollen throat. It offered a tiny bit of relief and she tried to smile at Mrs. Parker, thank her with her eyes. She inhaled a thin breath, the effort excruciating.

"There you go now, dear." It soothed Atta to simply look at the older woman. Her gray hair was smoothed back into a chignon, her appearance impeccable as usual, her expression peaceful.

It wouldn't be long now. She'd be released from her suffering. She'd be with God. But the same nagging sensation that had haunted her since she'd collapsed swooped down upon her with sharp talons. Seizing her. Searing her with worry. What would happen to Gertie? She clutched Mrs. Parker's arm. "Gertie." The word sucked up all her energy, so soft and hoarse it choked out nearly unrecognizable.

"She's right in the next room. I'll go get her, Atta."

Atta shook her head, pressed her arm against Mrs. Parker's. "Take care..."

Mrs. Parker's eyes shone with tears. "Now, Atta. Don't be thinking like that."

She widened her eyes, pleading with her. "Please."

Mrs. Parker ran a warm hand over Atta's forehead, smoothing aside tendrils of loose, unkempt hair. "Yes, dear. You know I will always be there for Gertie." She sat back and pushed the tea aside. "She's doing remarkably, you know. Her legs are still ulcerated, but their strength is returning. Even Dr. Parker called it a miracle."

Atta's breaths relaxed as she sent up a thanksgiving for Gertie's health. The patients had been praying for Dr. Mayhew, but God had something else in mind all along.

"Harry?" she rasped.

The corners of Mrs. Parker's mouth turned downward. "Dr. Parker won't see him until next week. We'll have more news then."

She may not be alive by then. Like Adskhan, who died two days earlier. Her fate would soon be wrapped with his.

Mrs. Parker opened her Bible and began to read. Atta closed her eyes, sinking into the ebb and flow of the older woman's voice. "Fear thou not; for I am with thee: be not dismayed for I am thy God. I will strengthen thee; yea, I will help thee; yea, I will uphold thee with the right hand of my righteousness."

Jesus would hold her up. Especially now. He'd wrap her in His arms. She would bask in His mercy, in this moment and in the many to come. Still, a bothersome thought robbed her of peace. She hadn't yet forgiven her father. She needed to write him a letter before she died, or at least give Mrs. Parker a message for him.

But Gertie would be all alone. The blame for that lay on her father's soul. He should have been a better father. He should have been more responsible, more loving, more—

No, she'd never be able to forgive him with this line of bitter thinking.

Her mind summoned sound from deep within her chest. Nothing came up, and she motioned for Mrs. Parker with a limp hand. Her nerves were nearly dead, her skin scarred from accidents she failed to feel. A coffee too hot, a hard bump against a doorknob.

The older woman turned, but not before Gertie barreled into the room, breathing hard with clear, unobstructed breaths. "Dr. Mayhew—Dr. Mayhew's here."

Atta's heart lurched. She looked to the door, willing Harry to appear, glad she'd be able to see him one last time. The disease had attacked her insides with ferocity. Every breath was a struggle and any moment—maybe with her next gasp—she'd fail to find air. They would grow thinner and thinner until, like Lucy, she'd suffocate.

When Harry appeared, relief crossed his face and he rushed to her bedside, taking her numb hand in his and kissing it. "My dove...I'm here. I'm here."

He didn't look well, swaying by her bedside, struggling to remain standing.

"Harry." She tried to lift her hand to his face, but only managed raising her elbow an inch off the bed. If only she could feel his stubbled cheek beneath her palm, his curly waves beneath her fingers. She wanted to tell him not to grieve her, that it was better this way. He should go on with a normal life, and she would be with God. She'd accepted her fate. If only he'd do the same.

But she hadn't the strength and when he noticed her lips moving, he put a finger to her mouth. "Sshhh, beloved." He rummaged around in the bag at his feet. "I am here. May I try one more thing to help you?"

Warm tears spilled over her eyelids and onto her bumpy cheeks. They flowed as they hadn't in years, in a cascade of love for the man before her. Oh, her dear Harry. Ever-willing, ever-hopeful that he could save her from the ugliness that ate her body. She started to shake her head no. If she died later today or tomorrow, she didn't want him to question his role in her death.

His ocean-blue eyes beseeched hers. He would not go through with whatever he planned without her permission. She remembered the first time they'd met and how much he'd changed, how grace had seized him.

"Please, Atta." His tone held a desperation she'd never heard before.

"Harry," she croaked. "I wait...heaven..."

His eyes shone. "Perhaps God has given me medicine. Please, Atta. Please, let me try."

And who was she to put a miracle past God, even in this hour of her life? She nodded, let her head fall to the side, wilting against the pillow. She barely felt the pinch of the needle in her arm but was acutely aware of the stinging liquid burning through her veins.

Struggling for another breath, she allowed the darkness to descend upon her.

Chapter Fifty-Two

"Harry, come lie down." Dr. Parker placed a sturdy hand on Harry's shoulder. "You are foolish to have traveled so far in your condition."

"There was no way to reach you. I had to try."

"Come lay down, son. There's nothing more you can do for her."

Harry shook his head, clutched harder to Atta's small, bruised hand. "I'm not leaving her." Yet, his body rebelled with weakness, and he struggled to keep his head off Atta's mattress.

Behind him, a bed frame scraped across the floor. When he turned, he saw that Dr. Parker had moved the next bed as close to Atta's as possible. "At least lie down."

Harry obeyed, getting in the bed with his shoes on, unwilling to let go of Atta's flaccid hand for a moment.

Dr. Parker removed Harry's shoes and tucked the blankets around him. "I should have kicked you off this island long ago, Dr. Mayhew."

Harry looked up, blinked back the wetness in his eyes. "Thank you for not doing that, sir. It's been the greatest pleasure of my life working here—working with you. You've been like a father to me."

"And you've been like a son." The older man cleared his throat. "I'll wake you for her next dose."

"Thank you." But Harry wouldn't fall asleep. He'd stay here and watch each one of Atta's precious breaths. He'd lie here and pray for a miracle.

Dr. Parker gave one last look at Atta, then left the room, leaving Harry alone to watch her chest rise and fall ever so slightly.

They were so close to one another, and yet so far. If she were healthy, he could wake beside her every morning. But he'd given her to God, who loved her infinitely more than he did. Surely, He'd take care of her, whether she lived or died.

"Please," he whispered. "Let her live."

"Jesus...ask you heal Atta." Gertie listened to Willie Goon's words. They were jumpier than a toad's but something about them sounded real pretty, too. She'd gone to the patients after Dr. Mayhew arrived and asked them to pray with her. She'd shown them how strong her legs were, how she felt the healing in her body in a strange way. Slowly, they trickled into the amusement room as white swirls of snow blanketed the hospital, blocking out the tumbling sea.

The patient's prayers were simple. Flavia now prayed in Italian, but Gertie recognized Atta's name followed by all of their names.

As they prayed, a warm, invisible *something* surrounded her. Almost as if God held her in His big hands and snuggled her up like a caterpillar in a warm cocoon. She'd be all right. No matter what happened, no matter all the bad things that had happened, God would take care of her.

Suddenly, being mad at Papi didn't seem so important anymore. And she understood what Atta said about being free. The anger inside her was like a toy top spinning out of control, knocking into things and denting them, but never slowing down.

With her decision to forgive Papi, the top came to a grinding halt.

Her heart was quiet, calm. Free.

ATTA fought for breath in that mystical place between sleep and awake. A voice came to her. Harry's. Then a warmth on her arm. But it was all so far away. So far away. Suddenly, the warmth radiated outward and up until it filled her sight. Half of her struggled to take in a breath and the other half stood in awe of the peace tingling through her.

"ATTA—ATTA NO, PLEASE HANG ON." Harry clutched at Atta's arm, willing her to breathe life into her lungs. Instead, a crackling rattle sounded in her throat. A death rattle. "God, don't take her."

He wept against the bed sheets. He'd given her over to God. But that was when he thought her chances of living were fair. How much harder it was to believe in the face of death.

"Jesus, help."

THIS WAS IT. She would leave this earthly life and move on to the next. The warmth beckoned to Atta, and then a voice—the most beautiful voice she'd ever heard, spoke to her. Instantly, she knew who it was.

"Beloved. I have loved you with an everlasting love. Remember my mercy."

"But haven't you come to take me home, Lord?"

"There is a time for everything, but yours has not yet come."

The warmth receded, and she tried to reach for it. "Father!"

"Remember my mercy..."

And then He was gone, but the air filling her lungs had returned. She gasped it in, her eyes flying open.

From beside her, Harry lifted his head, his cheeks wet. His jaw hung open, his mouth moving but no words coming out.

Atta inhaled another breath, this one not as thin as before. Something had cleared. She knew it sure as the wind, sure as the encounter with her Lord.

"Harry..." Her voice was still hoarse and raspy, barely a whisper, but her throat didn't hurt as badly.

Disbelief etched Harry's face. He clasped her to his chest and buried words of praise in her blankets before lifting his head to let them flow free. They stayed that way for a long time, and yet in that place, a deep sense of loss pressed upon her spirit. How close she had been to her Creator, how close to seeing His gleaming face. She couldn't imagine anything more wonderful.

But her time on earth wasn't through. She was here for a reason.

Harry kissed her eyelids, her cheeks, and finally her mouth. Their tears mingled with one another and she tasted the saltiness on her lips.

He rose, still holding her hand. "Dr. Parker," he yelled. "Mrs. Parker. Gertie. Everyone! Come quickly. Come see."

Gertie was the first to rush into the room. "Atta!" She put her arms gently around Atta's neck and Atta bore the pain in order to relish her sister's closeness.

Soon, all the staff and patients surrounded her bed. Dr. Parker probed his fingers along her wrist, took out his stethoscope and pressed it to her chest.

He blinked, shook his head. "Well, I'll be...Miss Atta, you—you seem to have made an improvement."

Improved may not be saved, but what did it matter? This time was precious and she'd praise God for every extra minute she had to see Harry and Gertie and all of the patients who had become like family to her.

"Please," Atta whispered. "Could we sing?" She reached for Harry's hand, then for Gertie's. Harry held Willie Goon's, who held Mrs. Parker's, who held Mary's, who held Nurse Edith's, until they all formed a circle.

Harry squeezed her hand, began to sing in a strong, soft baritone.

> "I hear the Savior say,
> thy strength indeed is small,
> child of weakness, watch and pray,
> find in me, thine all in all."

She joined him as best as she could, her mouth moving, the words still lost. Even when her faith was weak, God had found her.

Mrs. Parker joined in, her voice strong. Then Mary and Dr. Parker and Nurse Edith and Gertie, all filling in where Atta could not. Completing her praise.

> "Jesus paid it all,
> all to Him I owe.
> Sin hath left a crimson stain,
> He washed it white as snow."

The entire group now sang, and Atta had never known a closer bond, had never known what it was like to be so fully human, as she did in this time.

> "Lord, now indeed I find
> Thy power and Thine alone,
> can change the leper's spots,
> and melt the heart of stone."

Chapter Fifty-Three

"When must we leave?" Atta smoothed a hand over the quilt she'd been working on for the last four months, still experiencing a rush of pleasure at the feel of the fabric on her fingertips. Little by little, she improved.

With each dose of dapsone that entered her veins, her body became stronger and stronger. Her face had cleared considerably, as had her airways. The sores on her arms and legs had greatly improved. Harry estimated that in six months' time her skin would show only scars—a remnant of the disease that had wreaked havoc on her body. Her nose would never regain its original perkiness, but at least she could breathe from it.

"A few weeks."

The winter had been one of the coldest on record, surrounding the island with a solid layer of ice. Within the island's sanctuary, Atta had regained her health under Harry's protective care. But now, Penikese was closing. The federal government was opening a hospital in Louisiana, and all the patients on Penikese would be transferred there—including Atta.

The man she loved more than any other knelt at her feet where she sat in her cabin. "I wish we didn't have to leave."

The board would not allow for her freedom until she'd accumulated a year's worth of negative leprosy tests. Lord willing, that day would come.

"And Gertie?" she asked.

While Harry had not administered so much as a dose of dapsone to Gertie, her sister had been healed. While Atta's recovery proved slow and painful, Gertie's was effortless.

"Where else would she come but with us?"

Us. "Harry, you mustn't follow me everywhere. Perhaps it's best if you go back to Boston for a bit. Think. See if the city has something better for you than your stubborn continuance to pine over an outcast."

He grinned at her, a foolish thing to do.

"You think I'm funny, do you?"

Harry kissed her disfigured nose. She leaned into him, savoring the brush of his lips against her skin.

"Atta, when will you understand? I'm not going anywhere. And what better place to serve others than Carville? A place where patients need hope so desperately? We can work together. Minister to the sick. With God's grace and the dapsone, I don't see how you can question that my place is beside you." His eyes shone with excitement, and she captured his joy. Her future was nothing as she expected. In many ways, it looked so much brighter.

With that notion, came thoughts of Papi and of what she needed to do, of what she'd put off for too long.

Harry ran a finger over her slightly bumpy cheek, and she leaned into his palm, thoughts of her father once again forgotten.

"I love you, Atta Schaeffer." He licked his lips and shifted on his knee. "Marry me, my dove."

Her body trembled. Her heart thumped hard within her chest. "Harry—"

"We may lose the chance if we don't ask Reverend Bailey before we leave. I don't know how accommodating those in Louisiana would be."

"I may not be cured. Who knows if I'll have to fight this thing for the rest of my life."

"I want nothing more than to fight it with you."

Oh, she wanted to say yes. But what of Harry's well-being?

"Let me be a part of your life, a part of God's plan for you. Let me be a part of who you are. Let me be your husband."

She closed her eyes. What if she gave the disease to Harry? What if they had children and they were infected? What if they weren't allowed to be together once they arrived in Louisiana?

Take therefore no thought for the morrow: for the morrow shall take thought for the things of itself.

The verse, the peace, erased all the what-ifs floating in her head. She wasn't to live her life in fear. She wasn't to live it by constantly looking over her shoulder. She was made new. She would rest in that.

"Yes," she breathed.

Harry tightened his grip on her hands. "Was that the word I think it was?"

She smiled. "Yes."

He stood and scooped her up, kissing her on the lips. "Atta Schaeffer, I will cherish you forever."

She melted into his embrace, allowing his fervent kiss to warm her insides, to caress every corner of her being.

When a knock sounded at the door, Harry grudgingly placed Atta on her feet, ensuring she was steady before leaving her to open the door. When Atta glimpsed the figure on the threshold beside Dr. Parker, she fell back into her seat. "Papi."

Papi fiddled with the tweed hat in his hands, didn't make a move to step forward. He looked older, the hair on his head laced with gray, wrinkles at the corners of his eyes where none had been the last time she'd seen him. "*Hallo* Atta. I was—that is, I was hoping to visit with you and Gertie."

"Sir." Harry held out his hand. "Harry Mayhew, sir. I can't

thank you enough for your letters. For introducing me to Professor Hoffmeyer."

Papi shoved his hand into Harry's, and Atta tried to reconcile the image of the two most influential men in her life shaking hands. Harry bestowing thanks upon Papi for...her stomach lurched. Yes, if not for Papi, she would not be alive. She'd jumped at the chance to blame him in the past, so that thought was a new one.

"I'll leave you two to visit, then." Harry questioned her with his eyes, and she nodded, knowing what needed to be done, knowing it might not be easy, even after all she'd been through.

Harry left the room and closed the door. Atta stood, beckoning Papi to take her seat. He shook his head. "Please, Atta. I don't want to sit. I would have come sooner if not for the ice. I want to—" His lower lip quivered and he fell to his knees, right in front of the door. "I want to beg—beg your forgiveness. Daughter, there ain't no excuse. I haven't got one. But I swear to you I am changed. I'm done with liquor. I'm done with the past." He bowed his head and to her horror, began to sob. "I know I don't deserve it, but I'm asking you—you and Gertie both—to forgive me."

She tried not to let his blatant display of emotion affect her. She had Gertie to think about, to protect. How would her little sister react to seeing Papi? She'd come so far in her healing, both physically and emotionally. Papi's presence may cause her to revert. Papi shouldn't have come here at all. They'd been doing fine, he shouldn't show up and—

Remember my mercy.

Oh...but how quickly she forgot.

She took a slow step forward. Then another. When she reached her father, she held out a trembling hand, placed it on the scruffy shoulder of his coat. Her fingers inched around his neck and he fell against her waist, clutching at her like a toddler to his mother. Her own tears poured forth, spilling on his head, baptizing him in her forgiveness.

"I forgive you, Papi. Please, get up. Let's start new."

Her own soul broke free in that moment, growing wings and flying from the cage that had held it for so long. Forgiving didn't mean forgetting. Forgiveness didn't make what Papi had done all right. The road ahead would not always be easy. No doubt it would be fraught with pain. But this...this was certainly a start.

Together, she and Papi walked toward the hospital. Harry and Gertie waited beneath the pavilion. Atta's steps were still a bit unsteady, and Papi held her elbow, not releasing her until she was safely by Harry's side.

Papi knelt at Gertie's feet, whispered soft words. Her sister's bottom lip trembled. Atta started to go to her, but Harry held her back.

Papi continued to speak quiet words. Gertie nodded. A tear meandered down her cheek. She took a hesitant step closer, raised her arms, and finally embraced her father in mutual sobs.

Atta melted into Harry's side. So many miles of regret and guilt beginning to be buried. An adventure awaited them that she hadn't dared to dream until this moment.

The cross in the distant cemetery shone with the last light of day. Atta snuggled closer to Harry as a cleansing tear fell onto her cheek, and for the first time it felt healthy, good. The wind, like the very hand of God, caressed her face, drying it away.

Chapter Fifty-Four

1993

I stare at my aunt's grave marker, the gentle island breeze sweeping the tears from my face.

Atta Schaeffer Mayhew
April 4, 1897 – December 24, 1974
Beloved Wife and Sister, Champion of Outcasts
At Peace with God

My Aunt Atta had died two months before I was born. She'd lived much longer than any of her doctors had anticipated. She'd married my great-uncle.

I stare at the words *At Peace with God* and something within me is zealous for them. I want what my Aunt Atta had. Not just her healing from her physical afflictions but healing from her spiritual afflictions as well.

I know two things for certain in that moment. First, I must forgive my parents. I must forgive them, and at the same time, I must also separate myself from their unhealthy choices.

And the second?

"That story should be told." My words don't leave room for argument. "It should have never been hidden away. It should be written down and told over and over to our family and to anyone else who wishes to hear it."

"I agree," Sam says. He's been quiet through the end of Gram and Uncle Harry's story, as have I. Now, he stands with his hands in his pockets, contemplative, as the wind whips his t-shirt against his body.

The place we now stand is where my aunt and uncle first saw one another outside the examination room. The first time my Aunt Atta had given my uncle a grade.

"So, my grandfather kept his original surname," I say.

"Timmy was grateful my mother gave him a home and love," Uncle Harry says. "I couldn't have asked for a better brother. But yes, he loved his birth parents and wanted to keep their name alive."

Questions still swirl. "Why did Aunt Atta ask to be buried here, after all those years?"

"Atta said this is where she was born. She wished her final resting place to be here as well," my uncle says. "I've made plans to be buried alongside her when the good Lord takes me away. I think it's fitting."

I turn my face to the sea, sense a warmth within me, an unfamiliar but welcome presence.

"I think so, too," I whisper.

THE NEXT MORNING dawns warm and beautiful. A good thing, for the ceremony is to be conducted outside. In another hour, a boat will drop off nearly a hundred passengers to help commemorate the Penikese Island Leper Hospital and Frank and Marion Parker for their persevering love to the patients on the island.

I wear a slip dress with lace. As I brush my hair and work some curl cream into it, allowing loose waves to fall below my shoulders, something within me feels unsettled, unfinished.

Gram and Uncle Harry are chatting on lawn chairs outside. I go over to tell them I plan to take a short walk.

Gram eyes me. "Be careful, child—and Emily?"

"Yes?"

"You look beautiful."

"She certainly does," my uncle agrees.

I feel they mean it. I sense a rising glow within me.

I start up the hill toward the other side of the island. Flowers poke up from where the patients planted gardens outside their cabins all those years ago. New life in the dust of my aunt's story. Something about it feels good. *Right*, even.

When I find myself at the burial ground, I pause at each marking. I.U. Iwa Umezakia. The Japanese man who rowed to New Bedford. Lucy Peterson, my Aunt Atta's first friend upon the island. Isabelle Barros, the woman whose baby was born upon the island but was taken away from her after only twenty days.

Little Nugget pushes my right side and I press my hand back, certain I am touching his or her heel.

I walk to my Aunt Atta's grave.

"Hey, Aunt Atta. I wish I knew you, but I guess in some ways I do." I breathe in the salty air, lift my face to the sun. "You were a pretty cool lady. Thanks for being my anchor."

Because that's what it felt like Gram and my aunt and even Uncle Harry and Sam had done—given me an anchor when I'd floated helplessly out to sea. I'd been unwanted, a mess consumed with my mistakes. But they'd each grounded me in their own way. Each offered a part of themselves that served to give me hope.

I place my hands over my stomach and am overcome with a sudden longing. If I give birth to a girl, I want her name to be Atta.

But I will only have a say in her name if I keep her. She will only be mine if I wade through all the difficulties and perhaps impossible work of being a single teenage mother.

An unexpected sob breaks away from me.

I don't think I can give up this baby. I don't think I can allow her to leave my body and not be placed straight into my arms.

I walk down to the beach and sit among the grassy reeds. I allow the gentle waves to reach my toes. The ocean calls to me, the words of my aunt like a ghost on the swell of the waves.

I pray, dearest, that the God of hope fill you with all joy and peace in believing, that ye may abound in hope through the power of the Holy Ghost.

A single tear meanders down my face. I've been trying to figure everything out myself. I've been filled with anger toward my parents. I've been stubborn about acknowledging how horribly I've messed up. But here and now, surer than the babe growing within me, I know a love so deep and wide and long and sure that I want, more than anything else, to give myself over to it. To leave behind my old ways and embrace the new.

I stand and start toward the water.

"Emily!"

Sam runs up behind me. He is handsome in his dress pants and button-down shirt, and I immediately feel embarrassed for what I was about to do.

He shakes his head. "What are you doing?"

"I—I don't know. I wanted to feel the water." To allow it to wash over me, to symbolize a new beginning.

"Okay. I'll come with you." Sam unties his shoes and rolls up his pants. The fact that he doesn't ask questions is not lost on me. It's as if simply being with me is enough for him.

My face warms at the thought. I don't know what I have done to deserve his friendship.

When he offers his hand, we wade into the water together. The cool waves rush in between my toes and then swirl around my legs. I think of my aunt and grandmother on this same beach more than seventy years ago. My Aunt Atta lifting her hands to the sky. My Uncle Harry falling in love with her. My grandmother's miraculous healing.

Sam and I navigate the rocky bottom. He leads me away from a slight dip in the sand. "I had a dream last night," he begins.

"Tell me."

The tips of his ears grow pink and he stops walking. I do the same. "It wasn't an ordinary dream. It was like an angel spoke to me or something. About my brother. Telling me it was okay to move on." He turns his clear gaze upon me. "I want what Atta and Harry had. Have. I need it. I went to bed last night thinking that I want to be healed, too. In the way that matters most. In the way that only God can heal."

I laugh through another sob. He has put into words exactly how I feel. "I know what you mean."

When we come out of the water, the oppressive weight I've been carrying falls from my shoulders. It's as if I suddenly know with every ounce of my being that God completely and unabashedly loves me. That He doesn't care a whit about my past sins as I fall in the direction of His open arms. Despite my growing belly, I feel light for the first time in years.

The road ahead may be long and hard, but Gram is right—I am not alone.

I slip on my sandals and Sam ties his shoes. Again, he grabs my hand.

"Thank you, Sam," I say. My future is still so very uncertain, and yet an anchor of peace has latched onto my spirit. With it, I feel anything is possible.

At Peace with God.

That is the hope Gram was talking about all along.

Chapter Fifty-Five

2001

"Are we going to be late?" I wring my hands from where I sit in the passenger seat of our minivan.

My husband places his hand on my arm. "Relax, honey. We're on time."

A wobbly breath hitches in my throat. "It's just, this could be the last time we celebrate like this with her."

From the back, little Atta cranes her neck to see me better. "How old is Gram?"

"Ninety years old today," I say.

"Wow. That's old."

I turn around and smile at my oldest daughter, taking in her light blonde hair, her soft brown eyes. For the millionth time in the last eight years, I thank God that she is in my life. That I made the decision to keep her.

"That is old," I affirm. "Do you know Gram took care of you a lot when you were little so that I could go to school? She changed all your dirty diapers. Even the poopy ones."

Atta scrunches up her nose and looks at her twenty-month-old sister in the car seat beside her. I notice a smudge on my older daughter's dress. She was playing in the sandbox this morning. "Eww. Ava's poopy diapers are super gross. That was a big job for Gram."

Sam and I laugh. I study his handsome profile. His hair is shorter now, and I'm forever reminding him to shave, but we have walked through every path of life together these past eight years. Gram isn't the only one who made it possible for me to keep Atta. I wouldn't have made it without Sam.

I pick up his hand and kiss it. "So, we never did get to discuss our movie last night..."

We'd hired a babysitter so we could see *Jurassic Park III*.

"Book wins," Sam says.

"But there was no book based on that movie."

"But the *characters* are based off the books and there would be no movie without characters. Therefore...Atta, back me up here, honey."

Our daughter holds up a copy of *Charlotte's Web*. "Books always win!"

"That's my girl," Sam says.

"Don't you want books to win, Mommy? You're an author after all," Atta says.

I smile, thinking of the book that released a year ago. A novel based on my aunt and my grandmother's experiences upon Penikese. "You're absolutely right, honey. Books always win."

We pull into the church parking lot. We've chosen to honor Gram with a birthday Mass followed by a birthday luncheon. My parents are just getting out of the car when we pull in. They see us and wait until we are parked before they open the back doors of the minivan.

My father gives Atta a warm hug and holds her hand as she jumps out of the back seat. Mom unbuckles Ava.

Dad wraps me in a hug. "This was a beautiful idea, Emily. To celebrate your grandmother like this."

"Thanks, Dad."

The last eight years have been rough on our relationship. My parents didn't agree with me keeping Atta and were downright enraged when Gram said I could continue living with her. Dad thought it selfish and irresponsible of me to stay with my grandmother, to expect her to help take care of a newborn.

And sometimes, I wondered if he was right. But each time I would voice my doubts or apologies to Gram, she'd cover my hand with her own aged, freckled one and say, "God planned this a long time ago, Emily Grace. There is nothing that gives me greater joy than helping you raise my great-grandchild. Our little Atta."

And as Atta grew, she did indeed bring us joy. My parents couldn't stay away from their granddaughter for long. In an interview with a local news station, Dad even shared his mother's history on Penikese.

Sam worked days and went to school at night to get his degree in engineering. He asked Atta's permission to marry me. My then four-year-old had heartily agreed.

Now, we hustle into the church, where the organist plays *Be Thou My Vision*. Gram sits in the front of the church and we slide into the pew beside her. Atta throws her arms around my grandmother's waist and stays by her side, even as Gram embraces me.

I hold her close. Who knows how much longer we'll have together? But I am grateful for each and every day.

The priest extends his hands. "Grace to you and peace from God our Father and the Lord Jesus Christ."

I remember the day Sam and I waded into the waters of Penikese, beginning a journey of faith that consisted of the legacy started by my great-aunt and uncle. Continued by Gram. One we would pass onto Atta and Ava.

At peace with God.

Joy wells up within me and a single tear slides down my cheek, washing me clean, pressing me on toward the greatest gift of all.

Love.

Historical Note

The original leper colony on Penikese Island in Massachusetts opened in 1905 and closed in 1921. Dr. and Mrs. Frank Parker came to the island in 1907 and did not leave until the island's closing. At that time, Dr. Parker could find no patients and was—at the age of sixty-six, after fourteen years of service to the state of Massachusetts—refused a pension. Frank and Marion Parker are the true heroes of this story. I gained great respect for these two individuals as I read about them. I have strived not to distort their memories in any way.

All of the patients on the island, with the exception of Atta, Gertie, and Adskhan, who are fictitious, were a part of the colony. Harry Mayhew, who is also fictional, cannot take credit for the first cure found for leprosy. That did not come until 1941 in Carville, Louisiana, were Dr. Guy Faget first used a sulfone drug, Promin, in the treatment of leprosy. Additional sulfur drugs were then developed, including diasone, later called dapsone, to aid in the cure of leprosy. Dapsone was considered a "possible treatment" for Hansen's disease in 1909, at the Second International Leprosy Congress in Bergen, Norway, but was ruled out, considered too toxic for human use.

Hansen's disease carries an age-old social stigma. Fortunately, in this age of medicine it can be cured with multidrug therapy within a year.

The founding of the Penikese Island School is credited in its entirety to George Cadwalader, Herman Bosch, David Masch, and Carl Jackson. Fictional Timothy Robertson did not play a part in the forming of the school. If you would like to learn more about the current school and the work being done there today, please visit penikese.org for information, history, and some beautiful pictures of the island.

Acknowledgments

When I began writing this book ten years ago, I could have never imagined how contagious illnesses, masks, and impossible cures would be on so much of our minds. Part of me wishes this book made its way into the world before the pandemic, but another, bigger part is trusting that this is simply God's plan for this story.

A huge thank you to I. Thomas Buckley and his book, *Island of Hope*, which brought my attention to the fascinating history surrounding the island in the first place. Thank you to the Buzzards Bay Coalition and the Penikese Island School for allowing me to take a trip to the island back in 2011 to conduct my research.

A big thank you to Harvard's Countway Library of Medicine for allowing me access to the correspondence to and from the island concerning matters of the patients. I can't tell you the enormous help it was to have this precious glimpse into history.

Thank you to my critique partners and editors, Sandra Ardoin, Melissa Jagears, Edwina Cowgill, Nicole Miller, and Donna Anuszczyk. Especially to Sandy and Melissa, you knew how important this story was to me and you never once wavered in your belief of it. You both gave me hard, honest feedback—and I'm so appreciative of it. Thank you!

A big thank you to my amazing launch team and to Erin Laramore for giving this book a proofread.

Thank you to the many bloggers, booksellers, librarians, authors, and reviewers who support my books and help me get them out to readers. And speaking of readers...readers—my readers —you are the very best. I'm beyond touched by your sweet support and encouragement. Thank you for anxiously awaiting whatever I write next. Without you, this journey would be meaningless. You make it all worthwhile. Thank you.

Thank you to my husband, Daniel, who supports me in every way. To my son James, who went to Penikese with me when he was a little kid of six, and to my youngest son Noah, who always cheers me on.

And most of all to my Heavenly Father and Creator. This is the one that's all for You. In many ways, it's the story of what You've done for me. I will be forever grateful. Thank you, Jesus.

Discussion Questions

1. Emily struggles to feel understood and longs for just one friend. When was a time you felt misunderstood? How did you cope?

2. Atta is at first convinced that her sickness is a curse from God, but Reverend Bailey insists otherwise. What beliefs have you held about God's punishment that may not be truthful?

3. Atta takes matters into her own hands when she tries to escape the island. What would you have done in her shoes? Do you tend to wait before acting or do you tend to be more impulsive?

4. Emily feels it may not be wise to be friends with Sam. She even questions if men and women can be friends in a strictly platonic way. What are your thoughts on this?

5. Harry's goal is to prove himself and his place in the medical community. By the end, his goals are different. What has prompted his change? What prompts us as humans to change?

6. Robert betrayed Atta in a terrible way, and yet he thought he was doing what was right and what was safe for the community. Have you ever found yourself in that gray area between right and wrong? Have you ever done something you considered right but ended up hurting another person?

7. Reverend Bailey tells Atta that Jesus often scorned the religious leaders but "sought out the poor, the ostracized and oppressed, the sick and downtrodden. The outcasts."

How does this make you feel? In what way might you sometimes find yourself a "religious leader"? In what way might you sometimes find yourself an "outcast"?

8. Sam claims that books are always better than the movies they are made into. Would you agree or disagree? What's one book you read that was better than its movie?

9. Florence Whalen says that she's "been quick to sing of God's abounding grace" but also "quick to judge—to fail to show the grace we all need." At what times have you been quick to judge? What is one step you can take to better treat others with respect and compassion?

10. Atta struggles to forgive her father and to a lesser extent, Emily struggles to forgive both her parents. Have you ever withheld forgiveness? What happened when you forgave? How did you feel?

Where Grace Appears

Turn the page to read a sample of *Where Grace Appears*, Book 1 in
The Orchard House Bed and Breakfast Series
(a contemporary twist on *Little Women*)!

Chapter One

THE NATURE OF SECRETS is that they long to be kept and long to be told all at the same time.

At least that's the conclusion I came to as I stared at the solid wood door of my childhood home. Only a year away from my master's in clinical psychology at NYU, and the one thing threatening success...the secret lodged in my belly.

I knew all about the psychology of secrets—our need for self-preservation, why we held our confidences close to our hearts, the proven healing of mind and body that often comes with their release. And so I had followed James Pennebaker's advice and written my secret on a torn page of my journal. Then I burned it with a match over my sink, watched my words dissolve into ash, and convinced myself that it had been freed from my conscience.

I would put Pennebaker's theory to the test over the next several weeks. For yes, I had known all about the psychology of secrets from my textbooks.

And now, I would know about them firsthand.

I pushed open the door, remembering the many times I'd crossed this threshold to find Mom pulling a batch of oatmeal cookies out of the oven for the latest PTO fundraiser. Maggie would be pacing before the kitchen bar, fretting over an upcoming date, while Lizzie sprawled on the floor patting Scrabble's furry belly. Bronson would be laboring over an algebra problem at the dining room table, while Amie pasted wildflower petals onto cardstock beside him.

And Dad...Dad would be holed up in his office, of course, or out at the mission, saving the world.

"Hello?" I wrestled my suitcase through the doorway, filled with more books and notebooks than clothes and accessories. "I'm home!"

The rooms echoed back uncharacteristically silent despite the scent of freshly-baked brownies. I passed Dad's office and a pang started in my breastbone. I forced my gaze away from the partially open door, not yet ready to see what I knew was there—the hollow curve of his chair, the dust thick on his dear books. I'd crack at least one open in his honor this summer. Maybe a Bertrand Russell book, or Aristotle, maybe *Fate* by Ralph Waldo Emerson. It wouldn't be easy, but I'd pull on my big girl pants and do it, if not for Dad's sake this time, then as a sort of toast to his memory.

The roar of a compressor came from the back of the house and I left my suitcase to search out its owner. Where was everyone? While I wasn't vain enough to expect a welcome home party, I did think at least Lizzie would have ensured I didn't return home to an empty house. It had been five months since I'd seen them, after all. Five months, and in some ways, a lifetime.

"Hello?" I entered the dining room to see a familiar form standing on a small ladder, holding a nail gun to freshly-painted crown molding.

He turned, and my heart gave an unexpected lurch.

Tripp Colton was the last person I needed to see right now. I still couldn't think of that day last summer without a flush of embarrassment creeping over me. He should have never said those words. And he definitely shouldn't have kissed me like that. He had ruined our perfectly lovely, comfortable relationship in one stormy, steamy afternoon.

We'd never be the same again.

"Josie." His voice possessed a warmth I didn't expect. Maybe there was still hope for us to reclaim what we'd once had. Maybe there was still hope for our friendship.

These past silent months had been torture but now, glimpsing a promise of goodwill, I longed to fight for the old order of things. To not lose Tripp's friendship no matter how we got to this place. No matter the regret tied to that summer day. No matter the secret singeing my chest.

He stepped off the ladder and gave me a hug, eliciting a lurch of longing. I wanted to sink into those strong arms, into the spicy aroma of cologne and wood shavings and sea. So familiar. So achingly comforting. So unlike Finn's book and leather scent.

I shook my head free of the forbidden thoughts, glanced at Tripp's khakis and polo shirt, searched for solid ground between us.

"Grandpop didn't up the dress code for his best project manager again, did he?"

Tripp smiled that delicious smile, the one that drove all the girls in high school crazy. Curly black hair matched his deep eyes, the faintest five o'clock shadow making his mysterious dark looks and white teeth all that more alluring.

Not that I'd ever been one of the crazy high school girls, of course. I'd just been Josie, his best friend.

Tripp shrugged. "The old boy has high standards, what can I say?" His smile spread wider. "I'm kidding. I was on the way to the library but had a half-hour to spare. Figured I could put this up for your mother—I caught her with power tools last week."

I groaned. Ever since Mom had taken off a piece of her thumb with a belt sander when I was twelve, we'd tried to keep her away from the power tools. It had become a running joke in the family that she stick with what suited her best—books and good home cooking. "Then consider the Martin children—and Mom's fingers —forever in your debt." We laughed, and it felt good. Like the old us, instead of the after-that-summer-day us.

I headed to the adjoining kitchen and took a glass from the corner cupboard. I pushed it against the water dispenser on the refrigerator, noting the dispenser light was out. My thoughts turned to Dad again, just as hopeless as Mom when it came to handy house fixes. Poor Dad had always been too caught up in the mentally constructive to have anything to do with the physical improvement of anything. Lucky for us, Tripp didn't mind trading handyman services for dibs on whatever came out of Mom's kitchen.

I turned from the fridge, catching sight of a neatly folded sheet and pillow on the corner of the living room sofa. I wondered who Mom had allowed to crash on our couch this week. "So, a library visit, huh? They get in a new Calvin and Hobbes or something?" Despite my best efforts, I never could get Tripp to crack much more than an occasional graphic novel.

"Ha, ha." He shook his head, picked up a smaller molding, climbed the ladder, and fit it in the corner like a perfect puzzle piece before nailing it in place. He smoothed his hand along the wood, testing it out, searching for a bump or imperfection—something to fix. Because that's what Tripp did. Fix things.

Too bad he couldn't fix what happened between us just as easily.

"I'm going to the library for your mother." He climbed down the ladder and our gazes caught. For a terrible moment, I felt the awkwardness I feared would be ours from here on out. He shifted his attention back to the molding above.

I cleared my throat, grasped for words and understanding. Mom was one of the librarians. "Why does she need you to get something for her? She's working today, isn't she?"

"Her retirement party? At three o'clock?" Tripp rolled up the hose of the nail gun.

"R-retirement?" Surely, I hadn't missed that piece of information. Yes, I'd been distracted of late, but not so distracted I'd miss such big news.

And a party? I'd received a text from Maggie last week, something about the twins' Little League tournament. Nothing mentioning retirement. Lizzie called a few days ago to play me a new song she'd written. Had she said anything?

Tripp squeezed my shoulder. "Hey, you okay? No one has to know you forgot. It hasn't even started yet. We'll head over together...if you want."

His hand landed steady on me, solid if not a bit hesitant. I so needed firm ground right now.

But no, arriving at Mom's party together would never do. I needed to create clear boundaries between us. No mixed signals, especially now.

I pulled away from his warm hand. "I didn't forget. No one told me."

Right. That was it, wasn't it? I pulled out a chair and sat heavily. "Mom's really retiring?"

"That's the word."

We'd always been tight on money, and Mom was still young—too young to think about retiring. Unless...I gasped for sudden breath, chest tight. "Is she okay?"

"She's fine, Josie. Better than fine, I think. She's just ready for a change, you know? Even talked about renting some space over on Main Street, opening up a bookstore."

I stared, mouth agape.

Tripp's face reddened. "Amie talks too much sometimes."

"Apparently," I muttered. Still, it annoyed me that Tripp knew more than I did about what went on with my own family. I mean, a bookshop? That was *huge*. And no one thought to tell me?

An unpleasant twinge of guilt came as I recalled the many phone calls and text messages—especially the ones from Mom— that I'd either ignored or acknowledged with simple "likes" or smiley-faced emojis. I had my reasons, of course. Not particularly good ones, but reasons nonetheless.

Finn *had* been a distraction. One I'd kept to myself, hadn't even shared with Maggie, never mind Mom. He'd been from Dad's world, after all. It would be too much for Mom, especially not even a year after Dad's death.

Not to mention that my obsession with Finn was such an incredibly un-Josielike thing to do. Yes, I'd always been the wild Martin. The impulsive, blunt, opinionated, passionate Martin. But I'd never lost my head around a man and I certainly never let anything get in the way of my big career plans. Not until Professor Finn Becker came along, anyway.

My face burned as I remembered the moments we shared, how the alluring power of him had been enough to swallow me up, to create oblivion in all other areas of my life.

I'd forgotten the careful outline I'd sketched out for my life. I'd forgotten respectability and reason. I'd thrown myself into the dangerous. Played with fire. It shouldn't be a surprise I'd gotten burned. Torched.

Now, I had nothing but sizzling shame in the depths of my spirit. Too bad it wasn't enough to undo all that had been done.

I sighed. None of those memories deserved a place here, on my homecoming day. Mom's retirement day. Just think...a *bookshop*. How many times had Dad sat at this very dining room table talking about this long-held dream?

Tripp waved a hand in front of my face, and I blinked to see something like disappointment marring his features.

"I'm sorry. I'm more distracted than usual, I guess."

"Planning that next book in your head?"

I averted my gaze. "I haven't written since high school, and you know it."

"That's right. Too busy strapping all those letters to the end of your name in the Big Apple to consider silly things like stories, is that it?"

His scoffing tone rubbed me the wrong way. I breathed deep, pressed my lips together, and attempted to reign in that old temper. "Because you're such a huge proponent of deep, well-told stories, I suppose? Don't worry, Colton. I could never match the likes of Captain Underpants, anyway."

"Hey, that is a brilliant series concept." He grew serious, studied me without cracking a smile, a thousand unspoken words in his gaze. "You do know I would have gobbled up anything you'd written, Jo."

I bristled at his nickname for me. It was bad enough Mom and Dad had the entire *Little Women* thing going on with our names, but sometimes I wondered if our association with the March family hadn't cursed us in some ways. Mom had been so thrilled when I wrote my first story in elementary school. *I'd Cross the Desert for Milk*. It was awful. But you wouldn't have known it by Mom's enthusiasm.

Over the years, as Amie gravitated to art and Lizzie to music, as I bucked against the urge to write, and even last year as Maggie threw away her marketing career to be a wife and mother, I wondered if we'd inadvertently formed some sort of name-fulfilling prophecy. Had knowing Mom and Dad named us after the March family led us to mirror them in some ways? Many times, in ways we didn't even want?

Over time, I'd pulled away from creative writing and moved toward philosophy and psychology. Towards Dad's dreams for me. For who was I to compete with Jo March?

I shook my head, forcing myself back to the present. Back to Tripp stating he wanted to read my stories. Back to that horrid nickname he had for me. "Don't call me 'Jo.' Besides, we both know you never had the attention span for anything more than a graphic novel."

He leaned forward. "Remember *Noah and the Seed*? That was a brilliant story."

A grin tugged at the corners of my mouth. "It had pictures.

That's why you liked it."

Amie had drawn the pictures, and we'd presented it at story time at the children's hospital a month after Lizzie's thyroid surgery. There'd been nothing better than seeing those little faces light up as they transported from the bright playroom corner of a hospital to a world I'd created with words.

Enthralled by my story and Amie's pictures, the uncertainty etched on their small faces had disappeared, replaced by a look of wonder.

I pushed the memory away. I'd decided on a different route to help people now. Dad would have been proud of all I'd accomplished so far in making a name for myself in the field of psychology at NYU.

I sniffed, not quite able to push away the full memories of those times in the hospital—with Tripp leaning against a wall enjoying the stories as much as the children.

He pulled out a chair and sat beside me. "I loved all your stories, even the ones without pictures. Still love them." His gaze held mine, and something about it brought me to the edge of longing, so much so it was devastating.

I shot to my feet, familiar panic working its way to my chest. "Why don't you head on over to the library? I have to put some things away. I'll see you there?"

He swallowed, the thick bob of his Adam's apple moving along his smooth neck. "Yeah, sure. Whatever you want."

"Thanks." This was what I wanted. It was. To be left alone.

He gathered up his tools and ladder, seemed prepared to leave in silence.

"Tripp." I caught him before he headed out the back door to his truck. "It's good to see you."

His smile, etched with a sadness I'd expected to have disappeared by now, didn't quite reach the edges of his mouth. "You too, Josie."

I didn't breathe until the sound of his truck was an echo down our quiet street.

We would clear the air between us sometime soon. But it didn't have to be the very afternoon I came home.

Tripp started up his work truck and leaned back against the headrest, his thoughts filled with his encounter with Josie. She joked he wasn't much of a reader, and that might be true, but he read one thing very well, even if she'd never admit it—her.

That sad, desperate look in her sharp gray eyes, hidden beneath that mass of wild chestnut hair, covered something she didn't want him to see. It didn't matter that it'd been five months—five long months—since they'd seen one another. He knew.

Something was wrong. Was it just being home again, realizing the loss of her father anew? She used to confide in him, but those days vanished faster than coffees on a construction site.

Seeing her was like reopening an old wound. With much pain, he realized he still held out hope for them to be together someday. His best friend. The girl he'd loved all his life.

But she'd rejected him, tore his heart to shreds like one would an old bank statement. He'd convinced himself he was getting over her, even went on a date or two, but always found the poor girl, who sat across from him at dinner, lacking. Not with any kind of blatant physical or character flaw, but with the simple fact that she wasn't Josie, the girl who took up every inch and corner of his heart.

He put his truck in drive and sent up a quick prayer for whatever the future brought for them. How would he even survive this retirement party? Josie'd want to catch up with her siblings no doubt. Would she even acknowledge his presence?

But he wasn't going for Josie, he was going for Hannah. The woman had been like a mother to him all these years. He couldn't miss her big day. Seeing Josie again—even if she didn't give him the time of day—was just an added benefit.

His phone rang out over his Bluetooth and he turned left on Bay View Street toward the library, the sparkling Maine coast on his right. He picked up. "Hey, Pedro. What's up?"

"You at the office, Boss Man?"

"I can be." His best foreman didn't ask for much, so when he did, Tripp tried to accommodate.

"I gotta talk to you before I lose my cool."

Pedro didn't lose his cool often. Not over receiving the wrong materials on a job-site. Not over a picky homeowner who changed their mind a hundred times over tile backsplash choices. Not even over a four-hundred-dollar table saw gone bust.

An unpleasant knowing settled in Tripp's stomach. "I'll be there in five minutes." He'd have to be late to the library. Keeping his foreman happy trumped being on time for a retirement party. Better to keep Grandpop out of it all if possible. Especially if... "This doesn't have anything to do with a certain blond-haired college kid who'd rather be surfing than building houses, does it?"

"You called it, Boss."

Tripp groaned and hung up with Pedro, his fingers tight on the wheel. He probably should have fired that kid a week ago. Probably should have sent him packing, told him to get a job at a beach club where he could have smiled pretty for tips all summer long. If only it wasn't so complicated.

If only the lazy laborer was someone other than his own brother.

About the Author

Heidi Chiavaroli (pronounced shev-uh-roli...sort of like *Chevrolet* and *ravioli* mushed together!) wrote her first story in third grade, titled *I'd Cross the Desert for Milk*. Years later, she revisited writing, using her two small boys' nap times to pursue what she thought at the time was a foolish dream.

Heidi's debut novel, *Freedom's Ring*, was a Carol Award winner and a Christy Award finalist, a *Romantic Times* Top Pick and a *Booklist* Top Ten Romance Debut. Her dual timeline novel, *The Orchard House*, is inspired by the lesser-known events in Louisa May Alcott's life and compelled her to create The Orchard House Bed and Breakfast series. Heidi makes her home in Massachusetts with her husband and two sons. Visit her online at heidichiavaroli.com

Made in the USA
Middletown, DE
02 February 2023

23820180R00265